HEART OF
THE STORM

HEART OF THE STORM

SAPIENS BOOK 2

Persimmon

Podium

HEART OF
THE STORM

CHAPTER ONE

Voggo turned out to be easier to convince to allow her access to the village's records than Dorea had expected, but he was also more skeptical than she hoped for.

Wards were a complex and semipermanent form of ritual, which anchored to a boundary and enforced an effect by expending mana. Unless the effect was very weak, the natural mana in the air would not be enough to sustain them. Indeed, according to what she had found, doing so was a good way of turning a territory into a wasteland.

Mana wasn't something ordinary people could use or even perceive unless it was in large concentrations. However, it still was a necessary part of life, and to remove it entirely would mean the death of an ecosystem. The ancestors were very clear about that. Never anchor a ward to the ambient unless it was for something extremely simple, like an alert message that would go out when something passed through it.

At first, she had been excited about that, since even such a system would allow them much greater security. Still, it was apparently almost impossible for Journeymen to get them to have the proper sensitivity. This meant the caster'd get alerted at every bird's passing or only if a stampeding therium was charging through. It was something to be revisited when her grasp on magic was much greater, and such subtleties could be dealt with more easily.

For the moment, her interest was more toward elemental wards. Protections based on the caster's specific mana type always came out better than generic ones. The need to meditate upon one's fractals and find a particular pattern that worked for a stable ward was apparently just as complicated a process as crafting a new spell, which dampened her enthusiasm somewhat, but Dorea reminded herself of what she had witnessed just two days before.

Samos was a powerful mage, that was for sure, but the magic he brought to bear in defense of his people was simply beyond him.

She wanted that.

Dorea wanted to be able to sweep her enemies away like that, and while she was sure one day she'd get there with just her own efforts, doing so now would require a different approach.

Thus, wards.

Her main problem always circled back to sustainability.

She could probably cobble something together in terms of matrices and whatnot, but it wouldn't work if there was always a need for someone to supply it with mana to keep it running.

Well, at least I can probably make it multi-elemental based so everyone can contribute. That would make it easier.

It rankled her that their allies had what was evidently a powerful source at their disposal that they used to maintain their own wards, and Whitecliff didn't.

Unfortunately, as far as she could tell, most of their ancestral resources had been either lost to the earthquake that gave her grandmother her powers or abandoned after they left their original village in the mountains.

That meant they would have to make do with what they could bring to the table.

Already, the presence of a wall would help. In her reading, she had found that the more an object was related to the task its ward was supposed to do, the better it would serve as an anchor.

That meant better efficiency, greater effects, and all-around improvements.

And you can't get much better than a wall that has protected Whitecliff for forty years as an anchor for a ward to protect the village.

Still, she wouldn't cast it immediately. Not only did she want to ensure that the matrix she'd chosen would work in the intended manner, but since this was her first foray into more advanced magic, she had been sternly told not to begin her experiments by herself.

Now, Dorea was an adventurous teenager who liked to think of herself as capable of facing all of life's problems without help, as demonstrated by her forays into the wilderness to hunt powerful beasts, but she wasn't stupid.

She knew very well that trying her hand at setting up a ritual without supervision, at least the first time, could have terrible consequences.

Voggo had explained, at the beginning of his lessons, the various types of magic that existed but had then concentrated mainly on manipulation and spells.

Those were the bread and butter of every mage. They were what everyone used in their daily life and what they held in reserve in case of battle.

Rituals, on the other hand, were finicky and could have unpredictable results. If a spell went wrong, and it was quite the rare occurrence, it would simply fizzle out or, in the most extreme cases, explode.

While that might sound terrible, the side effects of botched rituals could go from turning oneself inside out to opening a gate for demonic creatures to pass through.

That last one was apparently real, since there were three different records of such things happening. They usually occurred when someone tried to find a way to shorten travel times by transporting either themselves or goods to another place instantaneously.

Voggo's notes on the incident suggested that such magics would require incredibly powerful Gifts to control them and a level of understanding of the weave of mana that was simply inconceivable, even for a Master.

The shaman believed such miracles were possible only when one ascended to Archmage, but since such a rank was little more than speculation and legend, it was functionally impossible to achieve.

But I don't want to do anything like that. I just want a barrier to protect us from attacks. And maybe something to tell if we are about to be attacked in the first place. Nothing too complicated.

Since she had been ordered not to start on the practical side yet, and Voggo would have his hands busy for a couple of days still—what with having to tend to the injured she had rescued and replenishing the village's stock of poultices after he sent a wagon of it to the Forest tribe—Dorea kept to the theory.

She'd have her moment to muck about in the field, she was sure, but for now, she was content with learning more about the mistakes of the past.

It also became a good way of learning what was possible at higher levels of power.

Whitecliff's previous generation of Gifted had also included Master-level mages, one of whom was her grandmother.

That meant they had much more leeway in their ability to experiment with rituals, even though most were focused on the earth.

Some attempted to create new, powerful weapons with the help of the metal mages they had, but most of those projects had been abandoned simply because the effort put into them wasn't worth the payoff.

The axe they used for executions to this day was apparently one of the few things to come out of those projects. While the village had gotten a lot of mileage out of it, the fact that it required three Journeyman metal mages to work in concert for a whole week alerted her to the fact that not only could rituals go catastrophically wrong, but they could also simply be a terribly inefficient way to go about things.

Which likely explains why there is no warding around the village. If the mages could sense things much better than what such a protection could, without having to feed it constantly, there would be no reason to build it.

Thus, she had to find a way to make it more efficient than simple patrols, which was a tall order.

That, or she could try for a more niche need.

It was unlikely that she could set up a ward to work so well that it could remove the need for patrols, and if people were already there to look for intruders or enemies, the need to keep such a ward up would lessen dramatically, which meant that she needed to build something that did a job patrols didn't.

That all built upon the premise that she'd actually be able to do it, which Dorea wasn't sure of.

Still, she'd try. It was unlikely that the Mondeans would stop with their attempts at breaking their resolve, but since they were so busy with the war in the north, there would be some time to prepare before the next attack.

Or that had been Voggo's conclusion, at the very least.

"They have spent too many resources trying to take us to heel. Men do not do that and then abandon the cause. The moment they have enough people to spare, we'll see them again," had been his words, and however much she might not have liked them, Dorea trusted the old man's wisdom.

Thus, the need to prepare. She would still hunt in the forest when possible, as killing enhanced beasts was the best method to grow her personal power, but something inside told her that they'd need more than what she could bring to bear.

Even just a barrier that could be powered by noncombatant mages during a siege would be enough.

Actually, that's not a bad idea at all. They can't get close enough without our notice because of the patrols. When they do, we have shown ourselves capable of dealing with it as long as they don't bring to bear their real strength. But giving ourselves another defensive option, one that would give me and others the time to attack properly, is a decent thought.

Of course, she'd need to figure out a way to implement the matrices used to mix earth and metal mana in a different pattern to use lightning, wind, and water.

That would be the bulk of the work, alongside putting together a barrier type for all those elements.

Converting them into one another is out. It was possible for the previous generation because they were both more skilled than I, and their mana types were much more compatible. There is no way I'm turning lightning into water, unfortunately.

But maybe she could empower a barrier with a separate element.

She'd need to think deeply about this, and it likely wouldn't be a short effort to bring it into reality, but Dorea was convinced this was the correct path to take.

Also, she had already started working on a type of air barrier, so using that as a base should make her life a bit easier.

With a sigh, Dorea gave up for the day.

She had been cloistered in Voggo's library for the whole morning, and speculating further about things she couldn't actually be sure she'd be able to do was not a good way of spending her time.

Instead, she decided to go check on her friends. Since Jonah and Beth had started their relationship, she felt that something like a rift had opened between them, even though nothing should have changed.

I just want things to go back to how they were, dammit. How is that so much to ask for?

She left the shaman's house, distractedly waving goodbye to her mother, who was busy mashing herbs into a paste, given the powerful smell coming from the room she was in.

Turning her senses toward the outside to their fullest extent, she went looking for them.

Unfortunately, it turned out that Jonah was out on a mission, as the scouts wanted to ensure no new incursion from the north was coming.

His father, Joe, relayed this to her gruffly, but by how he kept going about it, he was actually very proud of his son.

The two had a complicated relationship, as the boy had always been reluctant to express himself in as masculine a way as his dad, making it difficult for them to understand each other.

Still, there was love there, and seeing the baker talk about his son's exploits with a shine in his eye felt good. Jonah had been working hard in the last few months, and it was right for it to be recognized.

She left the building without a precise destination, unsure what to do now that her plans had been derailed.

Then, she felt her other friend come into her range, possibly having come to look for Jonah just like her and hurried her way.

"Beth! Here!" She waved from a distance.

The brunette turned her way, her expression obscured by her hair, which hung like a curtain.

She stopped once she got close enough to be heard without shouting, surprising Dorea, who was expecting one of her usual bear hugs.

"Can we talk?"

The blonde blinked. "Sure, what do you want to talk about?"

Beth shook her head, gesturing toward the open fields she had just come from. "Let's move away from here." And turned away, already walking.

Still confused by the abruptness, Dorea followed, albeit hesitantly.

What's going on? She's never like this.

They strolled past the verdant fields, which had finally fully recovered from the passing of the Nature's Wrath. The influx of refugees surprisingly had served as a boon to Whitecliff's economy, having plugged the labor gaps created by the storm.

In the past, such things would have meant many months of hard work and poorer harvests, but thanks to magic and manpower, they had matched up with the scheduled production and were in the process of expanding the fields farther.

That would allow them to reap much more than they used to, which they'd need, what with all the new mouths to feed.

They passed by several farmers, busy prepping the ground for the second round of planting already.

It felt weird to Dorea, seeing so many new faces she barely recognized inside the village, but these people had dedicated their whole to becoming part of Whitecliff and, so far, had managed to do so with minimal fuss.

She knew that most of that success lay at Voggo's and Noele's feet, as their attentive presence and control smoothed out any rising issue.

She turned to share her thoughts with her friend, only to find her accelerating away.

Now starting to get annoyed, Dorea matched her pace for the next several minutes until they reached an empty field where no one seemed to be working.

"Can you tell me why you brought me all the way over here now?" she asked, her tone waspish.

Beth finally turned to face her fully, and she got a good look at her.

She looked angry. Her teeth were gritted, her brow scrunched, and her eyes held a fire that spoke of a long-standing grievance coming to light.

"You," she began, pointing her index finger at her, "need to leave Jonah alone."

Her words were followed by a moment of stunned silence, where Dorea attempted to understand what had just happened. "What? What are you talking about?"

That seemed to make Beth even angrier. "You always push him to be more like you. Always congratulate him on his 'tough' missions."

Her tone was mocking as she got closer and closer, pretending to swoon. "Oh, Jonah, that was so cool. You were so manly, going to risk your life in the mountains, where the barbarians would have torn you into pieces."

Dorea's face became more inscrutable as the girl went on with her performance, but rage was boiling inside.

"You think I don't know what you are doing? Always wanting to bring him on your harebrained adventures? You need to let him be," she panted, finally done.

"Is it over? Can I speak now?" Dorea asked stonily.

Without waiting for a response, she kept going, "Not only have I never sought to bring Jonah on one of my 'harebrained adventures,' as you call them, but I've never encouraged him to do anything of the sort. I complimented him when he returned from dangerous missions, yes, but I had no hand in sending him there, and you know perfectly well that he could have simply said no if he didn't want to go."

She tried to keep her tone cold, knowing that if she let out what she was really feeling inside, she risked doing something she'd regret.

"I have never sought to take him away from you. And I know that this is what all this scene is about. You got together without telling me anything, but I've not been anything but supportive of you two. If you can't appreciate that, you are a fucking idiot."

Beth's face had steadily gotten redder as Dorea spoke, and her eyes were tearing up. "You dumb cow. I know you've always known he had a crush on you. The moment he moves on with another, you just have to do your best to destroy everything, huh?"

It was evident to Dorea that the other girl would never believe whatever she said. If she stayed any longer, she feared that the roaring of her blood might drown out the voice in the back of her head, telling her not to do anything stupid.

Frigidly, she turned her back to her once friend, but not before one last parting shot. "It's not me you are afraid of. It's him leaving you once he realizes how much you have been forcing yourself on him. Think about that."

She activated Air Boost and sped away, leaving behind a purposeful gust of wind that sent the other girl on her ass.

She only allowed herself that small revenge, not wanting to stay around for longer in case her patience finally snapped.

Dorea quickly moved through the fields, careful to avoid anyone who might have been working.

And if doing so, no one saw the tears that spilled from her eyes, well, it was no one's business but hers.

CHAPTER TWO

Dorea crashed through the forest with all the rage of a mother therium looking for her child.

She pushed into the depths, uncaring of the noise she was making and what it would call to her.

When she finally reached a clearing far enough from the usual patrol routes, she let go of Air Boost.

She screamed herself hoarse, tears falling in heavy, salty droplets.

Vaguely, she was aware that her reaction was disproportionate to what she had just experienced, but she was too far into her emotions' grip to care.

Whatever the correct response to a stupid argument with a friend was, she had gone far past it.

The winds whipped around her uncontrollably as her mana leaked in angry, disrupting waves. Arcs of electricity charred the surrounding ground, striking on beat with her screams.

Dorea sat at the center of the miniature storm, feeling betrayed, sad, and most of all, an animalistic rage that felt like it had no end.

Most of the forest residents knew to avoid such displays of power, and so birds flew away, just as squirrels jumped from tree to tree with their mouths full as they attempted to save their stocks.

Her tantrum was stopped when she felt a roar shake her bones. The ground trembled at its power, and what had once been a local evacuation became a general one.

The forest came alive as everything that could try to run, did.

Dorea had a moment of realization, where she understood that she had strayed too far into dangerous territory, before the thing that produced the deafening roar showed himself.

It was a gigantic bear, taller than some of the younger trees. His steps shook the ground as he lumbered in her direction.

Dorea sat in silence, paralyzed in fear.

All the animalistic rage that had filled her had fled in the face of what she knew had to be Old Titan.

The monster gave one last roar, powerful enough to send her hair flying even from where she was fifty feet away. He dropped down on all fours, causing further shakes, and slowly approached her.

He sniffed the air, curiously looking at the destroyed clearing.

She had evidently strayed too far east rather than turning north as she usually did when going on her hunts, and in her emotional state, she hadn't realized where she had ended up.

But now it's too late. Can't do anything about it. Can't even fight him, really.

Mana wasn't easy to perceive in another being, especially if that being was of a different element. However, the sheer power radiating from the bear was enough to put to rest any hope she might have had of running away or even putting up a fight.

The thing wasn't even doing anything, but she could easily tell that he was a Master-level creature. On the upper side of the scale, even.

Generally, people didn't go around broadcasting their signature like he was currently doing, but it was possible that he saw no need to avoid it.

Not only was Old Titan the most powerful beast of the forest, as far as she knew, but he had not faced a significant challenge since the days of her grandmother.

Nobody, in more than a decade, had dared try their luck.

It was possible that a few of the newer enhanced beasts, especially those crazed by the power received from the storm, had attacked him, but they were no real threat.

Unfortunately, from her, she posed no threat either.

Dorea could feel it in her bones. If she moved the wrong way, if she so much as attempted to call upon her mana, she'd die before she could realize it.

Through hard work, luck, and weird mutations, she had scaled the power rankings of Whitecliff, ending up close to the top. She had reached Journeyman level after managing to cast two spells of entirely different branches.

That was nothing compared to what was in front of her.

The great muddy-brown bear lumbered slowly, without a care in the world. The ground beneath his feet shifted minutely every time he was about to step on it, condensing to a level of hardness that allowed him to walk without sinking into it.

Such a level of mastery would have already been impressive, but she could tell he was doing it without paying attention. It was an unconscious act. Old Titan had such control over the earth that it bent to his whims before he could even form them.

To her senses, it was difficult to tell where the bear ended and the earth began. It was like a sentient bit of the ground, a living embodiment.

He finally stopped in front of her.

His face was larger than her two arms spread open, and his eye was as wide as her hand. He sniffed at her curiously, starting from her hair and slowly descending.

She could sense saliva pouring out of his mouth as he evidently anticipated a tasty snack.

Abruptly, he stopped when he reached just below her neck. There, he pressed his nose to her shirt and inhaled deeply, letting out a low sound.

Whatever he had found, and Dorea had a strong suspicion as to what it might have been, it made the bear back off.

The girl was shocked when a rough tongue the size of her torso licked her face from top to bottom, leaving her drenched in smelly saliva.

Somehow, that ended up being all that happened. The bear retreated at his usual slow pace, casually swiping his paw at a tree in his way and pulping its trunk, sending it crashing down the side.

Dorea watched it all happen with a mystified expression, her heart beating a thousand beats per second as she tried to find the logic in what had just happened.

Still, she dared not move until the monster was out of her sensing range.

Even then, she slowly got up, not using any magic whatsoever, and walked off in the village's direction, carefully stepping around anything that might make too much noise.

Her pace started slowly increasing as she got farther away from the clearing, until she was running at full speed.

A few minutes later, her brain started functioning again enough to remember that she was a mage, and she spun up Air Boost.

Dorea passed through the vegetation at speeds she had not been able to touch yet, desperately wanting to put as much ground between her and the thing that could have ended her life as easily as she could an ant's.

No matter how much she had grown, the only thing that had saved her life there had been the pendant on her neck.

Thank you, Grandma. Thank you.

She didn't know if it had activated its powers and made the monster lose interest or if Old Titan had recognized the magic within and decided she was a friend, but whatever happened had nothing to do with her.

The power she had felt back there had been crushing. So much so that any thought of resistance had immediately fled her mind.

She had been faced with a superior existence, and nothing she might have attempted would have mattered.

Dorea had known, since that first mission to the Heidels, that there were greater powers out there. People with enough mana in them to turn Whitecliff into rubble.

But what she had just witnessed was beyond that. The sheer weight of the bear's existence had been too much for her. A primal instinct, which she didn't know she had, had screamed to her that her fate was not up to her anymore.

She never wanted to experience anything of the sort ever again.

Whatever little problems might have bothered her before suddenly didn't matter at all. She had just been faced with the most threatening being she had ever met, and until the last moment, he had evidently thought of her as a snack.

Her thoughts kept running in circles for a while as she slowly came down from the state of terror she had just experienced.

Eventually, she reached the village's outer wall and stopped after an air-platform-assisted jump.

Her active magic released, Dorea lay down against the wall, taking in large breaths of air. Her eyes gazed into the blue sky, and she focused on the clouds, trying to discern shapes like she did when she was little and wanted to take her mind off things.

It took a while, but eventually, it worked, and she finally came down from her state of agitation.

She realized she had gone into full flight mode, as her mind couldn't comprehend what she had faced. Or rather, she knew all too well that she had no agency in such a situation and checked out.

Now that she was back, she realized her behavior had not been particularly smart. Not only had she allowed her anger at Beth to cloud her mind enough to end up in Old Titan's territory, but the moment she realized it, she should have sprinted as far away as possible.

She had been very lucky that, once again, her pendant had saved her life. But she couldn't rely on that to work every time.

Her hand unconsciously grabbed it, taking it out of her shirt.

It was such a simple thing. Her grandmother might have even gotten it from a caravan, but whatever ritual she had carried out to imbue it with such powers, she had made it into a priceless artifact.

Its polished silvery appearance told her that it likely came from a metal mage, who could churn out such things quickly and sell them in bulk to a passing merchant, earning themselves a quick buck for something that would take a nonmagical artisan quite a few hours of work.

Whatever its origins, Dorea knew that she'd forever be grateful for it. There was no doubt in her mind that without it, she'd have become bear chow.

She ended up staying there for a few hours, just relaxing, but eventually, she mustered the strength to get up and go back home.

Her rumbling stomach also alerted her that she had missed lunch, and since her breakfast had just been a baked potato with some cheese, she suddenly felt ravenous.

Surviving certain death made you hungry, who knew.

Despite her body doing its best to hurry her along, Dorea took her time. She breathed in the fresh air, happy to just be alive.

Her hands trailed the stalks of golden wheat as she walked through the fields, and she allowed the breeze to ruffle her hair.

At times, she realized being a mage isolated you from the world. You started to control so much of it that you thought yourself above it.

It's a good reminder. Not only am I not above nature, but I'm also very much a part of it. And I should partake in it as much as possible.

Once she finally saw her family's ranch, she realized she had been smiling for a while. The change in perspective had been pricy, but she had needed it.

Dorea had spent so long thinking of herself as a vital resource for Whitecliff and even the entire alliance—and her successes had only confirmed her feelings— that she had forgotten how easy it was for one's life to be snuffed.

Her parents had tried to tell her that several times.

They had attempted to ensure she wouldn't take on too many responsibilities she was simply not ready for, but she had stubbornly decided that only she could do it.

Now she realized how foolish that had been. Her role in the council was not a relevant one. She was there only as a possible future member, because Voggo believed it was essential to show the next generation of mages that they were involved in the decision-making, to prevent anyone from getting ideas.

Dorea sensed her father putting together a small spread of cold cuts and cheeses he'd make in his spare time. He'd usually only do so the few times he didn't have much work to do, but ever since he had hired the new laborers, his days had been freer, and he had started dedicating himself more to perfecting his craft.

She didn't really understand his fascination with the differences in aging and mix-ins, but so far, he had managed to put a few decent ones on the table.

During her childhood, fresh cheeses had been a staple, and at times they had even sold them to their neighbors or bartered them for other supplies, but it seemed that Dodro had decided to try his hand at a more serious effort.

It was nice, in a way, that he finally had the time to explore such fancies. The man had always worked himself to the bone to ensure they had everything they could possibly want, and while they certainly hadn't been as well off as some others, they had lacked nothing.

Lia, her little sister, was hanging outside with the anoas, apparently trying and failing to ride Bebe.

Luckily for her, the alpha was very patient and wouldn't hurt her, but Dorea made a note to tell her to try her luck with Mimi. The electric buffalo might be smaller, but he was still strong enough to carry her and was much more likely to accept being treated as a mount.

Her mother was in the back, taking in the dried clothes after the sun had done its job.

She still felt disconnected from how peaceful life was within Whitecliff's walls and how violent it could be outside, but she was over most of it.

Not wanting to be seen in her tattered appearance, Dorea created a few platforms of solid air to get to her room without going in from the front door, thus avoiding her father.

With a simple bit of further manipulation, she opened the wooden handle of her sunblind and got in.

She quickly changed and conjured some fresh water to splash on her face to remove any trace of her earlier turmoil.

Walking down the stairs, she used her powers to prevent any sound from escaping, and when she got close enough to her father, she yelled, "Aaaah!"

He jumped with a shriek, dropping a quarter wheel of cheese on the counter and grabbing his heart in fright.

Bright laughter resounded through the kitchen as Dorea rolled on the ground, holding her stomach.

The back door was then opened forcefully as Lilian entered to check on the noise, but she immediately relaxed when she saw the state her eldest was in.

"Don't do that!" shouted Dodro, sounding as if his heart was in his throat.

Dorea just kept chuckling, soon joined by her mother, who did her best to smother her hilarity.

"I see how it is. Just gang up on the only man in the house, why don't you?" he complained fruitlessly, only managing to make them laugh more.

The sound of small feet running alerted them that the last member of the family had heard the noise. The girl entered from the same back door but was quickly joined by Mimi.

That sent another bout of mirth through the kitchen, especially when she realized she had been followed and tried to push the anoa outside, to little success.

Taking pity on the girl, Dorea got up and waved her hand at the animal, lifting him into the air and taking him back outside, where he was joined by Bebe, who bleated angrily.

Shaking her head at their antics, Lilian joined Dodro in finishing up the dinner preparations, not before one last quip. "Since you had so much fun with your magic, little Dory, maybe you can use it to clean up your sister and the mess she made."

Rather than her taking it as a punishment, Dorea's face took on an evil cast. Quickly noticing that, Lia tried to escape outside but was stopped by a watery ring that formed around her.

It started spinning, cleaning off the muck she was caked in from the time she spent in the anoa enclosure but also making her sputter from all the splashes in her face.

Dorea held it until she was sure the little girl was immaculate before throwing it outside. Then, she conjured another batch to clean the floor, but this time, she somehow did so in far less time.

Fending off Lia's annoyed attempts at slapping her body with laughter, Dorea started setting the table and, after a sigh of defeat, was joined by her sister.

In short order, the family had dinner ready, and they all sat to enjoy it.

Spring was coming to an end, and that meant that the sun stayed up much longer, granting them the chance to eat with natural light.

They passed around the cheeses and cold cuts, enjoying the addition of a few pickled onions and cucumbers they had gotten from their neighbors in exchange for some cheese.

"I was wondering if you could tell me more about Grandma," Dorea asked once they finished the cleanup.

The two parents shared a long look over the table, seemingly having an entire conversation.

"What exactly did you want to know?" Dodro queried.

Even as he did so, Lilian dragged Lia to bed, much to her protest. The woman was undaunted, however, and brooked no complaint.

The man gestured to the living room, where he used to tell her stories before bed on stormy nights.

"Tell me about her powers."

CHAPTER THREE

As far as I know, she was the most powerful Gifted in the village. Not just in the way that one might think of, as simply being able to do what others could, but better and for longer. Mom was capable of *more*," Dodro began.

He reclined against the leather chair, his gaze lost outside the window as he reminisced.

"She never talked directly about the war, but from what I've been told by others, her presence on the battlefield was a guarantee that they would not lose. They had to retreat at times, and she was fought to a standstill more than once by powerful generals, but if Doressa was present, you could be certain you wouldn't be crushed."

As he spoke, Lilian rejoined them, having somehow wrangled Lia into her bed.

Knowing her little sister, Dorea was surprised that she hadn't already snuck out of her room to eavesdrop. Their mother must have bribed her with something good.

"My mother was a greater-than-life figure, and to this day, it's one of my greatest regrets that you could not meet her. She'd absolutely have adored you, little Dory," he continued, smiling slightly.

"You know I've never been too into the magic stuff—your mother is much better at it than me, but I can tell you what I know. After the war, your grandmama often took on the duty of clearing up the surrounding lands of those beasts that had become too aggressive. She's why the caravans come all the way over here, even though the risks are high, as she apparently saved them from certain death."

Dodro sighed, ruffling his hair as he thought back to what were evidently bittersweet memories.

"I wouldn't say she was a perfect parent. I don't think anyone can be, really. But I understood that she had an important role to serve. Her power made it so that she belonged to all of Whitecliff, not just us."

Lilian patted his shoulder in comfort. Revisiting such thoughts must not have been easy for him, especially since Dorea now knew that her grandmother had died exactly because of those duties.

Had she not needed to fight that poisonous beast, she would likely still be alive. According to Voggo, the more powerful a mage, the longer they'd live, as their bodies maintained a certain vigor thanks to their large mana reserves.

"What you want to know is probably what her magic was like, no?"

Dorea nodded. She would have been content with stories about the woman's escapades, but she cared most about understanding more of such a great mage's powers.

"I'm sorry that I can't give you technical details; for that, you'd need to check with Voggo if there is something in the archives, since I gave everything to him after she died," he apologized.

She had known about those journals he was referring to and, indeed, had checked them out as soon as the shaman had granted her access, but she had found them incredibly dry and almost entirely about specific matrices and their different usages.

Since her grandmother and she didn't share an element, Dorea couldn't take inspiration from it, as the underlying basis for spells worked under different principles.

She had an unfortunate amount of experience with it, as she had to test things out much more than her fellow mages, since transposing a spell from one element to another was a tiresome and incredibly complicated effort.

And that was with access to that element! Without it, it might as well have been gibberish.

"I remember that she liked to say that her strategy was twofold. A soft touch for when subtlety was needed, and absolute power for everything else." He laughed, drying a tear that threatened to fall from his eye. "She was a very 'do or do not' kind of person. No half measures with her."

Dorea smiled, liking that kind of approach. "I don't know why you are laughing. It sounds entirely sensible to me."

Her mother joined in the laughter, apparently having gotten enough of her exploits out of Voggo to know she enjoyed being a blunt instrument.

"Her signature move was something called The Rupturing. She'd break the ground with powerful tremors destabilizing everyone, creating cracks into the earth, and then used Stone Shower to annihilate anyone who still moved. It was apparently enough to end more than one battle by itself."

That had been the power she had expected. To totally control the battlefield with such ease was the privilege of a Master, and while she was still very far from such a rank, learning their tactics could only help her.

"Again, I've never been that curious about the specifics. I just knew my mother would always win, and since it wasn't a world I was involved in personally, it was enough. But I've been told that at least twice, she forced armies of thousands to retreat, on pain of complete destruction."

Dorea gulped. Even though she had just witnessed for herself the power of a Master-rank being, Old Titan was more like a force of nature, willfully taking what he wanted and uncaring of everything else.

Her grandmother had the benefit of human intellect. That made her an entirely different beast.

I don't doubt that the damn bear is smart. Smarter than some people I know, I'd say, but he doesn't operate on the same wavelength as humans do. There is no inherent ambition or planning. And honestly, he has no need for it.

"She was a sweet woman, but when what was hers was threatened, she could be rather forceful," Lilian finally added after a moment of silence.

Dorea snorted at the understatement, which prompted a laugh from her parents.

"I'm sorry I can't tell you her war stories, but know this. Your grandmother did everything she did for the sole reason of protecting our little slice of heaven. She was never deliberately cruel, nor did she risk herself or her allies to grant mercy to an enemy. That was one of the few things she told me herself. Do what is necessary for yours to thrive, not just survive."

Dorea flipped through the pages of the loosely bound tome on the table, once again looking for the last bits of confirming evidence that what she was about to attempt would not call a calamity upon Whitecliff.

It had to be remarked that she was doing so under duress, since she had been ready to start the practical side of the experimenting long ago.

Instead, Voggo had imposed upon her the onerous task of checking all her sources to ensure she hadn't missed anything.

And I didn't. The circle is perfect, and the function is clear as the day. Just because the last sketch was missing a power regulating function doesn't mean everything I make is inherently reckless.

She was pouting, she knew, but she still didn't see why they wouldn't want to have the shield always at full power.

After all, if they needed to call upon it, the threat had to be grave, right?

Voggo didn't seem to share such thoughts, and for all that he himself was known for his less than perfectly safe experiments, the old man had his own rigid way of doing things. And since she didn't have the experience with rituals necessary to understand at a moment's notice if something was starting to go wonky, and the shaman wouldn't be able to check the matrix for mistakes beyond the most basic stuff, as she was using an elemental one, she needed to ensure nothing could go wrong from the get-go.

Of course, what she was about to attempt was a pale imitation of what she would raise upon the village's walls once she was confident it would work, but prototypes had to come first.

Apparently, it was common practice everywhere to make smaller, weaker examples of one's future work as a proof of concept. It was how most artifacts got into the market actually, as mages sold functioning things, though useless to themselves, to nonmagicals that would serve as family heirlooms for generations.

What Dorea was making wouldn't serve much to anyone, especially since it required regular recharging and needed a mage to be present to switch from passive to active.

Strictly speaking, even the finished product wouldn't count as much more than a temporary ward. She simply wasn't skilled enough in the craft to make a permanent one, much less if she added even more complex functions to make it practical for other people.

But then again, we don't need a fancy artifact that operates by itself, feeding on the mana currents. We need to have further fortifications, especially up north, and since we cannot simply make the wall taller, as it would end up much weaker than the lower side, this is what we have to work with.

Her final concept had been brutally stripped of all the bells and whistles by an amused Voggo. While it might have been helpful to have several additional functions like progressively stronger air resistance against intruders or localized weather events, she had been deemed "overenthusiastic" and told to work with what was in the realm of possibilities.

What she ended up with was both more and less complex than she had expected.

More, because she hadn't accounted for all the little regulation mechanisms she'd have to put in place, and finding the proper fractals for those had been the work of an entire week.

Less, because having stripped all the cool functions, the ward would essentially only raise a silent alarm that they had been breached in passive mode and project a shield where needed on active.

She had initially thought to always have the shield be around the entire town, but that had been shot down, too, as entirely too expensive and possibly even counterproductive if they needed to evacuate.

It was humbling, having to go back to the drawing board so many times, being forced to explain why she thought her ideas would be needed even in cases where it should have been evident to all with a functioning brain that they were.

Unfortunately, she had been shown several times in the past week that her instincts weren't as keen when planning realistic wards.

Still, Dorea considered the whole experience as a learning opportunity.

She might not have been in the wilds, hunting powerful beasts and growing stronger every day, but after the scare she had had with Old Titan, she was content taking some time to explore the other branches of magic a bit better.

Especially because they still had heard nothing from the Mondeans, which made her nervous.

I know it's likely that they are just too busy killing other tribes up north and that we just aren't that much of a priority for now, but with all the losses we have inflicted on them, they are bound to come back one day. And I'd much rather know when that might be.

Thus all the preparations she had been busy with.

That it also allowed her to avoid confrontations with her so-called friends; well, she wouldn't complain.

It wasn't so much that she was scared of confrontation. If anything, she was afraid that her temper might erupt entirely, leaving no possible way of reconciling with Beth.

And for all that, she was still incredibly annoyed with the girl for dumping all her fears and accusations on her without even bothering to talk with her first; she still loved her like a sister and would like to one day make up.

She had better apologize soon, though. I can't really just ignore what she said to me.

Therefore, she had caught two birds with one stone. She could contribute to the village's defense in a significant manner once she was done with her project, and it also allowed enough distance and time to pass that, hopefully, Beth would start seeing reason.

Dorea shook her head, clearing it of any distractions. She would have the chance to clear things up with her friend, but for the moment, she needed to concentrate fully on the task in front of her.

"How's it going?" came the question from behind her.

She turned to give Voggo the stink eye, still annoyed that he had forced her back to the drawing table for the third time. "It's perfect, as I told you. I solved that little issue in no time."

He chuckled, smoothing his beard. "It was such a small thing that if I had not rechecked it, it would have blown us all up."

Dorea huffed, somewhat bothered that her first prototype had not been perfect.

A warm hand on her head made her look up to see the old man's kind gaze. "It's perfectly normal to want to be good at what you do, but wards and rituals are a complex craft. Mages much more powerful than I dedicate their entire lives to them and still do not make great breakthroughs."

His words reassured her, but she still felt somewhat insecure. He must have noticed this, because he continued, "It only took you a week of studying to get to this point, little Dory. I'd say that is remarkable in and of itself. If you ever manage to cast the ward on the whole village, you'll have done us all a great service."

He said this with fierce pride in his eyes. That, more than his words, made her smile back.

It wasn't that she had been insecure before. She knew very well what kind of contribution she had made to Whitecliff's safety. But she had somehow believed that she'd be instantly capable of crafting powerful wards. That she'd discover another secret power that would make her surpass everyone's expectations.

Instead, she followed the standard curve, somewhat aided by her magical control.

As Voggo had told her, it wasn't anything to scoff at what she was trying to do. If she succeeded, she'd be giving the tribe another powerful ace.

It might not have been the powerful wards that surrounded the Forest village, with all their trickery and illusions, but it was better than what they currently had.

"Remind me again, why haven't you built one of your own?" she asked the shaman. Given what he had taught her, he certainly had the skill to do so.

Voggo sighed. "I could. I could have made it many years ago, even. But back then, no one else could have sustained the cost, and I needed my mana to be ready in case injuries happened."

That was a good argument. It still stung somewhat that all her hard work was not strictly necessary, but she understood his point.

"There was no need for one either. For all that the forest is always dangerous, our walls served us well. And with no discord with other tribes, active defenses would have been a waste," he continued.

"But that doesn't explain why you didn't put up a ward after the Wrath. We knew, even then, that conflict was bound to arrive at our door." Dorea wasn't trying to put the old man on the spot, but she had wondered about it as she studied for her own attempt.

Again, he agreed, "I could have. I even started drawing up plans to do so. But there was one big problem. Something that, so far, has remained unsolvable. Something that, luckily, doesn't apply to you. Can you think of what it is?"

While he usually gave lectures more directly, when teaching people one-on-one, Voggo enjoyed making them think for themselves.

It was universally considered an annoying but practical habit.

Dorea pondered the question briefly before it hit her like a bolt from the blue. "Of course! Unlike me, you can't use three elements, which allows other people to power it up."

It was such an easy answer that she wondered why she hadn't immediately thought of it.

The twinkle in his eye told her that she was only partially correct.

"It is true that your peculiar ability should allow you to make charging up a ward much easier. But it's not the only reason. There are ways to convert elemental mana into unaspected, but they are horribly inefficient. Of course, after Noele came to Whitecliff, the burden could have been placed on the two of us. Still, I decided that our time would be much better served healing and replenishing our stockpiles of potions rather than maintaining a ward that could only be used passively."

And that was likely the real reason, she realized. Even if they could have put up passive protection, they wouldn't have been able to sustain its cost when going into active mode.

That meant that it wouldn't be feasible until a mage with an element common enough became proficient enough in rituals.

"But why haven't you encouraged those who do not want to fight to try their hands at this? Even if they weren't super talented at it, they should have managed to make something useful with enough time," she wondered aloud.

It wasn't that Dorea thought of herself as unnecessary, as her tri-elemental nature made her perfectly suited to the task, but surely an attempt could have been made.

Voggo laughed out loud, holding his belly as he unrestrainedly showed her what he thought of her words. Before she could get offended, he mustered the strength to reply.

"Most of them still haven't cast a spell, which entirely removes them from the equation. But some have, and they have been studying how to do so for a while. You just have never noticed them. A bit too inside your own world, eh?"

CHAPTER FOUR

To say that the shaman's words had been a slap to the face would have been an understatement.

If she forced herself, Dorea could vaguely remember seeing others enter the records room, but she hadn't paid enough attention to know what they were doing.

In her defense, she had simply taken the task set before her as seriously as possible.

Still, that didn't justify her utterly ignoring other people's presence.

Voggo hadn't seen anything too wrong with it, simply telling her to pay more attention to her surroundings herself and not rely on her mystical senses too much.

There might be something to that. I've been using magic only for a few months, but I already can't live without it. Just because I can tell someone is close to me doesn't mean I shouldn't acknowledge them anyway.

It made her wonder if she had offended anyone. She hadn't meant to, and people could probably tell she was just engrossed in her studies, but it still sucked.

It also made her rethink her social interactions in the past few months. Had she really been that self-centered? Could Beth have a point that she pushed Jonah to be more like her?

She ended up having to stop her work for the day, since she just wasn't in the right state of mind for finicky, detail-oriented practice.

I'm done with the theory anyways; now it's just a matter of attempting a prototype and, if that works, scaling it up.

Thus, she took the afternoon off. She'd need to check in for a patrol in a couple of days, but the influx of refugees they had received, and the accompanying mages, meant that the rosters were pretty full.

Usually, in a moment such as this, she'd go into the forest to look for a beast to fight, get a little bit stronger, and feel better about herself. She was starting to realize, however, that it might not be the best way to go about things.

First of all, she needed to face her problem head-on rather than avoid it.

Of course, growing stronger is important. I'm one of the main pillars of Whitecliff's defense, and the more time passes, the closer we get to the next Mondean attack. But I can't just use it as an excuse to avoid self-reflection.

Dorea walked determinedly toward the cliffs. It was the place she felt the most at peace at, and the fresh sea breeze would help her concentrate.

As she went, she made a point to say hello to anyone she met on the path, and given their surprise, she realized that the problem might have been worse than she had thought.

Everyone seemed happy to see her, which warmed her heart, but she knew their happiness came from gratitude for her efforts, not just because they enjoyed her presence.

The final nail in the coffin was that the electric trio, who had come with Noele, looked amazed that she had stopped to chat with them.

After a few minutes, she excused herself but swore she'd occasionally make the time to chat with her fellow mages.

I'm supposed to be their representative in the council! What am I representing if I don't know anything about them?

Finally, she reached the cliffs. Dorea breathed a sigh of relief, glad to find them deserted, even though she had expected them to be, since everyone had taken to avoiding the spot where the Trial had been held.

No matter how the days passed, the loss of so many young people would forever hurt, and no one wanted to be reminded of it.

Therefore, Dorea had the place all to herself. She plopped down at the edge, her feet swinging into the air.

Once, even she would have been too cautious about getting that close, since sometimes strong winds could draw one in toward the sea, and according to her parents, it had led to several deaths.

Nowadays, such a problem didn't touch her. Not only could she tell when the air shifted and thus would be made aware of it before it could happen, but even without that, she'd simply lift herself up in the air with her magic if she were to fall.

So much power makes you lose sight of an average person's problems. I thought I avoided the arrogance I can see in some Gifted, but it seems like I was wrong.

Hers was not the smug kind of superiority she despised in others, but she had evidently left behind things that would have been common sense to her months before.

That tied in with the problems she had been having. Not only had she been so deep in her mind to ignore other people's presence, but even their troubles sometimes seemed worthless.

That wasn't even to start on the bouts of rage she felt whenever challenged. She was well aware that it wasn't normal, but Voggo hadn't found anything specific during his checkups on her condition, and she was afraid he'd tell her to stop deliberately growing stronger if she pushed for more.

Again, she was self-aware enough to know that such thoughts only brought her more grief. The more she isolated herself, the more she'd suffer from said isolation.

And playing the happy family whenever I remember that I have one is not a long-term solution. I'm glad my parents support me, but they cannot protect me from this.

The way her father had talked about his own mother had told her everything she needed to know. He spoke as if Doressa was an almost divine entity, whom he simply couldn't comprehend. And his interest in her was limited to the few times she'd give him attention.

She didn't want to end up isolated from the people she cared about, but it might just be inevitable.

I cannot surrender so easily. Obviously, I live a very different life than most everyone else. Even compared to some of the mages. I need to actively try and keep some kind of link to them.

Dorea nodded determinedly. She'd need to change some things about how she operated, but she had always been social and saw no need for that to stop being the case.

The other problem she had, which she had been avoiding thinking about so far, was that she was slowly but surely becoming angrier and more irritable.

She hadn't worried at first, since she had had a temper even as a little kid, but whatever was going on was more than that.

It was no stretch to connect the dots and arrive at the unique condition that allowed her to grow stronger by killing magical beings.

She was trying not to think about it, but that had stopped working a while ago, and she feared it would become more and more of a problem.

I was ready to rip that guy's face off when he wouldn't let me talk to Samos. He was annoying but not enough to warrant such a response.

There were more moments where she felt close to the brink of doing something she'd regret, and the latest example of her talk with Beth could have led to terrible consequences.

That she had been forced to run away recklessly to avoid hurting one of her best friends, even if she had been excessively accusing, meant that the situation was officially out of control.

Her pendant had somehow allowed her to survive coming into contact with

Old Titan at that time, but she couldn't count on it to always save her skin at the last moment.

She needed to do something, but Voggo hadn't been able to notice anything wrong with her, which told her it was either a problem so complex that the shaman couldn't even see it, or it wasn't anything to do with her mana system.

She wasn't likely to do any better than her mentor if it was the first. He had decades of experience with healing all sorts of ailments, and even if he wasn't used to tackling magical problems since the last earth mage died years before, he was still the best expert in all the Loisosian coast, bar none.

If it was the second, she might have a chance to do something about it. Thus, Dorea went through the options.

It started when I began killing beasts, so it has to be connected to it. Any other external cause would have been noticed by Voggo. No way I'm being poisoned or anything of the sort since most of my meals nowadays are simple rations we get in bulk, and everyone else eats them too.

She scooted back from the cliff's end, trying to get into a more comfortable position. Dorea had never been a fan of meditation—even though the shaman had told them that to do so could allow one greater control over their mana—but she'd do anything to get a grip on the issue.

Since that had never been a problem for her, she hadn't felt the need to do it. She could feel within herself easily with her passive mystical senses, but this time, she believed she'd need to go further.

She took a deep breath, pulled her hair up in a messy bun so that it stopped swaying with the wind, and dove in.

Five minutes of silence passed before she let herself lie down with her back to the grass, annoyed that she hadn't managed to feel anything more than she usually did.

Dorea had never minded dedicating herself to a specific task for extended amounts of time, as she had demonstrated when she obsessively worked to be the first to cast a spell, but if she didn't see any meaningful progress, she'd quickly lose interest.

So far, she had managed to get by thanks to the sheer wonder she felt whenever she experimented with magic. It had allowed her to spend an entire week trawling through old records and ancient journals to see what a functional ward might have looked like.

But meditation? She had attempted it several times, but never with meaningful results.

However, this time she had decided she'd do it, and Dorea wasn't one to go back on her word, even if it was just to herself.

Thus, she attempted it again, this time not bothering with the uncomfortable position.

Reaching within her core was simple. Mana flowed smoothly in that weird way it always did, not fully there but still tangible to her senses.

That was the easy part. She could stay hours there, observing how it moved through a system that wasn't necessarily as grounded in reality as the rest of her was. Dorea had often asked herself questions about the true nature of mana, but beyond its uses, it seemed like people had simply decided to deem it as a gift from the gods.

There were several interpretations in the records, but they all boiled down to the same thing. Mana was too ethereal to be part of the mortal world; therefore, it had to be from the godly realm.

Whether the specific mage thought of it as a gift from above or the blood of a dead god that sacrificed themselves to save humanity, it didn't particularly matter. None dared think of it as something inherent to the world.

This was weird because Dorea was pretty sure Mother Nature was more than just a powerful person controlling a few types of magic. The Goddess was supposed to be the true incarnation of the World. She wasn't a being that became something else.

The Mother was the World itself, drawing breath.

Or that was how Voggo had taught them. But she liked that explanation much more than imagining a plump woman waving her hands around and making flowers bloom.

That was a mage, not a god. And for all their powers, mages were not gods.

And she had lost focus again.

That it was easier to be drawn into metaphysical debates within herself rather than meditating properly demonstrated the sheer lack of interest Dorea had in the practice.

Unfortunately, she had decided she'd do it, and by the Goddess, she'd spend the entire day trying if she had to.

She turned her focus back inward, this time determined not to be distracted by anything. She'd simply bask in the mana and let her mind be free of thoughts.

I never noticed how uniformly my mana is mixed together. I can call upon it in three distinct elemental types, but I can't really feel a specific one when it's resting. The presence of all three is evident, but there are no separations. It's almost homogenous.

She wasn't sure she could find any reference to something like this. Every mage had their own specific flavor of mana, and the way it was aspected changed from one to the other, but the basic theme of an element remained constant.

However, she had a mix of three elements, which had never happened in her tribe.

According to Voggo, it was a very rare condition even in the outside world, and the few people who had it didn't make their findings known.

Nonetheless, she was fascinated by the implications of what she was seeing. She had never thought of it much, but to be able to fully use her reserves on one singular element, meant her mana could convert itself fully to that specific one.

That meant that her magic was in a constant state where it was available in all three elements at the same time!

Dorea focused harder on the energy flowing inside her, now curious to see if she might discover anything else.

There was a kind of resistance at first, as if she was using a muscle she barely ever moved, but she kept at it and slowly started to make out the details.

Mana was generated in several different manners; this much she knew from Voggo's lessons. First and least important was what the physical body naturally produced by eating. Most of that energy went to essential functions, but some ended up becoming mana.

Secondly, there was what a mage absorbed through breathing and osmosis from the ambient. Natural currents couldn't be directly used to power a spell, but they left behind something with their passage.

These two methods generally accounted only for about five to ten percent of a Journeyman's reserves, according to Voggo.

He had, apparently, run several different tests using himself as a subject to figure this much out.

The last and vastly most important way was what sprung forth from one's soul as it touched the material world.

It was the most complicated to understand, as a soul was less a singular object and more the metaphysical weight of one's entire being.

That weight, in turn, pressing upon the fabric of reality, spawned mana. In the same way that pushing hard against something generated force, if one believed the shaman.

Dorea wasn't sure she fully understood the implications, but the gist of it was that as long as one existed in the material world, they'd produce mana.

What she was observing mostly matched those explanations. She could tell she was getting a bit more than she should have from her surroundings, but it was such a small amount that it was difficult to be sure.

Beyond that, nothing stood out. Which was weird since her situation was strange enough that something should have happened.

Instead, everything seemed to run smoothly. The weird mixed mana moved effortlessly through her system, and she felt perfectly fine.

That reminded her that she had been looking for a cause for her temper, and she barely managed to maintain the correct state of mind, frustrated at being sidetracked again.

Something has to be going on. It's impossible for me to feel like this all the time and not be caused by anything.

Dorea spent several hours there, flush against the grass, with her eyes closed as she desperately tried to find something wrong within herself.

Unfortunately, she got nothing. No matter how carefully she mapped out her own system, how she examined the composition of the power going through her, nothing at all explained her condition.

In the end, she decided that continuing when she was that frustrated was not a good idea. She'd try again once she calmed herself down, and in the meantime, she'd pay more attention to her feelings to prevent any outbursts.

Only as she was disentangling herself from the depths she had fallen into did a glimpse of something reveal itself.

There, at the edge of her metaphysical sight, something looked too dark to be right.

She would have ignored it easily had she not just spent hours watching her mana flow. She had memorized the eddies and currents of it enough that she was sure she'd dream about them.

Immediately, she turned her whole attention to whatever it was and found something she felt she should have known about but somehow didn't.

Her entire system looked frayed at the edges, like someone had taken a leather sharpener to it.

Minuscule amounts of her mana were leaking into the atmosphere before being reabsorbed. Nothing seemed to be happening beyond this weird cycle, but she knew it shouldn't be like that.

I have no idea what that might mean, but I've finally found something.

"Hem, hem!"

Jolting back into the real world, Dorea felt vaguely thankful that whoever it was had at least waited long enough for her to find something, but still annoyed at being interrupted. She sat up, looking toward where she sensed a presence.

"I didn't want to wake you up, but I've waited almost half an hour and wanted to talk before it gets dark."

Much to her dismay, the speaker was Mark, the farmer's son. The boy she had rejected months before and had subsequently saved from captivity, but who had lost a hand because of her.

CHAPTER FIVE

Her gaze was inevitably drawn to the empty spot where Mark's hand should have been.

"It's an ugly sight, isn't it?" he chuckled ruefully.

Dorea snapped her eyes back to his, not sure how to feel. "It's definitely better than the last time I saw it." She tried to break the tension.

The laughter that followed was a touch too hysterical, but she'd take what she could get.

It took the boy a few seconds to regain his composure, even as he shook with mirth. "You are the first to make a joke out of it. Thank you."

The way he smiled, more genuine than ever before, made him look so much like his dead brother that she couldn't bear it.

She affixed her gaze over his left shoulder to try and get through the interaction without making a fool of herself.

Dorea had been close enough to figure something out that she should have felt extremely annoyed, especially considering what her temper was like lately, but the shock of the encounter had jolted her out of such a mood.

"I bet you have heard enough condolences and reassuring speeches," she answered. There was a time and place for those, but if they became all you could hear about, it would grate on anyone.

She hadn't experienced the loss of a limb, of course, but even just being forced to stay in bed for days, like she had been after the Battle of the Rocky Hills, had been too much to bear. She couldn't imagine what he was going through.

"Yes, they are. If I have to listen to another old biddy trying to tell me how

I should swear off fighting and take care of myself, as if I was utterly infirm, I'm going to do something stupid."

A chuckle escaped her, as she was well acquainted with that general feeling.

Even if two people didn't particularly like each other, shared experiences made strange bedfellows, and Dorea found that commiserating with Mark wasn't as bad as she might have feared.

The conversation was kept light, as they didn't speak about what happened for him to lose his limb. Seemingly, the boy just wanted to chat with her.

He didn't hit on her, nor did he behave inappropriately, which threw her off enough that she treated him like anyone else and was surprised to find him to be a decent conversationalist.

"Well, it's not like this is a crippling problem like it would have been for a nonmagical, thankfully," he explained, calling upon the seawater from below the cliff to form a prosthetic hand.

It looked good, which meant that he had spent a lot of time on it to get all the details right.

"That looks well constructed. Is it a spell?" It wasn't, she knew. It had taken far too much time to put together, but given the proud smile she received, he took it as the compliment she intended it as.

"It's not yet. But it's gonna be one soon enough. I just need to work out all the kinks in the matrix, and it's gonna work perfectly."

He demonstrated how he could move it at will as he clenched and unclenched the watery fist.

It doesn't look that expensive to keep up, so he'll probably be able to always have it on. Definitely not as bad as it would have been for a nonmagical.

"It's not the real thing, but it can do things a normal hand can't," he said, twisting the fingers in ways that would have broken any fleshy limb.

She hummed in agreement before looking toward the horizon, where the sun had started dipping beyond their sight. "I'm glad you are better now. But we should get going; I have lots to do still."

He jolted, apparently having forgotten his promise not to take too much of her time. "Ah yes, sorry. Just wanted to thank you for rescuing us. We were in a bad spot."

Dorea forced herself to look at Mark for who he was. Seeing him like that hurt her heart, but this was not Rupert. Rupert was dead.

In front of her was his brother, who had many faults but had certainly not deserved what would have happened to him had she not saved him.

"It was the right thing to do. I'd do it for any of our comrades," she replied.

From his tentative smile, it seemed like he understood. She meant to convey that what had happened between them could be considered the past and that she thought of him as an ally.

Generally, Dorea wouldn't have been as forgiving. Especially lately, she had been so angry that simply treating someone she didn't like so decently was an effort, but she had decided to be more sociable, and if that meant starting with Mark, she would.

The walk back toward the village was done in awkward silence, as they had already said goodbye but were forced by the path to their respective home to stay close for more than fifteen minutes.

When they finally got to the split in the road that'd lead them to their houses, they merely muttered another "Bye."

Well, it went better than I thought it would. At least I didn't have to chase him away with lightning bolts.

Two days later, she was no closer to finding the connection between what she had observed at the edges of her system and her fiery temper, but duty called, and as such, Dorea left for a patrol toward the southern side of the forest.

Typically, people like her and Mark the Blue would be sent to the north in case the Mondeans thought to sneak in another attack. However, their scouts hadn't noticed any movement, and Jonah's presence there meant that it was unlikely anyone could pass by unnoticed.

On the other hand, an unusual amount of fires had been observed where the grasslands and the forest met.

Colossal fire salamanders had taken residence there many years before but had generally lived in their territory in peace.

Something had happened, though, and the overgrown lizards were becoming a problem.

Luckily, the Wrath had gifted water magic to many animals. This meant that such blazes were unlikely to ever pose a threat to the entire forest, especially since the salamanders, for all their dullness, were intelligent enough to know that burning it all down would bring the attentions of things they couldn't handle.

Still, the beasts could be a big problem if left unattended, and therefore, Dorea was dispatched to see if she could solve whatever was causing them to raise such a fuss.

Her team was mainly made of water specialists, as they would be needed if the salamanders became hostile, and among them was Nettle.

The teen looked much better than the last time she talked with him, considering how he had survived a deadly wound by the skin of his teeth.

In the intervening time, he had gained a much healthier color, revealing tanned skin and bright green eyes that had been lost in the sickly pallor he had been in.

Now that he wasn't at death's door, he could easily be considered attractive.

His mood was also much improved as he bounced around, delighted to be trusted with such a critical mission.

Dorea didn't have the heart to tell him that they didn't exactly expect to fight the salamanders, since they were supposed to either solve the cause of their irritation or gather information and report it back to the village.

Still, she was glad that he had found some happiness in Whitecliff. The Goddess knew what he and his people had gone through to get to safety.

I still haven't seen Mav since. I know he's alive because I've felt him walk around the village, but I should take the time to speak with him. The information they brought helped a lot in putting things into perspective.

It hadn't been the most accurate since the numbers he knew of referred to before the Mondeans began their conquest, but he had been able to give them enough to show them what the landscape was like.

Luckily, according to Nettle, all his companions had settled in properly.

Most people worked as laborers, building more permanent housing for the swelled population, or in the fields, tending to the crops that would feed them come winter.

It might not have been the most glamorous of occupations, but they were appreciated for their efforts, and it gave them something to be proud of.

That, according to Voggo, was even more important.

"People turn to trouble if they have unmet fundamental needs or feel alienated from the community. With all the refugees we took in, avoiding such a situation is a priority of the highest order."

The old man, for all that he mostly enjoyed spending time tinkering with potions, was very wise. He had led the village through tough times for many, many years and was experienced enough to tackle problems before they could rise.

Dorea shuddered at the thought of having internal discord at a time when all their strength was needed to resist external aggression.

That might actually be what helps people get along better. The refugees know that we didn't have to take them in, and that the Mondeans would have pounced on them. While the people of Whitecliff need more defenders to survive against the tide from the north.

And wasn't that a trip, realizing exactly why Voggo had pushed them to accept all those who asked for shelter after he ensured they weren't spies?

They needed more men to man the walls and more mages to fight against the enemy.

Basically, he had gambled that he could prevent social instability long enough that external pressure would forge the different tribes into a single one.

It had been another of his private lessons, where he took her aside after one village meeting and explained precisely what he was doing and why.

I wouldn't have guessed it by myself. Not because I think it's wrong or immoral, since it's evidently the only thing we can do if we want to survive, but because it shows such long-term thinking. He's really always two steps ahead of everyone.

That Voggo had chosen her as a possible successor scared her more than she wanted to admit, even to herself.

Not only did she not believe herself capable of plotting so intricately to ensure the village's survival, but she also much preferred fighting directly to staying in the back.

Luckily, she would have years before that became a problem. The shaman, for all his age, was still very healthy, and his ability to heal, magical power, and knowledge of the body allowed him to aim to live for many more years than a nonmagical would.

"And then, the glyptodon went *ka-pow*! And with a Whoosh, she dropped him. And I said, 'You are done!' and *boom*! Smashed it down."

The constant noise from the side would have generally been annoying, but Nettle was endearing enough that she tolerated him.

"That sounds like a very cool adventure," she replied, not having paid attention to his umpteenth recounting of his first patrol.

"Your voice doesn't seem very awed, Dorea. Maybe you should retell it again, Nettle. Make sure she hears all the details," Eddie commented slyly from her other side.

Dorea rolled her eyes. Beth's cousin had always been one for levity, but he seemed to enjoy taking the piss out of their newer members a bit too much.

Luckily, Nettle realized the real meaning behind his words but didn't take it to heart, instead pouting dramatically. "But it was cool! And Dorea was listening, right?"

"I was. You fought a glyptodon with Nora and Leo during your first patrol and defeated it using a water hammer. It was very well done," she replied, having heard him say the story enough times in the few hours since they had left the village that she could recite it by heart.

"See! She was listening to me!" Nettle cried out, rudely gesturing to Eddie.

The man chuckled, apparently content with the teasing he had done.

Feeling something enter her range, Dorea halted the group with a raised hand. "We have five people coming in our direction at walking speed."

Everyone scrambled to their positions, readying themselves for a possible fight. They all knew it was unlikely to be hostile since they were so close to Heidel lands, but it only took one instance of being caught with your pants down for an entire team to be disposed of.

As they got closer, Dorea was able to distinguish more. "At least two mages, one water and one wind."

The presence of someone shrouded in water-based armor also gave her a hint as to whom it might be.

As she spoke, she kept the noise of her voice from escaping their little formation to make it harder for any possible enemy to locate them.

Of course, since they're already coming in our direction, they must have a sensor with greater range than me and knew of our presence long before I noticed them.

Fortunately, a pulse of mana erupted from the unknowns, revealing them to be a Heidel group there to share information.

This was one of the cleverest things Voggo had insisted upon. Apparently, it had been quite common during the war with the Ergasters, and implementing the system—with some changes since there was a possibility that some of the older Mondean generation still remembered the code and could hijack it—had likely saved them from many accidents.

Dorea replied with her own pulse of mana, in the predetermined pattern meant to show that she was from Whitecliff and willing to talk.

A couple of minutes later, the Heidel group revealed themselves.

At their head stood Melu, the happy-go-lucky, fun girl that had taken part in the exchange for a few weeks.

"Dorea! I knew it was you! How are you doing?" the brown-skinned girl exclaimed as soon as she was close enough, rushing to give her a hug.

Dorea happily embraced her, having found her to be a wonderful person and a powerful mage. They had fought and bled together several times, and such bonds were not easily forgotten.

"What are you doing here? Is it about the salamanders?" she asked.

Melu shook her head, sending her messy curls everywhere. "No, no, it has nothing to do with those overgrown lizards. According to the chief, they like to make a mess of things during their mating season but should calm down soon enough."

That was a good piece of information, even if Dorea doubted that Voggo hadn't known it. The salamanders had resided in the southeastern side of the forest for decades, and if this kind of occurrence was cyclical, they should have had records of it.

Still, now wasn't the time to get lost in such thoughts. She'd simply ask the old man when she returned to Whitecliff.

"If it's not them, then why come so far into the forest? Is it the southern tribes?"

Again, the response was a head shake. "Not exactly. Although there have been weird movements in the south, so far they haven't dared test the chief. Her name still holds great weight in the grasslands."

That's a relief. Having to open another front down south would have been taxing—wait, not exactly?

"What do you mean with not exactly?" she asked, afraid of the answer.

"The chief has asked me to formally request Whitecliff to hold a meeting of the three tribes. The possibility of attacks from the north and the south, the recent advances in magical warding, and other things mean there should be a discussion about how to proceed."

There was a murmur in the Sapiens crowd as they digested what they just heard. The fact that there weren't any imminent attacks from another front was good news, and further cooperation had been Voggo's goal since the very beginning; this much was known to everyone.

But the Witch of Immolation had been resistant to such melding of their tribes from the beginning. She had obviously seen the need to have more allies. However, she had wanted to maintain her people's independence at all costs, and suddenly asking for a summit to discuss further cooperation was out of character.

Somewhat surprised, Dorea numbly replied, "I'll be sure to bring this to Whitecliff's leadership's attention as soon as possible. We'll send word as soon as we have reached a decision."

She was stiffer than usual, but her mind was busy trying to come up with reasons for the sudden change of heart.

Yaomi was not one to be underestimated, even when she was your ally, and she did nothing if it wouldn't directly benefit her people.

"Perfect." Melu smiled. "We have sent another group to the Forest tribe to inform them of the same, so we should be ready to meet within the week if your heads accept. Oh, I'm so happy to see you again, Dorea; this was a wonderful surprise."

Still feeling more out of sorts than she would have liked, Dorea tried to regain her bearing. "It was very nice for me as well. I hope everything is okay back home?"

"Yes, yes, nothing ever happens in that place. Oh! I almost forgot!" the girl exclaimed, gesturing for one of the accompanying Heidels to remove the large pack he carried over his shoulders. "This is a little gift from the chief. They are Transmission Logs. If you burn one, you can communicate through a fire made by another one and speak with the person on the other side as if they were right in front of you!"

The man with the pack opened it slightly to show a row of dried wooden logs with tiny scriptures and magical matrix carvings.

The detail work was incredible, and Dorea was sure she'd be able to learn a lot once she had the time to sit down.

"They should allow you to tell us when you have decided if you want to host the summit as soon as you are ready, without having to travel all the way to us." Melu grinned, apparently enjoying not letting Dorea get much of a word in and stunning her with more and more things.

"Well, we did what we had to, so we'll go back now. Let us know soon!" The girl gave one last wave, and as quickly as she had arrived, she left.

CHAPTER SIX

There hadn't been much to discuss about whether they'd host the requested meeting, as not doing so would have been a message they couldn't afford to give.

Voggo hadn't been happy with the way things had been sprung on them, but if it was true that trouble was brewing south of the Heidels, they needed to start preparing immediately.

Further cooperation between the three allies had also been Whitecliff's official stance for a while, and going back on it now would mean being left alone to fight the Mondeans.

And we'll still have to fight them, no matter how quiet they have been lately. We might not be a priority for a while, but no one doubts that they'll want to make us pay for the losses we have inflicted.

Therefore, the order had been given to start setting up tents for the delegations to reside in by the southeastern wall, so that they could show proper hospitality while also keeping them away from the most densely inhabited part of the village.

As soon as the decision was made, people scrambled to make it happen. Magic was handy in such moments, and luckily the Heidels had at least given them a week to prepare.

Dorea stayed behind in Voggo's house after it was made official, curious about how the carved logs would work.

Noticing her gaze, the shaman explained, "It's been a while since I've seen these. We used them pretty heavily during the war. They are surprisingly easy to use, as the magic is already contained within them."

He took out a piece of wood, admiring its intricate detail work and tracing it with a wizened finger. "It's almost a pity to burn them, but they definitely beat having to send a messenger all the way to the Heidel's village."

Dorea vehemently agreed with that. Although she could cross the distance much quicker than anyone else with Air Boost, it would still have meant two full days of traveling to get there and come back.

She was delighted that her services were not needed anymore. "But why give them to us now? Why not when we first agreed to be allies?"

Voggo hummed as he placed one of the logs in his fireplace. "Most likely because she didn't have any left. As far as I know, these things take a lot of time and effort to make and need another active fire to be on at the same time to work. They were useful during the war because we set them alight when the sun went down to report, but in case of emergency, they are just not going to cut it."

He gestured for her to do the honors.

Feeling ridiculous at being used as a flintstone, Dorea called upon her magic to create a lightning spark, holding it long enough for the wood to catch fire.

Smoke billowed out unnaturally, churning like the angry sea. This went on for a few seconds before it dispersed, leaving behind dark flames that crackled merrily.

"So you have received my present, you old fossil," came a slightly distorted voice, sounding as if it originated directly from the fire.

"I see that even old age hasn't taught you manners, my dear," replied Voggo, sitting close to the hearth.

Slowly, a face appeared in the flames, revealing the Heidel chief, Yaomi.

The image flickered alongside the natural movement of the light, but it was visible enough that Dorea felt as if the older woman's face was really there.

It was a piece of magic she had never seen or heard about before, and the sheer possibilities it allowed boggled her mind.

"Bah, I've not stoked a fire like a young wife waiting for her husband to return just to flirt with you. What is your answer?"

Yaomi's mannerisms were, as always, abrasive and shocking, but Voggo took it in stride with a chuckle, apparently not minding it at all. "As you might have suspected, we'll be delighted to host a summit of the three villages. We are looking forward to expanding our alliance in new directions."

The woman cackled. "Not like you had a choice, huh? Well, we don't either, so we need to stick together if we want to survive."

They continued talking for a few minutes, arranging for the size of the escorts and the amenities that would be given to the delegations; all the while, Yaomi threw in a casual insult or made a crass remark, and Voggo deflected, maintaining aplomb seemingly effortlessly.

Finally, they said their goodbyes, and without them doing anything, the fire winked out, leaving behind a charred log whose carvings had been wholly ruined.

"And that's that. We must ensure that nothing can interfere with this summit, which means sending scouting groups up north. Please call upon Mark and Ed so we can get started on that as well."

The day of the delegations' arrival was sunny, making Dorea hope for the best.

Technically, nothing bad was supposed to happen since they were all allies and openly sought greater integration. Still, Voggo had been clear that you never knew who could take offense to what in these situations and send the whole thing up in the air.

A part of her was dreading the thought of Yaomi herself coming to lead the Heidel group, but the rational side of her brain told her that, since the very reason for calling the meeting was that the Witch was worried about possible incursions from the south, she wasn't likely to leave her village.

The old woman was by far the most potent deterrent they had on hand, and abandoning her people in such a moment would have been a terrible mistake.

On the other hand, she would likely see Samos again, since the Forest tribe was well protected by their natural wards and mystic illusions.

I'm still curious about how exactly they are powering them. My experiments with rituals so far have shown that they require a surprising amount of energy to maintain, and I'm more and more sure that they are hiding some kind of energy source or an ancient artifact.

Her thoughts were interrupted by the blast of a horn from the southern gate.

It seemed like the Heidel delegation had arrived first.

Dorea dropped all that she was doing and immediately spun up an Air Boost, speeding through the fields toward the origin of the sound.

Though she wouldn't have a speaking role at the table since her experience negotiating anything wasn't great, she had still been tasked with overseeing the whole thing. She had her successes, but they came about in a more unorthodox manner than most were comfortable with.

And Dorea honestly didn't mind that much. She would still be present since she was considered one of Whitecliff's most promising mages and also the one with the most connections to the other two villages, but not having a speaking role would allow her to learn rather than be forced to make things up in an effort not to bring about war.

It's not that I never want to do diplomatic missions again, but I'm definitely not distraught at being told to just watch.

Finally coming into sight of the wall, Dorea noticed a larger crowd than usual, as people snooped.

They had already been exposed to the Heidels when the first group came for their exchange, but Whitecliff's residents were not used to so many outsiders. Differently from the seasonal caravans, these people would soon become even more important for their daily affairs.

The village was not big enough that anyone could miss what was happening. While some people preferred not to think about leadership matters, trusting Voggo entirely, others wanted to know the reasoning behind certain choices.

Hosting the summit would hopefully show the more reticent tribesmen that their differences with their allies were minimal compared to what they shared.

Releasing the spell, Dorea made sure that the wind dispersed harmlessly into the environment, having been scolded one too many times when she allowed the compressed air to be released carelessly and sent clothes and sometimes people flying.

At the head of the delegation stood a familiar face. Masi, the boy whom she had chatted with during her brief visit down south and who had fought alongside her at the Battle of the Rocky Hills, was accompanying an older man who looked to be of an age with Voggo.

Behind them, Melu greeted people she recognized from her stay, receiving a much more enthusiastic welcome than the others.

That girl is dangerous in a way I'm not prepared to deal with. I'm pretty sure I could win a fight, but she's too good with words. People just get wrapped around her finger.

The entire delegation was made up of only ten Heidels, but given who their chief was, Dorea doubted they would be spending the time slacking off.

A luxurious tent had been set up for them, as it was the most that could be done in the short amount of time they'd been afforded, and as Voggo had said, if they didn't like it, they could always camp out in the forest.

There hadn't been much time for chatting with the people she knew, especially since the Forest tribe delegation was expected to arrive within the hour, and no one wanted to waste time.

With the Heidels settled down, Dorea marched toward where the talks were supposed to happen.

A pavilion of sorts had been set up, where a large wooden table that was usually reserved for feasts took up most of the space, with thirty leather chairs meant to sit everyone.

Normal people weren't technically supposed to be present, as they could distract the delegations from the talks, so two guards had been placed at the entrance, though they didn't do anything to stop her from entering.

Although she didn't have a speaking role, Dorea was considered an important figure and, as such, had been given a seat close to Voggo.

Inside, the shaman was already present, busy directing the preparations for the refreshments. Such duties were traditionally left to the host, but Voggo wasn't strong enough to do everything by himself anymore, not without using magic, and to blatantly do so could be taken as a negative sign by the others.

As such, they needed to set everything perfectly before the talks could begin so that Voggo wouldn't have to do much more than open the summit.

Dorea spent some time with the old man, aiding him in simple, manual tasks that she hadn't done in months but remembered well enough to do without supervision.

Shortly after they were done, another sound alerted them to the arrival of the Forest delegation, this time through the eastern gate.

As she had expected, Samos, the chief, was at the head of the group and had brought alongside several elders and only one mage, Jasper.

The boy bounced around happily as he took in the sights, evidently not having ever left the forest.

He seemed particularly taken in by the sight of the sea in the distance, and Dorea made a note to remember to take him there once things kicked off and their presence wasn't needed anymore.

Summits such as this were apparently common during and even after the war. As the mages got older, though, they fell out of favor and people started thinking more about their own business.

It wasn't necessarily a bad thing in her eyes, as after the war, things were peaceful for quite a few years, but now that the Mondeans and the southern tribes had started poking around again, they needed to rekindle the old alliances.

"Welcome, my friend. It's been too long since we last saw each other," Voggo greeted the much taller man.

Samos was wearing his usual headdress and looked mostly recovered from whatever he had done to repel the Mondean attack the last time she had seen him.

He walked forward confidently, with a charming smile. "Elder, you don't look a year older. You must tell me your secret because my knees are starting to hurt."

Her grandfather in all but blood roared in laughter, patting the other shaman on the shoulder. "It is the start of a slow and miserable decline, then. Drink more willow tea before you go to sleep if they bother you that much."

"I wouldn't listen to this old man if I were you," interrupted a reedy voice from behind.

Of course, Dorea had felt the group approach, just like every other mage in the pavilion, but she hadn't expected the older man to speak that way.

Instead of taking offense to his words, both Voggo and Samos looked mildly amused.

"I see that even old age hasn't managed to mellow you out, Mort."

The older Heidel scoffed, but Dorea spied the hint of a smile on his lips. "There wasn't anything to mellow out. I've always been perfectly pleasant."

From the giggles that Masi and Melu were desperately trying to hide, it didn't seem like his statement was close to the truth.

Apparently, all the men chosen to lead the negotiations knew each other and were on friendly terms.

It shouldn't have been that shocking, since she had known that they had all fought together in the same war, but Dorea still found herself surprised.

Voggo had never spoken of a Mort in the Heidel village, even when sending her south for a desperate request.

That meant that either he hadn't believed the man to still be alive—given the wrinkles that carved his face, it was a decent assumption—or for all their apparent friendliness, he hadn't believed that he would grant them any aid.

The second is much more likely. If he's been chosen as a representative for the Heidels, Yaomi must trust him a lot. That means he wouldn't be swayed by any kind of relationship if it meant going against his people's interests.

The three men took their seats at the center of their own set of chairs, adorned with a blue scarf for the hosts, a red one for the southerners, and a green one for the Forest tribe.

The prepared dishes were placed in the middle of the table, where everyone could easily access them.

Apparently, it was another tradition to eat together before any business could be done.

When she had been tasked with the two diplomatic missions she ran, there simply hadn't been the time to alert the hosts of her coming, and so she hadn't been offered a feast, but now that things were a bit less frenetic, they could observe all the proper rituals.

And it's much harder to get angry at people you just shared a delicious meal with. That's probably the origin of this tradition.

Two anoas had been slaughtered for this feast, and their meats had been cooked in various manners.

Ribs coated in sticky pomegranate sauce sat to Dorea's right, and she reached for a piece. Next to them sat a loin, carved open and then stuffed with the last of the dried figs they had from the previous year's harvest.

Herbs of all kinds adorned the cuts, releasing a mouthwatering fragrance.

A cask of mead was opened, and everyone partook in a toast dedicated to the longevity of their alliance, as Voggo lifted his glass up. " My friends, dear allies, I want to extend my personal gratitude to everyone here for your willingness to forge an alliance and bolster our tribes. As we break bread today, please enjoy this scrumptious feast. May this food fortify us, as our dialogue strengthens our ties. With unity, we'll organize formidable defenses in the north and the south that shall allow us to continue prospering in peace. Let this meal be the start of many fruitful discussions and the reforging of an alliance rooted in resilience and mutual respect. Here's to our collective triumph!"

A loud cheer rang out through the pavilion as everyone drank their glass.

Voggo has always been good at speeches, no matter how much he grumbles. He set the mood perfectly.

The lunch passed quickly, leaving everyone stuffed to the brim. The talk had been kept purposefully to light topics only, as they wordlessly agreed to tackle the main issues later.

Almost licking her chops, Dorea finished the last bits of apple pie that had been set in front of her, only to find the amused gaze of the two Heidel siblings Masi and Melu.

"What?" she asked confusedly.

A chuckle of amusement escaped the two as the girl replied, "Nothing, it's good to see that you know how to fill your stomach. Too many girls think they need to appear dainty in front of men. It's nice to see that you don't care."

Dorea met her eyes, looking for any sign of mockery. She knew she wasn't exactly the most feminine of girls, but eating became more of an all-day activity when one consumed as much energy as she did. There was simply no time for manners. Or at least she thought so; her mother certainly didn't agree.

It seemed, however, that her words were sincere, and so Dorea graced the two with a smile. "I know what I like. And the grannies who prepared the feast are *really* good at their jobs. It would be a pity to leave something."

Their chat was interrupted, as it seemed the delegates were finally ready to start the actual event.

The table was then quickly cleared with the assistance of a few of the older women who had lent themselves to preparing the feast.

"Well then, shall we start?" asked Voggo.

Surprisingly, it was Samos who took word first. "Yes, let's begin. First of all, I want to thank both of your people for the help you gave us when we needed it the most. Some aided us in unorthodox ways"—he looked directly at Dorea— "but you all contributed to our safety."

There was a short applause before he continued, "That said, I'm here mostly because I heard dangerous whispers of movement both to the south and south-east. Is another Great War coming?" he asked, directly looking at Mort, the Heidel leader.

CHAPTER SEVEN

There was a beat of silence as everyone contemplated Samos's words.

A war with the Ergasters would be absolutely disastrous. Nobody could afford it, and they would be swept away by unending waves of men and mages.

The last time the eastern people turned their attentions to the coast, it had taken the might of all the tribes and villages working together to throw them back, and such an effort had cost them dearly.

The Great War had weakened their mages enough that few remained alive today, even though mages who reached a certain level usually lived longer.

Considering how forging an alliance with the northern tribes was entirely out of the question, and given the suspicious movements in the south, Dorea sincerely doubted they'd last long.

We'd be picked apart one by one and crushed into dust. It wouldn't even be a competition.

Her forays into the records room to learn more about warding also had the benefit of teaching her about the war. She had learned that if the Ergasters brought even just half of the troops they used the last time, they'd gain control of the Loisosian coast within months.

Tens of thousands of nonmagical troops, thousands of mages, and entire corps made of beast tamers and siege engines.

Even if they didn't bring any Master-level Gifted, their sheer numbers would be enough to crush whatever resistance they could hope to mount.

"We do not have any evidence that would lead one to think a war with the Ergasters is imminent," the reedy Heidel began. "Indeed, as far as we could tell, they are locked in internal conflicts as the new generation of mages jockeys for more resources and higher positions. Likely, they won't be able to start a campaign for a few years."

Mort was evidently a different beast than Yaomi. The chief had been almost brutally straightforward, and such was her personal power that she could run through any kind of opposition.

On the other hand, the old man seemed to be well versed in the song and dance of diplomacy. He gave them enough information to reassure them that disaster wasn't about to strike while telling them that, somehow, the Heidels had a deep knowledge of the happenings within Ergaster's lands.

Since that should have been impossible, they must have informants inside or sent spies. Both are terrifying because they imply a level of reconnaissance or subversion capability we didn't know they had.

Of course, Whitecliff's leadership had known, since the first meeting in the grasslands, that the Heidels were sending scouts into faraway territories to gain information.

But there was a difference between doing so by avoiding discovery, thanks to the forest being too chaotic to keep control of, and infiltrating an entire society.

It might be that he's lying. Or the information was a onetime thing, like what the caravan leader gave us. But we don't know, and even if we were to ask, he'd probably deflect. Damn, old men can be so scary.

"But"—Mort raised his voice to be heard over the murmuring that had started after the firebomb he just dropped—"that doesn't mean we are entirely safe. The southern tribes have been observed to be congregating in a few different spots, and while this is just speculation, we believe there might be several concurrent attempts at forming cities."

That sent the room into an uproar.

While cities were not unknown to them, as the Ergasters had several, and a few were known to exist in the northeast, well beyond the mountain ranges, they were considered to be far away enough to not be a problem.

If they started popping up in the south—and likely at least a big one in the north, given the Mondeans' efforts to unite the tribes under a single banner— they would become their problem, whether they wanted it or not.

Cities are not just big congregations of people, though. They need infrastructure, trade, armies, and much more.

Evidently, her thoughts were shared by others as well, as Voggo finally raised his hand to indicate his desire to speak.

Luckily, everyone in the room was polite or curious enough to let him, so silence fell in the pavilion.

"You say they want to build cities, as in several of them, but the southern tribes have always been fractious. I have difficulty believing they could be forced to the table so easily. Not to speak of the issue of population. There can't be more than five thousand of them."

His words had the immediate effect of calming everyone down. His concerns were entirely reasonable, and they didn't even start addressing the difficulty of building a city from scratch.

The old Heidel merely smiled sadly. "Those had been my doubts too. But our scouts did a thorough job of confirming the information, and it appears that at least two sites are likely to be successful, with another two attempts being made."

He took a moment to drink from his chalice, smacking his lips. "As for the population concerns, unfortunately, they seem to have spent the last twenty years breeding like rabbits and have increased their numbers by at least threefold. My suspicion, and this has not been proven by any evidence, is that several new shamans were made thanks to a few Mana Geysers, which allowed them to increase their childhood survivability by many times."

On the one hand, they didn't know everything as it seemed before, which relieved her; on the other, Dorea would have much preferred having a clear picture of the happenings down south.

Can't be too greedy. Already knowing this much is a lot. We didn't have to send any of our men to the desolate grasslands or, even worse, the Kame Desert. Well, we'll probably have to send someone to confirm it, just to be sure, but going there with a clear idea of what might be going on is miles better than being blind.

Voggo looked to be in deep contemplation, as the news of several new shamans existing in the south severely changed his calculations.

If more of their men could be healed and sent back to the battlefield, the tribes' ability to wage war so far from home would increase several times.

If their population had exploded as Mort claimed, then they would pose a threat as significant as the Mondeans', if not more.

Evidently, they needed confirmation for all the information that had been dumped on them, but being able to start preparing plans for these new threats was a boon.

"That still doesn't explain how they ended up working together. Even if split into four major groups, something must have pushed them to it. If anything, the Wrath should have made things even worse, as every tribe tried to grab more land," Samos spoke. The Forest chief had stayed silent all throughout Mort's speech, merely tilting his head to one side or the other to better hear his advisors' murmurs.

It might have sounded unfair to question the Heidels so much on the information they freely shared, but extraordinary claims required extraordinary evidence.

Also, since they had been the ones to push for a meeting, going so far as to hoist it on Whitecliff rather than hold it themselves, they must have had an angle to all of this.

By the glint in Mort's eye, that angle was about to be revealed.

"You are correct in your assessment, Chief Samos. It was also our belief that they wouldn't be able to put aside their differences, no matter the opportunities that would come, should they manage to do so. But something shifted the region's balance," the reedy man revealed.

His dark eyes glinted with intelligence as he paused to meet Voggo's and Samos's gazes.

"Volgora the Flying Death and Mussad the Maw met in combat sometime last year and wounded each other enough that they didn't survive to see the Wrath. This has freed the ruins of Kamadar and Katmasou. It's there that the two major attempts are being made."

Shock ran through the pavilion as news of the deaths of two of the greatest beasts of the last generation was revealed.

Even with the incredible distance, Dorea knew those names very well. They had appeared several times in the records of the last war she had perused lately, and beyond that, they were considered almost to the level of legends.

Volgora the Flying Death was a monstrous feathered reptilian creature of a kind that no one had ever seen before, and was known for its absolute mastery over the element of air.

It had devastated entire battlefields when roused to anger. It was known to periodically target human settlements, catching a few as prey and destroying the buildings as a claim of dominance.

Mussad the Maw, on the other hand, was a sandworm that had gorged itself on all life in an area of the desert as large as the land under the three allies' control. Its earth magic made it an apex predator in the desolated territory, as it controlled everything without exception.

More than that, the two monsters were known to have taken residence in the two ancient cities of Kamadar and Katmasou's ruins, respectively.

No one knew precisely why they had fallen, as it had happened ages before their times, but countless people had, over time, resided within their still mighty walls.

The presence of the two beasts had meant that the two main trade hubs of the Kame Desert had been taken out of the equation entirely for the last few decades. Their sudden liberation would be more than enough for the tribes to start congregating again.

The three delegation heads were all busy fending off questions and worries from their people and advisors, and the meeting looked to be over for the time being.

Such momentous revelations would require all three groups to take some time and rethink their approach. The Heidels, being the ones who brought the news to the table, had obviously had the time to digest it, but they likely would still want the pause to ponder on the other two delegations' response.

Just as she thought, Voggo rose from his chair and clapped his hands, getting everyone's attention. "I believe we might be due for a recess. Some time is needed to ponder all the implications of the news our friends have brought, and we'll be able to meet again tomorrow morning with a fresher perspective."

The afternoon was turning into evening, and things would have been wrapped up soon anyways, as the delegations had been traveling for days in the case of the Heidels, and talks such as these were not ones that should be rushed.

At his words, people rose up and started leaving, directed to the area their tents had been set up in the case of those not native to Whitecliff.

Dorea sneaked away soon after, knowing that Voggo would be busy discussing everything with Mark and Ed and that she would have little to add.

Usually, she was more than welcome to take part in their council meetings, but here her inexperience would have rendered whatever she might say practically worthless.

If he wants my opinion on something, he can just send a messenger to call me. Or ask me tomorrow morning, after I have the time to digest the news and the food.

Subconsciously, her feet directed her toward the cliffs, where she'd be left alone with her thoughts.

Somehow, the macabre feeling that had accompanied the place for everyone else had melted away for her shortly after she visited the spot for the first time after the Trial.

That it was avoided by everyone else made it the perfect spot to get some much-needed space.

The day's revelations would immediately affect all their plans, from how much food they should attempt to produce to patrol schedules and missions.

Indeed, Dorea expected to be sent down south to check on the tribe's movements. Others could do it, but she was the only one who'd be able to do it by herself and in much less time too.

That alone would probably push Voggo to send her.

It's not that we can't trust what the Heidels are saying. This is too big to lie about. But having a direct source is fundamental when drawing up long-term plans.

To her surprise, Dorea felt someone approach from the village. As they got closer, she recognized the signature as Masi's, the Heidel boy who fought alongside her and who was Melu's brother.

"I don't want to intrude on your special place, but I thought this might be a good moment to talk," he said once he had gotten close enough to be heard.

Dorea turned, taking him in. Masi was a couple of years older than her and almost fully grown in body. He was much taller than her, almost reaching the height of Whitecliff's tallest man, Ed the hunter.

He wore a simple tunic adorned with the typical geometric patterns preferred by the grasslands people. An animal teeth necklace completed the look.

Dorea knew it was tradition for the Heidel hunters to wear the teeth of the first beast they fought to remind them of how far they had come. Considering the length of the teeth, it must not have been a small one, which implied he was either very skilled or had waited until he received his Gift to hunt.

"Not many people come here. It freaks them out, knowing kids died at this place undergoing the Trial," she replied, looking for signs of discomfort in his expression.

He didn't even twitch. "Yeah, I know. Melu told me about it. It's a nice idea to turn the spot where you got your powers into a memorial. We just had a big feast to commemorate the lost ones and went on with our lives."

That was interesting to hear. Dorea hadn't given much thought about how the other villages had dealt with the Wrath's fallout, but it made sense that not everyone would want to dedicate a piece of their land to be a reminder of what they lost forever.

"I doubt that discussing our respective people's funerary rites is what you came here for. So what is it that you wanted?" she finally asked when it looked like he wouldn't continue speaking.

Masi hummed in thought, looking into the horizon as the wind ruffled his hair. "You are aware that our tribes are likely going to be more and more involved with one another, correct?"

Dorea rolled her eyes. "Yes, of course."

"And that shows of support like what we did at the Battle of the Rocky Hills and the fight at Tumbling Lake, while useful, are not enough to cement such an alliance?" he continued in a leading tone.

This time, she took his words seriously.

Is he saying what I think he's saying?

"Spit it out. What are you implying?"

His hands rose up in defense. "Hey, hey, I'm just the messenger here. You know as much as I do that things aren't going to calm down for many years, if ever, and one of the only few ways of cementing alliances is marriage."

Dorea had been purposefully avoiding thinking about that. While it was a fact of life that one day, she'd have to shack up with someone and pop out a few kids, she wasn't particularly enthusiastic about it, and no one in Whitecliff had brought up the subject with her.

"Bleeding on the battlefield together is a much better show of unity than bleeding on the birthing rack," she replied scathingly.

The boy rolled his eyes at that. "Oh, come on. I'm not saying that you should marry tomorrow. But it is something to keep in mind. External forces will try to squash us, and we need to be certain who we stand with. This is just one of the better ways to do that."

Dorea sighed, knowing that he was telling the truth. It was unlikely that Whitecliff would be able to survive the coming difficulties by itself, and the Heidels had been a stalwart ally.

She truly looked at Masi for the first time, scrutinizing every inch.

He was easy on the eyes, that much was evident, had a good smile, and was a powerful mage. She could remember the strength behind the bolts of lightning he had thrown around, which boded well for his future growth.

That he had been leading a group when she first met him so many weeks ago also told her that he would likely receive a leadership position.

All in all, if he had been a fellow tribesman, she would have put him at the top of her list.

But even having to consider a list of marriageable prospects felt yucky, and Dorea definitely didn't want to have such a conversation in the place where her last crush had died.

Noticing her expression turning into a frown, Masi shook his head with an easy smile. "There is no need to make any big decisions now. This summit doesn't have anything to do with it anyway. I just wanted to alert you to the possibility that this will be something to consider in the future."

Dorea nodded at that and purposefully lightened her facial features. While this wasn't a subject she was a fan of, she could understand that it was a valid issue to raise.

"I get it, and I'm not mad. I'll have to think about this more before I can give you anything, though."

He relaxed his shoulders, apparently having tensed up in wait for an answer. "That's perfectly fine. I won't take more of your time, then. See you tomorrow."

He left, sedately returning to the tents prepared for the Heidel delegation.

CHAPTER EIGHT

The following day, the talks resumed without a hitch. The previous revelations had been shocking, and everyone had needed time to fully process them, but they didn't change the original plan.

If anything, they increased the need for further cooperation. Not only would there need to be a more significant presence of each other's warriors in every village to show support and inform their people of coming conflicts, but sharing more precious information was now also being discussed.

The Forest tribe wasn't about to give away all their secrets, and certainly nothing about how they powered their wards, but they had an abundance of low-level artifacts that could be useful for various tasks.

Samos brought out a few as an example, like the water-collecting cup. It would automatically condense water from the air into itself and would stop any spillage when full.

While it might have seemed entirely useless with the presence of water mages, not all teams could afford to have one on every mission, which would make such a thing very precious indeed.

Others, like a spear with inscriptions that rendered it heavier when swung, were more obviously useful.

Voggo, on the other hand, brought more than a few things to the table. The thing everyone wanted the most was, of course, access to his potions.

Even though Samos himself was a shaman, he recognized that the older man was a much more experienced potioneer, and his healing salves would save many lives in future conflicts.

Furthermore, Whitecliff's contingent offered to cast wards on the two other villages once they completed their own.

Considering that she was the one working on that specific project and hadn't been informed of the need to have it prepared and ready as soon as possible, Dorea felt justified in being a bit miffed.

They should have talked about this with me before announcing it as if it's a done deal. I still haven't even started casting with the prototype, for Goddess's sake!

Admittedly, after the talk with Masi, she hadn't made herself available for any such discussion, but they could have at least told her that morning before going in.

The Heidels, beyond the information they had already shared, offered to put more people in the other two villages as protection than what they would receive.

Everyone understood this was only possible because their population was the largest, being over a thousand people, and thanks to Yaomi's presence. As long as the Witch of Immolation resided within the village, little could threaten their safety, no matter the southern tribes' movements.

Nothing short of a full-scale invasion, at the very least, which they would hopefully learn about before it started. The entire reason behind the exchange program was that, after all.

Well, supposedly, it's so we can slowly integrate better with each other's culture, but everyone knows it's so there is a stake in the protection of every village.

No one would dare withhold aid if their own people would suffer for it. It was basically a hostage exchange, where the hostages would work to defend the kidnapper's home.

"Ah, my dear friends, it brings me great joy and heartfelt warmth to express my deepest gratitude for our commendable progress thus far."

Voggo's hands were raised as if to hug all of them. "It is indeed a remarkable moment to stand before you all today, witnessing how far we have come from the somber shadows of the past. I have seen the walls of misunderstanding and mistrust that might have held us back crumble before our eyes, only to be replaced with bridges of shared respect and unity."

The old man, for all his distaste for grandiose speeches, was actually very good at them, and it seemed that the sentiment was shared by others in the room as they directed all their attention to him.

"Yes, it is true. Our old alliance, that ancient beacon of unity, seemed lost to the sands of time. It lay dormant, deceased, and buried deep within the earth of our history. Yet, here we stand, not to mourn its death but to celebrate its reincarnation. However, it is not a mere echo of a once mighty pact that we hold in our grasp now. Oh, no. We hold something far more significant. We have rekindled the spirit of the alliance, not as it was, but as it ought to be. A spirit forged not only in the fires of necessity but in the profound understanding that we are strongest when we stand together and most prosperous when we share in each other's bounty.

"In this newfound unity, we see a light that will guide us toward a future bright with promise, toward a dawn that holds the potential for a harmony our ancestors could only dream of.

"I firmly believe that this cooperation, this harmony of our tribes, will guide us to not merely survive the trials of the future but to thrive in its midst, to mold it into an era of peace, prosperity, and mutual respect."

A bright smile was affixed on his face as he beheld the congregation of the three tribes.

Dorea had known that the shaman had considered the loss of the grand alliance against the Ergasters to be something of a missed opportunity. That they could have achieved much if they had stuck together, but the sheer emotion in his voice now made her think that he had suffered more than previously implied because of its dissolution.

"We walk this path together with open hearts and eager minds. The alliance may be old, but the spirit that guides us is fresh, filled with hope and the shared dream of a better tomorrow. Here's to nurturing this spirit, to strengthening the bonds that unite us, and to building a future that benefits us all, leaving no tribe behind. After all, it is not our abilities that show who we truly are. It is our choices, and I am grateful we choose unity, respect, and cooperation. The future awaits, my dear friends. Let's embrace it, hand in hand, and stride confidently into the dawn of our shared destiny."

As Voggo finished, the very air stood still, as if unsure of what would happen next. Then, the pavilion erupted into applause.

The old man's words had been heartfelt and moving and, for many, had touched deep within. What they were all doing wasn't just a desperate gamble to survive but a way to honor their ancestors and light the way for a more prosperous future.

And there is the political hook. If I didn't know him as well as I do, I would have fallen to his charm. He's really damn good at this.

The leader of the Forest tribe, Chief Samos, rose from his seat, his eyes shining with a combination of gratitude and determination. He was a tall, stoic figure with a powerful presence. His voice reverberated through the room as he began to speak.

"Elder Voggo, your words have moved us. It is an honor to be part of this renewed alliance, to stand side by side with our fellow tribes, not as adversaries but as allies. We pledge ourselves to this spirit of cooperation. Your wisdom has illuminated a path for us, a path that leads to shared prosperity and a brighter future. The Forest tribe will not shirk this commitment."

There was another round of applause as Samos nodded solemnly and retook his seat.

Ah, so we're going for the portentous and weighty speeches from all sides. Since Voggo's had such great reception, the other two can't just stay silent, or they'd be considered weak. But they can't disagree since their own people were so enthusiastic about the old man's speech. He got them again. Damn.

Dorea did her best not to show her mirth as she took in the situation. It wasn't like the shaman had imposed himself on the others, but he had forced the others' hands by capturing the audience in his grandiose and impassioned call for unity.

It was basically what they all wanted in the first place, but now Voggo had given their desperate attempts to survive a shinier new coat.

They weren't simply weak little villages banding together to survive the depredations of their stronger neighbors. Instead, they were noble warriors who sought to reforge ancient alliances and whose values couldn't be questioned.

Just a little bit of thinking would reveal this farce for what it is, but why would anyone want to do that?

Voggo had taught her, during their private lessons, that people liked to think of themselves as righteous. That applied when attacking innocent people to steal their valuables, which they justified by thinking of the lives their ill-begotten gains would help. It also applied here, where everyone shed the look of a scared victim and took on a righteous image.

The fact that she could see it working on people of all ages just went to show how persuasive the old man could be when he wanted to.

Then, the Heidel's top delegate, Mort, rose. He was a man whose frail body contained an indomitable spirit, and for all his age, his voice rang clear amidst the gathering.

His words echoed Voggo's sentiments, reinforcing the strength of their new-found unity. "Dear allies of Whitecliff and the Forest, I thank you for not only sparking this flame of unity but for helping it burn bright. Your belief in our ability to rise above our past and build a future together inspires us."

And he's trying to regain control of the meeting. Given how he went through us as if we were made of parchment yesterday, he probably didn't expect Voggo to co-opt the whole thing. So he needs to agree in a way that will not put him in a subordinate position to the old man.

"Us Heidels pledge to uphold this spirit of the alliance. We will honor it, nurture it, and ensure that it leads us to a harmonious future. Your vision for unity and shared prosperity is one we wholeheartedly share. Together, we will see it realized."

As Mort took his seat, another round of applause rang through the room, louder and warmer than before. The air was thick with promise and hope, a testament to the power of unity and cooperation. The old alliance's spirit was reborn, stronger and more determined than ever.

Or rather, that was the impression the three leaders had decided to give. Although Voggo had started things off and taken the initiative, the effort would have failed if the other two had opposed it.

That meant that for all their dislike of how things had slipped from their control, the Heidels still believed this to be the correct course of action.

Which tells us more about how dire things really are. This entire thing was likely supposed to be their way of taking control of the alliance, but even if it failed, that they still wanted to go through with it means that Yaomi told them to push for more cooperation, even if their bid for leadership failed.

Dorea didn't particularly enjoy having to speculate so much about her allies' real intentions, especially because she, too, would have much rather believed that the union of the three tribes was a pure and valorous effort brought about simply by their desire to honor their ancestors.

Unfortunately, she had peeked behind the curtain too often to miss what was going on.

I have to wonder if Yaomi actually believed that this would work or if she just wanted to test us. No matter how much she likes to say she doesn't deal in subterfuge, I wouldn't put it past that canny old witch.

"My dear friends," Voggo began, a bright smile lighting up his face. "It swells my heart with immense satisfaction to witness your unwavering valor. Often, the corridors of memory have a curious way of draping our failures and follies in gossamer veils of nostalgia. However, standing before me today are individuals whose actions shine brighter than any embellished remembrance could cast upon them. You have each proven to be paragons of virtue, far surpassing even my most optimistic hopes."

Puffed chests and proud grins were a common sight in the pavilion. The shaman was evidently stoking their self-worth, but Dorea considered it a job well done since it seemed to work.

"The strength of an alliance such as ours is akin to the sturdy oak, its roots reach deep and its branches stretch wide. It is in gatherings like this one that we water these roots, that we nurture these branches. And so, my friends, I propose that we reconvene six months hence. Let us continue to stoke the embers of collaboration, to fan the flames of understanding, and to keep this beacon of hope, our alliance, burning bright. For in unity, we find strength; in strength, we find victory; and in victory, we find the promise of a harmonious future."

The loquacity displayed here would have felt like too much in any other situation, but Dorea could recognize a momentous one when she saw it.

While their alliance had already been forged in the heat of battle, so far it had all rested on solitary meetings where the respective leaders decided by themselves.

And though no one in Whitecliff would gainsay Voggo on it, having the matter be put through a larger group made it that much more official.

When more people were involved, it became much harder to break the pact, as the leaders would have to justify their choices to those who had participated in its forging.

More discussion was to be had, as the specific number of resources and people to be sent around had to be decided, and the schedules needed to be worked out, but the most crucial bit was over.

The alliance had been forged more permanently than anyone expected even just a few months before. Having it out in the open, where the people of all three villages could talk about it, giving it an ideological twist, meant that it was now cemented into reality.

After the less important details were dealt with, Voggo gestured for the people who had volunteered to cater for the summit to bring out the food for the last feast.

Normally, they'd only hold one on special occasions and never so close to another. Still, the shaman had wanted to celebrate the successful talks with something that could be remembered and thus had given the order to prepare enough food for the whole village.

It had taken days for the ladies to cook up for the feast, and people like Jonah's father, Joe the baker, had pitched in, but they had managed to make it in time.

Whitecliff's center was decorated with lanterns and garlands as people spilled into the streets. Tables had been set up, with the help of mages, to host hundreds.

The two delegations looked surprised and delighted at such a festival being prepared in mere hours.

As soon as word got out that the talks had ended on a positive note, the work began, and while Dorea was aware that it was mostly a way for Voggo to cement the alliance further in everyone's minds, she still enjoyed it.

Large boars that had been hunted mere days before adorned the tables, glistening with fat. They had been split open and roasted on charcoal, low and slow, so as to make the meat as tender as possible.

The skin had been later glazed with honey and tangy berry juice, giving it a crackling, sweet and sour taste, in the tradition of the Heidel people.

Even Mort, the reedy old man, looked delighted at the offering.

As sides, roasted vegetables and roots had been tossed with fragrant herbs found in the forest, with cheeses of all kinds serving as accompaniment.

Freshly caught sea bass was also present, grilled directly over the coals and then cleaned of its scales. The tender meat was a delicacy that the other two tribes weren't often able to have, and given the ravenous hunger with which the delegations threw themselves on it, they had been greatly appreciated.

Freshly baked bread adorned all tables, its wonderful aroma inviting all who sat down to eat a piece. Dishes with salted butter were also provided, and many enjoyed the simple treat with gusto.

Finally, after the main meal was over, the desserts were brought out.

The last dried figs they had prepared during the previous summer had been mashed into a coarse and sticky rustic paste. With the addition of ground, roasted hazelnuts from the nearby forest, they were shaped into small bite-sized balls.

They were delightfully chewy, sweet from the sun-dried figs, and satisfyingly crunchy thanks to the nuts.

Dorea happily gorged herself, aware that she'd likely pay for it with a stomachache but more than happy to be there, having avoided patrolling duty unlike a few others who'd have to miss the feast to ensure its smooth completion.

Some food had been saved for them, but it just wasn't the same.

Dorea conversed with everyone she found, for once not feeling the dark shadow of the future looming over her head, and even her temper appeared to have decided to let her rest.

Her decision to be more social was not necessarily simple to put into practice, but moments such as these, where everyone was merry and in a good mood, made it much easier to accomplish.

CHAPTER NINE

In the center of the sun-kissed beach, Dorea and Masi stood, surrounded by an electrified crowd.

Sand whispered between their toes, cooler now that the sun had begun its descent. The waves crashed behind them, creating a serene background noise that did little to quell the tension in the air.

After the summit ended, the Heidel delegation had left behind a small group of three, consisting of Masi, the team leader, and two teenage boys who seemed to be perpetually bouncing around in excitement at having been trusted with such an important task.

No one had had the heart to tell them that since no attack was expected this soon, their only role would be to ingratiate themselves with the population of Whitecliff.

It's not as glamorous, that's for sure. But Melu made it work, so they might be able to do it too.

After a few days, the team of three was joined by seven others, and the exchange program pioneered by his sister began under Masi's leadership.

Two teams of Whitecliff's Gifted were then sent to the Forest tribe and their southern ally to do the same, one led by Lara and one by Leo.

The two refugees had volunteered for the role on Noele's recommendation. And while both were decently powerful mages, Dorea had been surprised that Voggo had readily acquiesced to the request.

"We need to show that we trust them to deal with important things, and this is a good, safe opportunity to do so. Integration can only happen if both sides show willingness. And, between you and me, the actual mission will happen in a few weeks when the Heidels have finished preparing for it. I'll be sending you down there to scout the southern tribes' movements."

That cleared things up. Voggo was using this occasion to test the refugees and not risk his most valuable mages.

It was ingenious and scary in a way that she was becoming increasingly used to.

Still, since she was present in the village and had nothing better to do, Dorea had been tasked with showing the Heidel contingent around.

Luckily for her, however boisterous the boys might have been, they followed behind Masi like ducklings. Their behavior was much more respectful than one might have expected by teenagers, which likely explained why they had been sent at all.

While a first exchange had already happened, Melu had set the standard for future interactions very high, and immediately dropping the ball after formally signing the alliance would have been a terrible signal.

Therefore, she brought them around Whitecliff, showing the fields that were seeing the first harvest, where laborers and farmers worked together to make the most out of it.

Food stores would need refilling after the influx of refugees, and since Voggo believed that more such groups might come their way, they had to reap and then plant again as soon as possible.

The forest would always provide for them, what with the abundance of wildlife and plants, but relying on it entirely for all their needs was a quick way of attracting the attention of the old monsters that resided in its depths.

Such conflicts had to be avoided at all costs. Ever since Dorea had come face-to-face with Old Titan, she had been more confident than ever that the beast was capable of taking on the entirety of Whitecliff's mages by himself. Luckily, he was content to remain in his territory. Doing anything to provoke him was foolish to the extreme, and she was very glad that Voggo agreed with her there.

Their tour had taken them up north, toward her family's ranch, where the mating season had started.

The boys had been incredibly amused at the sight of rutting anoas, which Dorea thought was somewhat immature, and the dances the moas did to entice partners sent them rolling with laughter.

Finally, they arrived at the beach. It wasn't as deserted as it had been the last few times she had seen it, as the summer was now in full swing, and people liked splashing about in the water or even just resting after a long day of work, being caressed by the breeze.

It was there that the idea for a sparring match took root. The boys that made up Masi's entourage had been curious about her power ever since they first met, having apparently heard of some of her exploits but being doubtful of the more unrealistic ones.

When Dorea confirmed that she had indeed killed ten men from a distance without being noticed, they started speculating about whether she was stronger than their leader or if he still held the lead.

By this point, Dorea was long used to being underestimated, so she didn't take it to heart when most boys agreed that Masi was still more powerful. Still, when he commented that he could probably take her on, even if it was in a joking manner, she couldn't help herself. "Care to put your money where your mouth is?"

A beat of silence followed the question before excited grins and hoots of laughter escaped the group. They all started pounding on Masi's shoulders, egging him on to take the bet.

He looked at her seriously for a moment, dispelling the easy image he had maintained so far. His eyes were asking, without the need for words, if she believed it would be a good idea to fight.

"It'll just be a spar, no need to get serious. We have fought together in the Battle of the Rocky Hills, so we both know we can handle a little bit of heat," she replied to the unspoken question.

"Very well, if you think it's a good idea, I don't mind getting down and dirty with you," he answered, his roguish grin back in place.

"Care to take the first swing?" Masi's smile was rakish, his posture relaxed, yet his eyes bore the sharp intensity of a striking serpent.

Fondly exasperated, Dorea raised her hands. With a delicate motion, she tugged at the fabric of the sky overhead. A crack echoed in the air, and a silver whip of air darted from the heavens toward her opponent.

Unfazed, he danced around it with the grace of an eel in water, his speed surprising her. He then returned her playfulness with a bolt of lightning.

"Your courtesy is rather . . . shocking," she bantered, surrounding herself with a barrier of swirling winds as his electric retaliation raced toward her. Their collision was an explosion of raw energy, sending ripples through the audience.

"And yet, you seem unharmed, Dorea," Masi fired back. He moved, carving elegant arcs in the sand with his feet, a predator circling his prey, awaiting the opportune moment.

Unyielding, Dorea answered by coaxing the waves into action.

At her command, a towering surge of seawater raced toward the boy. Standing resolute, he wove a shield of lightning around himself.

The clash of elements was deafening, reducing the wave to a cloud of steaming mist.

With the cover of steam, Masi moved, his silhouette a phantom shadow.

Suddenly, he emerged, a radiant whip of lightning in his hand snaking toward Dorea. Swift as the wind, she took to the air, jumping from one platform to the next, avoiding the strike and retaliating with a bolt of lightning of her own.

As the mist cleared, Masi redirected her attack with his whip, catching the electricity and making it his own. "I know you can do better than that. I've seen you fight," he challenged.

Dorea rolled her eyes, not falling for the taunt. This was a sparring match, and as such, she would avoid using her full might simply because one could never know what could happen when clashing so recklessly.

"The show has just begun," she declared, landing on the sand gracefully.

Seizing the opportunity now that she was back in range, Masi shot toward her, his whip snapping with power.

He launched it forward, crashing it against her reformed shield of air. With a grin of challenge, the boy started striking her construct from all sides, attempting to weaken it enough to break through.

Surprisingly, he dropped the whip shortly after, letting it disperse harmlessly. Instead he punched the condensed air, his fist bursting with power.

The impact was enough to break the shield, sending Dorea skidding across the sand with the backlash.

The crowd gasped at the show of power, impressed that a single punch was enough to do what the whip hadn't been able to.

For just a moment, she felt a flash of anger at the subterfuge. He had let her believe that the whip was his trump card while he had developed physical enhancement spells to such a high degree of mastery.

Empowerment was a complex field, especially where lightning was concerned, which told Dorea that he likely had direct supervision from someone with a great deal of experience.

In her rage, she reached for the sea, swiftly condensing the water and preparing to cast her Exploding Water Bullets.

Masi's laughter rang through the beach, breaking the tension that had fallen and the haze that muddled her thoughts.

With a jolt, Dorea let go of her spell. If she had gone through with her intention, she would have definitely won the spar, but it would have meant escalating too far.

I could have killed him with that. This is so stupid. Why would I ever get this angry about a simple fight where the stakes are this low?

Luckily for her, Masi seemed utterly oblivious to what had just almost happened.

"What a . . . shocking result," he teased, coming closer and offering her his hand. She glanced at it and took it, causing cheers to erupt from the spectators.

"That was a terrible pun. You just copied me," she commented teasingly after he let go of her.

With an exaggerated flourish, the boy bowed in apology. "I'm terribly sorry. I'll study the ancient art of puns to a much higher degree before our next spar."

Although his tone bordered on mocking, the spark of amusement in his eye told her he was just an incredibly sarcastic person.

With a huff, Dorea left him behind, walking toward the crowd. "Make sure to actually learn how to win next time. Just because you broke my shield doesn't mean it was over," she called out without looking.

"Hey, hey, I won fair and square. You put up a good fight, but my power was too much. There is nothing to be ashamed of; many have lost to me," he said as he quickly moved to join her.

"Victory means that you had a clear shot that would have incapacitated me. You didn't, as you stopped well before that," she commented, speaking as if to a very simpleminded child.

"Yeah, Masi, were you afraid to get hurt if you got any closer?" one of the Heidel boys jeered.

Loud laughter ensued, and her opponent ended up the object of much teasing, ranging from being scared to get cooties, to being too chivalrous.

It didn't make much sense to accuse him of completely opposite behaviors, but Dorea knew that friends making fun of you didn't necessarily have to follow a logical process.

"That was well fought," commented a familiar voice from behind, startling Dorea.

She had gotten so used to always sensing everything surrounding her that when someone developed the ability to hide, either through a spell or a special skill, she ended up being extremely surprised.

This time, Jonah's familiar face and voice prevented her from responding violently, and she dispelled a Lightning Sphere with a cough of embarrassment.

"How did you get here without me noticing?" she asked the boy, moving in as if to hug him, only to stop when she got close.

Would Beth think me hugging him now means I want to steal him away?

"Oh, come off it," Jonah muttered, closing the distance and embracing her. "I don't care what kind of fight you and Beth have going on; you both need to drop it and make peace," he said in her hair.

Dorea tensed up, ready to explain to him exactly how things had gone and how she had absolutely no fault in the whole mess, but she stopped herself.

Do I really want to keep this thing going for much longer? Is it worth possibly losing my best friends?

And the answer she gave herself was a resounding no. No matter how annoyed she might have been with Beth, she didn't want to lose her.

She let out a long breath, releasing her anger and frustration, and stepped away from Jonah.

"We'll talk more about this later. Possibly when Beth is also present." Then she turned to face Masi, who had been observing the interaction keenly. "Now, this is Masi, the leader of the Heidel contingent. Masi, this is Jonah, my dear friend and our best sensor."

The two boys looked each other in the eye for a moment before a cough from her prompted them to move. They shook hands, still maintaining eye contact.

"A pleasure," the darker-skinned of the two said.

"The pleasure is all mine," Jonah replied.

There was a weird tension between them, but Dorea decided it wasn't worth trying to budge in. Boys sometimes were strange, after all.

"You still haven't told me how you evaded my senses," she interrupted after a while.

That seemed to break whatever was going on, and they let go of each other. Jonah turned to face her with a somewhat forced smile. "That's my newest spell: Silent Steps. It makes me invisible to passive sensing of all kinds."

"Whoa! That's fantastic! How did you do it?" she asked excitedly. The awe of learning a new piece of magic had luckily never faded for her, making spending long hours on experimentation much easier.

"Wait!" she interrupted him before he could reply. "Is that what those guys so long ago were doing? The first few Mondean groups? Is that where you got the idea?"

"That's definitely where I got the first glimpse into the world of stealth. But Mel already developed a way of hiding herself, remember?"

Dorea stood still for a moment before scratching her head embarrassedly. "Oh yeah, I forgot about her."

Loud laughter interrupted Jonah's words as Masi held his stomach. "Oh, that was too funny. You just live in your own little world, don't you, Dorea?" he asked.

Rather than taking offense, the girl chuckled herself. She was well aware that she had a problem with paying enough attention to what went on around her.

She had genuinely never thought about the girl since she rescued her from captivity. "Is she still active, then? Has she recovered?" She turned to Jonah.

He rolled his eyes at the question but still answered, "She has gotten much better. I've actually just returned from a mission with her. Her suggestions are what allowed me to refine my spell, after all."

"That's good to hear. She was in rough shape last I saw her," Dorea commented distractedly. She then turned toward Masi, gesturing to the other Heidels still at the beach. "I think I've shown you guys everything important. If you have more questions, I'm sure you can find someone to assist you. I'll see you guys around."

She grabbed Jonah's hand without letting the boy answer and started marching away.

They walked for five minutes before she realized she had no idea where Beth might be.

"She's just finishing her shift at the wall. We can wait for her at the benches outside the bakery; I'll send her a message to let her know," he said, not even waiting for her to ask the question.

"You know me too well," Dorea replied, taking off toward their destination.

He just chuckled, following closely behind. "So, are you ready to bury the hatchet?"

She groaned, knowing that she'd have to make the first move. No matter how much she wanted to be stubborn and wait for Beth to crawl to her and apologize, she knew that if they didn't solve their quarrel there and then, it would become a much bigger thing.

Considering how I'm going to get sent down south to check on the tribes' movements, it could be weeks before we have another chance of making up. I don't want to risk my life knowing my best friend hates me.

Once they got to the bakery, Jonah went inside to pick up a few pieces of sweetbread, well aware that having a dessert on hand could act like a magical potion of calming.

Shortly after, Beth joined them. The girl looked rough, as if she hadn't slept well for days.

Her hair was a mess, and heavy bags pulled beneath her eyes. Still, she brightened up when she saw Jonah, rushing to his side for a quick peck and hugging him.

After a couple of minutes of silence, she released her boyfriend and turned to look at Dorea.

Before the blond girl could even open her mouth to start speaking, Dorea was tackled to the ground in a bear hug.

"I'm sorry, I'm sorry," Beth blubbered. "I was so worried about Jonah since he's been going on such dangerous missions, and I thought you were encouraging him. I'm sorry; I shouldn't have taken it out on you. I didn't mean anything of what I said."

Dorea sighed, rubbing the girl's back comfortingly. "I shouldn't have been as waspish as I was either. We both have had a rough time lately and had a blowout. I'm sorry too."

The two girls laughed wetly at their foolishness. Some things remained unsaid, problems that would undoubtedly arise in the future, but for the moment, they were finally back together.

INTERLUDE

Kannis the Wolf

No matter how many times I see it, I can never get used to it.

As he walked through the corpses of the enemy mages, Kannis stopped at every single one, searching their clothes and bodies for anything of value.

He wasn't ashamed of his current role. That kind of emotion had long left him.

This was the tenth such battle he participated in, although saying he had fought would be an exaggeration.

He had shot his quiver of arrows and was almost certain that he had hit at least one man. That was nothing compared to the carnage the mages had left behind.

The nonmagicals served primarily as harassing troops before any fighting could occur and, once it was over, as cleanup.

Some would take offense to being rendered so useless. For their skill and strength of arm to be relegated to such menial and demeaning chores.

Those people had all died. Or rather, some might still be around, but at the very least they had learned to keep their tongues from wagging.

Kannis himself had been outraged at the beginning, after not only seeing his village bent under a tyrant's heel but being ordered to fight so that more could be enslaved.

That outrage had left him the first time he saw Olnar turn a defector into a bag of skin and bones.

The sight had never left him. There had been no time to scream for help, no last words. Just the horror was left, etched into Markus's face and in his memory forever.

He didn't want to end up like that. That was something he swore to himself.

Death didn't necessarily scare him, but there was a difference between going out swinging, fighting to take down a great beast or in battle to protect one's loved ones, and what Markus and so many others went through.

By now, he was almost used to the sight of so many desiccated corpses. The problems came when he looked too closely, and young eyes stared back at him, accusing him of their death.

I'm sorry, but there is nothing anyone can do about it. They say Olnar's about to cross into Master level, and then no one will be able to stop him.

His initial hope, after witnessing the casual cruelty of his new master, had been that one of the few truly powerful mages left in the mountain range would deal with the new chief.

Unfortunately, Olnar was not just given incredible power by the Mother or the many other gods he worshipped—honestly, Kannis was not sure any god could call themselves that and allow such horrible things to happen. No, he had a sharp intellect to go with it. Military matters were either quickly dealt with overwhelming strength or thanks to careful planning.

Impossible-to-surpass roadblocks, like Ghionn the Invisible Hand, were courted until they fell under the boy's charm.

Kannis still didn't understand how exactly the old Master-level ice mage had been convinced that his people would be perfectly safe under Olnar's aegis, but somehow it happened.

Well, everyone knows Ghionn wanted to leave his village and go back to fighting the monsters in the True North, but he managed to keep himself in check for over three decades. Something has to have changed . . .

It wasn't really his problem anyway. Once, he had been in line for a leadership position in his tribe. Not chief, as that was generally reserved for mages, but he could have led the hunters. He had been groomed for it.

That life felt more like a dream at times. He sometimes saw his old tribesmen, but no one was allowed to recreate their own groups once absorbed within the Mondeans.

They were supposed to be the start of something much grander. The entire Sapiens population of the Loisos region under one banner. They'd be greater than any Heidel or Ergaster could ever hope to be.

Or those were the claims repeated by the officers. Kannis didn't believe them one whit, but again, he had long since surrendered himself to the tide of history.

Some people truly bought into the rhetoric spouted by the Mondeans and fought with the aggressiveness only true believers had.

He always made sure to stand behind them on the battlefield. Few shields were as efficient as an entire line of rabidly obsessive humans.

An explosion shook the land, causing him to drop everything and dive between the corpses.

His commander had given the order to start scouring the battlefield after Olnar was done with his magic, but it seemed like a few pockets of resistance still existed.

Hiding between the fresh bodies of his slain enemies was not one of his favorite things to do, but it beat being caught in the crosshair of a battle between Gifted.

As the light of the setting sun illuminated the battlefield, Kannis observed the renewed fighting.

Two separate groups of enemy Gifted had apparently faked their deaths or escaped notice long enough that the Mondeans had lowered their guards.

Taking advantage of that, they had tried to strike the group's center from two sides, likely aiming to take down Olnar, thinking he would be too tired after the battle.

The fact that they hadn't been rendered into skin bags made it clear that they had been right, but given the massive waves of water crashing against the enemy's hastily constructed shields, the young chief still wasn't out of the fight.

The clansmen tried to regroup. Their air and lightning mages attempted to retaliate while all the water-aspected Gifted fought for control of the liquid with Olnar.

They likely would have managed to break it if he had been alone, but the chief almost never traveled without his entourage—aside from the scouting missions he insisted on doing by himself, for some reason. And it was those people who interfered, casting terrible bolts of lightning that caused the very earth to shudder, making his teeth chatter involuntarily.

Kannis didn't see what happened next, too worried about his own safety to care to sneak a peek at a battle between what might have been gods to him.

Helping himself with his elbows, the man crawled through the piles of bodies, huffing at the effort, until he arrived beneath a large stone's shade.

The mountains were never as hot as the south, but even here, staying under the summer sunlight for too long was a good way of burning yourself. Also, and more importantly, desiccated bodies didn't make for a great shield against the force of nature being thrown around.

Thunderous bangs and heavy tremors continued for a few minutes before they finally stopped.

Before Kannis could think of raising his head to check on the situation, one last resounding crash echoed in the valley, signaling one of Olnar's favorite moves.

He had taken a liking to using the water he pulled from his victims' bodies to crush the remaining resistance, and Kannis had gotten unfortunately familiar with the sound a wave that big made when it smashed into humans.

Few would remain alive after that, and honestly, it might have been a mercy not to survive it. Seeing your families captured and turned into slaves in all but name was a terrible thing.

He had been lucky to be part of the first wave of conquered tribes, since there had been more of a need for fighters and workers rather than the abundance that led to the terrible conditions those who were integrated now received.

Of course, Olnar wasn't stupid enough to simply force everyone into servitude. People could prove themselves by going on dangerous missions, like those who went to the south.

For whatever reason, the people there had managed to resist several assaults, one in which he had taken part.

Coming face-to-face with Ed from Whitecliff had been a bit of a shock, and he could admit to himself to have been ashamed. Ashamed of being forced to attack people who had done nothing to deserve it.

Still, orders were orders, and Kannis, for all his experience, was not in a high enough position to be able to challenge them.

Maybe if he rose through the ranks enough, he'd be able to convince the Mondean leadership to send him south to entreat with the Sapiens tribes there.

There was no chance for them to survive the coming conflict, no matter the few victories they had collected. If he could make them see reason, they'd be spared the horrifying death that so many of Olnar's enemies went through.

For the moment, that remained a daydream. He had acquitted himself decently well lately, but the bias for mages to be in leadership positions was great, and even amongst the nonmagicals, the Mondean-born ones had precedence over the second-order citizens.

After five more minutes of silence, Kannis slowly and carefully rose up, checking several times that no more fighting was about to erupt.

His skills at noticing dangerous animals in the wilds had served him well in dealing with powerful mages, but he could only push his luck so far.

Therefore, with a heavy heart and defeated mindset, Kannis the Wolf, the once proud hunter who ranged from the great forest of the south to the high peaks of the north, returned to his duty of scavenging corpses without so much as an imprecation.

If he found enough valuables, he'd be able to skip having to look through those defeated last, thus avoiding their mangled bodies, which was, to him, the most important thing.

CHAPTER TEN

The relief she felt at making up with her best friend was incredible. Dorea hadn't even realized how much she had missed the easy companionship she had with Beth, but now that she had it back, she couldn't be happier.

Jonah hung around for a while before bowing out, too tired from his mission to stay awake much longer.

Beth looked like she severely needed to sleep too, but she kept talking for hours, sharing all the fears, happiness, and emotions she had experienced during the days they hadn't spoken.

While Dorea was all for making up for lost time, she drew the line when she noticed her friend's eyes starting to close.

Between the worries about Jonah's missions and their fight, Beth hadn't been sleeping well, and having just returned from a shift at the wall, she was dead on her feet.

Therefore, Dorea executively decided that she needed to sleep, and unheeding the girl's protests, she lifted her up in the air with a platform and brought her back home, where she dumped her in the capable hands of Eloise, Beth's mother.

The woman thanked her and promised she'd make sure her daughter would get to bed and sleep until the next morning, chuckling evilly as Beth protested her treatment.

Having done that, and with the promise that she'd dedicate an entire day to her two best friends where they'd go on an old-fashioned adventure like they did before the Wrath, Dorea set off toward the gates.

Her only duty for the day had been to show Masi and his group around the village, and having done that, she was free to do as she wished.

With her reconciliation with Beth done, one of her main problems had been resolved.

Since she was nowhere close to solving the much bigger one, the fiery temper that was starting to rear its ugly head more and more, Dorea decided to work off some stress in the forest.

The sun still hadn't dipped, and even then, to a mage like her, the night was almost as clear as the day.

Most people had grandiose spells and extraordinary rituals in mind when they thought of a Gifted's life, but to Dorea, the main improvement came from the sheer utility of one's mystical senses.

Being able to always know where everything was gave someone a level of assuredness in their movements that was impossible to find in a nonmagical.

I haven't stubbed a toe ever since the Wrath! I don't need to light a candle to go to the bathroom at night, and I am never surprised by anyone's presence. Well, almost never.

She couldn't possibly live without it nowadays, having gotten too used to it.

The other main quality of life improvement was her movement spell, Air Boost. However simple a concept it might have been, it allowed her to cross distances at speeds that would have once been unthinkable.

When it turned into a spell, its efficiency and maneuverability also increased enough that she could use it without worrying about crashing, even in the forest.

And while Dorea knew that others would soon start developing their own mobility magics, she was the only one who could do it at the moment.

She took full advantage of her skill and reached the wall in only a few minutes, jumping above it with a cheeky wave to Nora, who was manning the gate.

She couldn't see it, having already left the area, but her senses told her that the girl sighed in exasperation, shaking her head.

Dorea sped off into the wild with a laugh, taking great care to angle herself away from Old Titan's territory.

She plunged into the verdant maw of the forest, the heart of a world where nature told stories through rustling leaves and bird songs. The melody of life echoed around her, still not quietened for the night. Yet beneath the serene serenade lay a vein of raw tension.

This wasn't an ordinary walk through the woods. Today, Dorea was on a hunt.

She wanted both to try her hand at something bigger than her usual targets and to see if she could hunt her quarry with the skills she had seen many hunters use during the patrols.

She hadn't learned enough by watching to replicate all their behaviors, as it took many years to reach such a level. Still, Dorea suspected she might be able to make up for her deficiencies thanks to magic.

Thus, she slowed down, dispelling Air Boost with a thought. If she wanted to do things well, she needed to move quietly enough not to be noticed.

Each of her footsteps was an exercise in deliberation and subtlety. Her fingers teased the heavy, moist air, tracing the soft pulse of electricity hidden within the atmosphere. She kept her ears open for that distinct sound—the signal of a prey's presence.

Dorea ignored most animals that would have seen her stop for a fight any other day.

Boars and birds weren't her targets for the day, and even the solitary glyptodon's presence she felt at the edge of her senses couldn't arrest her march.

No, she sought something she had wanted to fight for many months. Ever since her first mission, if she was to be honest.

Being in the presence of Old Titan had taught her that power was inherent, and even if the monster had been a quarter of the size, it would have been terrifying.

That, however, didn't mean that a large body wasn't a weapon of its own. And if she wanted to keep growing in power, she needed to start hunting greater beasts.

While she was not ready to face the older enhanced animals of the forest, and she wouldn't be for a while, there were creatures who had gained their powers at the same time as her, who had risen amongst the ranks.

She was seeking something that could give her a fight, as she was still somewhat frustrated by the little sparring match she had had with Masi.

While she could understand that such things were closer to demonstrations rather than true battle, she felt like she had been given a taste of something delicious, only for it to be taken away.

Therefore, she was going to get that delicious thing for herself.

As she got deeper into the forest, she came to find that one of the tributary rivulets of Tumbling Lake had changed course.

After the Wrath, no weather event had happened with enough strength to do such a thing, which meant deliberate action.

She was familiar with this specific stream because it was the one she'd fought the glyptodon in so long ago. That meant that something had either fought there with enough force to change the landscape—Dorea doubted that was the case since the forest looked untouched—or that something had decided to change the course for mysterious reasons.

Following the water upriver, Dorea looked for traces.

No human would do such a thing since they would be immediately found out by the Forest tribe or Whitecliff's patrols. That meant it was either a strong enough person to not care about the two villages, but she couldn't fathom why they would want to do such a thing, or an enhanced beast.

Dorea was almost certain it was the latter.

She found more instances of change in the stream's course as she walked. None of them were particularly dramatic, being only a dozen feet on one side or the other, but they definitely showed a pattern.

Her quarry enjoyed playing around with the waters, which showed a certain level of intelligence and sapience. Dumb animals wouldn't see the need to do such a thing, after all.

Beasts like the glyptodon she had fought splashed around, submerged themselves, and used the water as a toy, but they never went out of their way to change the landscape, even if they had the power to do so.

That meant there was a will behind it. A relatively dumb one, for sure, but still.

This marked her first encounter with an intelligent beast. Or, well, the first encounter where she had a chance to do anything beyond hope for a swift death.

Putting aside the terrifying memory of Old Titan's very sharp teeth so close to her, Dorea quickened her pace, excited to get to her target.

Finally, she started noticing deep, large imprints in the muddy soil. The change in the stream's course had left its previous path full of sludge, and she found the tracks she was looking for there.

Dorea barely restrained herself from whooping in joy. Not only had she found something strong enough to give her a fight, but its traces pointed to it being a massive being. And there was only one type of creature this far north that it could be: a therium.

The gigantic sloths liked eating all kinds of plants, and since this area had been cleared by her of pesky predators, it would have free rein on its bounty.

Excited but cautious at the same time, Dorea slowed her pace. If it genuinely was a therium powerful enough to have developed intelligence, she needed to ensure not to make any mistakes.

Strategies she had developed against the dumber beasts wouldn't work as easily on it. She had to approach this fight as if she was about to fight a human. A very big one, for sure, but still something capable of adapting on the fly.

But if it's that smart, should I even try to fight it? I want to release some steam, but that shouldn't mean I become a rabid animal. I need to show some restraint.

With a heavy heart, she decided to approach it with an open mind. If the therium was as intelligent as she suspected, establishing a friendly relationship might be worth it.

If, on the other hand, it wasn't, or it was but still decided to attack her, then she'd use her full might to bring it down.

While our food stores are filling up nicely, bringing back something that big will go a long way to replenish what we used for the feast. It won't always be summer, after all.

With her senses fully extended, Dorea approached what she believed to be the beast's territory. The stream had been warped beyond recognition here, turning it into a chain of small ponds, where signs of a giant creature rolling around told her she was on the right path.

Trees were knocked down, and their foliage and fruits were eaten entirely, painting a picture of laziness and gluttony.

She could already imagine what she'd see. A fat therium, cooling off in an artificial pool and consuming all around it.

Okay, I need to stop with the preconceptions. I have absolutely no proof it's doing anything bad. And even if it is eating all the vegetation, as long as it doesn't consume everything, it's not that big of a deal.

A few minutes later, pushing through the underbrush, Dorea finally started sensing something.

At the edge of her range, something was moving. Something big, so big that it could only be her quarry.

With great care—and cursing herself for not learning more about Jonah's new spell that would have rendered her invisible to passive sensing—she approached.

Luckily, it seemed that the great beast was sleeping. A large area had been cleared, with dozens of trees having been felled and piled up on the side of the clearing.

Some spotted signs of having been snacked upon, while others had been neatly stacked as if in a pantry.

In the middle was an unnatural pool. The forest ground had been dug up and compacted to form a small lake, deep enough for three of her to stand on top of each other.

Inside, her target slept. It wasn't as big as the therium the hunters had felled so many months ago, but it was definitely much bigger than anything she had ever fought before.

Still, she hadn't yet decided if she could justify attacking the animal. While she enjoyed hunting very much and had somehow started taking some pleasure in fighting against Whitecliff's enemies, the therium had done nothing to deserve death.

Its actions had been destructive, but not enough to justify attacking it.

Unfortunately, the choice was ripped away from her. With a great bellow, the beast rose from the water, sending a destructive wave in her direction.

Dorea had been expecting it, though, never having let down her guard, and immediately activated her Air Boost, flitting through the trees, her form blending seamlessly with the swirling air currents, a wraith amidst the foliage.

"Wait, I don't want to fight!" she yelled, moving her hands to show she didn't mean any harm.

The therium apparently took that wrong, as it recalled the water it had sent out and condensed it into a drill, shooting it her way.

It missed her by a hairbreadth, crashing through several trees behind her.

That level of power could only belong to something well within the Journeyman rank. The way it used the waters, not just instinctively but with developed manipulations, also told her that she had been spot on with her guess about its intelligence.

Unluckily, it seemed to have no remorse in using that intelligence to kill her.

Firming up her resolve, she decided that if the therium wanted to fight, she'd definitely give it a fight. She had come here looking for one, and she'd certainly never back down when her overtures of peace were so rudely dismissed.

Sapience is not a necessary indicator of intelligence; the Mondeans should have shown me that.

Taking aim thanks to the clear line of sight, she called upon her lightning magic, never letting go of her Air Boost in case the therium took another crack at turning her into mush.

Energy crackled at her fingertips as she formed her Lightning Sphere and released it at the colossal creature.

Instead of using the pond's water to shield itself like she had hoped for, the beast showed further cunning by conjuring a water barrier using only its mana, thus creating a pure liquid that wouldn't allow the electricity to reach it.

Dorea's eyes hardened, undeterred by the failed attempt. She called upon the air, sending forceful gales in her adversary's direction, intending to break its concentration and unbalance the water shield.

The therium retaliated with defiance that shook the forest, repelling her gales with ferocious jets of water. Dorea evaded as best she could, but the onslaught was relentless.

A stray shot clipped her, stopped from breaking bone and flesh only by a last-second move, through which she hardened the winds of Air Boost into a shield.

Changing spells like that was not easy, especially under duress, but necessity was the mother of invention.

Uninjured, Dorea was left soaked nonetheless, and by the mocking bellow of the therium, it, too, knew how close it had gotten to victory.

Cold but determined, Dorea reached deeper into her reservoir of magic. She closed her eyes, listening to the symphony of elements around her—the crackle of electricity high up in the air, the subtle rhythm of the water, the whispers of the wind.

Gathering her power, she renewed her assault. It was evident that blunt force wouldn't work this time, as the therium was both too powerful in its defense and too canny to fall to provocations.

Thus, she decided to take full advantage of her Gift. The water that had soaked her and the ground rose up, condensing into acorn-sized balls.

The Bullets she had harnessed shot toward the beast like a hail of liquid arrows. It expanded its shield, fortifying it to catch all the projectiles. It buckled severely but held under the onslaught.

With a triumphant grin, Dorea spun up another Lightning Sphere and shot it into the shield. To the therium's surprise, the spell exploded on contact, and this time the electricity passed through, severely shocking it.

Taking full advantage of its inability to do more than twitch, the blonde shot three more Spheres into the artificial lake. The water immediately superheated, exploding into a cloud of hissing mist, and the mighty creature was sent crashing on its side.

The bellows of pain were almost like music to her, the sound raw with shock, and she started approaching the creature.

Still maintaining her shield up, wary of a last-minute attack, she finally got close enough to see the damage she had wrought.

Its fur was matted with blood, angry welts littered its form where her lightning had hit. The twitching of the muscles belied its inability to do anything beyond glare hatefully.

The beast was so weak that, although she could sense it trying to move the waters into a last desperate push, she merely needed to swat at its mana like one would an annoying fly.

Having lost in its gambit, the therium turned away from her, looking up to the sky as laborious gasps escaped it.

Dorea wanted to explain that they hadn't needed to fight. That she had come with good intentions, seeking to build a good relationship, but she respected the great animal too much to turn its last moments into a litany of complaints.

Instead, she put her hand on its fur, and with a final surge of electricity, she shut down its heart.

Silence again reigned in the forest as birds restarted their chorus and insects returned to buzzing. It was as if the fierce battle they had just fought had merely been a ripple in time, but even if no one else cared, Dorea promised herself she would.

This hadn't been an ordinary hunt, after all. It had been closer to a dance, a clash of wills. The therium had been smart enough to understand that fighting wasn't the only choice, and it still attacked her.

Dorea could respect that.

CHAPTER ELEVEN

The rush of power Dorea felt once the therium exhaled its last breath was great. Much more significant than any single hunt before that and comparable to what she received after the Battle of the Rocky Hills.

Back then, she had been too out of it to properly appreciate it, but now she was at full capacity. And she enjoyed everything, from the tingling of new mana being absorbed to the slight stretch and feeling of fullness as her reserves expanded.

That a single beast could give such a great boost could only mean that great rewards awaited her if she dared hunt more powerful opponents.

Of course, that came with much-expanded risks. If the therium's water drill had even just clipped her, she would have been done for.

That, by itself, was a blaring reminder that she needed to work on her defensive repertoire. An elemental armor like what Masi or the Forest people used could be an option, or she could work more on her spherical wind barrier.

It had saved her from inevitable defeat just a few minutes before, and if she could manage to turn it into a spell, she'd have a decisive advantage.

It wouldn't allow her to get in for close combat, but that wasn't her style. Masi might enjoy jumping like a rabbit all around the battlefield, strengthening his body to punch things harder, but she couldn't really see herself following that path.

Voggo had been clear in his explanation that magical enhancement would only increase what was already present. For a trained warrior, that was a perfectly reasonable choice.

It would allow them to use what they had spent years learning, even as they transitioned from rank-and-file combatant to mage.

Therefore, the path of body enhancement was not for her. Beyond the lack of experience and muscle, Dorea enjoyed having enough distance from her opponent to control the battlefield.

She'd need to learn a defensive spell sturdy enough that no one, not even people like Masi who used their power in a concentrated manner, would manage to break her barrier. Considering how she had once held for thirty seconds against the entire Mondean force sent to attack the Forest village, Dorea believed she was on the right path.

Every day that she fought, she learned something more. And as long as the Goddess allowed her to stay alive, she'd continue to do so.

For the moment, she had a carcass to bring back to Whitecliff. The benefit of the therium having been so destructive was that it had chased away any leftover predator that might have attacked her during the trip back, so she could take her time with it. The noise of battle should have also served as a deterrent, at least for a while.

Deciding to use the water accumulated during the fighting, Dorea motioned with her hands upward, collecting the liquid from the ponds scattered all over the clearing.

She then turned to the still half-submerged therium and considered it. Had she been able to establish communication with it, she would have felt some trepidation at taking it to be butchered and eaten, but it being so antagonistic from the start had removed the problem.

With another gesture, the collected water merged with the artificial pool and rose up.

The rushing sound, as more than half of the small lake's volume was lifted in the air, was great, reminding Dorea of Tumbling Lake.

For a moment, she entertained the idea of crafting her own beautiful spot one day, changing the landscape to fit her whims. But that day was still far off.

Though she could likely do it with hard work and long hours, if something just a bit stronger than her came along, she wouldn't be able to protect it.

And she already had her hands full with defending Whitecliff.

No, it's a stupid idea. It sounds cool, being so powerful that nature has to bow to my whims, but that's a bit too much like blasphemy to suit my tastes.

There was a definite allure to the thought, but she shelved it for the future. For the moment, her hands were full.

With the therium in tow, held aloft by an enormous bubble of water, Dorea set off in Whitecliff's direction.

Since the creature was so large, she needed to keep it above the tree line to prevent it from being caught in every other branch, which increased her mana consumption enough that using Air Boost was out of the realm of possibility.

She wouldn't have used it anyways, since she couldn't lug around her trophy with it, but it was still necessary to pay attention to the amount of mana she had available.

The refill she got from winning had allowed her to return to comfortable levels, but she needed to consider that something might come along and attack her, even if everything she knew about the wilds told her nothing would.

Many experienced hunters and scouts had been lost to freak accidents or powerful beasts wandering where they had never been spotted before.

Luckily, she had mystical senses to alert her of anything that got too close.

Or I would if Jonah hadn't shown me that passive sensing isn't enough to stop anyone with a stealth ability from sneaking on me.

She had known that it was a possibility, of course. Voggo had covered it in his lessons, and Mel had learned the skill soon after. Even some of the Mondeans had shown proficiency with it, at times using it to hide entire teams.

Having it used on her, although Jonah had simply been playing a harmless prank on her, made it evident that she had become too reliant on her passive sensing.

Dorea needed to use her active ones more often, just like Voggo had told her to do, but it was hard to break out of the habit.

Still, she periodically extended her mind to check that nothing was hiding. Fortunately, her only encounters so far had been curious squirrels and terrified shrews.

Floating a therium corpse encapsulated in a water bubble a few dozen feet up in the air, like a child would with a kite, made for an impressive sight. Or at least confusing enough that not many things wanted to try their luck.

Finally, something pinged at the end of her range. It was the work of a couple of seconds to realize she had intercepted a patrol, and she sent a pulse of mana in the pattern they had decided upon at the beginning of the week.

Changing it so often was annoying, but no one wanted their system to be breached. There were horror stories about that happening during the Great War, where entire battalions were wiped off the map simply because they believed the approaching enemies were friendly.

There was a separate system for those going on missions that would take them away from the village for more than a week and an even different one that they shared with the two allied tribes.

It was all very complicated, but Dorea appreciated the fact that everyone was putting in the work to keep Whitecliff safe. Not all could face an army by themselves, but everyone had a specific role to play, and if they did their job well, everything else would work smoothly.

She received a ping back of acknowledgment and relaxed a bit. Although she hadn't ever met anyone capable of faking a mana signature, some beings could do so.

Not many wandered this far east, but preventing those things from getting in was also a significant benefit the system provided.

The first person she saw approach her was Nora, the girl whose spell, Swarming Void, she had complimented at the beach.

Her hair was tied in a severe ponytail, but her expression was too flabbergasted to go with her look, making for a comical sight.

"What in the hell have you managed to do this time, Dorea?" the girl asked, her eyes affixed on the therium corpse.

Dorea grinned unrepentantly. She knew very well that many in the village considered her actions beyond reckless, but none of them knew about the benefits only she could get from such hunts.

It definitely wouldn't hurt them to fight outside of those perfectly safe battles that happen when a patrol finds a hostile beast. Even if they can't get a power boost like me, it would grant them some much-needed experience.

Beyond that, Dorea had found that spell crafting required some inspiration that went beyond simple calculations. One could definitely construct a perfect matrix in a safe environment and even complete a spell, but magic was a wild thing.

The very act of finding oneself in danger, the body and mind firing at full power to get out of there, or to overpower the opponent, was a great motivator to complete a spell.

It was, Dorea suspected, the reason why her repertoire was so much more extensive than almost everyone else.

The only person who could compare, beyond Voggo, who had decades to hone his craft, was Mark the Blue. The man was a fully-fledged scout before he underwent the Trial and was no stranger to danger.

Indeed, he hadn't rested on his laurels even after being proclaimed the Gifted with the most power and had pushed himself hard.

Dorea had never had much to discuss with him, but she could respect his drive. If only he could be a better conversationalist, she'd even find him pleasant, but the man only had fighting in his brain, which made for a dull experience after the first few times.

"It's exactly what it looks like. I found this therium diverting a stream's course for its own purposes and took it down after it attacked me on sight."

However much she might have liked Nora, she wasn't about to tell her of her condition. No one beyond her parents and Voggo knew about it, and if she had her way, it'd stay like that.

Dorea trusted the people of Whitecliff to watch her back in any kind of situation, and she had risked her life many times to protect them herself, but that didn't make her blind to their faults.

Most were simple artisans, farmers, or fishermen. They lived lives where each day was like the previous one and liked it that way.

Magic was something other to them. It was an inevitable fact of life, as the Mother's Wrath was, and to not have mages after it passed was a death sentence, but they didn't like having to think about it.

If they ever discovered her condition, they'd believe she was either cursed or a demon wearing a girl's face. There wasn't much they could do to her, but their rejection would be crushing.

No, it's much better to keep it this way. Only people I trust unconditionally know, and that's the only way to prevent a secret from spilling out. I haven't told Jonah and Beth for a reason, after all. However much I might love them, their discretion isn't exactly top-notch.

From the exasperation on Nora's face, she hadn't exactly been that convincing, but there wasn't anything she could do about it.

Strangled gasps from farther in the forest told her that the others had finally come into sight of her prize.

Dorea allowed the corpse to slowly float downward, keeping an eye out for obstructing branches.

Up close, the thing was even bigger than it looked at first sight. Theriums could reach immense sizes, after all, and while this was a juvenile specimen, it was still impressive.

When standing upright, it must have been close to twenty feet, and given how much mana she was expending to bring it along, it was around three tons in weight.

Most of it would be bones and organs, but even just one ton of meat would go a long way to helping refill their stores.

"How in the hell have you done that?" asked a hunter from the back.

Dorea laughed out loud. "That's what she just asked. The answer is very simple—I fought and defeated it."

"It was enhanced, then?"

Her smile must have given her away because the others looked even more amazed at that.

"Our meat stores were looking a bit too empty for my tastes," she said in lieu of a direct answer.

No one likes a braggart. It's an impressive feat, yes, but I shouldn't let it go to my head. If I had been just a bit more careless, I wouldn't be here now, after all.

"Can you manage floating it for the remaining distance?" Nora questioned discreetly.

That was why Dorea liked her. She was a hard worker and, even with average talent, managed to rise through the ranks thanks to her dedication.

The fact that she had enough tact not to embarrass her in front of all the hunters showed that she had a good head on her shoulders, even beyond her determination.

"It's fine. This thing is very heavy, but I'll manage," she answered, underplaying her power.

Dorea's reserves were now rivaled only by Mark the Blue, whose growth continued undaunted.

Most mages experienced an explosive initial increase in mana reserves, which tapered off after the first few months. Those had now passed, and consistent hard work was the only thing that would see a mage's pool expand now.

Mark the Blue was an idiot savant. It might have sounded harsh, but for all his talent in the field of magic, he was just passable in almost everything else.

It was excellent news, then, that he didn't appear interested in the village's leadership, at least for the moment. Not many would have supported his bid, but his personal power would have made it difficult to reject him outright, even for Voggo.

The old man was barely above the scout-turned-powerhouse in terms of reserves, and he was likely to be surpassed in the next few months.

For the moment, Mark the Blue seemed perfectly happy undertaking dangerous missions where he could push himself to the limits, which was something Dorea could well understand.

Does my getting him on such an instinctive level mean I'm an idiot too?

Shaking the thought off, Dorea started moving again toward the village. This time, she was surrounded by the patrol she had encountered, who served as guards for the fresh kill.

It had happened quite a few times, that the hunters would bring down a great beast, only to have it snatched away by a powerful enhanced animal.

Everyone hated when that happened, but before the Wrath, there were few things they could do to prevent it. Now, the Goddess had given them the tools to fight back.

To say that the reception at the gate was shocked would be an understatement.

For all that Whitecliff's residents had started expecting great deeds from her at this point, the sight of such a slip of a girl levitating a great mass of water that contained an entire therium carcass was still a lot to take in.

Cheers broke out once they got over their surprise. The capture of a therium was always an occasion to be merry, and though normally they would hold a feast like the last time they got one, they wouldn't this time, since the end-of-summit party had just happened, but people still yelled their congratulations.

Voggo came out to check on the commotion, and after a moment of silence where he took in the ridiculous sight, he laughed.

"You always manage to surprise me, little Dory. What will you bring back next time, I wonder?"

Dorea silently shook her head, relieved to finally lower her prize to the appointed spot at the back of the triage tent.

It had once been where hunters dressed their catches, and it could still be used as such.

She hadn't done all that a professional would have, like cutting the beast open and cleaning it on the spot, but magic made transferring it to the village much easier than it was for the hunters, and she'd gladly leave the rest of the job to them.

Indeed, soon after, a pair of burly men from Noele's tribe came out of their tent and, after a moment of shock, started walking around the carcass to take its measure.

"Let's leave that to the professionals. I have something to talk to you about," Voggo whispered from her side.

Nodding absently, Dorea waved at the two butchers, who distractedly shooed her off, and followed her mentor back to his house.

The place was as messy as ever, even with all her mother's efforts to keep it clean. However, Lilian had been too busy to do her typical sorting sprees lately, since most of the brewing processes had been dumped on her, and it showed.

Avoiding several objects and gizmos placed around the way, they finally reached the room in the back, where the village councils were usually held.

Yet, neither of the two leaders was present, and Dorea turned to Voggo questioningly.

"I have been worried about your condition for a long time, little Dory. I'm afraid it might have some side effects, from what I've observed, and I want to run some tests to ensure it's nothing too serious."

The old man's tone was casual, but his words sent an ice-cold shiver down her back.

Suddenly much more present, the girl strangled out a question, "What have you seen that makes you think so?"

Voggo sighed, sitting in his chair heavily and gesturing for her to take the opposite one.

He waited until she did so and only then replied, "Your behavior has been somewhat erratic lately, and not only in ways ascribable to teenage woes. There are several different possibilities here, and I want to be certain that you'll be fine. Will you let me check?"

For a single moment, Dorea seriously contemplated blasting her way out of there. She had been well aware that something was happening, but being confronted with it made her more afraid than she liked to admit. Still, that moment passed, and with a heavy sigh, she acquiesced.

"What do you need me to do?"

CHAPTER TWELVE

W e have already tried with brute force, and nothing happened. I'd say
that the subtler road is the only one left to us," Voggo stated, gesturing
with a hand to his left.

An ornate box rose up in the air with a telltale blue glow. Its silvery color and
beautiful inscriptions might have told the story of a jewelry container, but Dorea
knew it to be an artifact from the mana she sensed.

It gently floated to the table that divided them, and once it touched down,
it opened by itself.

Inside was something she hadn't thought of in quite a while, and Dorea let
out a gasp once she recognized it.

It was the fruit she had bought at the market months before! She hadn't
thought of it ever since, what with the important information she received at the
meeting in the very place she was at now.

"How do you have that? I thought I lost it!" she asked in a surprised tone.

Voggo chuckled, carefully taking the fruit out. "You did lose it. Here, in fact.
Luckily, I immediately noticed its signature and placed it in this nifty little box,
preserving its qualities."

"But that was months ago! How's it possible for a fruit to still look as fresh as
the day I bought it? Even the vendor's artifact, which generated enough cold to
keep things from rotting, wouldn't have managed to maintain it," she countered,
her mind telling her that what her eyes were seeing was ridiculous.

"That's because of this wonderful little gadget. It's one of my better creations,
I like to think," the shaman replied.

He placed the fruit on a small plate, carefully maneuvering it so that it wouldn't move. Then, he took the box in his hands, closing it and turning its bottom toward her.

There, a myriad of tiny fractals was etched in the silver. Too many to properly understand with a single glance, but her gut told her that their purpose had something to do with isolating whatever was inside from the outside.

When she said it out loud, Voggo clapped his hands in praise, smiling proudly. "That is almost entirely correct. Its purpose is to keep whatever is inside in the state it was in when it was put in. To do that, I had to spend months experimenting with stasis wards and medical spells. A surprising amount of work had to go into making sure that it wouldn't simply freeze its contents in place. That'd kill any organic matter."

However much Dorea might have usually enjoyed their talks, at the moment, her more pressing need was finding out whatever the shaman had in store for her.

"That sounds fascinating, and if you'll give me your notes, I'll make sure to study them to see if there is anything I can add to my ward prototype. It still doesn't explain what that has to do with me."

Voggo startled, jolted out of his focused state. "You are right; while it is a fascinating creation, this is not the time."

Coughing to cover his embarrassment, he gestured toward the fruit. "What you have here is a Prune of Punishment. Unfortunately, it's not as amazing as the fruit of a mana tree. It won't give anyone access to unaspected mana. Still, what it's known to do, is clear up any corruption in affected mages and kill any that have gone too far."

Dorea looked at the fruit with different eyes. She had bought it back then because she had felt power within it and some kind of weird affinity.

"Do you mean to say that I just have to eat it, and I'll be cleared of whatever is going on with me? Why couldn't I have done this earlier if you were so worried?" If there was some heat behind her words, Voggo made no comment of it.

The girl had been worried about her situation ever since the Wrath, and having known that there could have been a simple solution, such as eating a fruit, she would have breathed much easier.

"I'm sorry to say that it's not that easy. I have personally confirmed that there is no corruption within you. If you just ate it like that, you'd probably feel very refreshed, and that'd be it," the shaman replied.

That makes sense. He wouldn't have left me in such a limbo if he had a simple solution at hand. I need to stop getting angry so quickly. Well, I would if I could . . .

"Thus, I have spent the last few months working on a possible solution. A few came to mind initially. While eating the Prune as is wouldn't do anything per se, I believe it would allow me much greater access to your mana network for at least a few minutes before the pendant's effect kick back in," he commented, gesticulating to show his point.

"And while having a better look would be useful, you found a better way to go about it," she replied knowingly, now following his logic.

Voggo smiled proudly, showing that she was on the mark. "That is correct. If there is one thing I can rightfully say I'm good at, it's potion-making. And making a potion out of the Prune of Punishment to draw out only the uses we want is likely to be one of my best creations."

Now Dorea was starting to get excited. While she would have liked to have known about the magical fruit earlier, the fact that Voggo had spent months working on it made her smile.

However dedicated the old man might be to Whitecliff's people, he wouldn't have spent so many weeks on just any of them, especially with other, more pressing matters that needed tending.

"So, what have you come up with?" she asked eagerly.

"Something I like to call the Draught of Determination!" he revealed, looking incredibly proud of himself.

When he didn't add anything further, Dorea sighed. "And what is that?"

"Mmmh? Oh, of course. It's a brew that should enhance your mana system's ability to respond to foreign influences. It's obvious to me that while whatever started what is going on with you didn't necessarily leave a noticeable taint behind, it certainly changed you in some way. This is a way to see if we can strengthen you enough to prevent any further side effect and purge you," the shaman answered as he got up.

He started collecting all kinds of ingredients from various shelves and even two different cauldrons.

"Now, to do that, I shall first extract the greatest distillation possible from the Prune. Well, not the strongest one, as that'd probably kill you, but the most useful one."

Dorea knew, from having been witness to this process several times, that when Voggo started buzzing around like a bee, flitting between herbs and mushrooms, it was impossible to get him to speak coherently.

The man was a genius, that much was plain to see, but like most geniuses—and Dorea was starting to learn more about them thanks to reading the village's records—he operated on his own frequency.

His explanation had aroused more questions than it answered, but she settled back down in her chair, aware that it'd be counterproductive to interfere now.

Strengthening my system sounds good, but the idea that there is something that needs purging in me is an uncomfortable one, even if I was already aware of it.

Her attempts at meditation since the last success had been mixed. She could generally go back to that in-between state of consciousness where she wasn't wholly focused on her system but was still not fully present outside.

She had then observed that her first impression had been correct. The edges of her system were "frayed" in a way that didn't necessarily mean ruined. Instead, she believed that her brain was interpreting what it couldn't comprehend as broken.

She could catch a glimpse, with her mystical senses, of something being there. It was as if an additional layer of mana system was present in the space where her own original one was.

In a way, it feels very much like what sensing myself for the first time was like. I became aware of the additional layer imposed upon the world, and this feels like there is something that looks to be missing and instead is on a separate realm.

Dorea was aware that her thoughts didn't make much sense. She struggled to find the logic within them, but she had come to find that when speaking of the most fundamental concepts of magic, human language often lacked the proper words.

Still, she was hopeful that whatever Voggo was cooking up might reveal more.

It obviously wasn't supposed to be a definite solution to her problem, but having more clarity might make it easier to reach one.

Well, it doesn't sound like anything bad could happen anyways. The Prune of Punishment—and what a ridiculous name that is—is the kind of solution that seems too good to be true, and given what he implied at the beginning, if I was entirely corrupt, it'd just kill me.

Fortunately, Dorea didn't believe that to be the case. Something weird was going on, but she didn't feel like a demon.

I think I would know if I somehow became a demon. That sounds like the kind of thing you'd be aware of, to be honest.

Half-suppressed flashes of memory of her Trial told her that she had encountered at least one extremely dangerous being in the dream world, but how much it was her tripping balls from the brew and how much it was real, she couldn't tell.

Rather, she knew something had happened, because she firmly remembered her grandmother's pendant protecting her from a *thing's* attention.

If that was the cause of her condition, however, it remained a mystery.

Going by the fumes starting to come out of the two cauldrons, Voggo was fully in the middle of his craft, so Dorea relaxed further in her chair.

Although she had never felt the desire to become a potioneer herself, she had learned the basics thanks to her mother's teachings and to her spending so much time hanging around the shaman's house.

That beginner-level knowledge told her that she had absolutely no hope of recreating what the old man was doing.

It's one thing to intellectually know that he is the best of the best, but to see him actually brew a high-level potion is entirely different. His usual medicinal potions are like child's play in comparison.

Ingredients flew around the room, either called by Voggo's magic or thrown by the man's hands. It was like a symphony without music. Every movement was perfectly calculated to be the most efficient possible.

Materials that were prohibitive to work with for anyone else because of their volatile reactions were docile in his hands. The stirring, mashing, and bubbling all melded together, creating a rhythm that gave the old man's movement the feeling of choreography.

Finally, he grabbed the Prune, gently cutting into it with an obsidian knife.

The fruit's flesh was a bright yellow, with red filaments extending from its core. Voggo carefully removed the pit, ensuring no pulp was left behind.

Juice almost dripped from his fingers, and he quickly moved to a mortar, where he dropped it and started mashing. The stone pestle made short work of it, rendering it into pulp.

He then transferred the whole thing into a glass contraption he had placed over the fire, mixing the fruit with a clear liquid she didn't know the components of.

It started bubbling immediately after, lighting up her mystical senses in a way that nothing in the process so far had done.

Something deep within her, an instinct she didn't know the origin of, told her that she needed to eat that.

She remained still only thanks to a flex of her will, as her rational mind battled with her subconscious. Dorea knew perfectly well that interrupting the brewing now would likely lead to ruining it, but she still felt the need to reach in and scoop the fruit paste out.

Luckily, she managed to keep it under control, not making much noise, afraid of bothering the shaman.

The old man kept up his frantic pace for several more minutes before finally slowing down.

A golden vapor came out of the paste and cooled down into a liquid in a connected vial.

He unscrewed that off the contraption and put out the fire, turning to face the last cauldron, whose contents she couldn't see from where she was sitting but that her senses told her contained at least some water.

He scooped out a ladleful of the pot's contents and poured it, together with the golden liquid, into another bowl.

There, it fizzled angrily, only calming down when he passed a glowing blue hand over it.

There was a beat of silence as he observed his brew, scrutinizing the still surface for any imperfection. Apparently, it passed his standard because he turned to face her triumphantly. "There, it's done!"

Dorea jumped up from her seat, extremely relieved not to have to contain herself anymore. The need to drink whatever Voggo had cooked up had been building up as he worked, and she had barely kept herself from doing something stupid.

"I feel this ravenous hunger, deep within, for whatever this thing is. I have never experienced anything like that before. Is this going to be okay?" she asked worriedly.

Usually, she liked to trust her instincts, but when the stakes were so high, she wanted to ensure all the negative variables were accounted for.

Voggo hummed in thought, stroking his beard. "Many things could cause such a feeling, but none of them are worrying. If I had to pinpoint one, it's like a sailor's need for fresh fruit when coming ashore after a long sea voyage. Only it comes from the metaphysical mana system. There is an unaddressed need within you for what's in the Draught of Determination," he finally answered.

That sounded good to Dorea. There would be time for further questions later, but with her most pressing one resolved, she moved to grab the bowl.

Voggo didn't stop her, merely looking on with an amused smile, and sat back to observe. His eyes glowed blue, signaling an active spell, and a journal and quill floated to him as he took his place at the table.

Dorea lost all awareness of the outside world the second the golden liquid touched her lips. If she had been thirsty for it before, she was now ravenous.

She guzzled it all down, uncaring of the uncomfortable feeling in her stomach.

While her physical body wasn't enjoying the experience, her mana system sang in joy. The brew's power coursed through her, cleansing aches she didn't even know she had and strengthening the metaphysical veins through which her power moved.

Dorea slid down, unaware of her contact with the hard floor, as all her concentration was locked on whatever was happening inside her.

It left her feeling raw wherever it passed, but it was closer to what a good stretch was like rather than anything nefarious.

Small amounts of dark muck were scraped off, though nothing close to what she would have expected when she was truly infected by the demonic taint.

Beyond that, the most significant change happened to the edges of her system. The golden light pressed through in the place that didn't feel real, where she had only speculated something to be happening.

It became harder to follow as it started operating on a separate layer of reality, but it was tethered to her enough that she could tell the scraping happening there was much more vigorous.

Finally, with a great heave, an opening widened just enough for her to peer through.

Something she had believed to be only a dream greeted her as the confounding world she experienced during the Trial stretched on infinitely.

She was just a lonely light in a place of great currents of power, but her form suffused the environment, as if staking its claim.

Then, she snapped back into herself. Dorea had a single moment of clarity, where she realized the implications of what she had just seen, and then her eyes rolled back into her head, and she fell limply to the ground.

CHAPTER THIRTEEN

Dorea woke up groggy. Her hands groped around, trying to understand where she was.

They found well-cured leather wrapped around moa feathers. The cushions had a familiar smell, and it only took her a few moments to realize she was lying on Voggo's couch.

When she had been a little girl and accompanied her mother to work every other day, she'd often find herself napping in the same place she was now.

Then, reality rushed back in, and she sat up with a gasp. That was, apparently, the wrong thing to do, as her head started pounding.

It was as if a hammer-wielding warrior had decided that her brain was the perfect target practice.

Dorea cradled her forehead, gently massaging her temples in a vain attempt to make the pain go away.

"That won't do much. Drink this—it'll help," a feminine voice said from her side.

Without even looking at who had just spoken, Dorea extended a hand. A cup was placed in her grasp shortly after, and she brought it to her lips, drinking it all down.

Considering how her last experience with mysterious liquids had gone, she should have shown more wariness, but her condition was such that she'd take anything that could take the incessant pounding away.

A strong herbal taste greeted her, though it wasn't necessarily unpleasant. Satisfied that she wasn't drinking anything foul, she drained the last of it.

The pain slowly started subsiding in the following few minutes, going from all-distracting to barely bearable and, finally, to merely annoying.

Finally free from it, Dorea looked up, taking the room in. As she had suspected, she had been taken to Voggo's living room, which was adjacent to her mother's brewing chamber.

Sitting opposite to her, Noele reclined on a chair, observing her in return. "Feeling better?"

Dorea cleared her throat, shifting on the couch to sit properly. "Yeah, thanks. My head was killing me."

"I bet it was. Whatever it was that Voggo gave you to drink brought so many impurities out of you that I'm surprised you are even alive," the one-legged woman commented casually.

"Wait, what? Impurities? Voggo said it wouldn't do much about those, just strengthen my system!" Dorea replied confusedly.

"Mmm, I'd wait for the old man to tell you exactly what happened, but given what he told me and what I can infer, I'd say that while the potion wasn't necessarily meant to cleanse you, it empowered your metaphysical system to rid itself of all the additional bits that stuck to it."

While Noele's appearance was somewhat frightening, what with the pronounced lightning scars crisscrossing her face and hard expression, her tone was gentle. She wasn't trying to dumb down an explanation but was evidently taking into account her distress.

Before Dorea could ask another question, Voggo entered the room, interrupting her, "That is remarkably close to what exactly has happened. Thank you, Noele. You have been of great help looking after little Dory while I was occupied with healing those foolish kids."

Taking it as the unspoken dismissal it was, the middle-aged woman hobbled up, using two wooden crutches to leave the room after giving the two other occupants a nod.

Dorea thanked her absentmindedly, more focused on the old shaman, who had taken the now empty spot with a sigh of relief.

"I'm sorry I couldn't be here when you woke up, but your mother and I were both needed after a patrol drifted too far south and came into contact with those pesky salamanders. Instead of retreating, they tried to fight them and barely managed to run away with grievous burns." Voggo sighed.

The salamanders had been the focus of the mission that a week ago took her south, where she had met Melu and her contingent and had been informed that the Heidels wanted a summit to be held.

After that, the problem was relegated to another time. After all, for all the chaos they created, the beasts still hadn't spilled beyond their claimed lands, and the fires they started hadn't expanded enough to be a problem yet.

"Are the salamanders leaving their territory, then?" she asked, unconsciously slipping into a more serious leadership role.

Voggo smiled briefly as he looked her over. "No, it was just those idiots who pushed beyond the line they had burned into the forest. They didn't even learn what has them so riled up, so it's all around a failure."

"But they are okay now? And who was involved?"

"Leo and Mel were between the group, though luckily they were the least injured," the old man answered, tiredly pushing a lock of silvery hair out of his face.

With a jolt, Dorea remembered that she had a more pressing issue she wanted to know about. "Oh! The potion! What happened to me after I drank it?"

Voggo chuckled at that, the mirth at her distraction evident in his eyes. "I'd say it went better than expected. The potion was, like what Noele told you and we talked about, supposed to strengthen your mana system. However, it meant that, unexpectedly, it gave you the power necessary to rid yourself of all the accumulated baggage of the mana you absorbed to strengthen yourself," he explained.

Now that her headache was gone, Dorea started to stretch her senses again, pushing both into the outside world and within herself.

Surprisingly, even after going through such a harrowing experience, she didn't feel anything more than mild annoyance.

Even just hours before, she was sure she would have gone on a rampage about it. Instead, her emotions were entirely under her control. She hadn't experienced it in months, and she had almost forgotten what it was like.

"You should be feeling exceptionally refreshed now. Well, after the headache fades completely. Expelling so many impurities is a painful endeavor, and though you were unconscious for all of it, your body is definitely overstressed," Voggo continued.

He raised a hand to halt any further questions and continued explaining. "Impurities are something everyone builds up over time, but our systems have ways of dealing with them. My theory is that, in absorbing your slain enemies' mana, you took some of theirs in. How exactly it escaped my notice, I don't know for certain. There are a few possibilities, but that's in the future," he finished, gesturing for her to proceed with her questions.

Instead of vomiting all she was thinking, Dorea took a moment to ponder what he had just told her.

If it's true that I absorb more than just mana when I defeat my opponents, and it's perfectly reasonable to think so since everyone has some minor impurities in their own system, it would explain the mood swings. But how have neither I nor Voggo noticed anything before? It can't just be that the pendant is hiding me so well! Wait, if I remember correctly, there was something close to a secondary system in a different space there at the end . . .

She immediately relayed this thought to the shaman, whose face took on a grave cast.

He stayed silent for a few minutes, evidently deep in thought as he considered her words. Finally, he lifted his head up. "There is something that comes to mind, but I want to check on a few sources before I give you an answer. The important thing to remember at the moment is that, for the time being, you are clean of any taint. Still, you should take a couple of days off, spend some time with your friends, and give your system the leeway it needs to recover. After that, I'll have a better answer for you."

Somewhat unsatisfied but aware that when Voggo got like that, it was better not to push him, Dorea acquiesced.

She'd demand a better answer once she felt more like herself, but for that to happen, she'd need to rest.

That the thought of enforced rest is not making me go crazy like it did last time is definite proof that the Draught of Determination worked perfectly.

Some time would also be needed to settle her thoughts about the matter. Suddenly getting control of her emotions back was jarring, and she would need to ensure she felt wholly like herself before she made any serious decisions.

Thus, she thanked the shaman, who gently hugged her, and left the house.

Although she had just woken up from sleeping for several hours, she felt a deep tiredness inside that could only come from the apparently exhausting process of expelling the accumulated impurities of months of hunts and fights.

That's another thing to keep in mind. The Prune of Punishment is not nearly as rare as a Mana Fruit, but it's still not something you'd come across easily. I need to understand precisely how many impurities my system can expel now that it has been strengthened and if I'll need to periodically drink another draught . . .

She did not feel ready to face such thoughts at the moment, but the worries for the future remained, so she decided that a distraction was in order, changing course despite her tiredness.

Soon enough, the bakery came into sight. She hadn't exactly brought money with her, but considering how she had just carried back an entire therium and that Joe would receive a share of it to braise and stuff in his buns, Dorea felt quite confident that she wouldn't have to even attempt paying for whatever she wanted.

Walking inside, she greeted the burly baker snoozing behind the counter.

Joe was one of the few people who'd have benefited much from taking in one of the refugees as a worker, either as a help in making bread or in standing behind the counter where Jonah had often filled in the vacancies when his father got too tired.

The work of a baker is a surprisingly harsh one. You need to wake up before dawn, mix the bread by hand several times over, time the rise properly, take into account the humidity and heat, and finally bake everything perfectly. If you miss even one of these steps, your product is ruined and you can't sell it.

Dorea had a surprising amount of knowledge of the inner workings of a bakery, mostly because she had to listen to both Jonah's complaints and Joe's lectures when he caught his son trying to skive off.

With a start, the man woke up from his slumber. He lit up when he saw her and reached past the wooden counter, dragging Dorea in a bear hug. "You little devil! You managed to bring back an entire therium by yourself!"

After a few seconds where he held her up in the air as if she weighed nothing, he finally let go, dropping her back on firm land.

Dorea rubbed the back of her head bashfully. Though she had gotten more used to praise lately, receiving it from the well-known grump somehow meant more.

"Thank you, Joe. It wasn't an easy battle, I'll tell you that!"

They kept chatting about her latest escapades for a while, the older man showing surprising interest in her dangerous activities.

Considering how much he had been against Jonah going on missions, it felt weird that he'd encourage her so much, but it was more likely that he simply didn't consider his son to be capable of defending himself if anything went wrong.

Which isn't necessarily incorrect. He's no slouch, but his focus is not on fighting, and it shows.

Once they were done, he filled her arms with all kinds of bread products, from sweet lavender and honey doughnuts—her favorite!—to savory fish-stuffed ones.

Finally, as she was leaving, she got an idea. "Would you please tell Jonah and Beth when they come by that I want them to meet me at the beach tomorrow morning? I know they have the day off, and I have an idea."

The man readily agreed, and she set off, grateful that she could make platforms of air to unload the burden on.

The next day, the summer sun shined brightly, and a refreshing breeze cooled the otherwise hot air.

The sea shimmered like glass, reflecting the brilliant, clear blue of the sky.

Dorea waited at the pier, her white linen dress fluttering with the wind, a woven basket sitting at her feet filled with snacks and food for later.

When her mother learned about her plans, she insisted on preparing enough food for a battalion. To say that the woman was enthusiastic about her taking the day off to relax with her friends was an understatement.

Pies of three different kinds had joined some of the cheeses her father had added. An herby one with fresh cheese and eggs, one with braised moa, and the last one was, much to her delight, a honey and rhubarb one.

It was the last rhubarb of the season, which ended with the spring, and she was delighted that her mother had baked it for her.

Finally, she felt her two friends approach the beach. They were hand in hand, though luckily for her, they didn't seem interested in jumping each other like before.

Jonah's other hand was busy holding a sack full to the brim, and if her senses didn't betray her, Dorea believed its contents to be more food.

"It looks like they want us to eat until we get sick to keep us away from the wilds." She laughed, gesturing toward the basket at her feet.

The boy shook his head with a rueful smile, sending his golden curls flying everywhere. "My dad would rather I die in the mountains than present myself somewhere without enough food to feed a small army."

Both turned to face Beth, who appeared to have brought nothing. "I can conjure the water?" she replied with a shrug.

Dorea could too, but she decided not to make it an issue. They had enough food for three more people, and if necessary, she was confident they'd be able to catch a couple fish.

"Will you tell us why you wanted us to come here now?" the only brunette asked.

A grin appeared on Dorea's face, stretching almost from ear to ear. "Well, I've been told to relax as much as possible, and I intend to follow that command to the letter."

Her two friends rolled their eyes, knowing better than to take her at face value.

"Which means," she continued, "that I have to do what I haven't had time to do ever since we became mages. We're going on an adventure!"

Her cheer was met with somewhat unenthusiastic smiles, much to her consternation. "Oh, come on, what's with those frowns?"

"Dorea, when we went on adventures as kids, it meant reaching the spot where the wall touches the sea in the south or swimming at the beach. Do you really want to do that kind of thing now?" Beth asked, speaking as if to a small child.

Jonah lightly slapped her shoulder to tell her to knock it off, which she did with a laugh.

Dorea merely smirked, undaunted by the reception. "That's because your minds are too limited! We can now go on a real adventure! Brave the seas, tempt fate, and all that stuff!"

Her enthusiasm was enough to break her friends' resistance. Although they had more points they could raise, like if Dorea had been ordered not to do anything strenuous, leaving the village's confines, especially in an area they hadn't explored before, was entirely counterproductive.

Still, they knew their friend very well and knew that when she had an idea in mind, she wouldn't let go until they caved.

Thus, they reluctantly boarded the small boat Dorea had requisitioned for her use. Luckily, the fishermen hadn't needed it. Ever since they had started bringing along a few mages to ensure no enhanced beast would attack them from the depths, their catches had gotten much bigger than what the rickety boat could hold, and therefore, they hadn't complained when Dorea requested it for the day.

They set off, deciding to move north toward the caves in the cliffs, where the sailors had told stories of crystal clear waters and wondrous sights.

Although none of them had ever received instruction on how to operate a boat, their magical ability made it all trivially easy.

There was no need to row and tire themselves out when Dorea and Beth could direct the currents to push them in their desired direction.

The three of them, out on an adventure, the salty tang of the sea air, the wind teasing Dorea's hair, the rhythm of the waves against the boat's hull. It was exactly what she had hoped for.

The little boat skimmed over the water, carried along by the sea's natural currents and Jonah's playful gusts of wind. Laughter and lighthearted banter filled the air.

The last few months had been hard on them, and though they had gotten used to the frenetic pace and the high stakes, taking a day off to simply enjoy being teenagers without the looming shadow of conflict in the distance was fantastic.

They kept following the coast for almost an hour, having left Whitecliff's northern walls behind a while before, until they finally saw something in the distance.

Dorea charted the course, sensing an empty space in the rock wall. She turned to Jonah to ask him if he felt the same, and he wordlessly nodded, his gaze affixed to the cliff.

"There," she pointed out, where the coast dipped into a cove, the mouth of a cavern just barely visible from the distance.

As they drew nearer, they could make out the details of the cave. The entrance was large enough for their boat to pass through, the rocky walls streaked with minerals that sparkled in the morning light.

All of a sudden, the currents that had docilely accompanied them until that moment were ripped from their control.

Beth and Dorea barely had time to realize that something much stronger than them had seeped its mana into the waters before the boat lurched into the cave.

CHAPTER FOURTEEN

Frantically trying to wrest control back had no visible effect, so Dorea quickly abandoned the attempt.

Whatever it was that had caught them in its grip was simply too strong to fight directly. Thus, she rose up in the air, levitating her two friends along, turning to fly out of the cave.

Their yells of shock were drowned out when a wall of water rose up, closing the only exit.

Dorea attempted to disrupt the obstacle with a few different attacks, mostly leaning on air magic, but the wall didn't even budge.

Instead, the little boat floated back underneath them, as if inviting them back on.

"Whatever it is that's doing this, it's smart enough to communicate and probably doesn't want us immediately dead. Otherwise, there'd be nothing we could do to stop it," Dorea pronounced finally, gently lowering herself and her friends back down.

"I can't feel any other exit," Jonah commented grimly, his carefree smile now a thing of the past.

Stupid, how could I not think of the possibility that a Master-level beast was here. This is all my fault.

"Is there anything we can even attempt at this point? My magic is sliding off the water. I can't even try to take control back," Beth asked worriedly.

The girl was the least experienced of the three, but she had still seen her fair share of fighting, and however much she might have wanted to curl up and cry or scream her frustration, she knew that this was not the appropriate moment.

Unfortunately, all their attempts ended up failing. Even a concentrated effort from all three didn't yield any result in opening the way.

All the while they struggled, the boat drifted deeper into the cave.

At any other moment, the sight would have amazed them, as the crystalline growths and shimmering lights provided a fantastic spectacle, but none of the teenagers were in the mood to appreciate it.

Finally, the way opened into a large chamber. If the outside had been fascinating, the inside was another thing entirely. Columns of twisted coral rose from deep below until they touched the high ceiling. The water was so pure that they could see the sandy white bottom even at a hundred feet of depth.

Schools of colorful fish swam around, playing between the bright green and red algae and the corals.

The whole thing was like a completely separate environment from the outside world. And in the middle stood its guardian and their captor.

Invisible to their senses but unmistakably there to their eyes, a gigantic sea turtle rested, half-buried in the water, basking on a ledge.

Its shell was a beautiful mosaic of colors—greens, blues, and even soft pinks mixed together harmoniously. It was like looking at a living piece of the sea, and as they got closer, they started to sense it.

Whatever it was doing to conceal its presence made it so that no one who wasn't standing in front of it could distinguish it from the waters it rested in.

It would have been an interesting application of magic if the user hadn't forced them to be there, shrugging off all their attempts to leave with casual ease.

None of the three attempted to attack the beast, as its presence exuded power and age. If they hadn't been able to do anything to it at hundreds of feet of distance, assaulting it this close would be a death sentence.

Then, Beth gasped in surprise. "It's Harlech! The turtle from the fishermen's stories!"

The other two turned to her with a confused expression, neither being familiar with it.

The girl huffed, relaxing now that she recognized their captor. "C'mon, you must have heard him at least once. He's the magical turtle that will help you back to shore during a storm if you say his name and give him an offer every time you go fishing!"

That niggled something in Dorea's memory. It was something she hadn't heard about for years, but if she concentrated, she could remember one of the elderly fishermen—a bearded old man whose lame leg didn't allow him to go on extended voyages—narrating fantastic tales of sea creatures and dangerous monsters to an audience of captive kids.

"Oh! Harlech the Kindly Guide! What the hell, why did he capture us, then?" she asked confusedly.

By now, they had come to a stop in front of the creature. He was truly a massive specimen, easily spanning twenty feet from flipper to flipper, and he peered at them groggily, as if he had just been awoken from a nap.

"Maybe it wants an offering?" questioned Jonah from the side. He dug into his sack before taking out a few buns and waving them at the animal.

Surprisingly, he reacted, following the boy's hands like a trained dog.

With a shrug, he threw them toward Harlech. Two tendrils of water exploded out of the still cave, catching onto the morsels and bringing them to the turtle's mouth.

Harlech gobbled them, almost licking his beak. Then he returned to staring, this time directly at the basket, which had luckily survived the harrowing experience.

Almost in disbelief, Dorea opened it up and picked the three pies stacked on top of each other. As soon as she took them out, Harlech rose from his position, eagerly moving toward them, somehow without disturbing the waters.

The tendrils reappeared, this time insistently pointing toward the bottom pie.

Dorea stood still, incredulous at what was happening, until Beth nudged her with an elbow. "Give him whatever he wants," she whispered.

With a whine of discontent, Dorea put the top two pies back down and threw the last one toward the turtle, who snapped it up and eagerly devoured it. "That was my favorite rhubarb and honey pie," she complained softly.

Her two companions looked at her as if she was completely insane but quickly returned to warily observing the turtle when he finished his meal.

Harlech—Dorea was sure that was his name now—closed in the distance, bumped his head against the boat, making it rock back, and dipped into the waters.

Their ride was rapidly brought out of the chamber, back into the cave, and then outside. They received one last push toward Whitecliff, and once they were almost a mile away from the grotto, a tendril of water rose up, cheerily waving at them.

Silently, the three friends decided that they had tested their luck enough for the day and, having regained control of the currents, quickly returned back home.

The rocky hills in the north had always served as something of a natural barrier between the lush forest and the harsh mountains.

They were too barren for anyone to attempt building a town there, and dangerous beasts roamed in search of unwary travelers.

Magic made traversing them much easier, but while that meant they had become a less dangerous environment for the people of Whitecliff, it also meant that any invading force from the north wouldn't find much difficulty passing through.

That all translated to increased patrols in the hills, and though no one liked having to go, they all did since it was by far the most dangerous border that needed guarding.

The harsh conditions also mean that if you find traces of a large number of humans, they are either an army coming to pillage or desperate refugees.

Dorea stood on top of a hill, ahead of the team she had been assigned to that morning. The summer sun was glaring down harshly, and had she not been a mage capable of creating a refreshing breeze for herself whenever she wanted it, she would have been sweating buckets.

Instead, she comfortably descended the hill, stopping in front of large tracks in the dried mud.

It had rained quite harshly two days before, one of those summer storms that even the whitebeards couldn't predict.

Had it been a year before, it would have been a tragedy for their crops. Luckily, the presence of water-aspected Gifted meant that removing the excess liquid from the ground was trivially easy, preventing most of the damage.

Some plants had been knocked down and would still see reduced growth, but it was a manageable loss compared to what it could have been.

And considering how much our population has ballooned lately, we will need every last grain we can squeeze from the ground.

Since the tracks didn't seem to be directed precisely toward Whitecliff, and there were small imprints belonging to many children, Dorea felt reasonably confident that what she was looking at belonged to another caravan of refugees rather than another Mondean army.

At least four different carts were being pulled by hoofed animals, which she supposed might have contained enemy soldiers, but the vibe she got was more fleeing desperate people rather than conquering warriors.

Still, she could always be wrong, and she'd prefer to get a second opinion before choosing between following the tracks to see where they ended or rushing back to the village to raise the alarm.

She only had to wait two more minutes before a voice spoke up from behind her, "Those don't look like the tracks left behind by an army. Probably another group of northerners running away from the Mondeans."

Dorea turned to face the speaker. Matt looked pale and emaciated still, and a noticeable scar ran down his brow to his chin.

Still, the man had managed to finally wake up from the injury the Mondeans had inflicted upon him, and after a short period of rehabilitation, he had insisted on returning to patrolling.

Voggo's tonics could almost be called miraculous for how much they helped Matt recover, but it would take some time before he looked like himself again.

Still, his expertise was almost unmatched in Whitecliff, having served for many years as a scout—second only to Mark the lead scout and Harlan, the gruff elder who refused to retire. Dorea had learned to trust the man almost instinctively, and that his words confirmed her thoughts reassured her greatly.

"That was my thinking as well. I don't know where they might be heading, though. This path would take them farther east than even the Forest village is," she commented.

"Well, I guess we'll be able to ask them ourselves. The tracks are less than a day old, and with that many people, especially with kids, they won't be able to make it that far. We could catch up in a few hours if we leave now," Matt said, looking at her to make a decision.

The protocol in this case wasn't exactly clear, since the refugees were evidently not heading toward Whitecliff. Still, Voggo had expressed more than once that even should they meet a group fleeing from the Mondeans that didn't want to settle with them, they should still try and learn as much as possible.

Although they sent the occasional scouting mission in the mountains that told them their enemies were still engaged in their war of conquest there, the information one could learn from the natives was much better.

Especially for those clansmen who have fought until now. If they were part of a tribe defeated in the last few days or even weeks, what they know could be worth more than their weight in gold.

Thus, Dorea made an executive decision. She'd go by herself to check on this group, using Air Boost to shorten the trip by an order of magnitude; Tom, the water mage, who was with the rest, would go back to Whitecliff to inform them of what they had found so far, while the rest continued their patrol.

It was a bit of a gamble since the weakened patrol could be more easily ambushed without two mages, but Dorea didn't feel comfortable sending anyone back by themselves on an hours-long journey if they couldn't at least protect their lives from a beast attack.

She was actively choosing to believe that the suppositions they made about the Mondeans, that they would wait until they could dedicate a much greater force to crush them once and for all, was true.

She explained this to the others, who all nodded gravely.

Unfortunately, there were no easy solutions, and the weight of responsibility would fall on her should anything go wrong.

"I'll come back as quickly as possible to inform you guys of what I've found, but that might take a few hours. Stay safe, everyone."

Tom left immediately toward Whitecliff, using something he was calling Surfing Steps to increase the speed of his run.

It seemed like more and more people were starting to develop their own mobility spells, which, while great for the village as a whole, also meant that she should start expecting her enemies to use them.

With one last nod to Matt, she also set off. Air Boost came to life around her, and with a mental push, she blasted away from the team.

The increase in speed and efficiency of the spell had made it an integral part of her fighting style. Not only could she maneuver much better than when she had to adjust everything manually, but its cost was so little now, thanks to her increased reserves, that she could keep it up for days.

The Draught of Determination might not have granted me immense power, but my mana system feels like a well-oiled gear compared to a rusty one. I wasn't even aware of how sluggish everything was until it was cleaned up.

When compared to the average mage, her speed and efficiency when casting had increased from one and a half as much to twice more.

Although it hadn't necessarily fixed her impurities accumulation problem, according to Voggo, it had still strengthened her enough that it would take years before she returned to the condition she had been in before the draught.

She would have the time to find another Prune of Punishment, especially if things settled down enough by then that she could leave the village for longer periods of time.

Well, that's in the far future. Voggo said a minimum of five years, with an upper limit of ten, depending on how much I absorb from fallen enemies.

That gave her enough leeway that she was confident she could find another of the fruits before it became a problem.

While pondering all this, she kept following the tracks, noticing when they expanded significantly, meaning the group had stopped to rest at one point and shrunk back to their original size when they set off again.

Finally, three hours after she had started her journey, she saw a dust cloud on the horizon.

Ordinarily, such things happened in nature when the winds were strong enough to whip up the sediment, but there was nothing of the sort at the moment.

This meant that someone was purposefully creating the cloud, likely to use it as cover against dangerous beasts.

It wouldn't work against a human with more intelligence than a toddler's, but given the tracks the group left behind, they weren't trying to hide from humans.

Dorea slowed down, not wanting to spook them by appearing like a wraith on the hunt.

As soon as she got close enough, someone picked up her signature, because a group of three young men peeled off and moved in her direction.

"Who goes there? What do you want from us?" called the tallest one.

He had a scraggly beard and appeared like an awkward teenager, but his hard eyes prevented any thought that he might be a pushover. This was someone who had gone through terrible things, and Dorea wouldn't be surprised if he had personally killed more than one person.

"I'm from Whitecliff! We were on patrol to protect us from the Mondeans and saw the tracks you left," she replied, careful not to get too close.

Generally, she would have been more casual in her approach, but these people seemed traumatized, and she didn't want to spook anyone into doing something stupid.

The response she got wasn't what she expected. Disbelief was painted all over the three's faces, and their eyes looked to almost pop out.

"Impossible—Whitecliff must have been destroyed months ago!" the shortest one shouted. He had more delicate features than the other two, and his long brown hair was tied in a low ponytail.

Dorea laughed out loud. "Whitecliff destroyed? What world do you live in? We gave those bastards quite the black eye every time they tried us!"

More expressions of shock followed, but soon enough, she convinced them that she truly was from the coastal village.

No one raised concerns that she might be a Mondean in disguise, mostly because she dressed nothing like them, lacking the furs even in summer and the typical earrings. Beyond that, if she was somehow the vanguard of a party made up of the bloodthirsty maniacs, they could do nothing about it.

The three boys looked exhausted. They were trying their best to conceal their desperate hope that she was telling the truth.

It seemed that they had been told by older members of their tribes that the southern villages had been visited by the Mondeans and had assumed it meant that they, too, had been destroyed and their people taken.

That was why they had headed east, moving through the rocky hills in the hopes that they'd reach the end of the mountain ranges and thus escape their enemy's influence.

It wasn't necessarily a terrible plan, but they all looked dead on their feet, and when they allowed her to get closer to the caravan, she saw that it was mostly made up of kids and teenagers, along with a few women.

"The men and elderly stayed behind to give us the time to escape. They promised they'd join us, but we heard terrible explosions in the village's direction just a day later, and we knew there wasn't anyone there who could stand up to a powerful mage's wrath," the tallest of the three young mages explained.

This ragtag group had started their journey more than two weeks before, having to navigate through the mountains and then the arid hills, but thanks to the dozen or so mages they had, they had managed to make it through mostly unscathed.

The promise of shelter and aid in Whitecliff might have pushed the boundaries of her authority, but Dorea knew that it was what Voggo would have done.

He can interrogate them once we get there to ensure they told the truth, but we need them as much as they need us, even if they don't know it.

It left a sour taste in her mouth, having to weigh the value of their future contribution against the cost of taking them in, but twelve new mages, even if they weren't all combat capable, and the fact that there were no men to make a fuss about the inevitable cultural assimilation, made the prospect of "helping" them a favorable one.

Well, we will give them safety and stability. That's what they wanted, right?

CHAPTER FIFTEEN

Turning the entire caravan of refugees around proved to be a more complicated endeavor than Dorea would have liked.

Some simply didn't believe that anyone could survive the Mondeans' attention like she tried to explain Whitecliff had done, and while others did trust her word, they just didn't think the village would last much longer.

She could understand their desire for a peaceful place to settle in, but since the Wrath had hit the entire Loisos region, the possibility of them finding one was infinitesimal.

She tried to explain this, and luckily the three mages who had first met her seemed to agree.

There were no elderly who might have remembered the Great War against the Ergasters, where most of the mountain clans joined hands with the southerners in an effort to repel the invaders. Still, a few of the adult women knew of the event well enough to remember that Whitecliff had served an important role.

That seemed to be the tiebreaker, as the refugees finally chose a known quantity over an unknown and likely very dangerous one.

Dorea didn't even feel that bad after, since she had saved these people from being beset on all sides by perils.

They had no plan beyond getting as far away as possible from the Mondeans. And while it might work to stop being harassed by them, they'd likely just have to face similar forces, which they know nothing about.

That they would need to contribute to Whitecliff's defense in case of attack seemed to be the most contentious of her demands to grant them shelter and aid, but even that was eventually agreed upon when she specified that only the mages would need to do so.

Had there been nonmagical adult men, it would have applied to them as well, but unfortunately, they had all been lost in their desperate attempt to grant the rest time to flee.

Thus, they turned the caravan around, much to the curiosity of the two dozen kids running around.

Seeing them so carefree, even in such a dangerous situation, lessened a weight on Dorea's heart. They were mostly too young to have taken part in the Trial, which explained their high numbers, and for the two who were Gifted but were being hidden as nonmagical, well, Voggo could decide what to do about them.

The trip toward Whitecliff was a long and exhausting one. The rocky hills didn't have any road running through them, and the few beaten paths were made for much more agile groups, like the patrol she had been a part of.

Moving an entire caravan through them required much more effort because it served as a beacon for hungry beasts to converge upon, and she wasn't surprised at all when she ended up having to fry two smilodons who must have scented the kids' presence.

Also, the carts weren't exactly made with the rough terrain in mind. It surprised her to learn that an ancient road network in the mountain range connected the vast majority of the villages there.

It was one of the sacred duties of every chief and shaman to ensure that their portions were well maintained. That usually meant removing the weeds and, every once in a while, fallen rocks since the roads themselves hadn't shown any sign of deteriorating, even after at least a few centuries.

It fascinated Dorea to learn the history of the region. She hadn't known of such infrastructures, mostly because her latest research had been focused on the wards used during the last war, but she promised herself that once all the fighting had stopped, she would spend some time simply traveling all through the region and maybe even farther beyond.

Suddenly, she understood her father's brother. She had always considered him a deadbeat, since he had abandoned his family and tribe just to explore long abandoned ruins, but now she thought she might get his fascination.

It took them two days to get close enough to be picked up by a patrol. Dorea sent a pulse of magic as soon as she first felt a human presence at the edge of her senses and received a correct one back, making her slump in relief.

She then turned around to face the rest of the caravan. "I have just sensed one of Whitecliff's patrols. They should be here in a few minutes."

A murmur of tension and happiness went through the crowd. Everyone wanted to be done with their long voyage, but some still harbored the belief that this was all a complicated ruse to make them lower their guards.

It was the reason she hadn't been able to leave the caravan behind to alert either her team or the village proper of their coming. These people were very skittish, and she didn't want to do anything that might spook them.

Not only do we need their mages if we ever want to put up a fight against the Mondeans, but the information they know about their fighting habits is simply too precious to lose.

Dorea had kept the conversation casual but had also interspersed a few questions about what had happened to the tribe after the Wrath's passing. She learned that there had been a few initial skirmishes against both Mondean raiding parties, like those they had faced the first two times, and other tribes looking to expand.

It didn't surprise her that their enemy wasn't the only one with dreams of conquering land and people since that was an unfortunately common human instinct. The Mondeans, however, were undoubtedly the most successful ones.

When she had asked why the gangly teen who had taken to accompany her thought it was so, he had barely answered that their chief was a monster before clamming up.

Rather than being upset at his reticence, Dorea felt relieved that he knew anything at all. It had been a slowly simmering fear at the back of her mind that she might have made a wrong choice promising these people shelter, if it turned out that they couldn't contribute enough to make it worth it.

Luckily, it ended up being unfounded, as Thed, the awkwardly proportioned air mage, showed that he knew enough to make it worth it and that he was no slouch in the power department.

Shortly before the patrol picked them up, a blast of magic and the screech of an eagle resounded through the hills. Looking up and extending her senses in its direction, Dorea was able to determine that an air-aspected bird was stalking them, waiting for their guards to drop or for a kid to wander too far.

Its plans had been ruined by Thed, whose left hand was extended in the eagle's direction. A massive arrow, looking more like a siege bolt rather than one that could be shot from a bow, had torn through the beast's left wing, leaving it to sustain itself only through magic.

It was bleeding, though, and having been discovered, it apparently decided to go for broke. Thed didn't allow it to get close enough to threaten anyone, as another bolt ran through the bird's head, pulping it instantly.

Considering the size and power she had felt from it, Dorea believed that only the top ten most powerful mages in Whitecliff could have dealt with it so quickly, at such range and while using the same element.

The whole thing had taken only a handful of seconds, explaining exactly how the caravan had made it so far. For all his gangly limbs and awkward manner, Thed was a powerful mage and a ruthless one at that.

He will serve well.

Once they met up with the patrol and it became evident that no Mondeans were lying in wait for them to lower their guards, especially since they continued walking southwest, away from the mountains, even the most suspicious ones settled down.

Since there was no gate up north, they had to hug the wall through the forest until they reached the main entrance, but by then, everyone had relaxed, realizing that their long flight was coming to an end.

Voggo met them at the gates, accompanied by two dozen mages, some standing on the wall while others formed a half circle around him. Dorea could sense a few more hidden in the trees, and while she would have liked to call it overkill, she knew how important it was to filter anyone new they took in.

"It's fundamental that we increase our numbers fast enough that when the Mondeans come knocking, we can field an army large enough to fight them. That also means that we need to do everything in our power to address all the fears of those who were already living here before. Internal discord can be a terrible thing to behold." Those had been Voggo's words, and they echoed with truth even now.

They couldn't afford to turn away such a group, especially if they brought enough mages to make a significant difference in their defensive plans. Still, if those very mages became the object of strife, it could all come tumbling down.

I'm very glad it isn't me who has to deal with that. I know Voggo wants me to eventually start taking on more responsibility, especially since he fears that his personal power won't be enough to stifle leadership contests for long, but that's a problem for future me.

As she contemplated the complexities of leading a village in the middle of a conflict with a much more powerful enemy, the processing of the refugees began.

Like he had done for Noele's and Nettle's groups, the shaman cast truth-telling spells and several more subtle ones meant to catch even the barest hints of deception.

It always amazed Dorea how many utility-based pieces of magic Voggo had at his disposal, but then again, having to lead a village by himself for so many years was likely very conducive to developing such skills.

There was a bit of a commotion at one point when two of the older women refused to answer a few questions and aroused the suspicion of everyone around them. After Voggo had managed to calm down every spell-happy mage in the vicinity, it turned out that they had simply been hiding an affair behind their husbands' backs. Since the men had sacrificed themselves to give them time to leave, they wanted to conceal that fact to not lose face with all the other women.

It left everyone baffled that they would raise a fuss for such a stupid issue, but it seemed like humanity would always find a way to put matters of the heart above even the most important things.

Having been forced to reveal their affairs, the two women were then subjected to several more questions, not from Voggo or anyone from Whitecliff but from their own tribesmen.

The shaman shrugged, apparently deciding that it was a trivial enough matter that it could be left to those who would care for it.

A bit curious despite herself, Dorea manipulated the air currents enough so that the sound of the confrontation would carry to her.

"How long has this been going on? How much of a mockery have you made of my brother's death?" another woman harangued, this one with fiery red hair and a matching temper.

"Do you think I would have done this if your brother had ever done his duties as a husband without being exceptionally drunk? He was so disgusted with himself whenever he had to lie with me too. I couldn't go on like that forever," was the harsh response from the first woman. She was clutching a sleeping toddler to her bosom, apparently the fruit of the failed marriage.

Her words seemed to have a ring of truth because her husband's sister sighed, looking up at the sky desolately. "I had told him several times that he could have simply never married, but our parents' expectations were too much for him to bear."

That was enough for Dorea. She might have been curious, but listening in for longer than that would have been too much.

Fortunately, there was much to distract herself with. Thed was being processed by Voggo at the moment, and going by the expression of the people around them, his answers revealed precisely what she had learned from her observations.

That's a lesson to be remembered. Never underestimate anyone, no matter how they look. A mage can be the most ungainly guy you'll ever see, and they could still put you six feet under in a second.

Whitecliff received the new influx of refugees with grace. They had all long since learned of what awaited undefended groups outside their sturdy walls. Though no one really liked it when their land became overrun with strangers, their solidarity with the poor people was greater than their annoyance, at least for the moment.

Three things made it so that this specific group required less work to be accepted. First, the village's population was already made up of a fifth of recent immigrants, and with the latest arrivals, that number would go up to a fourth. Those people were immediately sympathetic and worked hard to ensure proper housing and essential necessities were available.

Secondly, the group was made up entirely of teenage mages, kids, and women. Their ragtag appearance tugged on heartstrings, and the story of how all the men had sacrificed themselves made all the fathers nod proudly in agreement. They were naturally inoffensive to the natives' minds.

Thirdly, it was made eminently clear to everyone that the new mages would be put through a short course to teach them the basics everyone in Whitecliff knew. Then they'd start contributing to construction-slash-agricultural efforts or, more likely, to the village's defense.

With the latest influx, their number of mages was over fifty, although not all of them were battle oriented. It was still nowhere close to what they needed if they wanted to pose a serious challenge to the Mondeans, but with every new group they took in, they got closer to that goal.

"Quality is the name of the game here," explained Dorea to the newbies. Somehow, she had once again been roped in to serve as a guide since she had already done so for both the Heidels and the previous refugees.

"Our numbers are much greater when you count our allies as well, but beyond that, we have shown again and again that Whitecliff's Gifted are second to none. In a fair fight, I'd put money on any one of ours against theirs."

This wasn't strictly true, but the speech served to reassure them of the village's capability to stand for itself.

No one wants to lay down their lives to fight for a place that doesn't have a future; Voggo is right. We must continue building a sense of unity and duty toward Whitecliff if we want people to put their all into this.

Dorea would have never thought of it herself, but having access to much greater experience and wisdom, the shaman could easily pull such ideas out of his hat.

It would take time to give the village's mages a definite structure, but apparently, that was important. It would serve as a way to remind everyone of their place, grant a clear path to advancement, and serve as a reassuring force for the nonmagical.

Voggo didn't mean for an actual army to be established, but their numbers were getting big enough that they couldn't operate in a direct manner anymore. Structure was needed.

They'd apparently take inspiration from the last war, where generals, lieutenants, and commanders were appointed at the head of respectively sized groups of fighters.

"It was a harsh lesson to learn," the shaman had explained. "We had believed that convincing everyone to fight together would be enough, as it had taken immense effort just to get that far, but the Ergasters' organization on the battlefield made it immediately obvious that we couldn't go at it in such a haphazard manner. Our first battle remains to this day the greatest loss of lives I know about. Four thousand men died that day on our side, and it's in their blood that we reforged ourselves anew."

While that was very interesting, it still left it up to her to begin assimilating these new people.

The only saving grace was that she was slated to go down south soon, to take part in the alliance rotation and check the situation with the southern tribes' attempts at city-building.

"The Mondeans have some terrifyingly powerful mages on their side," commented Beor, the short teen who had come to face her alongside Thed.

Dorea nodded in agreement. "I know; I fought one of their elites myself. Those are very rare, though, and even then, for all their power, their skill is not on par with what we have here."

Her rebuttal seemed to convince some, but the majority remained skeptical. That was okay, though, since she hadn't expected to win them over so quickly.

It would be a long process before they felt completely safe in Whitecliff, if they ever did. What she wanted to do was to engrave in their minds that they had a chance of beating their hated enemies here.

"But I can see that words are not enough. How about a demonstration?"

CHAPTER SIXTEEN

Unsurprisingly, no one wanted to fight Dorea. Be it because they were still too new to Whitecliff and didn't want to risk their place there by possibly hurting or offending her, or because they had heard something of her escapades, she still had no volunteer.

"I promise there won't be any consequences, even if you beat me badly," she cajoled.

Another long moment of silence followed before Thed finally stepped up.

The boy sighed, ruffling his hair. "I don't really think this is necessary, but I'll do it to allow you to make your point."

Dorea smiled gratefully at him. He might not be the most socially agile person she knew, but Thed had repeatedly shown that he had a good heart behind the rough exterior his circumstances had built up.

"Just to be clear, our purpose here is not to hurt each other. I just want to show you what I mean when I say that the level of training you get here makes the difference."

Of course, she wasn't being entirely truthful, since her special circumstances weren't exactly repeatable with training, no matter how intense. Still, she just needed to make a point.

Since the back of Voggo's house was, for the umpteenth time, filled with tents to house the new arrivals, she directed the mages toward the beach.

It's starting to become a habit. I take them down here, spar with the best, and let them know their place in the hierarchy.

Now that her mind was clearer than it had been for months, thanks to the

Draught of Determination, Dorea could recognize that her last spar with Masi had been much more involved on her part than it should have been.

If she hadn't caught herself there at the last moment, she might have broken the newly forged alliance beyond repair. Luckily, she was in an entirely different situation now.

As they walked toward the beach, their group picked up a few strays, amongst whom was the Heidel boy she had just been thinking about.

"Is it becoming a tradition for you to fight the newcomers?" he asked cheekily, unknowingly echoing her previous thoughts.

"I just want to reassure them of what Whitecliff is capable of," she responded, not giving away anything.

Message received, the tan teen slipped back toward the crowd of onlookers. She didn't want to broadcast anything to the refugees, and he wouldn't go against her wishes.

I can appreciate someone with a functioning brain. He's a bit arrogant, but he's powerful, well respected, and handsome. I guess it just comes with the territory.

Shaking her considerations off, she finally reached the spot she held the last spar in.

With but a thought, an invisible gust of wind carved a deep line in the sand, delineating the limit of the impromptu ring.

Since everyone spectating was a mage, or close enough to one to be protected by them, they didn't bother with setting up shields, especially since they had explicitly stated that they wouldn't use directly harmful magics.

Although the scene was the same as just a few weeks before, the situation was very different.

Firstly, for all of Thed's skills, the boy wasn't as talented as Masi, nor had he received the tutelage of arguably the most powerful mage on the Loisosian coast.

Secondly, Dorea herself had changed since then. Not only had she received all the benefits of the Draught of Determination, but she had put in many hours of hard work to expand her repertoire.

The fight with the therium had shown her that, no matter how she managed to steal the win from beneath the beast's nose, she needed more flexibility and defense if she wanted to last in a battle with powerful opponents.

Indeed, her focus these last few weeks had been almost entirely on filling those gaps.

Even as she guided the refugees through the rocky hills, she had kept up her practice, though subtly.

The fruits of her labor were what she intended to use this time. If she could defeat Thed with never-before-seen magics, word would come back to him and his companions, showing how the distance between them was even greater than first imagined.

I guess that competitiveness is still one of my natural personality traits. No matter how much muck the draught might have scraped off, what makes me "me" still remains.

Dorea and Thed took their positions, though he gave a long look at the deep furrow she had created seemingly without effort.

She just grinned at him, bright and innocent, for once appearing like the teenage girl she was.

"I'll act as a referee if no one minds, being impartial as an outsider," Masi declared, pulling himself from the crowd and standing just at the edge of the ring.

Thed gave him a look before shrugging. He then widened his stance as if a warrior preparing for combat.

Dorea stayed still, waving distractedly to the Heidel boy to go ahead.

"Very well. This is a spar meant to showcase the participants' skill level, and as such, any kind of truly dangerous offensive magic is forbidden. Start on three. One, two, three!"

Immediately, the sand blew up in an angry whirlwind. Thed stood in the middle of it, a concentrated furrow to his brow. With a gesture, the miniature whirlwind was thrown toward Dorea in an attempt to blind and confuse her.

Without bothering to acknowledge his efforts, the girl ripped his control away from the air.

She brought to bear the power and finesse she had been cultivating for all these months, forged by fight after fight.

It still wouldn't be enough if he had used a spell, but luckily he wanted to show off with a visually impressive manipulation.

Instead of pressing the advantage, Dorea merely allowed the sand to settle back down on the beach and for the concentrated mana in the air to dissipate.

She kept a bored look on her face all throughout, baiting the boy into attacking her again.

With a grunt of annoyance, Thed called upon the winds again, funneling them into a true sandstorm. Cries of irritation rang out from the spectators, as shields of various make blinked into existence to protect them from the sand.

"Let's see how you like this," he taunted, getting into the swing of things.

Having unleashed his magic, he immediately prepared a second attack, knowing that she wouldn't go down simply because of poor visibility and some annoyance.

Three rotating arrows made of compressed air spun dangerously, before he sent them where he felt her presence.

Inside the sandstorm, Dorea was cocooned in a dense sphere of air. Studying wards had finally made her take a look at the defensive aspects of magic, and her latest exploits had shown her the need to protect herself and move freely.

While Air Boost would likely remain her best mobility spell for quite a long time, it didn't mean she could rely only on it, as shown during the flight from the Mondean camp before the battle with the forest tribe.

That, combined with her efforts for the last few days, had finally culminated in a successful new spell. Wind Bulwark served as both an omnidirectional shield and a movement option, especially when coupled with Air Boost.

While taking to the skies was not necessarily always a good idea, since many mages had a long-range spell at their disposal, this fight wasn't about doing everything right.

It's about sending a message. And few things get the meaning across as ignoring everything your opponent is doing and ending them with a bolt from the sky.

Having assessed the sandstorm still raging around her and the occasional arrow being sent her way that splashed against her Bulwark with little damage to show, Dorea finally took the initiative.

She had a few different ideas in mind of how to show off without threatening Thed's life. Watery tendrils like those used by the gigantic turtle living in the cave up north had seemed like a good idea, as they would give her both flexibility and, if she pumped enough mana in them, the power necessary to break through any static defense.

Her spells Lightning Sphere and Exploding Water Bullet had both been rejected on grounds that if they hit, she couldn't guarantee that the boy wouldn't be maimed.

In the end, the solution was given to her by her opponent.

Sandstorms were very peculiar things in that, depending on their fury, they could build up enough electrical charges to have lightning happen naturally.

While what he was doing wasn't enough to make it happen by itself, she needed only to give it a nudge, and she'd have a lot of power at her disposal without even needing to tire herself.

What happened then could only be described as a beatdown.

Dorea called upon the natural forces that Thed had unknowingly prepared, turning potential charge into very real lightning.

Careful not to direct it at the boy, she gestured downward with a hand, lazily tracing the path that she wanted it to take.

With a roar that shook the beach and made several onlookers cry out, seven separate bolts ripped through the air.

The hasty shield that Thed threw up lasted less than a knob of butter on a heated pan.

The lightning hit all around him, sending sand blasting everywhere and pushing him on his knees.

A few seconds later, the storm finally calmed down, revealing the changed battlefield.

Inside a perfect heptagon, Thed faced up, a look of wonder mixed with fear painted on. Around him, seven spots emitted smoke where the magic had struck.

Fulgurite rods were all that was left of the sand there, having superheated enough to clump up into a glass-like substance.

"I'd say that this should be enough for today's purposes," Dorea lightly commented as she descended from the sky.

Hearing her words, Masi shook himself from his stupor and announced, "The winner is Dorea from Whitecliff! She broke through her opponent's defenses and could have easily hurt him, instead applying her control to prevent any injury!"

Touching down, she dismissed her Bulwark, looking untouched. "You have more than enough power to be a dangerous opponent, but whipping all that sand up against a lightning mage just gave me the charge I needed."

Thed finally rose up, looking more embarrassed and confused than angry. "I know that, but I saw you using air magic both today and before, so I assumed that it was all you could do! Who would think that you could use more than one element?! Is that even possible?" he asked, scratching his head.

"The world is a much larger place than you could imagine," was her only reply as she turned around and left.

That sounded mysterious enough. He'll probably ask around and get a dozen different explanations, so this should be enough for my purposes.

Luckily, no trouble started between the residents of Whitecliff and the new refugees in the following days.

Her little demonstration had served its purpose of putting the new arrivals in their place and assuring them that their new residence had people strong enough to protect them.

Dorea felt a bit embarrassed after the fact, having realized that she had basically used Thed as a tool to show off, but he didn't seem to take it badly, instead looking more determined than ever to better himself.

She hadn't used proper spells to attack. However, her knowledge of the environment and skill at handling magic made her words about the teachings one could receive in the village much more convincing, and Voggo had found himself swamped with requests for additional lessons.

Not even just from the new group, as a few of the less combative mages who hadn't participated in all his lectures wanted to join in.

"As if I didn't have enough work on my hands," the old shaman grumbled, puttering about as he fixed the tea for the council meeting he had called.

"Oh, come off it," interjected Mark, the scout leader. "You love having those little kids running to you for help. Makes you feel all warm and gooey, helping the next generation."

These occasions had gotten more casual as time went on. Initially, the men had treated her as respectfully as possible, not having spent any time with her before and being careful of possibly offending a powerful mage.

Getting to know her better had relaxed both significantly.

Dorea had only recently realized that they had feared that either she or Mark the Blue would attempt to challenge Voggo and their leadership, as it happened for the Mondeans.

Not that the shaman believed she would do such a thing, but that irrational fear had likely remained with them for a while.

"I think it's a good thing if they feel welcome enough to start asking for lessons," she commented, getting a nod of approval from Ed.

"Integration is fundamental at this point. We need them to start thinking of themselves as belonging to Whitecliff as soon as possible if we want to trust them on the battlefield," he added.

Dorea had come to find that the burly man, despite his appearance and choice of trade, was very thoughtful and good at long-term thinking.

He was very explicitly all for Whitecliff's superiority, which rankled a bit when he spoke of their new arrivals as pieces on a board game, but she had come to accept that he was simply made like that, and since Voggo kept him on the council, he must have valued his point of view too.

"I don't think we need to fear them deserting a battle against the Mondeans," she responded. "But I can see how they wouldn't really care for the southern border."

Her conclusion was met with nods of agreement from all sides. It wasn't just Thed who coveted a deep hatred for their enemies, and having survived only thanks to their fathers' sacrifice had made it so that no one was inclined to run away.

"There is a problem with their dedication," Voggo finally interjected. He poured a grassy-smelling tea for everyone before taking his seat and resuming his speech. "Not only for these latest arrivals but for those before them too. Their assimilation is ongoing, that is true, but in their minds, they still don't feel like they belong here. Only through spilling blood together can we overcome such a hurdle."

His words rang heavy, and however much she didn't like the idea that they needed a bloody affair for the people they were sheltering to commit to their side fully, Dorea trusted Voggo to know what he was talking about.

He was the architect of the entire decision behind taking them in; thus, if he believed there was such a need, it was likely to be true.

"And we can't send them off south to skirmish with the tribes there because they have no attachment to that fight," Mark finished, rubbing his chin in thought.

Voggo sighed, taking a deep drink of his tea. "That is the unfortunate truth; we need to wait for the Mondeans to attack us before we can start trusting them more."

It's a terrible situation. No one wants such a thing to happen simply because we are not ready to take them on yet. But if it doesn't happen, our bonds with the refugees will not solidify enough.

Such calculations always left a bitter feeling behind, but Dorea had come to realize that they were an inevitable part of ruling. Though she had no actual power, being made privy to these councils had pulled the curtain back, and she had to readjust her morals and worldview accordingly.

"Well, there isn't much we can do about it. I'm not about to order our scouts to bait the Mondeans here before they come down themselves." Voggo closed the discussion.

Everyone agreed silently. When the time came, and if they managed to survive such a confrontation, they would reap the benefits, but the risk was not worth the reward.

"For the time being, we should continue with the integration processes that have worked so far."

Finally, they got to the last issue of the day. In two weeks, a new rotation would happen between the villages, and Dorea would lead the group who'd go south.

"Of course, your primary mission is to find out what is going on in the Wastes. But you shouldn't forget to forge new ties with the Heidels. This alliance of ours could crumble tomorrow, but we should aim to keep it going for as long as possible. Just the safety and trade it provides are enough to make it worth the hassle," Mark explained.

The man had been the village's primary negotiator for years at this point, and while before the Wrath that duty consisted mainly of maintaining neutral status with the surrounding villages, he still had a lot of experience. Enough that she closely listened whenever he spoke, hoping to glean something to make her task more manageable.

"I'll try my best. Already, I have good relations with the two siblings, Masi and Melu, and Chief Yaomi treated me well during my last visit."

"More than that will be needed," interrupted Voggo. "Your role isn't that of simple team leader, there to prove that we can repay the debts we have incurred with our allies."

Dorea looked at him curiously. She knew he had plans for her future, but pushing so fast seemed a bit premature.

"You will one day become the leader of the entire alliance; there is no doubt of that in my mind. But to do that, you need to start your climb now," he declared, stunning her into silence.

CHAPTER SEVENTEEN

Voggo's words echoed in Dorea's mind long after leaving the meeting.

Dorea had always known that the shaman had grand plans for her but had assumed there would be much more time before anything serious needed to be discussed.

Instead, the old man and the two other leaders had explicitly told her that they wanted her to actively propose herself as the future leader of the alliance.

Her objection that Yaomi's presence made a successful bid impossible had been completely ignored, as they believed the old witch to be either grooming her own candidate in Masi or, more likely, to be waiting for someone to emerge organically.

Yaomi could have easily pushed for the position herself, on account of her immense personal power and prestige even in the two other villages, but that she hadn't done so already meant that she wasn't likely to do it now.

"Yaomi is not the kind of person who wants power for herself. She's the type who gets burdened with more and more responsibilities as time goes on until she wakes up one day to find that everything depends on her," explained Mark, being well versed in diplomacy. "That means she's likely to abhor answering to all three villages. She has enough experience to know that little benefits will come with the position, at least in the beginning, and that it's mostly going to be a hassle."

"And why would I want to do it, then, if it's such a bad thing?" she had asked, confused as to how anyone would want it, if it had no positive sides.

The older scout had smiled then, looking like a father teaching a naive child about the way of the world. "Yaomi doesn't need more power because her personal strength is more than enough. But for everyone in your generation, this is a chance to put their name out there and receive accolades and recognition. While you might not necessarily see it as something to pursue, I can assure you that for many young men and women, there is little they would want more."

And that had been the crux of the matter. Whitecliff's council didn't necessarily think she deserved the position at the moment; they had been clear in that, but they had seen the power vacuum and wanted to claim it before anyone got ideas.

"This isn't anything you need to be worrying about immediately. You just continue doing what you have so far: growing stronger and making bonds. We simply wanted to include you in this conversation because we value your point of view." Voggo's words had reassured her, and although she would have preferred the problem not to exist in the first place, she was okay with being informed in advance.

I just need to do what I've been doing so far; no need to worry about the future more than I already do.

Unfortunately, that was easier said than done, as Dorea found herself brooding over the situation more than she would have liked.

While it was nice to know that the village's leadership continued to believe in her, the amount of stress this whole thing gave her was frankly too much.

Therefore, Dorea did what all teenagers with problems bigger than themselves do and went out to look for her friends to distract herself.

She found Beth and Jonah on the path to the beach, apparently having just returned from a quick swim, given their still-dripping forms.

She contemplated for just a moment hiding from them, not wanting to be subjected to their sickly sweet behavior, but then she realized that Jonah likely had already noticed her long before she did them and continued walking.

"Dorea! We were looking for you, but you were in the meeting for so long that we went ahead by ourselves," Jonah explained, scratching the back of his neck awkwardly.

These kinds of trips to the beach used to be something they'd do together, but ever since they started their relationship and Dorea's duties took more and more of her time, they became a rare occurrence.

"Don't worry. Waiting for me in the heat would have been torture; you were right to take a dip," she replied, sounding a bit off even to herself.

The other two looked at each other in worry, turning to her.

"Is everything okay? Did they say anything we should be concerned about?" Beth asked.

Dorea shook her head, sending her hair flying in the light breeze that was starting to pick up. "No, nothing serious, just things about my next mission south that I need to be prepared for."

Neither seemed particularly convinced by her words, but she brushed them off, deciding that a dip in the sea would do wonders to calm herself down. "I mean it, I'm just going to swim for a while to take my mind off things, but I'll catch you guys later."

She didn't give them the time to respond, accelerating her pace with a subtle use of Air Boost. She avoided sending any winds their way, not wanting a repeat of her last confrontation with Beth, but made sure there was no mistaking that she wanted some time by herself.

Even after the Draught of Determination, I'm still kind of a mess. This time I don't even have the excuse of whatever was going on with me.

It was an unfortunate reality that not everything could be solved by drinking sketchy brews prepared by slightly insane elderly shamans.

With her mood thoroughly ruined, Dorea reached the beach in a few minutes. She thanked the Mother for magic, which she wouldn't know how to live without at this point, and dove into the water, not bothering to remove any clothing.

Her water manipulation would help her clean them of any salt after she was done, and considering how many people were present, she didn't feel like skinny dipping.

The cold water served immensely better as a distraction than what she had been trying so far. It shocked her out of her spiraling thoughts, sending her back to the present.

With a twist of her will, she conjured an air bubble around her face, so she could breathe while under the surface and used the surrounding water to guide her path, swimming deeper than she ever had before.

Why did I never do this? It's been hot enough to go swimming for weeks now, but it never occurred to me that I could simply become a fish myself.

Silently laughing at the silliness of her thoughts, Dorea pushed farther into the ocean.

She had come this far only a few times, always with her father nearby and ready to rescue her in case the currents started getting stronger.

Now, she was the master of the sea. Nothing without a mind could harm her, and even then, she had her doubts she'd meet anything this close to the coast that could put up a fight.

Well, there is that damn turtle, but I sincerely doubt he will fight me. For all that his methods are very scary, he just wanted some food. Never going back there, though.

Such powerful beings were also much rarer than the recent encounters would suggest. Typically, Master-level beasts had their territory well demarcated and resided there long enough that no local would mistakenly go in.

Harlech the turtle was an exception in that while he was known to the village, almost no one, even in the previous generation, had ever interacted with him, given his preferred element and location.

Only sailors reported of having seen him once in a while, but everyone knew that sailors liked to tell tales and couldn't be trusted to be perfectly objective.

No other Master-level creature was known to dwell this close to the coast.

Now, if she suddenly became an idiot and swam for many more miles, uncaring of the dangers, she'd enter the Deep Sea, where true monsters lived, but she had no intention of doing so.

With a thought, she changed the current's direction, pushing herself out of the water at great speeds with a whoop of joy. Diving back like a dolphin, Dorea stopped to admire the undersea environment.

Pure white sand was constellated with rocks of different make, some being the dark purple of obsidian while others having flashier oranges and yellows.

Colorful fish swam in great banks, darting through the coral reefs, their scales gleaming like gemstones in the sunlight that filtered through the water's surface. Sea anemones waved their delicate tendrils, inviting curious creatures to take shelter within their vibrant embrace.

Lost in the underwater paradise, Dorea allowed herself to absorb the serenity, the calming rhythm of the sea.

Little after, something teased at the edge of her sensory range. A sudden shift in the water's temperature alerted her senses. She turned, her gaze narrowing as she peered into the dark expanse. The tranquil atmosphere shifted, replaced by an undercurrent of tension. Something was coming.

And then, emerging from the shadows, its body shimmering with iridescent scales, appeared a sea serpent. Its eyes burned with a fierce intensity, a challenge reflected in its poison-yellow gaze.

The beast had to be at least twenty feet long, given how big it looked even at such a distance. Emerging fully from the reef, it looked both beautiful and terrible; a mix she was coming to find was becoming more familiar when powerful creatures were involved.

She hadn't known of its presence previously, no sailor or the mages that accompanied them having reported it, which meant that it was either very new or had no interest in what happened above the surface.

Watching it approach with murder in its eyes, Dorea considered her options.

Lightning was immediately discarded. Although she could protect herself from its aftereffects even in the water, many others were enjoying the ocean's cooling effect, and they would be caught in the aftermath.

That left water and air magic to work with, and so she started preparing.

Once it got close enough, the sea serpent lunged forward, jaws gaping wide, rows of razor-sharp teeth ready to snap shut on its prey. She had expected the explosion of movement, though, so she pushed away from the strike with the help of a current she commandeered at the last moment.

With a flick of her wrist, she directed a torrent of water toward the serpent.

The creature's scales shimmered as the blow crashed against its mighty frame, momentarily stunning it.

Aware that it hadn't done much more than gain her time, she called upon her newest spell, expanding the bubble of air that granted her oxygen to cover her whole body into the Wind Bulwark.

Now feeling safer behind its protection, she turned her attention to her opponent. It had seemingly recovered and, by the gleaming of its fangs, was preparing something.

Not wanting to give it the time to finish what it was doing, Dorea sent a barrage of Exploding Water Bullets against it.

Blood bloomed in the depths like deadly flowers greeting the sun, a soundless screech of pain resounding all around.

The beast attempted to finish what it had started, pushing through the clouds of its own blood with mangled muscles to crash against her Bulwark.

Its teeth crackled violently with power as they closed on the shield, making it buckle. Still, it held, and she took the opportunity to finish the fight, sending another barrage of Bullets down its gullet.

The creature didn't even have the time to realize it was making its last mistake before its head blew up.

It's becoming an unfortunately common tactic. I can't say it's not effective, to be sure, but you'd think I could find less brutal ways to finish a fight.

Dorea floated in the water for a few seconds, observing as the mangled carcass finally came to a stop against one of the larger rocks.

With a sigh, she released her Bulwark, slowly, so as to not be crushed by the water. She made a come-hither motion toward her slain opponent, grasping it magically, and floated away, feeling more emotionally than magically drained.

She emerged from the ocean, followed by the body, and quickly reached the beach.

No need to leave some perfectly fine meat out there for the fish. A nice stew will soften it up enough to be perfectly palatable, and we need as much to eat as possible with all the people I keep bringing back to the village.

Unfortunately, the fight hadn't given her much power, as the serpent's danger had been its size and physical strength, rather than magical might. She hadn't even recouped the mana she had spent to kill it, but Dorea supposed that not every engagement could be a perfect win. Even just a few months before, such a creature would have sent her gibbering in terror, but now defeating it felt more like a chore than anything.

Her musings were broken by the sound of cheering and clapping. Dorea checked with her senses to see what all the beachgoers were so happy about, but was surprised that they all seemed to face her.

"Woohoo! Good job, Dorea! That's how you do it!" yelled Tom, the friendly water mage, from where he was perched on a rock at the end of the beach.

Others quickly joined in, congratulating her on the victory and oohing at the size of her catch.

A bit embarrassed, Dorea realized that even though what she had done seemed par for the course to her, to others, it had to have looked like an incredible feat.

Of course, only the mages whose sensory range reached almost a mile would have witnessed the fight, but there had likely been some explosions visible from the shore that would have alerted everyone else to the ongoing battle.

And seeing her emerge, completely unscathed, accompanied by the mangled body of a massive sea snake like a warrior out of a legend, had to have an impact.

Although Dorea wasn't exactly in a festive mood, she recognized that it was important for Whitecliff's defenders to make a show out of their might once in a while, to reassure the villagers that they were well protected. So with a sigh, she raised a fist in victory.

A roar of approval immediately hit her, the crowd shouting their compliments, well-wishes, and even just inarticulate screams of joy.

It's been a tough time for everyone. Even for those who didn't have to fight. Maybe especially for them, since they could do nothing but hope that we would prevail, praying for deliverance to a Goddess who seemed not to care for their plight. They need heroes.

Finally, something clicked in her mind.

It wasn't so much that Voggo and the two other councilors wanted a teenage girl to take the reins of leadership. They didn't believe that she'd be the best possible candidate.

It was apparent that she was both inexperienced and unenthusiastic about the job. Any of them would have done a better job, and if Voggo was to be excluded from the running because of his old age, Mark, the scout leader, was much younger than him and experienced in both leadership and diplomacy.

No, what they were looking for was a symbol. Someone whose image they could rally the people to in hard times.

And since she had shown a surprising ability to befriend their allies' most important mages and had a very successful track record, she was the best candidate.

That, and the other mages from my generation, wouldn't accept someone who didn't go through what they did. Yaomi could, but she seems not to want it. That leaves few candidates, and I'm the least likely to go crazy with power.

Dorea was well aware that at least part of the reasoning behind giving her a seat at the council was that the leaders wanted to check her mettle.

Had she started lording her position over the others—it was an unfortunately common thing since she had seen a few team leaders do so with much less power in their grasp—she would have been sidelined shortly thereafter.

However, she hadn't done so. That, more than any affection that Voggo might have toward her, had made her into the perfect candidate.

With this in mind, Dorea floated the sea serpent's carcass until it was in the middle of the semicircle of people that had formed up, and dropped it in the sand.

Away from the heightened state of a fight, she thought the beast seemed even bigger. Considering how weak it was, it couldn't have belonged to a previous generation's Wrath, meaning it had been a juvenile animal when it got its powers.

For it to be so large and yet not fully grown, its final size would have truly belonged to a legend. Instead, it attacked the wrong thing, bringing a swift and brutal end to its life.

Watching the awed looks of the gathered people, the bright smiles on the kids' little faces as they ran around it, poking with sticks and trying to climb it, Dorea decided that she had to think bigger than simply growing stronger to protect her family and friends.

She had a responsibility to all these people, whether she liked it or not, to defend them with the power she had been given.

The serpent, she decided, would be a stepping stone for her legend.

CHAPTER EIGHTEEN

The morning sun had just started shining through the cracks of her window when Dorea woke up.

She grumbled internally, annoyed at the singular ray of light that had somehow managed to hit the exact spot where her eyes were, but rose nonetheless.

She stretched her limbs, anticipation mingling with a tinge of apprehension. Today was an important day for multiple reasons, but the most relevant one was that it was her birthday.

It wouldn't be a large celebration, as those were reserved for when one reached two or sixteen, thus showing that they had survived until the end of infancy and, in the latter's case, the true beginning of adulthood.

Dorea was turning fifteen, which meant she was still technically considered a kid. It was both an annoying reminder of her young age and a shield she was grateful for.

Already, her responsibilities had multiplied in the last few months, and she expected them to continue growing.

Voggo had been very clear in his hopes that she would, one day, take up the reins of the alliance's leadership, and even if the time had not yet arrived, she still needed to sow the seeds.

And to sow those seeds, I need to go to the field. In this case, the field in question is the Heidel village.

I'm grateful that he waited enough for me to spend my birthday here, but it still feels like time has passed too quickly.

She had been worried that another Mondean attack would happen in her absence, but she had been reassured that their enemies were busy pushing eastward in the mountains, thus having little time to spare for them.

The presence of the Transmission Logs, the wooden pieces that Yaomi had carved intricately to communicate over long distances, also reassured her that should such a thing come to pass, she'd at least know with some time to spare.

Shaking herself from such grim contemplations, Dorea finished dressing and went downstairs, where she could feel her family waiting for her.

It was tradition for them to hold a small celebration at dinner, but it seemed like her impending departure had changed things.

As soon as she stepped into the kitchen, a little blur snatched her waist in a hug. Little Lia looked at her with big, teary eyes, and Dorea already knew that if she allowed herself to think too deeply about it, she'd start crying too.

Putting on a bright smile, she pinched her sister, successfully distracting her, making her shriek and run away.

She gave chase, following her all around the table until she was stopped by a warm hand.

With a rueful chuckle, her father gathered her in his arms and hugged her. The rumbling of his laughter served as a soothing balm, further distracting her from her dark thoughts.

Once Dodro had gotten his fill, he passed her to his wife, Lilian, who embraced her tightly, giving her a sweet kiss on the forehead. "My little girl, all grown up. Look at what a wonderful woman you are becoming."

Dorea swatted the air in embarrassment, pushing away from her mother, much to her parents' mirth.

"I never would have thought that you'd be what you are now last year," said her father, drawing her attention, "but I can tell you this, I have never been prouder of you."

"Thank you, Dad," the girl muttered, overwhelmed with the love and affection she could feel radiating from her parents.

The sound of tapping against the table broke them out of the moment, and they turned to see Lia already seated. She was perched on a stool, her eyes wide with anticipation and mischief. Her fingers danced along the table's edge, impatiently waiting for the food to be served.

Rolling her eyes, Lilian complied with the unspoken request and returned to finishing the preparations.

A simple but hearty spread of freshly baked bread, still warm from the oven, soft cheeses made by Dodro specifically so as to not be too funky, and blueberry preserves, made with the fruits that Lia had picked the day before.

Honey wouldn't usually be wasted on such things, but an exception had been made for her birthday, and Dorea felt very grateful for it as she spooned a thick layer of the jam over buttered bread.

Joe's bakery's confections might have been delicious with their intricate fillings and complex preparations, but for Dorea, there was little better than what she was having at the moment.

A fresh minty tea was then served to cleanse their palates of the fatty, sugary foods, and she took a grateful gulp, enjoying the sensation.

"Has the mint been giving you trouble again?" Dorea asked her mother, gesturing toward the bundle of freshly picked plants on the counter.

Lilian pursed her lips, nodding. "It's an invasive species, and it keeps growing everywhere. Fortunately, I can sell the plants we don't use for tea, but it has been annoying."

The conversation flowed easily as they chatted about the duties of the day, the condition of the animals, and the new hires.

Dodro was still not fully convinced of one of the new women he had been asked to take on, as she seemed more interested in making doe eyes at the laborers than helping with the anoas, but Lilian convinced him to wait before throwing her out.

"The poor girl has been through all kinds of terrible things lately. If she found a safe place to work, where manly men work up a sweat, it'd be obvious that she'd be a bit distracted. Just give her some time, and if necessary, I'll talk to her about being more discreet."

These were the kinds of discussions they used to have every day before the Wrath's arrival.

Lately, though, Dorea hadn't spent much time with her family, especially at mealtime, and she found that she missed even such inane conversations.

Sitting there, sipping her mother's mint tea while her parents complained of the workload and Lia tried to sneak in a spoonful of jam in her mouth, Dorea felt at peace.

Like all nice things, it, too, unfortunately had to end.

A pulse of mana from the village's direction told her it was time to move, and with a sigh, Dorea stood up.

She made sure to kiss her parents on the cheek, ruffle her sister's hair, and gather her rucksack before leaving for the last patrol before she'd go down south for a month.

It sounds like a short amount of time when I think of it like that, and I'm sure I'll be back before I even know it, but leaving Whitecliff behind just doesn't sit well with me.

Dorea had been allowed to take the entire day off since it was her birthday. Still, since no one else did so for theirs, wanting to contribute to the village's defense, she felt that it would have looked bad for her future run as leader of the alliance, to already take advantage of her privileges.

I kinda hate having to think about this stuff all the time. It makes everything into a question of positive or negative value, even though I understand its importance.

In the end, she was aware that this kind of thing wouldn't really matter all that much, since personal power and accomplishments on the battlefield would be much more relevant in choosing a possible chief.

It didn't mean that she wanted to give a bad impression to people, however, and thus, she set off toward the main gate.

There, she met with her squad and greeted Ted and Leo with a smile.

"Happy birthday, Dorea!" Ted called out, alerting all the others.

What followed was a deluge of congratulations and well-wishes that felt more awkward than anything, but she realized it was a necessary social formality.

With that done, and after she gave Ted the stink eye enough that he got her annoyance, they exited the village, entering the forest.

Patrols such as this were something Dorea was well used to, having gone on dozens by now. And that was without taking into account her own forays into the deeper woods to hunt for beasts and grow her personal power.

The air inside the forest was already warm, though the shade the trees provided dampened the sun's heat to a comfortable level.

One of the older scouts, Harlan, led the group, having the most experience traversing the terrain. His rough-hewn face bore the marks of countless fights against animals, but his eyes gleamed with the wisdom of experience as they flitted through the trees, looking for marks.

It was especially important this time to have such a person leading them—the reason why Dorea hadn't taken command of the patrol—since their path would take them to the borders of Old Titan's territory.

Since the monster would kill anyone who dared brave his wrath, many believed that getting so close would be foolish, and a small, fearful part of Dorea agreed with them. But the possibility of the Mondeans sneaking in a force by leaving the mountains from a different, more eastern path than their usual ones and entering the forest by closely following the forbidden territories was a very real one.

Which meant, unfortunately, that they needed to check to ensure no one was there or had been using such a path in the past.

As they ventured deeper into the forest, the air grew thick with the earthy scent of moss and the sweet perfume of wildflowers. The trees stood tall and ancient, their foliage forming a lush canopy that dappled the forest floor with patches of sunlight.

Dorea kept her senses alert, ready to respond to potential threats lurking within the shadows.

Harlan signaled for them to stop, his hand raised in a silent command. The group fell into a hushed silence, attuning their senses to the forest's subtle rhythms.

Dorea's range encompassed hundreds of feet, and she could feel a family of deer grazing peacefully nearby, their graceful forms blending seamlessly with the foliage.

On their left, up on an old oak, a troupe of playful squirrels darted among the branches, their tiny paws creating a symphony of rustling leaves.

Ahead, a group of rabbits, with their twitching noses and alert ears, seemed to sense their presence, yet they remained unafraid. As of late, the forest had been a violent place, and animals had learned to either hide, blending perfectly with the environment, or face the oncoming threats head-on, throwing themselves at any who'd dare step on their territory.

Luckily, it seemed that none of the animals she could feel wanted anything to do with them, so she nodded to Harlan, showing that she believed the path to be clear.

Satisfied that the forest held no immediate threats, the grizzled man motioned for them to move forward.

Stopping for regular checks wasn't exactly needed, as Dorea always kept her attention on anything that moved. Still, she could appreciate an abundance of caution when getting so close to Old Titan's territory.

Her last meeting with the monster might have ended with just a scare, but she had absolutely no intention of coming face-to-face with the thing again until she was well above Master level.

After several hours of exploration, Harlan called for a rest. They settled in a small clearing, where a gentle brook gurgled nearby.

Dorea sat beside Tom and Leo, the three mages sharing an easy camaraderie. Given how well Leo had integrated, it was hard to think that the redheaded boy had arrived in Whitecliff only a few months before.

This is how we should be. No matter where you are from, standing together against the Mondeans' depredations should be our main concern. To do that, we need to put aside our differences.

"I guess you have been pretty busy lately, but have you learned to hide your presence?" Leo asked her as he finished his jerky.

Dorea tilted her head in confusion, not getting what he was talking about.

The two boys looked at each other and sighed. "We have been holding lessons to teach each other new skills we pick up; you remember that, right?" Tom asked.

When she nodded, thinking back to that day at the beach when she took part in the demonstration and had to leave because of her heightened emotions, he continued, "We don't just clap at every little trick we come up with, you know? Mel has taught us how to conceal our presence, and it's pretty obvious you either don't know how to do it or don't care."

Rather than taking offense, like she would have once, Dorea merely gestured for the boy to go on.

His words aren't exactly the kindest, but it is true that I haven't dedicated enough time to that skill, even after Jonah surprised me with it and I said I would learn it.

"It's not that complicated, but it requires some practice to keep up for long," he said, relieved that she hadn't made a fuss.

That, too, was an essential quality for a leader in Dorea's mind. Knowing when you are lacking and either having someone else fill in or having them teach you.

"So, you know how you can feel others because of their interaction with an element and their mana?"

She nodded again, pushing a blond lock away from her eyes with an absent-minded motion.

"The trick is to pull your mana inward, still the way the elements within you and around you interact with the rest of the world," he finished. At the same time, his presence became lessened until finally, she could only tell he was there when she actively focused on the spot her eyes told her he was in.

She had already known that it was how it would feel, having encountered the phenomenon a few times already, but it was always jarring to have such a disconnect between her natural senses and her mystical ones.

"You can't really cast any magic while you hide, and it's difficult to keep it up for long periods of time; still, it's a valuable skill to learn before you go down south," Leo interjected, bringing her attention to him.

"Yeah, I agree," she answered. "It's something I wanted to work on, but things have been kind of hectic lately."

Neither of the two boys had anything to say to that, so they both shrugged and turned to finish their meals, leaving her to contemplate what they just told her.

I can appreciate that they just wanted to help me. They probably could have said so in a kinder way, but it is true that I've been focusing too much on combat skills. I have my pendant, but I cannot rely on it to always save me. And they don't know of it, so it'd look like I'm being extremely foolish to them.

Dorea wasn't about to reveal it, having agreed with Voggo long ago that it was better for her to keep it a secret, but she still thought it would be worth learning the skill herself.

I like fighting, but having the choice of going through a place unmolested by beasts sounds terrific.

Thus, she turned her focus inward, though not going as deep as during her meditation. Grabbing her mana, she slowly pulled it toward her core, attempting to stop it from interacting with the physical world.

It turned out harder than she had expected it to be.

The mana wanted to flow through her mystical channels freely; it longed to affect reality with its sheer weight. Preventing that required her whole focus, and in the little time they had to rest, she only managed to successfully do so for a few seconds.

Opening her eyes, she met the stunned expressions of her two companions.

"How in the hell have you done that? It took me a week to actually do it for the first time!" asked Tom in a high-pitched voice.

Rather than replying verbally, Dorea rose up, having sensed Harlan getting ready to move, flicked her hair to the side, and left.

Behind her, she sensed the boys looking at each other in bafflement.

"If you are done horsing around, we can start doing our jobs again," Harlan commented gruffly, though the smirk that tugged at his lips revealed that he wasn't as annoyed as his words implied.

As they resumed their patrol, Dorea avoided testing her newest skill since it would limit her focus too much, and she was the mage with the broadest range present.

I'm going to train this until I can hold it without even thinking about it and then see if I can somehow hide while using magic, but now is not the time.

For toddlers to learn that obstacles existed, they had to smash against a wall hard enough to remember the lesson. Dorea felt very much the same about her experience with Old Titan.

She had been like a kid running around in a dangerous place, and only luck and her grandmother's providence had saved her life.

Thus, she had no intention of risking missing anything because she wasn't paying attention.

A few minutes later, an earth-shaking roar alerted everyone that *something* was happening.

Dorea paled dramatically, however, because she recognized that sound all too well.

It seemed like the bear had come out of his den.

CHAPTER NINETEEN

Again, the earth rumbled, followed by a loud bang. The screech of an eagle informed the patrol of who dared awaken Old Titan.

And there was no mistaking where that roar came from.

With a tremendous crash, violent winds smashed down from the heavens, blasting entire trees to the ground.

The group of humans fell over, destabilized by the howling gales and shaking earth. Through her terror, Dorea had the presence of mind to cast a Bulwark around them, protecting everyone from the flying debris.

Although they had been careful not to get too close, it seemed like they would still be drawn into the ongoing fight.

Luckily, neither of the two beasts who were squaring off appeared to care much about them.

"No one move. We cannot hope to make it if they take notice of us," ordered Harlan, his voice carrying just far enough to be heard by everyone.

The man looked like he had seen a ghost, pale and sweaty, with his gaze affixed to the center of the newly formed clearing.

Before them stood the colossal figure of Old Titan, a bear of legendary size and strength. His fur, a dark brown tinged with a weathered silver, shined in the dappled sunlight now that the forest canopy was no longer there. His every breath sent a rumble through the ground, the edges of his form looking almost indistinguishable from the earth he controlled.

Opposing Old Titan was a smaller but no less formidable-looking opponent—a majestic eagle, its wings spanning wide, feathers shimmering with a silvery iridescence. With each beat of its limbs, a gust of wind unfurled, and its screeches of challenge sent gales in every direction.

This is a fight between two Masters.

The realization struck her to her core. Dorea was aware that it had always been a realistic possibility for another great beast to decide to face off against their ancient neighbor, but she never imagined she'd see it with her own eyes.

The thought of fleeing was one she was sure had entered everyone's mind, but she knew that Harlan was correct. To draw attention to themselves now could spell their doom.

She wasn't sure if her shield, even reinforced by Tom and Leo, would hold against the stray hits coming their way. But were one of the two beasts turn their attention toward them, they'd be done for.

Finally, the standoff seemed to come to an end.

The eagle screeched again, but this time with intent. A hurricane materialized out of nowhere, boring down the forest and threatening to rip swathes of trees.

Dorea and the two other mages put their all into strengthening their barrier, and though they barely managed to hold it, it felt as if a giant had tried to take a chunk out of it.

Even if they were obviously not the target of the terrible spell, just being in its vicinity threatened to suck them into it.

Dorea's Bulwark, alongside Leo's solid air rectangles and Tom's water shield, expanded to cover the entire group. The spells were expensive enough that they couldn't hope to last more than just a few minutes, but leaving their safety to flee would mean certain death, while trying to run as they held the protection was sure to get the beasts' attention.

Much to her shame, Dorea contemplated, for just a moment, leaving her companions behind and fleeing by herself.

With her Air Boost and Bulwark, protected by her grandmother's pendant, she likely had a better chance of surviving than by staying there, but she reasserted her will over that little voice and quashed it.

Meanwhile, Old Titan weathered the sudden storm with little more than a grunt. His paws had half-sunk into the ground, holding him in place.

Seeing this, the eagle ended its attempts at wide-area effects and concentrated its might in much smaller buzzing wind blades.

To Dorea's shock, the power contained in each of them was twice as much as she held in her whole body. Her senses were almost useless, as the sheer might being thrown around blinded her as if she were staring at the sun.

As the eagle let the razor-sharp blades go, a deadly blow meant to end the fight at its inception, the bear called upon the power of the earth. The ground beneath his massive form quaked and rumbled, mud and stone rising to form an impenetrable barrier.

A dark brown dome was erected in half a second, covering the entirety of Old Titan's form from sight.

When the blades struck, a deafening blast resounded as a shower of rocks was sent flying everywhere.

Some hit Dorea's protection with enough force that they cracked her Bulwark, sending her to her knees as she tried to stop the deadly projectiles from skewering her companions.

On the other hand, beyond a few external layers being scraped off, the bear's shield showed almost no sign of being hit.

The eagle's attacks had been deflected, unable to breach the fortress of stone that Old Titan had erected.

With a mighty roar from within the earthen dome, stones as big as a horse lifted into the air, turned until their point faced the eagle, and shot toward it with such strength as to crack the air.

Seven mighty booms mixed into one, with enough power to deafen anyone not being protected magically.

Even just the aftershocks left behind were enough to rival Thunderclap, one of Dorea's mightiest magical attacks, and its entire purpose was just creating that explosion.

The eagle screeched in pain as one of the pillars managed to hit it. One instant, it was flying with both wings, crafting more terrible constructs, and the next, it was being held aloft only by its mastery over the air, one of its limbs missing entirely, with no sign of where its remains might be.

A low sound, more like a chuff than anything Dorea had heard so far, rumbled through the clearing. It took her a moment to realize that laughter was coming from within the earthen dome.

Old Titan's amusement felt jarring in such a high-stakes battle, but she remembered the sheer level of power he had exuded when she met him the first time and realized that he had been toying with the eagle all along.

Although both were Master-level creatures, the disparity in their reserves and power output was enormous. The protection the bear had hidden behind crumbled into dust, revealing the monster to be entirely unharmed.

For a while, he just stood there, staring at his foolish opponent, who still dared face the true master of the forest.

The eagle's bravery would have been commendable in any other situation, but here and now, it was nothing short of foolishness.

Still grievously injured and barely holding itself in the air, it glared down, the hate filling its eyes visible even in the distance.

It couldn't be a juvenile, not with the mastery it had shown so far, but its vigor was that of one. Even in its state, it didn't flee, choosing to continue its last stand.

Air rushed toward the eagle in a vortex that threatened to uproot the few remaining trees. Even the Wind Bulwark almost fell apart to be absorbed.

A great sphere of condensed gas came into being in front of the avian, its density such that it was visible to the naked eye even at the distances Whitecliff's patrol was sheltering at.

The power constrained within it was such that to compare it to Lightning Sphere would be like saying that a flame was similar to the sun.

The air pressure in the whole forest changed as the eagle crafted a masterpiece of magic, fusing individual currents of such strength that one alone would have been enough to threaten an entire village.

If that thing hits, we're done for. Not just us, but the whole forest might get destroyed.

Such was the power being displayed that it would irrevocably change the landscape for decades, if not centuries.

Old Titan, it seemed, shared the same thought because he stopped staring in amusement at his opponent and dropped back on all four.

The earth shook as he prepared something, but Dorea believed he might have waited too long.

The eagle screeched in victory, having been allowed to prepare its masterpiece without interference, and readied the final blow.

Just as the immensely dense ball of air was leaving its caster, and Dorea was saying her last prayers staring in the face of the incoming death, sure that nothing she could do would change the outcome now that the sphere had been completed, the earth split open.

A spire of white marble shot from the fissure too fast for her eyes to follow. In an instant, it had reached hundreds of feet in height.

The noise it made as it broke earth and sky at once was deafening, and Dorea again thanked her foresight in dampening the incoming sounds, as such a blast would have ruptured everyone's eardrums.

There was another loud bang as the white spire connected with the eagle and its spell before it was obscured by dust.

That was followed by the release of all the winds within the sphere in every direction. Dorea's shield was flattened into the ground, barely holding together enough to protect her charges. Trees hundreds of feet away were crushed into splinters and sawdust, looking like the fist of an angry god had struck them.

Dorea instinctively lay flat on the ground, a gibbering part of her brain telling her to make herself as small a target as possible. Even then, her whole focus was on maintaining the Bulwark.

She had no care for keeping a fair amount of mana on hand for the future. Her whole mind, body, and soul were dedicated to funneling as much power into her only protection as possible.

By now, Leo and Tom had fully exhausted themselves, having put more energy into the shield than anything they ever had before. For all their efforts, they would have still died had she not been there.

Leo's barriers easily rivaled hers in toughness and skill, but his tank had run dry much earlier than she would have expected.

Finally, silence settled over the clearing as the patrol absorbed the outcome of the intense battle. Dorea's heart was filled with both admiration for the courage displayed by the eagle and a sobering reverence for the immense power wielded by Old Titan.

Whatever the result, she knew she'd forever remember witnessing a clash of Masters.

As the cloud of dust finally dissipated, it revealed a gnarly sight.

The once proud eagle, commander of the winds, had been skewered on the marble spire.

Life had long since fled the creature, most of its body missing and being held aloft only by the wickedly sharp edges of the magical construct.

Upon seeing that victory was his, Old Titan roared to the heavens, shaking everything.

Once done with his celebration, he padded softly toward his creation until his snout almost touched it. He then raised a paw as big as a burly man's torso and pressed it against the marble.

The tower shook and started sinking back into the very earth that had given birth to it.

The process took a few minutes, though none of the humans dared make a sound to disturb the ruler of the forest in his effort. Finally, the dirt swallowed the last of it, leaving behind an unnaturally smooth surface and the eagle's mangled corpse.

The bear lowered his snout, sniffed it, and evidently deemed it acceptable, because he caught it in his mouth and dragged it away.

The group of humans silently stared as Old Titan ambled off toward the center of his territory, his prey secured.

No one dared emit a sound until he was out of sight, and even then, until Dorea relaxed, having sensed the monster leave her range. She finally dropped her Bulwark, feeling a deep ache in her system that she hadn't felt since she was just starting out.

"That was . . ." Ted tried to say, but nothing more came out.

Still, everyone nodded, understanding exactly what he was trying to say.

"I sincerely doubt that anyone's going to brave this area for quite a while," Harlan said finally, having taken the time to finally gather his wits. "But that doesn't mean we don't have a job still. The Mondeans would be incredibly foolish to come here now, but that wouldn't be a surprise, now would it?"

Going by the long faces, more than one person would have dearly liked to return to Whitecliff and try their best to forget what had just happened, but no one complained out loud.

It took them a few more minutes to be ready to move, but they did, keeping a wary eye toward the direction Old Titan had disappeared in.

Soon, they left behind the new clearing, reentering the forest. The unnatural quiet that had settled didn't do them any favors, but as they walked, sounds finally started filtering back in.

Birds tentatively chirped to each other, as if to ask whether it was now safe. Squirrels poked their heads out of their nests, wary of any new presence.

Dorea could sense the entire forest slowly starting to unfreeze. Its king had brought to bear a terrible power, but it appeared like the storm had passed without it spelling disaster for everyone.

As they walked on, silent in their duties, the blond girl did her best to pay attention to anything suspicious, despite her reserves being far from combat-readiness.

She had had to put her all into her Bulwark, but she didn't regret it. She didn't regret witnessing the titanic fight, even though it felt like her heart would bust out of her ribcage with how fast it beat.

If given the possibility of going back in time, she would still have come to where she had seen two Master-level creatures fight for the first time. Not only because she had always been very curious about the might of such a rank.

No, the reason she would have still risked her life was that she had gotten something out of it.

Her mind hadn't just been expanded on the possibilities that magic still held in reserve, but when she had focused all her senses on the great eagle as it crafted its last spell, something had clicked in her mind.

It wasn't anything like a new spell taking form, but more like a place her mana didn't know it could go to had finally been unlocked inside her.

The sheer level of control, the beauty of the flow, and the speed at which the winds were called upon and condensed into a deadly weapon had been breathtaking.

The tragedy of the eagle's loss didn't discount the might it had displayed. Indeed, it might even have engraved it further in Dorea's mind, as she attempted to retain every crumb of knowledge she had gleaned from the display.

She was sure, now, that she'd be able to craft a Wind Sphere, based upon her first spell, with little trouble, save for her lack of mana.

It'll be the first thing I do as soon as I get back. I might need to leave shortly, but this feels like something I need to crystalize into a concrete action before the inspiration fades away.

That Old Titan had merely been toying with the eagle just went to show exactly how far she was from the monster.

Even just his first attack, the boulders he had shot at the eagle at speeds that beggared comprehension, would have been enough to level Whitecliff to the ground.

The fact that such a monster had lived close to the village for decades and never even attempted to harm them reassured her that it wouldn't happen now, but the awe and fear she had felt toward the bear ever since her first meeting with him had been stoked further.

She knew she'd never forget the sight of a marble spire, as tall as a mountain, rising from the ground with all the effort of a child building with sand.

The return to Whitecliff had taken longer than Dorea would have liked, not because they had met any more mighty beasts along the way but because Harlan had insisted upon being as thorough as possible.

Dorea suspected that the older man had been spooked much more than he was giving away and wanted to do something he could fully control. That, or he believed that it would be helpful for everyone to explore every nook and cranny of their path with almost obsessive attention.

Still, they had made it back and relayed what they had witnessed to Voggo and the two other councilors, who all seemed keen on knowing more. The village had been on high alert, having heard the sounds of the confrontation, and an explanation was gratefully received.

After everyone but she had been dismissed, they questioned her further, knowing that she'd have been able to pick up more with her senses.

Dorea did what she could to impress upon them the sheer power she had felt being thrown around in the fight. The grave expressions on the two councilors' faces told her she had managed at least a little, but Voggo looked weirdly relieved.

"Old Titan is an extremely powerful creature, but he has shown again and again that he has no intention to attack us," he explained when questioned, unknowingly echoing her earlier thoughts. "If he had weakened, we would have had to prepare for more challengers to try their luck, and not all of them would have been so kind as to avoid collateral damage."

In the end, there wasn't much they could do about what the patrol had seen. It would forever serve as a reminder of the difference between magical ranks and even within them, but they would have to make peace with it.

Dorea left Voggo's house with much on her mind, a spell to attempt, and a bag to pack.

After all, tomorrow, she'd leave for the south.

CHAPTER TWENTY

Having left behind the lush forest, Dorea sighed. The grasslands stretched before her, the wind blowing the yellowed strands as the sun beat down on her.

Unlike her previous times traversing these grounds, she was constrained to walking speed, as the entire Heidel contingent that had resided in Whitecliff since the summit was coming down south with her.

They had waited a day longer than expected, as the new group was delayed by having to put out a small fire coming from the salamanders' direction.

It's becoming more and more of a problem. We really need to get on that, or at this rate, they'll try to burn the whole forest down.

Still, the wait had been welcomed, as she managed to spend some more time with her family and friends, and, equally important, she succeeded in cashing in on the revelation the monstrous fight between the eagle and Old Titan had given her.

More than just developing a new spell that would have served a similar role as her Lightning Sphere, Dorea had pushed herself to the limit, straining her mind to recall every little scrap of information.

The result, she felt, was more than worth it.

She had never seen such fast progress, even in the first few weeks of gaining her powers, which were supposed to be the time when the most growth happened.

The price she had paid for it, though, had been steep. Luck had played a significant role in her and everyone else's survival that day, and had even just one attack gone astray and hit them directly, no barrier of hers would have been enough.

Still, she had been curious as to why Voggo hadn't told them during his earlier lessons that such epiphanies were possible.

"Because I didn't want foolish teenagers to go look for trouble. Bothering a Master-level creature just because you want to take a look at what they can do when they let go is an incredibly efficient way to die young." That had been the shaman's answer, and honestly, Dorea couldn't really fault his reasoning.

She had been careful in her forays in the forest to avoid any of the old monsters, even before coming face-to-face with the gigantic bear that towered over all others. Still, Dorea wasn't sure she could say she would have done the same if she had known that such leaps were possible.

Dorea felt that she had grown, not just in age and power, but also in wisdom as of late.

Her newest spell would definitely come in handy when the occasion called for it, but she wouldn't go looking for a similar experience, even if the thought had come to her a few times.

Returning back to the present, Dorea sighed again.

"Already homesick?" asked Masi from her side.

The young man had successfully led the first exchange rotation and returned home triumphantly, having proven his leadership skills. More than one of his companions had already congratulated him, as if his future had become all but assuredly bright.

Still, he managed not to appear too smug, settling for a slightly happy but constrained look of celebration.

"Not really. I don't mind leaving the village for a while, but the grasslands are so boring it somehow always manages to surprise me," she replied, only half-joking.

From the shocked outrage on the boy's face, he was more than ready to start back up the old argument between the two of them.

"Please, please, flirt when we are back home and you don't have an audience. Not everyone is interested in your weird courtship rituals," interjected a weathered voice.

It was the older man she had seen accompany Masi back when she first met him, and by his long-suffering expression, he wasn't about to hear any backtalk.

Dorea regarded him severely for a moment, somewhat annoyed at him. The man didn't flinch, evidently used to being stared down by mages, and she sighed, deciding that it wasn't worth putting up a fuss.

My goal here is to establish good relations, put myself forward as a possible future leader, and learn as much as possible about what's going on in the south. I don't really need to start getting into fights with anyone, if possible. Not for something like this, at least.

Seeing that the situation was still somewhat tense, Masi bumped her shoulder. "The old man might look grumpy, but he has a soft spot for Melu the size of a therium."

At that, the man rolled his eyes, threw his arms up, and walked away, evidently done with the boy's antics.

Once he was out of earshot, Masi explained, "Sorry about him. He hasn't been very happy with the alliance since he had bad blood with one of your mages. Well, one from the previous generation."

Dorea hummed, twisting her mana just so, to ensure no one overheard their conversation. "I'm not surprised that there are some who are reticent. Even in Whitecliff, all this change is enough to frustrate many people."

It might have sounded stupid to reveal such a weakness, but since Masi had opened up first, she decided that sharing this kind of information would be more beneficial than hiding it.

After all, if their villages were supposed to become more intertwined with each other, it would be better to know beforehand about possible troublemakers.

"He won't do anything since he'll follow whatever the chief decides, but his impression of you guys has been colored by that encounter during the war, and little will change his mind," the boy finished.

"Well, as long as he won't deliberately sabotage the alliance, I have no problem with some dissent. I find that it's a sign of a healthy tribe to be able to disagree safely without consequences," she replied, thinking back to the many council meetings she had attended in the last few months.

Voggo, Mark, and Ed had not always shared the same opinion about what they should do, and though the eldest among them had much greater personal and political power, he never exerted it on his fellows.

Instead, the shaman valued their opinions greatly, sometimes asking for further clarification and engaging in lively debate when he wasn't convinced. But to quash that dissent would mean erecting himself as absolute ruler, something he had purposefully avoided for all his tenure.

Dorea wasn't sure exactly what type of leader she wanted to be. To be honest, she wasn't even fully decided on whether she did want to lead the alliance, despite her earlier determination, but her circumstances were obviously pushing her in that direction.

Others would also make their bid in time, that much was inevitable, and she suspected that Masi might be one of those, but whether she or he won that fight, having good relationships with one another was a no-brainer.

It's not even because of what he said to me that day at the cliffs. I know I'm gonna have to marry someday, but that kind of thing can wait until I feel ready for it.

"He won't," Masi assured her, bringing her back to the present. "He might be a bit of a grump, and he doesn't like outsiders, but he is brave and true."

Dorea decided that if the problem arose again, she could deal with it then, but for the moment, she'd extend a measure of trust to the boy.

"Very well, I'll leave it in your hands, then." She then walked away, moving toward the rest of Whitecliff's contingent, feeling Masi's eyes on her the whole time.

The Heidel village didn't have an official name, mainly because it had never been meant to be anything more than just a temporary camp.

Indeed, if one really wanted to ascribe one to the settlement, it would be Camp.

Before the Great War, the Heidel tribe had been nomadic, wandering through the grasslands, settling for a season or two before picking their things up and moving again.

When traveling became unwise thanks to their eastern neighbor's movements and because of the increasing power wielded by the Witch of Immolation, the reasons to move again started to dwindle.

Their traditions dictated they did so, but when faced with several excellent arguments not to, they quickly adapted.

What the result ended up being was a mishmash of sedentary and nomadic. This was apparent to anyone who gazed upon their village.

Camp was aptly named, as tents of various make stretched in all directions, covering a good length of the river's course.

Leather, rather than cloth, seemed to be the most popular material, but its shiny black and brown told a story of great skill. The quality of the tents was such that Dorea wouldn't be surprised if some had survived the Wrath's passing even without magical interference.

Others looked shabbier, almost unkempt, and their leather was dull and lifeless. These were relegated to the outskirts of the village.

From up the hill where they stood, Dorea couldn't feel inside them, but she was sure she'd be able to explore Camp in depth in the month she'd spend here.

For the moment, she contented herself with observing what she could and keeping an eye on the approaching welcoming party.

At its head, standing slightly before anyone else, was the most powerful woman Dorea had ever known. Yaomi looked exactly the same as the last time she had seen her, a fierce mage with dark silvery hair and eyes that bore into the soul.

Her dark gray tunic accentuated her figure just enough to remind her that she was a woman, but still modestly, as proper for someone her age. She was more handsome than beautiful, Dorea noted, but once, she might have been contended between several suitors.

Now, the hard lines on her face and the power brimming beneath her skin would be enough to send even the bravest men running.

Even at the distance she was standing at, a mere few dozen feet away, Dorea had trouble picking up her signature. She had believed that the advancements in skill and power she had gone through might have allowed her to finally pierce through whatever technique Yaomi was using, as it appeared to be fundamentally different than what was being spread in Whitecliff, but if anything, she seemed even more elusive.

Instead of pulling herself inward, making it much harder to pick out her mana but still possible if one knew through other means that someone was there, she blended in the ambient currents, appearing as if a mirage.

Is that what it is? An illusion? I know high-level mages of any element can do it, but it seems a petty usage of her time and skill. And given the extreme power I felt when she killed that beast during our first meeting, I doubt it's just a mirage.

Finally, after an almost uncomfortable silence, Yaomi spoke up, "Welcome, to our new allies, to our sons and daughters who undertook the fundamental mission of protecting and nurturing this burgeoning camaraderie. You will be fed, watered, and sang to very shortly, but allow me to take a moment to commemorate this event."

Yaomi lifted her hands in the air, slowly turning so that everyone could see her. Her voice reached even the farthest of the onlookers, and even though Dorea couldn't sense any mana being used, she was sure there was magic at work.

When her hair caught the light of the dying sun just so, as she had it to her back, looking more like a divine agent than a mortal woman, she continued, "Today we rejoice as the first group to go on such a mission comes back, bearing good news. They were welcomed and treated like family by the people of Whitecliff, respected for their work and sacrifice, and held in high regard. That is all a mage and a warrior could ever ask for. I assure you that the same is true for those Sapiens who stayed with us and have now returned to the forest, just as it will be for those who have just arrived."

Her proclamation was met with cheers from everyone. Young children ran to the returning warriors, greeting them as heroes.

It all looked a bit overdone to Dorea since it wasn't as if this batch of Heidels had to fight anything beyond a few daring animals. Still, she supposed that ceremonies such as this were necessary to cement the importance of the alliance in everyone's mind.

When she looked back at Yaomi, she found the woman staring at her. Dorea inclined her head in greeting, respectful but not submissive, and got a crooked grin back.

She knew that she'd have to have a talk with her, even though she wasn't looking forward to it. Unfortunately, any possible bid for leadership would have to go through the Witch, and trying to circumvent her would just bring troubles.

I don't really feel like doing this, but since someone is going to, and there aren't many who I'd trust with that kind of responsibility, I guess I can at least try.

That had been the conclusion of her brooding in the last few days. Voggo had made it clear that if they went through with further integration, people would start looking for someone to lead them and that he very much wanted that person to be her.

Her thoughts were interrupted by a small girl, dusky-skinned in the way of all Heidels, with black hair tied in a dozen small braids, who ran to her.

She couldn't be older than Lia, and the sight made her heart ache.

Curiously, the girl poked Dorea's thigh, seemingly startled that she was solid. "You are real! I thought you were a ghost!"

Laughter bubbled up unbidden at that. Dorea crouched down at the girl's height and held up an arm close to the little one's.

That seemed to open the floodgates, as she was subjected to all kinds of poking and prodding. The stark difference in skin tone and hair color seemed to be what shocked the girl the most, but her blue eyes also got an amazed look.

More children got close then, having noticed that their friend hadn't been rejected, and Dorea found herself almost submersed in kids, all trying to get her attention to ask questions about Whitecliff, from inane ones like "Is it true that you all live in dark caves and never see the sun?" to more direct "How many kids survived the Wrath?"

Luckily for her, Masi was within earshot, and when he heard that, he stopped the assault. He waded into the crowd of kids, picking some of them up and pushing others away until he stood next to her. "All right, that's enough! I'm sure you'll get to know Dorea more in her time here, but mobbing her like this is not polite. Go play with something—we brought back a few toys from Whitecliff."

Though some had looked mulish at his words, when he got to the final part, everyone darted toward where their bags had been placed in search of the promised toys.

"Thanks." Dorea sent Masi a grateful look.

The boy shrugged, scratching his elbow as he looked toward where the kids swarmed the poor people who had been picked to unload their luggage like locusts. "It's no trouble. I know that they can be a bit too much."

Shortly after, they were brought into the village proper, toward the main square, where the river had been hemmed in by polished blocks of granite that looked to have been melted together.

Given the presence of the Witch of Immolation, that was a very likely possibility.

Now that Dorea had no pressing need to solve, she could take in Camp much better. Although it was mostly made up of tents, there was evident attention to communal living all through the settlement.

The main square was open to the skies at the moment, but she could see large rolls of leather hanging from tall wooden poles that told her that, in case of necessity, it could be covered from the pouring rain to give the tribesmen a place to come to even in the shortest days of the winter.

Beyond that, the roads were mostly well-beaten dirt paths and cobblestones, giving the whole thing a rustic but well-maintained feel.

Large tables had been set up at the edges of the plaza, where roasts, cured meats, and vegetables of all kinds were laid for everyone to enjoy.

Attending a feast in a different village than Whitecliff was a weird experience for Dorea, especially since, for the first time, she wasn't expected to help at all, being a guest.

She flitted through the tables, sampling everything from glazed hams to savory mashes of various roots. The food was different from what she had experienced all her life, tending more toward sour and spicy than her home's herbaceous and braised flavors, but she didn't mind it.

"I hope you are enjoying our hospitality," called a voice from behind her, startling her enough that she barely caught her plate with a last-second air platform.

Turning around while she held her hand over her heart, Dorea found the Heidel chief, smirking at her surprise.

Oh, this damn . . . I really need to find a way to rely less on my senses or, preferably, pierce through whatever technique she's using.

"I apologize. I just have a lot of fun startling you kids. The first couple of years, you all depend so much on your new and expanded perception that it's too funny to startle you," the older woman explained, holding two glasses of milky white liquid.

She proffered one to Dorea, which she realized was more of a peace offering than anything else, and lifted the other to toast her.

"We'll talk more in the coming days. We have much we need to share and even more to decide, but for now, enjoy the feast."

CHAPTER TWENTY-ONE

Dorea rolled out of her cot with a groan, absentmindedly conjuring some water in the bucket next to the small dresser to wash her face.

Camp didn't have as many amenities as Whitecliff, as the Heidels were more rugged people thanks to their nomadic origin, but she made do thanks to her magic.

Without it, she'd have found it difficult to even tend to her more basic necessities in such a place, and thus she had taken to sending a prayer of thanks to Mother Nature for her Gift every time.

The day started early, mostly because the tents, for all their high quality, didn't really do much to dampen sounds coming from the outside, and when the early risers started to do their jobs, be it stoking the fire for a blacksmith—who was the only one afforded a stone building, for obvious reasons—or letting out the animals, everyone who wasn't used to sleeping through the racket also woke up.

Dorea was the daughter of a rancher and, as such, wasn't a stranger to an early rise, but the sheer level of noise that assaulted her had been much more than expected.

And they gave us the tents farthest from the trade district! I can't imagine what it would have been like sleeping next to the forge. I'd have gone insane.

Grumblings done for the morning, she finished tying her hair in two braids, in the style that the little girl she had met when she arrived at Camp—who she had learned was named Hana— had shown her.

Usually, she'd leave it loose or tie it with lazy hairstyles, but she had found that the tight braids were working for her, as she didn't need to push them out of her face so often.

Dorea put forth more effort than she usually would that morning because she was expected at Yaomi's tent for lunch after she got her daily training in. Although she was still irritated with the woman, she didn't want to appear slobbish.

Exiting her abode, she met Nora's eyes. The girl had also been among those sent south for the current rotation, and Dorea was grateful for her presence.

Though they had never been particularly close before, given her friendship with Beth and Jonah, she found her to be a lovely girl with a surprisingly biting sarcasm.

They greeted each other, both with bags under their eyes, and left for the tent set aside for Whitecliff's contingent, where they could all gather and eat together.

That specific one was closer to the river, so they enjoyed a quiet walk in the early morning, even as Camp woke up.

The fresh air of the dawn might have led someone to believe that the grasslands were a cool place, but Dorea had been literally and figuratively burned by the harsh summer sun, and she would not lower her guard.

Inside the tent, which was a hundred feet wide, was a table filled with food and pitchers of fresh water, teas, and the same milky drink that Yaomi had toasted her with.

Dorea had come to find that the Heidels all had a preference for that specific beverage, though she couldn't really understand it. Fermented horse milk didn't sound particularly appealing to her, even though the one served in the morning was fresher than the one reserved for the evening.

For one, the acidic taste didn't really sit well with her, preferring the sweeter, more palatable anoa milk. Beyond that, the consistency was, at times, slightly pulpy, as clumps of milk fat gathered together.

That was not to her taste, so she purposefully avoided it ever since she had been forced to drink it at the party.

I couldn't really avoid it back then. Yaomi had given it to me, and we toasted. To throw it away would have been an insult.

Dorea had the sneaking suspicion that the Witch had once again been pranking her, as she seemed to have taken a liking to do. What alerted her was that the first time she had come to the Camp, she had been served tea.

If it truly was as common a drink as it looked now, Yaomi had purposefully avoided giving it to her back then because she didn't want to make her uncomfortable.

Which means that now she has no such compunction. That woman is testing me, and I have a few ideas why.

Dorea greeted the others, who slowly filed in, blearily rubbing the sleep from their eyes. Everyone got something to eat and sat down at the sturdy oak table.

Seeing that no one was missing, Dorea started speaking, "Today we have the morning free for personal training, or if you feel like you need it and somehow can manage with the racket that's always going on, you can go back to your tent and sleep some more."

Her words were met with half-hearted cheers, as the prospect of having some personal time was enough to put energy back into them.

"I know that the past few days have been more exhausting than expected," she continued, referencing both the early rises and the patrols that they had been slotted for. "But things should start settling down soon. I have a meeting with the Heidels' leadership in a few hours, and we'll be discussing this. I believe they wanted to parade us around in the south to show the more aggressive tribes there that they have backup, but I'll be getting clear answers from them."

It was a conviction she had matured during the long hours spent walking through the southern reaches of the grasslands, where the sun gave no mercy and wildlife was highly aggressive.

The Heidels, she believed, had developed a strategy similar to a poisonous frog. If provoked, they could be extremely deadly since Yaomi's power was incontestable, but they still much preferred not having to engage.

For all their martial preparedness and the weight they gave to military prowess, they knew that getting into a fight on a new front, while they were already wary of eastern and northern incursions, could prove to be too much even for them.

As such, they made periodic shows of force, where they paraded their allies on longer-than-normal patrols, to send the message that an attack on them would see retaliation from the entire alliance.

At least, that's what I think. It's what I've gathered from speaking with those who returned from the first rotation and observing the Heidels who accompanied us on the patrols. No matter what they said, those were not just to show us the lay of the land.

"Oh Goddess, does that mean we'll finally be able to get some rest?" Tom asked from the back. The water mage had been the most annoyed of all at having been made to work so hard, rightfully saying that no one had tried to make the Heidels in Whitecliff do more than they were supposed to. Still, Dorea had shut down that line of thought early, since any dissent would be detrimental to the alliance's stability.

"Our schedules should be much more manageable now, though I want to remind you that if their plan works as intended, just a few more hours of patrolling means that we'll avoid having to open another front here in the south," she gently rebuked.

Dorea could understand her companions' frustrations at being employed in such a manner without even consulting them before, and she fully intended to bring that to her meeting with Yaomi later in the day—appearing to be too passive would be even more detrimental than looking too proactive—but that was something for her to worry about. If the mages under her nominal control started making problems, it could undermine everything.

Tom settled down at that. Though he didn't look satisfied, he trusted her enough to let it go if she said it wouldn't happen again.

"All right, if that's all, you can finish your breakfast in peace. I'll see you all for dinner, where I'll go over what we discussed in the meeting," she concluded, getting nods of acknowledgment from all around and tucking in her own plate.

Yaomi's tent looked the same as the last time she had seen it.

It was the most ornate and well constructed in Camp, signifying the woman's status as the chief; but its interconnected network of smaller tents made it almost look like a palace.

It was the center of the Heidels' government, where decisions ranging from declaring war to the amount of water that could be diverted from the river were made.

Not all of them by Yaomi, of course, as that would require her to spend hours every day on the most inane subjects rather than furthering her craft and increasing her power, thus better defending the village.

Rather, a score of tribesmen ran around between the canvas, shouting requests for an increase in production of this or that, arguing over grain harvests and hunting rights.

It was the heart of Heidel society, and it gave a glimpse to Dorea of how their allies managed it.

In Whitecliff, things were very different. Voggo had long since established rules that everyone knew of, and in case something had to be decided on the spot, they all trusted him and the two council members to make the best decision possible.

As for the day-to-day, unless there was a contention between two villagers, people were left to manage their lives. After all, why would a hunter tell a farmer how to till their fields?

Still, Dorea could see the appeal of a hands-on approach. It granted Yaomi much more control over the village without having to spend so much time on it herself, and if a class of people could be taught from the beginning how to rule, leaving them to it would probably work better than the laissez-faire they employed in Whitecliff.

At least until a bureaucrat that has never set foot outside the village tries to tell a hunter, or worse, a mage, where they can and can't go. Can't see that working well.

There had been no need for a superstructure such as this in her hometown so far, but if they kept expanding their population at the rates they were doing right now, it would be inevitable.

Still, as Dorea walked through the tented halls of Yaomi's palace, she had to ask herself if this was the most efficient way.

She hadn't paid any attention to it the first time; it had been very close to night and as such well beyond usual working hours, and her mind had been clouded with the task she had come to do.

Now that no such thing preoccupied her, she could observe more carefully. A middle-aged man, looking surprisingly thin for what she had seen of the Heidels so far, had come to look for her at the training fields half an hour before.

Then, when she had expressed the desire to wash up before her meeting, the man, who had presented himself as Lindus, had waited patiently outside her tent.

He sported a well-groomed mustache, thick and dark, much unlike his balding head. His tunic barely hid his frail frame, and he appeared to always be sweating excessively.

"And here you can see our best and brightest, conducting a study of possible incursion from the two ruined cities in the south." Lindus grandly gestured to another connected tent, where two women and three men, all dressed like warriors, argued fiercely with one older man dressed like her guide, gesturing toward a map that was laid on the table.

Dorea craned her neck to try and catch a glimpse of it, though it was too far away to make the details, and her mystical senses couldn't help her decipher its contents.

"You'll have all the time you want to go over that later," Lindus politely called for her attention.

Dorea coughed in embarrassment and stopped her more obvious snooping, though she still subtly redirected the sounds from all over the pavilion so as to overhear anything interesting.

Unfortunately, no one was talking about anything of import, and even the argument going on next to the map seemed to be more about who could go on a specific patrol rather than specific objectives.

Dorea had expected it, since she would make sure not to speak of anything sensitive with a mage she didn't know around, even if they were allies. Still, sometimes people slipped up, and it paid to have one's ears to the ground.

Yaomi runs a tight ship, it looks like. At first glance, it's chaotic, but people are exactly where they need to be, and no one's slacking off. It might just be because I'm here and they want to put up a good front, but something tells me that's not the case.

Finally, they reached the farthest tent from the entrance, which was also the largest, where the Witch resided. This time, it seemed like the older woman hadn't seen the need to hide her presence, as Dorea was able to sense her well before she entered the complex.

"The chief is waiting for you. I wish you a productive meeting and hope you enjoy your lunch." Lindus bowed once, then wiped his forehead with a handkerchief and left.

The two guards at the entrance, their spears gleaming even with the filtered sunlight, remained still, making no acknowledgment of her presence. When she made to enter, they didn't stop her.

Not that they could stop me, even if their skill is great. Well, I doubt they are there for more than just appearances. The Witch of Immolation herself is here, after all, and she needs protection from no one.

Inside, she found the woman she had been expecting, alongside two men. One, she quickly recognized as Mort, the delegation leader who had come to Whitecliff for the summit. The other was an older portly man, shorter than any adult Heidel she had met but still recognizably from the same tribe.

Dorea had seen him once before, at the party held at their arrival, and could remember being surprised at the fluidity of his movements and the assuredness of his steps.

That had lasted until she sensed him shift the ground beneath his feet more than once, and she realized that he must have been a mage too. But given his element, he had to belong to the previous generation, meaning he'd have to be at least eighty if she assumed him to be the youngest possible age at the Wrath's coming.

The man didn't look a day over sixty-five, which told her he was either a very powerful Gifted, as they were known for their slower aging thanks to the abundance of mana in their system, or simply someone blessed by the Goddess.

I doubt he's that strong, or Voggo would have talked about him. But underestimating an older mage is a terrible mistake, so I'm just gonna assume he's genuinely strong until proven wrong.

"Welcome, Dorea, granddaughter of Doressa. We have watched your ascent to leadership with great interest and can say that we look forward to seeing how much you'll grow in the future," Mort greeted, his voice just as reedy as she remembered.

That he had announced her as the granddaughter of Doressa rather than the more common "of Whitecliff" or "daughter of Dodro" told her that these people only cared about personal power, and by calling her that, they recognized her as a worthy heir of the previous strongest mage in her village.

Yaomi was reclined on a sofa, looking like a big feline enjoying a lazy moment, but her eyes were as hard as flint, and Dorea didn't for a moment think that the older woman was taking her without all due seriousness.

For all that she enjoyed levity and even the occasional prank, the Heidel chief had held her position for decades, not just because of her personal might. She was a consummate leader and could run rings around her if she wasn't careful.

"Thank you for hosting me for this lunch. I think it was needed and look forward to the following discussion."

Dorea had decided since the moment she had been invited over that she'd try to keep the tone light but professional. Although Yaomi might enjoy directness, she couldn't afford to make mistakes and assume a familiarity that wasn't there, especially with other people present.

The portly man approached her, extending a hand to shake hers. "I have to say, you look very much like your grandmother. I can only hope you'll match her fierceness on the battlefield, and from what I've been told, you are well on your way there."

Dorea shook his hand, filing away the admission that he had personally seen her grandmother, who hadn't been south since the Great War ended decades before.

"It's nice to meet you, sir. I'm Dorea, as you might already know. I can only hope to have inherited some of Grandma's skills."

A snort interrupted their talk as Yaomi finally rose from her couch. "Doressa was a monster; if I were you, I'd try to look for a different path."

A beat of silence followed the proclamation as Dorea tried to reconcile the most powerful human she knew calling her grandmother a monster, and the two other men looked at each other in evident exasperation.

"Forgive her," seamlessly interjected Mort. "What she means to say is that your grandmother's path to power was difficult to repeat, and the heights she reached were great. Your path is your own to carve."

Dorea looked at the three, recognizing them as the true leaders of the Heidels, and steeled herself for a difficult lunch. She was in shark-infested waters and needed to figure out how to swim soon, or she'd get eaten.

CHAPTER TWENTY-TWO

Oh, don't look at us like that. We didn't bring you here to bully you," Yaomi exclaimed upon seeing her expression.

Dorea didn't bother responding. If the three Heidel elders wanted to make her feel at ease, they could have arranged the meeting differently. Instead, this felt almost like an ambush or a test.

"I do not believe that young Dorea has been given any reason not to suspect us," interjected the portly man who still hadn't given her his name.

He then gestured for her to take a seat at the circular table that had been set on the left side of the tent, where the canvas was made of cloth rather than leather and allowed more light through.

She acquiesced, sitting farther away from the entrance, and the three joined her.

When she still didn't speak, merely looking at the one man she hadn't met before, he startled.

"Oh! I forgot to introduce myself." He chuckled, patting his belly. "When you get to be as old as I am, you start thinking that everyone knows you already. That was my bad. My name is Seshi."

Dorea took note that the newly named Seshi didn't offer any more information about himself. She doubted it would be difficult to find out more once she had some time to ask questions, but that didn't help her at the moment.

Yaomi then clapped her hands to signal the three people Dorea felt outside to enter.

Three young women filed in, each with a wooden tray holding a food course.

They all looked too old to have taken part in the Trial, and it made Dorea wonder whether they resented the missed opportunity or were happy not to have been made to risk their lives.

That train of thought stopped when an entire roasted suckling pig was placed in front of her. The skin looked to have been crisped up at high heat, and juices flowed freely from the rendered fat, barely holding the meat together.

Grilled vegetables and fruits had been artfully placed on another dish after having been drizzled with a fragrant oil.

The last plate held three different spreads, one yellow, one beige, and one red, and from what she had learned so far of Heidel culture, they were likely to all have some kind of spice inside.

Yaomi then gestured for the women to leave, which they did after placing four pitchers of water, each in front of one of the commensals, and one of the fermented horse milk they seemed to enjoy in the middle of the table.

For a few minutes, the important matters were shelved as everyone tucked in. The conversation was kept light as they discussed the specific spices used in the spreads—a yellow root called turmeric, which Dorea had only known to be used for its medicinal properties before, and several kinds of seeds, which, when ground, released various aromas.

Dorea noted that all three elders showed no reaction to the spice levels in the food, though to her, it felt more like a building inferno.

Sneakily, she conjured more water in her mouth, swishing it while muffling the sound, and thus managed to keep up appearances.

Finally, they cleaned their hands with the provided handkerchiefs, and everyone's expressions became more serious.

I have a few points I want to raise, like the overuse of Whitecliff's mages in the patrols, but since I have been invited and not requested an audience, I should let them state their case first. No need to put myself in a disadvantageous position from the very beginning.

After a moment of silence, where it became clear she wasn't about to speak up, Mort sighed. "We need to stop treating each other like dangerous beasts if we want this cooperation to bear fruits."

His words made sense, but Dorea couldn't be the one to lower her guard first, not when she was in the wolf's den.

Yaomi snorted at that. "Mages, especially powerful ones, will never stop dealing with others like them with caution. We know perfectly well what we are capable of with just a thought."

Mort took her rebuke with an incline of the head, though he didn't look particularly chastised. "I did not intend to say that you three should forget what you are. But there are matters of great importance we need to discuss and to do so on edge would be extremely counterproductive."

This time, it seemed like it was the older woman to have lost the verbal exchange.

I wonder how much of this is infighting, how much is simply a debate they have had many times, and how much is mummery they are putting up for my sake.

Although Yaomi's personal power was great, she wouldn't have kept her seat as chief so easily if she had to face internal discord. That meant that the three elders were likely to be free in how they expressed themselves to each other, as long as it was in a private setting.

Which made her wonder why they were making her privy to it.

"This might look like an old fools' argument, young Dorea," Seshi interjected, speaking directly to her. "But we have long debated it. You are by far the most likely candidate to come out of Whitecliff for a leadership position, be it just for your village or the entire alliance."

His words jolted her out of her contemplation. She had known that the Heidels had to have been having this kind of discussion since it had happened in Whitecliff, but for them to come out with it right out of the gate was a surprise.

Still, she wouldn't be baited into confirming her ambitions, especially since she still wasn't sure of them herself. "There are many in my tribe who have a bright future ahead of themselves. I can't say what the Goddess will plan for each of us, but as for me, I'm focused on furthering our alliance and protecting our lands at the moment."

It was a much more diplomatic answer than she could have given even just a few months ago, but being made a part of the ruling council—although not in an active manner—and taking part in several such missions had developed her skills.

The three elders looked at each other for a moment, and something passed between them.

"And that we can actually believe you mean at least some of that is why you are here today," explained Mort, stroking his mustache.

"Bah, let's just get this over with." Yaomi, it seemed, had much less patience than her two companions. "Girl, it's obvious to us that old Voggo is angling to have you fill his role in the near future and, if possible, that of alliance leader."

Dorea wanted to deny that, but the assuredness with which the woman had spoken told her that they had no doubt about it, and lying now could damage their relationship in ways she felt weren't easily recoverable. Still, she couldn't outright admit to that, so she kept silent.

Apparently, that was fine with Yaomi, so she continued, "You are far too young for such a role at the moment, even if your potential is high. Circumstances, however, are forcing our hands."

The way she said it made her sit up. Yaomi was, if she got it right, saying that something was happening that would necessitate a leader of the alliance to be chosen relatively soon.

"That's right. I can see that you get it. There are many reasons for this, and the incursion from all sides is contributing much, but the most important one is that I don't have a long time to live."

Her tone was casual as if she was talking about the weather rather than her impending demise.

Seeing that Dorea was too shocked to ask questions, Seshi took over the explanation after giving a warning look to his leader. "What the chief means is that her condition is expected to deteriorate in the next few years, not immediately."

Dorea exhaled in relief, suddenly feeling like she had been wrung dry. The difference between having Yaomi's support taken away immediately and in a few years' time was massive, as they could start preparing for the moment.

"Are you sure this condition cannot be cured? You have some good healers, but Voggo might be able to do more about it, given his skill and experience," she commented once she had calmed down enough.

All three elders shook their heads at that. "We have consulted with your shaman about this already, though we haven't explicitly said it was for her." Mort's response took the wind out of her sails, but she should have guessed they would have already explored that possibility.

Is that why Voggo suddenly started pushing me to become a leadership candidate? Because he was asked about an incurable condition and understood that Yaomi's position was suddenly much more fragile?

Those were questions that would have to wait for an answer until she was back in Whitecliff, but she was confident that she had gotten it right.

"I won't lose my powers soon and won't die for a while after that. But I'm not foolish enough not to start preparing for that moment. I would have done so anyway, even if I didn't know I had an incurable illness. This just accelerated things," the Witch continued, casually sipping from her chalice. "My sickness comes from within; my mana network is working against me. And my power is too great for anyone to be able to interfere with it," she explained, her eyes half-lidded.

To think that your magic could betray you so. Dorea felt it would have been a tragic situation even if it hadn't happened to the strongest mage in the alliance.

I don't know what I would do if it had happened to me. It sounds like she has been looking for answers for a long time and only recently received the last blow. That has to weigh heavily on her.

"That still doesn't explain why you felt the need to inform me. Telling Voggo would have been more than enough for him to start making plans. So, why?"

It would have been more proper to give the woman her condolences and engage in the song and dance expected of a sick person who didn't have much to live, but Dorea believed Yaomi would have hated her for it.

Indeed, the woman gave her an approving smirk. "As I told you earlier, you are the most likely candidate to become alliance leader, having established good relations with people in both villages and having gained the respect and gratitude of Chief Samos. You might still die in the coming conflicts, but if you survive and continue growing as you have until now, few will be able to match you."

Somehow, her words didn't feel as complimentary as they should have. A cold analytical mind was at work here, and Dorea was like a bug being observed. Yaomi was simply stating facts, and considered Dorea a worthy successor only because she respected certain parameters.

"You are not the only one we are considering, but you have gained enough of my respect that I felt it was correct to inform you."

From the pinched faces of the other elders, this was an old and unresolved argument too. They likely hadn't seen the need to disclose their weakness so soon.

Still, Dorea appreciated Yaomi's forthcomingness. Being informed this soon meant that she'd be able to act accordingly. Not having the protective umbrella of the Witch of Immolation for long was a setback, but if she could last a few years, Dorea felt that the future could still be safe.

"Now, nothing can be done for me, but I still have a lot I want to give our people. And yes, I do consider our people to be one, different races or not. Our fate is tied together, and to fight it would spell doom for everyone."

I doubt she would have been of the same opinion had she been healthy, but I guess sickness can change people's perspective.

"I want to thank you for including me in this information. I wish you the best, but knowing that one day your protection will not be here means I can start preparing for it," Dorea added when it was evident that Yaomi wasn't about to keep speaking.

The two other elders nodded at her words, recognizing her politeness for what it was. A way of showing that she still considered their chief to be a valuable asset for the alliance and not just a crippled old woman.

That she could turn me to cinders instantly if I dared utter that sentiment also played a role in my choice of words . . .

"That said," Dorea continued, "while you have hinted several times at my possible future, you still haven't said outright what you want me to do with this information. I doubt you invited me here just to alert me to your condition."

Some life returned to Yaomi's features at that, and she abandoned whatever dark thought had been taking her attention. "You are correct. All this pussyfooting around is not good for anyone."

She then grinned, gesturing to herself and her fellows. "We have decided that you should be put through the initiation trials of Heidel leadership."

It took Dorea a moment to realize all the implications hidden between her words, but when she did, she sat up straight in her chair. "Do you mean to say that you want to make it clear to your people that you have chosen me as a possible leader, even now?"

She had believed that there would be more time before such a thing was needed and, beyond that, that the Heidel leadership was about to offer her a deal to either ensure one of theirs would still have a prominent position or to slowly induct her into their government.

To have the process of choosing a leader start so soon, especially with an outsider, would send an unequivocal message to the population.

"Yes, I can see that you understand. I want to make it clear from the start that you are my choice for leading our people. Unfortunately, there are no others in your generation that I believe have what it takes." Yaomi looked genuinely regretful. She had likely spent many long hours agonizing over the possible consequences of having someone not from Camp lead the Heidels, but she also looked resolute in her choice.

"Of course, as long as I'm alive and well enough, I'll keep things running by myself, but having the leadership dropped on you when you are not ready for it is a harsh burden to leave behind. I won't repeat what was done to me." Her words explained more about her reasoning. If she had been forced to take up the mantle of chief without having had time to plan for it, she would not want to impose the same on whoever came after her.

"You have something like five years before I'm incapable of defending our lands anymore. It should be enough to grow some more in power and prestige," Yaomi finally revealed.

Having a timeline would greatly help her efforts to prepare herself for when the moment came, and knowing that she could count on the Witch of Immolation to defend their southern and eastern borders for that long was immensely relieving.

If she had said one or two years, I honestly would have contemplated picking my family up and running away. Already this puts a very tight constraint on my wish to explore the world after the war with the Mondeans is done . . .

"If we had ten more years, I genuinely believe we could train Melu or Masi enough to take over for you," Seshi said to Yaomi comfortingly.

The old woman waved him off. "Bah, those two have a good head and will serve well but aren't leaders. Even if I dedicated my last years to training them until they were powerful enough, it's useless if you don't have the spark in you."

Mort looked like he had just eaten something very sour, but he kept any disagreement to himself.

"So what does taking leadership trials mean in practice?" Dorea finally asked when it was apparent that no one would explain things to her further.

Yaomi turned to look at her with a grin, raising her chalice in a silent toast. "Oh, that's simple. You must prove yourself in several missions, defeating beasts and leading our people well. I have already decided what the first few will entail, so you should prepare to leave tomorrow in the early morning: you will hunt down some of those pesky salamanders and either figure out what is agitating them so much and remove it or kill them."

CHAPTER TWENTY-THREE

The sun's light had barely begun illuminating the grasslands as Dorea and Masi moved through it at high speeds, disturbing sleeping animals and the environment alike.

She had been surprised to find that the Heidel boy had developed a movement spell of his own that allowed him to keep up with her Air Boost, but she should have expected it to start happening more often.

Many months had passed since the Wrath, and the new mages had had the time to explore their powers enough to branch into utility magics.

Dorea still believed herself to be the most advanced of her generation, mostly thanks to her wide variety of spells and studies into wards, but she could feel the pressure of having others close in.

She had known that it would happen as people gained more experience, but it still felt bad not to be the dominant one in a field.

Lightning sparked around Masi as he ran fast enough to look like a blur to any nonmagical. Dorea looked much more elegant, as the principle behind Air Boost allowed her to look like she was strolling through the blades of grass, even as she easily maintained the same speed as her companion.

The landscape passed them by, and the blond girl felt grateful that her new friend could distinguish the hills enough to guide them.

I feel like I would have ended up getting lost quite easily otherwise. The road between Whitecliff and Camp is at least beaten enough to be recognizable. However, venturing toward the salamanders' territory from the south would have been almost impossible for me.

Dorea was still somewhat uncertain about the whole leadership trials thing, as it felt like Yaomi had decided everything by herself and simply informed her of it.

She hadn't even had the time to bring up what she wanted to talk about at all, as the conversation had been monopolized by the topic of the Witch's sickness and the alliance's future.

She had ended up going along with it simply because it aligned with her plans, but it felt more and more like the elders were forcing her into a position she wasn't sure she wanted.

If it wasn't for the obvious and present dangers we face, I would have told them all to stuff it, even Voggo, but I can't in good conscience just ignore their—unfortunately—sound arguments.

She had to explain things to the rest of Whitecliff's contingent the previous evening, and luckily they had been awed enough by the news that Yaomi was considering her as a possible leader for the whole alliance to forget that she hadn't talked about the issues they had discussed that morning at all.

Still, if her suspicions were correct, she wouldn't have to worry about any further excessively long patrol. Dorea was almost certain that it had been a way to test her and her grip on her team, which meant that now that she was officially undergoing the trials, there wouldn't be a need for it.

Meeting Masi that morning had been a bit awkward, as he had obviously heard that she, too, was being evaluated to succeed Yaomi. And given the ambitions he had talked about during their chat in Whitecliff, he had to be feeling conflicted about accompanying her.

Well, he doesn't know that his chief has already rejected his candidacy. He just thinks that I have been added as a competitor and that he has a good shot at it still.

It felt dirty to not tell him immediately, but if she did, she'd have to explain a lot more than that, and Dorea had sworn, before leaving Yaomi's tent, that she'd not say a word to anyone of her condition.

The girl felt like the more involved she became with political games, the more she was forced to compromise her morals, but there was little she could do about it.

In the end, she'd kept quiet, and they had left Camp very early to hopefully reach the salamanders' territory before noon.

It would have been impossible to do if Masi hadn't developed his newest spell, Lightning Enhancement. Since he was the only one who could keep up with her, he had been assigned as her guide and to serve as backup.

Dorea sneaked a look at the boy, finding him concentrated on the road ahead. They hadn't exchanged more than the usual pleasantries and basic information about the mission, but even that had been stilted enough to let her know that he was still digesting the news.

Finally, after hours of the landscape flashing by, Masi signaled for her to slow down.

They had reached a copse of trees that sparsely populated the grasslands. Within it, as was typical, passed a stream of water, where the fauna usually went to sate their thirst.

This time, no animal was present beyond a few insects—and even then, in a smaller amount than usual. Dorea curiously extended her senses to check and was surprised to find that the more north she pushed, the less life she could find.

"Why is this place so barren?" she asked. They were still a while away from the forest's edge, where the salamanders resided, and they couldn't be the reason.

Masi shook his head, dropping down to sit on a flat rock. "Consequences of the Great War. The earth mages that battled here put the land back together after they were done, but some compound that kills anything that drinks it for too long was released in the water."

Dorea looked curiously into the stream, finding it crystal clear, if almost bereft of any life. "Does it not affect the plants, then? I can feel some algae in the water, but none of the fish and insects that should be there."

"I keep forgetting that you can use all three elements. That's such an unfair advantage to have," he grumbled. Thankfully, his tone was more self-deprecating than angry, telling her they would be fine in time.

He then shook his head, replying to her question. "Nah, as you can see, the plants are not affected. It's something that affects the blood, so I'd stay away from it if I were you," he cautioned, seeing her get close to the edge.

Dorea laughed, not that worried about the danger. Even if she somehow lost her balance and fell in, her control over the water would make it impossible for any to touch her skin without her permission.

Still, noticing how stressed Masi was becoming, she acquiesced. They enjoyed a quick lunch together, made of cold cuts and a loaf of dense bread that the Heidels seemed to favor, and rested.

Although neither of the two had even come close to exhausting themselves, they both wanted to be ready when they entered salamander territory. It was possible that whatever it was that had the beasts in such a tizzy could be resolved without much trouble, but Dorea doubted it'd be that easy.

The chance that a more powerful being had encroached on their territory and was forcing them to move west was unfortunately real, and they'd have to assess whether it was better to deal with the origin of the problem or eliminate the salamanders.

If the latter ended up being the case, they could expect a very dangerous battle. The five beasts were not considered to be at Master level, and individually they were nowhere close to Old Titan's power. However, they could still pose a dangerous threat, especially when together, and underestimating them was a mistake Dorea didn't intend on making.

"We should start moving soon; we want to have enough time left to observe them for a while before we decide what to do." Masi's words made sense, and since she had already finished eating and her mana was comfortably full, she agreed.

This time, they only had to keep their spells up for about an hour as the forest became visible on the horizon. A plume of smoke had informed them long before that something was happening, and so they accelerated, intent on preventing a widespread fire from happening.

The salamanders had so far limited themselves to their territory and little beyond that, never straying too far even when evidently angered. This time, on the other hand, they had spilled into the grasslands proper, and their fires were spreading. It wasn't alarmingly quick, but it could develop into a nightmare if not stopped. The massive creatures had been described as easily reaching ten feet in length, the air warping around them from the heat.

The two teenagers looked at each other, silently deciding that the stealth approach they had planned would have to be set aside.

Since Masi couldn't exactly do much against the flames, given his elemental affinity, he took it upon himself to go in and check what was going on.

The sounds of battle were loud enough to be heard even from outside the forest proper, and the rumblings and roars made them both very cautious.

Until now, the salamanders hadn't actively fought anything, merely venting their anger at something in their surroundings. If there was a battle going on, it meant that they might have found their culprit.

Dorea conjured enough water to drown out the fires closest to them, and Masi went in, pulling his mana within so as to not be noticed immediately.

Dorea, on the other hand, kept herself busy by putting out the fire. It stretched in a ring, with a diameter of a mile, which made it impossible to stop easily, but leaving it to grow was not an option.

She spent almost half an hour doing so, slowly getting the ring under control, when Masi returned. Just one look at his ashen white face told her the situation was much worse than anyone had expected. He gestured for her to follow him, and they walked away, not using any magic, for more than half an hour until the sounds of battle faded away.

Finally, he stopped, looking a bit better. "We cannot go there."

Dorea contained herself. She had a deluge of questions she wanted to ask, from what exactly he had seen to what possessed him to want to leave on foot and without magic.

Still, she waited patiently. There usually was a team leader during regular missions, but since he was present only to act as an observer and she was the observed, there was no direct line of command.

This meant that the person with the most information would take the lead. It was what they had done for the whole morning as he guided them through the grasslands, and what was happening at the moment since he was the only one to have seen what was happening within the circle of flames.

That, however, didn't mean that her patience was endless. Possibly sensing this, he finally explained, "The salamanders are even bigger than what we were told, and the powers they wield are closer to Master level than what I'm comfortable with." He wet his lips with his tongue, clenching and unclenching his hands and looking back to where they had come from, as if expecting something to pursue them. "But there is a much bigger threat there. A mage, much more powerful than the beasts, is toying with them. I don't know what he wants and why exactly a Master of the earth element has come here, but going in there and interfering with his plans seems like a terrible idea."

His words left her stunned. She had contemplated the idea that a foreign mage could be behind the problems, of course, but for it to be a Master? It was hard to believe that such a powerhouse would waste weeks, if not months, occasionally harassing the family of salamanders.

Beyond that, the fact that such a dangerous man had been so close to both of their villages for so long made her skin crawl.

If a Master had come to Whitecliff, even if everyone pooled their strength together, she doubted they'd be able to do much about it. They would be blown away by the first attack if she took the battle between the eagle and Old Titan as an example of their capabilities.

She refrained from asking more simply because she doubted Masi had had the chance to learn more. It wasn't like the man would conveniently spout his plans out loud for them to hear.

"We need to go back and alert Chief Yaomi. She's the only person who can do something about it," she finally said. It would mean failing her test, but this matter was much more important than a pesky examination.

I'll have more chances in the future, but we cannot leave a Master so close to our territories without doing anything about it.

Masi, still pale, agreed without hesitation. Still, he didn't immediately start his movement spell, making her falter. "What's going on?"

"I have no idea how far he can sense, but I sincerely doubt he's not aware of us, being an earth mage," he murmured, as if afraid of being overheard.

It was true that earth mages were famous for being the best sensors amongst the Gifted. But waiting too long before returning could mean they would miss the opportunity to alert Yaomi.

"I think we just have to take the risk. He must have felt me dousing the fire if he knew about us. That means he knows we are mages, and us leaving in the direction of Camp, whether on foot or by magic, means that we'd likely inform the leadership of what we witnessed," Dorea finally commented, determined about the course of action they needed to follow.

Whatever Masi wanted to reply with was lost in the rumble because the earth started shaking beneath their feet.

Dorea subconsciously used her magic to levitate them both, thus avoiding a fall into the dangerous fissure that formed as the ground broke.

From below emerged a small man, much shorter than she would have expected from Masi's description. He was wearing a travel cloak with a raised hood obscuring his features. Coming to the height of less than five feet, the Master mage floated lazily on a rock, coming to a stop slightly above them.

She didn't try to run away, even though the primal part of her brain told her to. While this man was likely not as powerful as Old Titan, he was, without a doubt, strong enough to catch up and stop any attempt to leave she could make.

Instead, she bowed in greeting. "My name is Dorea of Whitecliff, O Master of the earth. I'm honored to meet you."

Politeness might not necessarily save her, but rudeness would certainly accelerate her demise.

Dorea still couldn't feel the man at all, even though her eyes told her very clearly that he was there, and she refrained from squeezing the air around him to get a sense of his presence, as that might anger him.

A croaky voice answered her, seemingly not having been used in a long time. "So that dump still stands, huh? I'm surprised that damnable bear hasn't eaten the lot of you."

The man then threw back the hood, revealing an unpleasantly broad face. He had a flat forehead, a crooked nose, and even more warped teeth. No blemish marred his skin, but it was a rancid white that could be found only in the very sick. His hair was thick around the back and almost absent on top, a graying color that reminded her of a rat.

His fingers were much longer than a Sapiens's or a Heidel's and looked especially disproportionate on his short stubby body.

For all his weird appearance, Dorea didn't dare react in any way and was grateful that Masi kept his silence, even if he was looking mighty uncomfortable, being held aloft in the air.

Not knowing how to reply, she didn't speak, merely looking at the man holding their lives in his palm. She would have questioned him about his dealings in their territory if he had been a Journeyman, but a Master could not be approached so brazenly.

"At least they taught you to hold your tongue. That's better than what you people were like the last time I was in these lands." The earth mage looked to be mostly speaking to himself, his gaze having left them almost immediately and bouncing around erratically.

"Well, I suppose you'll have to entertain me to make up for distracting me from my task." He grinned unpleasantly, and Dorea barely had the time to put up a Bulwark as rocks of all sizes started pelting her.

Their strength wasn't great, being barely enough to crack the shield—which told her that the man was toying with them for some reason—but the intensity was enough that she couldn't do anything beyond stand there and concentrate on the spell.

"You can't let us down, or he'll simply entrap us immediately," Masi shouted over the roar of rocks breaking against the Bulwark.

At the same time, he started shooting bolts of electricity from his hands, aiming at breaking up the biggest rocks before they could hit.

"We need to last as long as possible. He said he just wanted to be entertained," Dorea whispered, dedicating the little slack Masi had gained her with his interference to bringing her words directly to his ear, inspired by Jonah's spell.

All of a sudden, the rain of rocks stopped. "Well, it's just not fun if you turtle down and never move, you know?"

At that, a gigantic stone worm shot out of the open fissure in the earth, unnaturally silent, and broke through her Bulwark as if it wasn't even there, sending the two teenagers crashing painfully to the ground.

CHAPTER TWENTY-FOUR

To touch the ground at any point in a fight with a Master earth mage was to sign one's death warrant. It gave them the ability to strike from all directions. Unlike the air, which was too ephemeral to hide the concentration of magic necessary to harm with it, the earth allowed a Gifted—when beyond a certain level of power and skill—to prepare their attacks unnoticed.

This was what had been repeated again and again in the war journals Dorea had read to learn more about warding. She had had to go look for tidbits of useful information in between recountings of battles and had therefore absorbed some of that knowledge for herself.

Having witnessed firsthand the level of damage that an earth-aspected creature could wreck, even if its opponent never touched down, during the fight between Old Titan and the eagle, Dorea knew it wasn't a perfect solution. However, it remained the number one recommendation when facing such a mage. Never touch the ground.

This meant that, even though the stone worm had broken her Bulwark with little trouble, Dorea used all her faculties to catch herself and Masi to prevent them from coming into contact with the dirt.

As soon as she had reacquired control over their tumbling forms, she crafted another Bulwark and shot away from the Master mage.

He wants to chase us, and he'll force our hand if we don't do it. I don't know if we can survive this, but defiance at this point seems more foolish than brave.

"Run, little kiddies, run!" the mage screamed gleefully. His construct reared up before throwing itself in pursuit.

It dove into the ground like a sea serpent in the water, disappearing from her senses. Dorea knew, however, that the thing was not gone. It would track them down immediately if the mage willed it, but he apparently enjoyed the thrill of a hunt too much, and she could only hope to make enough of a racket that others would notice.

"We need to get back into patrolled lands, or we're gonna get killed!" Masi shouted, helplessly looking down to see if he could notice the worm before it could breach the ground.

Dorea set her face into a grim expression. If they managed to meet with another patrol, they'd also get drawn into the fight, and she doubted any of them could do much to the man hunting them. Their only hope of survival at this point was to either give the man what he wanted—meaning a chase—and hope that he'd be satisfied with that or get to Camp to be rescued by Yaomi.

The Witch of Immolation would be more than enough to deal with the earth mage, especially since he operated close to her territory for so long while hiding himself. That told her that he wasn't confident in facing the Heidel chief.

Still, Dorea seriously doubted he'd allow them to get that far. Even going as fast as she could, it would take them a few hours to be close enough to be sensed by the Witch. Unfortunately, they couldn't count on her.

Fleeing as fast as she was, Dorea didn't even have the time to set up traps or one of her more complicated manipulations, instead relying on her easier spells to chip at the gigantic worm chasing them.

Once every couple of minutes, it would breach the surface and attempt to break her Bulwark like it did the first time, only to be pelted by everything she could spare, though Masi was doing most of the work there. His lightning bolts were not well suited to taking down an inanimate enemy, so he had switched to causing as much wide-area damage as possible.

Large blasts left his hands in succession, exploding on contact with the worm or the ground and causing enough shaking and destruction to divert its lunges enough that she could maneuver away.

The situation, however, wasn't sustainable, as, after a dozen repetitions, the boy started to flag. The power he had been emitting was more than what she had believed him capable of, but he now looked to be scraping the bottom of the barrel as he panted with exertion.

"I don't know how long I can keep it up," he confessed, gaze firmly on the rapidly moving ground.

Dorea just grunted, having known that already. Even as they fled, they kept attacking, and the worm started to look worse and worse, losing its definition until it didn't have any at all.

Though its mouth was now just a hole, devoid of the teeth it originally had, Dorea was sure she wouldn't survive being eaten all the same.

In her desperation and knowing that help was too far to reach, she had directed them back toward the stream they had encountered that morning.

It was still oddly devoid of animal life, and though she knew the worm wouldn't feel anything from the poison in the water, the mage might be careless enough after they showed themselves to be at his mercy.

It's not a perfect plan, not even close, but I can't think of anything else, and I refuse to go down without a fight.

Any hope she might have had of resolving this peacefully had steadily vanished as the elder mage cackled maniacally at the sight of them desperately keeping away its construct.

No one who intended on letting you go would go to such lengths. If she needed to die so soon, Dorea wanted to do it while looking at her killer in the eye, knowing she had done all she could to keep him at bay.

Finally, the copse of trees came into sight, and with a burst of speed, she reached it, finally letting go of her mixed Bulwark and Air Boost. Individually, they weren't particularly draining spells, but when used together and in such conditions, they had taken well over a third of her mana.

I still have enough for this. I'm sorry, Mom, Dad, and Voggo. I know you had high hopes for me, but take heart in knowing that I did not go down like a coward.

"What's this? Do you think you can simply stop when you get too tired, little girl? Do you believe yourself to be the master of the games?" their pursuer croaked unpleasantly.

Though she hadn't said anything to Masi, he was smart enough to recognize her plan for what it was, having been the one to inform her of the peculiarities of the stream just a few hours before, and so he spoke up, trying to gain her time. "It's obvious that you are superior to us in skill and power, sir. We gave as much as we could, but you have bested us; that much is evident."

Though he kept up a respectful tone, it was hard to miss the disdain in his eyes.

"Boy, if you think whatever little plan you have cooked up will get you out of this, you are even more of an idiot than you look like. But then again, you surface dwellers are all the same, so confident that you know everything and that you'll always be able to make it."

At his words, it finally clicked to Dorea what exactly the man was. "You are an Ubag! And to have earth magic means that you were from one of the mountain villages destroyed by the previous Wrath! Why would you attack us, then? When we used to be allies?!"

He seemed to find her question very funny as he cackled, holding his stomach. "Oh, that's too good! Your ally? After you left us trapped inside the caves for months?! You dare say that we were allies?!" At the end, his words had become a roar, and the very earth shook with his anger.

The man was still floating on a rock, his stature was still that of a child, but at that moment, he appeared as a giant. It became difficult to breathe, and his power blanketed the air.

Dorea had never felt the direct intent of a Master mage, and the experience almost brought her to her knees. She slid down the tree she was propped up against, barely catching herself on a lower branch.

Her magic didn't want to respond to her calls, moving sluggishly. It was as if everything that she was was within the earth mage's control. To her side, Masi was almost choking, taking in strangled gulps of air as the man's intent hit him.

The ability to project one's will through their mana was something that everyone had—Whitecliff used mana pulses as code for a reason—but it became useful only after becoming a Master, letting people share impressions without words.

Some, however, learned how to weaponize it, turning all their willpower to crush their opponent's mind. It was considered taboo to do so against someone evidently weaker, even if one had already decided to kill them.

Respect for the sanctity of the human mind was baked into every culture, no matter their provenance, and to turn their gift into a weapon made to crush another's consciousness was blasphemy to all gods Dorea knew of.

It was unlikely that the man didn't know it, however, and for him to have chosen to attack them like that meant that he believed himself above the laws of gods and men.

Weakly, Dorea tugged on the river water, having just enough presence of mind to realize that she had to do something, anything, or she'd be crushed by the man's sheer magical presence.

With a push that took everything she had, a jet of water shot from the stream, overcoming the magical resistance just enough to splash against the Ubag mage.

By passing through the aura being emitted, it had been sapped of all its strength, meaning that when it connected, it did so with the power of a child's punch. The man sputtered, some of the water having entered his mouth, and with an angry wave of his hands, he conjured a cloud of dust that rapidly absorbed the liquid.

The Master at first looked even angrier but then laughed, realizing that it was the extent of her defiance. "Is that all you are capable of? Where did all your willpower go, little girl?"

Dorea slumped back down, exhausted from the effort beyond words. It wasn't so much that she had used a large amount of mana, but even just moving it outside of herself and directing it into a shot strong enough to overcome the resistance had been incredibly hard.

Under the enemy's will, her magic barely worked. It was as if she was weighed by rocks on all limbs and had to dash away from an enraged animal. She'd do it—her instincts wouldn't allow her not to—but it would drain her much more than if she was unencumbered.

"Why? Why are you doing this? Why attack the salamanders for so long? Why hunt us down like beasts?" she finally screamed, frustration and pain coloring her tone.

Even just speaking was exhausting, but it had all bubbled up for too long, and she needed answers.

Instead of dealing the final blow, the man considered her words. He was evidently someone who enjoyed hearing himself talk, and he'd happily waste some time to monologue about his intention if put into a situation where all control was his.

"Why have I attacked you two? Well, you interrupted me, and seeing your faces reminded me of unpleasant memories. You might not be directly related to the people I have a grudge against, but I'm petty enough that even a substitute like you will give me satisfaction," he finally replied, unbothered by her hateful stare.

"Why did I attack the salamanders? Those overgrown lizards might not seem particularly useful, but their blood can substitute very rare ingredients in the creation of some rituals, and now that I have found a steady supply of it, I don't see why I should not take advantage of it."

The tendency of powerful men who believed themselves to be winning to gloat would always be a constant, and Dorea felt very grateful for it. Although her plan was desperate, she needed as much time as possible for it to work, and if that meant having to listen to a megalomaniac talk for hours, she'd do it.

"No one would have bothered you if you simply took the blood, but you actively riled them up, causing them to spread fires that could threaten the whole forest!" she rebuked, now well and truly beyond any fear.

The magical pressure of the Ubag's intent was still pressing down on them, but it had let out enough that she could speak without feeling as if she was exhaling her last breath every time.

The man smiled crookedly. "I don't care. It's just as simple as that. I'll take what I want and leave you bugs to deal with the aftermath."

This is like dealing with an evil toddler who's too powerful to say no. How can an earth mage not care about the damage he's doing to the environment?!

Seeing that that line of questioning wouldn't give her any satisfying answers, Dorea switched it up. "I can understand the rule of the strong. No one can stop you, so you do what you want. But if you have found a good resource, why abuse it so? Why go out of your way to make the lives of everyone more difficult?"

That seemed to strike a chord, much like her initial question about his motives had, and the man's expression darkened. "Is this not what your ancestors did to me and my people?" he questioned, his voice dangerously low. "Did they not take what they wanted, uncaring of how it would leave those weaker than themselves? Did they not mine too deep in the mountains in their greedy search for resources, causing the whole thing to collapse on my village when the Wrath struck?"

By the end of it, he was screaming, with foam and spittle coming out of his mouth, and when he looked down at them, Dorea was sure he wasn't seeing two teenagers, but something else entirely.

"You don't right a wrong by committing another wrong!" she yelled back, even as Masi shifted uncomfortably. "You don't take it out on those who had nothing to do with it! Your anger is justified, but we are not its rightful target!"

In truth, Dorea had absolutely no idea what he spoke of. The records had been clear that the earthquake that struck their previous village had been mighty, causing collapses in every mine or cave for hundreds of miles.

Still, one look at the heaving man told her that trying to reason with him would be a foolish endeavor. He was simply too bitter and angry to see that his belief was wrong.

A few seconds passed as the Ubag regained his composure until he finally answered coldly, "I don't care. I did not mean to say that what your ancestors did was wrong. It took me a long time to understand this, but in truth, they had all the right of it, because they were more powerful! That's how the world works, no matter how much the weak scream and shout."

He had a maddened look, his eyes unfocused and his long fingers twitching as if yearning to close around something. He was, however, still a Master mage, and even insanity would not bridge the gap between them.

Dorea had been looking at the changes in his demeanor very carefully, trying to see how much was his natural personality and how much could be induced by external factors.

Being the daughter of a potioneer, she knew very well that one of the first symptoms of poisoning was erratic behavior, and her only hope at the moment was that she had managed to get enough of the tainted waters in his mouth.

Suddenly, the man refocused, his whole body language shifting. He looked like a completely different person, and the twitchiness that had started to overcome him disappeared in an instant.

Instead, a look of deadly seriousness was left behind as he looked toward the horizon in Camp's direction.

"I'm sorry to cut this little game short, kids. Pretending to slowly get sicker and sicker would have been fun, and quite honestly, I thought I was putting on a magnificent performance, but it seems like external factors will prevent me from completing it."

Ice flooded Dorea's veins, and Masi looked little better, his face pale and skin clammy. The whole thing had been a mummery, another lie to get them to lower their guards so he could toy with them. But then they simultaneously realized the real meaning of his words and turned to look in the same direction as the man.

In the sky, toward the southwest, was a bright light. It looked like a star had decided not to be dimmed by the sun, shouting its defiance against the heavens.

In just a few seconds, that light became bigger and brighter, and Dorea knew it was coming closer at incredible speeds. It was a red comet, streaking across the sky and leaving behind a burning trail.

Indeed, half a minute later, that very same star hit the ground a hundred feet away from them like a meteor, sending debris and dust everywhere.

A flash of light blinded everyone when it touched down, and when they could finally open their eyes, the two teenagers found a very welcome sight: the most powerful mage of the Loisos coast, the Witch of Immolation, had come to their rescue.

CHAPTER TWENTY-FIVE

When the dust finally settled, it revealed exactly what Dorea hadn't had the heart to hope for. Yaomi had arrived.

"It seems that I have been remiss in my duties if insects like this have been nipping at my territory," the woman casually commented.

Although her entrance had been very dramatic, she didn't carry a spec of dirt on her form. Instead, her black-and-silver dress looked immaculate, as if she had just exited her tent. As she got closer, the pressure forcing the two teenagers down finally abated, replaced with the toasty warmth of a fire on a winter day.

Finally, Yaomi stopped in front of them. She gave them both a cursory glance, her eyes briefly stopping on their tired expressions, and turned to face the man who had put them in that state.

"That seems a bit harsh," the Ubag replied, no hint of mania or joking in his tone.

"What else would you call someone who has to sneak by, hidden by little tricks, and tries to hurt my people when my gaze is turned elsewhere?"

Silence was her answer, but the woman didn't seem to care. Without taking her eyes off the floating man, she spoke to the two teens, "You two need to get out of here. I don't care how tired you feel; run until you truly can't anymore. I'll come to pick you up when I'm done here."

Dorea wanted to refuse, to say that now that her mana wasn't being suppressed, she would be able to help, but her rational mind stopped her. Even throwing her all at the man hadn't made a dent; staying would simply mean being a hindrance.

Thus, she gathered herself up and activated Air Boost with an effort of will.

Next to her, Masi did the same with his own spell. They left, this time not pursued by the seemingly mad mage or his creations.

Only five minutes later, Masi's magic collapsed around him, though Dorea caught him without trouble. The boy had exhausted himself keeping the stone worm at bay, and even though it had been fruitless in the end, she was still grateful for his effort.

Five minutes after that, the explosions started, and Dorea stopped atop a higher-than-normal hill.

Her vision was barely good enough to cross the distance they had traveled, but the scale of the fighting there made it feel much closer.

The shining star they had seen moving across the sky at insane speeds was now stationary, hovering above the burned-out husk of the copse of trees they had just left. No smoke left the area, appearing as if a wildfire had passed through days before, leaving behind just charred, crumbling trunks and melted stone.

Great pillars erupted from the earth, reaching for the sky like the hands of an ancient giant.

Or rather, that's an actual giant.

Indeed, the ground had split open, sending vibrations that reached their position, and from it rose the titanic statue of a man, which readily grasped at the air in an attempt to crush the Witch in one blow.

The statue's size dwarfed anything Dorea had seen moving so far, reaching hundreds of feet in height, but its movements were deceptively quick. It moved with the speed of a well-trained warrior, and its lunges shifted enough air that some of the winds it created reached them.

Even from the distance, it was possible to notice that its features were perfectly crafted, signifying a spell with which the mage had great experience.

To think that it is possible to get so strong, that creating something like that is a matter of simply flexing your will, as if I was making a Lightning Sphere.

Even as the giant tried to swat at the fiery comet as if she was a bug, great boulders were hurled from the earth, the Ubag mage directing everything while apparently encased into a stone bunker. A dome had emerged, looking extremely sturdy and similar enough in make to the houses of Whitecliff that Dorea knew it would take a lot of punishment.

Though the stones didn't have the obliterating power that Old Titan's had—she was still capable of tracking their ascent, and the sound of the very air breaking at their passage was absent—Dorea could recognize that getting hit by one was almost certainly enough to kill anyone.

Yaomi, on the other hand, seemed content simply taking on the assault, limiting herself to avoiding the statue's swats and melting those few stones that were protected by another one for long enough to get close to hitting her with fiery blasts.

The corona of flames that surrounded her did most of the work, turning almost every shot into molten slag, and even the statue's features appeared to be losing their definition as they were exposed to the insanely high temperatures.

Dorea would have expected the woman's style to be different, with a name like the Witch of Immolation, but for the moment, she appeared to want to crush her enemy's will by showing that nothing he could do would affect her.

All of a sudden, the pattern changed, and a concentrated beam of fire carved the grasslands, charring and melting the ground below a hundred feet deep.

When the Ubag mage emerged from the newly created fissure, missing a hand and clutching at the stump, Dorea realized that the man had tried to run for it while his barrage made it look like he was engaged on the offensive.

Dorea and Masi looked at each other silently, recognizing that the ongoing battle was well beyond them but unwilling to leave.

Though the man had been wounded, he didn't appear ready to back down, and he waved his hands, turning the giant statue into hundreds of stone worms, all arching through the air to get at the Witch.

Each one was bigger and faster than the ones that had hunted them earlier, and the casualness with which the Ubag had crafted them, even in his injured state, told her that he truly had been playing around.

In response, Yaomi exploded into a maelstrom of flames.

The corona that had surrounded her pushed outward, going from a red color to a bluish white, increasing the temperature so much that the very air looked to be melting, making it much harder to see exactly what was going on.

Still, even through the haze, Dorea could make out the stone worms melting like candles, and having experienced firsthand precisely how tough the constructs were, she gulped, understanding that the heat Yaomi was emitting was incredibly deadly.

Indeed, the grass close to the fight had not even had the time to catch on fire. It had burned out to ash. The temperature was so high that even from the distance, Dorea felt the need to craft another shield, using the last dregs of power left in her system.

"I have never seen her fight like this. It always ended with just one attack before."

The blond girl turned to look at her companion to find his gaze fixed on the fight, mesmerized, as he watched his chief fight for them.

"Something tells me she's still not going all out," she replied, noticing that most of Yaomi's attacks had been carefully aimed.

It's possible that if she were to truly let loose, the grasslands wouldn't survive it. Fire is a destructive element, and controlling its spread even as you fight a powerful enemy would be too distracting.

"She's not. But she doesn't need to. That bastard is gonna get all he deserves."

Masi might have been a bit biased in his leader's direction, but there was truth to his words. As they watched, it became evident that the tide had truly turned.

No matter what the Ubag mage tried, it was instantly countered. No attack of his managed to penetrate the aura of flames surrounding the Witch, and he was becoming increasingly desperate with his attempts.

At one point, hundreds of feet of earth rose up as if they were liquid, and with a heave, they were sent crashing against the fiery shield that Yaomi crafted.

Though the force of the attack had been immense, and its scale simply boggled the mind, not even a speck of dirt touched the fire mage's skin when she emerged.

That kind of attack would be more than enough to destroy Whitecliff. I don't know how our wall and buildings would fare against it—as they were made with earth magic—but everything else would be simply gone. Everyone would die.

And even then, with all that power at his disposal, the man hadn't managed to do anything to Yaomi. She still floated in the air, surrounded by her aura, as if nothing had happened.

It must have been a terribly demoralizing sight, and the attacks ceased. Dorea could see the two small figures floating there, talking, but neither moved to restart the conflict.

"Do you think he's gonna surrender?" she asked Masi, who was more unfamiliar with Yaomi's modus operandi.

"I doubt that. He's either negotiating to be let go, though I genuinely don't know what he could promise that would grant him his freedom at this point, or asking for a painless death. Could be either," he answered, never taking his eyes off his chief.

If he had just wanted to take the salamanders' blood, he could have probably paid a tribute of some kind and then harvested as much of it as he wished to, but since he did so by himself and then attacked us after we found him, I sincerely doubt he's gonna get away.

One simply didn't get the title of Witch of Immolation by letting their enemies go, after all. Yaomi was either interrogating him or, more likely, just letting him talk until whatever trap he was preparing was ready to be sprung, before finishing him.

"I doubt she's gonna allow him to go free after what he tried to do to us," she commented.

Masi finally took his eyes off the battle site and looked at her, taking in her frazzled state, and then examined his own. "Yeah, we are both the pride of the new generation. It would have been a terrible blow to the alliance if we had died here. She really can't just let him go, can she?"

It was an unfortunate reality of their world that you simply couldn't allow your enemies to live. Dorea would have very much liked a way of ensuring that people couldn't attack again after being defeated, but any method that could enforce such a deal was too blasphemous to consider.

Mother Nature, like many other gods, forbade subjugating another's will by mundane or magical means. But while slavery of the non-magically enforced kind could be explained away as paying off debts—not that Dorea would consider that a valid point—the more mystical ways of binding a human's mind were heresy, and all who took part in them had to be removed from the world of the living as soon as they were found out, with no exception.

That meant defeated prisoners of war would be given an out only if they hadn't had a choice before attacking and would otherwise be executed, just like they did after the Battle of the Rocky Hills.

And no matter how much the Ubag mage might argue, he hadn't been under duress when he decided to hunt and torture them to death.

Yaomi was the alliance's unofficial protector, being by far the strongest mage, which came with some responsibilities. If they were attacked by a Master mage, she was the only one who could mount a response, and she had to deal with any such occasion in a way that would severely discourage anyone else from trying their luck.

In the end, it turned out that Dorea's suspicions were correct. The man had been stalling, probably offering treasures, knowledge, or even servitude, as he prepared one last great attack.

Where the giant statue he had used at the beginning of the fight had been massive and beautifully crafted, the construct that emerged from the earth now was small and rough, but something within Dorea's mind screamed that it was truly dangerous.

She was far too distant to use her mystical senses on it, but if she had been, she was sure that they wouldn't have been able to penetrate the thing. It looked simply too solid, even beyond the material it was made of.

The thing had ungainly broad shoulders, looking like pauldrons made of stone. Next followed a humanoid waist, though it looked out of place given its much smaller size than the top. Legs made of white marble, more like a spider than anything found on a mammal, and arms as wide as the shoulders, ending in gigantic claws. The head was encased in the pauldrons and would have been easily missable if not for the two gemstones that made up its eyes.

It was almost entirely dark brown, except for the legs, and from the distance, it appeared almost like the sort of thing that a boy might make with mud, all incomplete forms but with an intimidating overall look.

The construct rapidly rose from the ground below its caster and absorbed the man within itself. It levitated there momentarily, tons of condensed stone and dirt held up in the air just through magical might. Then, it shot toward Yaomi with alarming speed, its claws extended to cut through her aura and end the fight in one hit.

Dorea had barely tracked its ascent when it was already there, and something told her that the protection that the Witch had employed so far wouldn't work this time.

A flash of light followed, enough to blind the two observing teenagers and send them to the ground in pain. The Bulwark shook as it barely held against the shock wave that followed, protecting them against what could have been a perilous situation.

The earth rumbled, shaking with enough strength to toss them around until Dorea regained the presence of mind to catch herself and her companion with the surrounding air.

It took a couple of minutes before they managed to blink away the sudden blindness, and a scene of absolute destruction was revealed before them.

What little of the copse of trees and stream that had remained had been completely obliterated, and a cloud of steam and smoke hung through the grasslands.

Nothing had managed to retain its green color, as even the plants closest to them had turned yellow with the absurd heat that had been emitted.

In the center, a hole the size of a small lake had been formed, going as deep as a hundred feet. It sizzled, molten stone bubbling as if in the heart of a volcano. Yellow-and-red magma flowed, slowly gathering in the middle, cooling off even as it twisted the air above it with its sheer heat.

Behind, it left darkened soil, with obsidian and ash scattered everywhere. No trace was left of the terrible construct the Ubag mage had employed, even with the sheer power that Dorea had felt radiate from it.

For a moment, she entertained the idea that the man might have managed to run away, tunneling through the earth, deep within the bones of the Mother, but then she shook away that thought. It simply wasn't possible, having been far too close to Yaomi when she attacked.

If he had stayed down, in contact with his element, he might have had a chance, but the sheer destruction that had been enacted made her doubt even that.

Dorea's most potent piece of magic so far—excluding the newest spell she had gotten from observing the eagle fight, which she unfortunately hadn't had the time nor the strength to cast against the Ubag mage—had been the lightning storm she had unleashed on that first Mondean patrol, and that had been nothing compared to what Yaomi had just done.

To change the landscape so profoundly—Dorea suspected that a new lake would form once the stream recovered from having that much of its water evaporated—was the work of a being of a higher level.

Yaomi was truly the master of the coast, and if she weren't suffering from a debilitating illness, she would continue her reign uncontested for many, many years.

Before the clouds could clear up to reveal the skies, a flash of orange pierced them, approaching them with immense speed. Dorea barely had had the time to recognize the Heidel chief when she was there, floating in the air in front of them, her corona of flames still on, looking absolutely unbothered by the destruction she had wrought.

"I distinctly remember telling you two to get away from here, not to find a good place to spectate the fight," the older woman commented drily.

Sheepishly, the two teens picked themselves up from the ground, wobbling as the day's exhaustion made itself known, and Masi apologized, "I'm sorry, Chief. I was out of mana and had to slow down. Dorea was just protecting me as I recovered."

Yaomi chuckled at that, not looking like she believed one word of Masi's speech but also not caring at all. "Well, I'm not your mother. If you want to die because you wish to look at what a real fight is like, it's no skin off my back."

That wasn't true, and they all knew it, but it was an out, and the two gratefully took it.

There would be a time to discuss precisely what had happened, learn from any mistakes they had made, and reflect on what other options they might have had, but for the moment, they were safe. And that was all that mattered.

CHAPTER TWENTY-SIX

To say that witnessing the battle between two Master mages had put a fire beneath Dorea's feet would be an understatement.

She was perfectly aware that she had survived the encounter only thanks to Yaomi's intervention, and all her shiny new spells hadn't done anything against the Ubag mage.

I haven't even been able to use my newest spell! That should have at least done something, but the requirements for it are not easy to set up, and in such a desperate situation, to stop and prepare to cast it would have meant the death of Masi and probably of me too.

It frustrated her to no end that she had developed something strong enough to at least give a powerful enemy a bloody nose and that she hadn't been able to even begin casting it.

The aura the man had emitted had simply been too overwhelming for any sophisticated usage of magic, and throwing poisoned water in his face had been all she could think to do.

That it did nothing to him at all was just another slap to the face. Dorea had deeply thought about the matter ever since her return to Camp, and had concluded that the man had either been poisoned, but it had simply been too slow acting to do anything in the short term, or more likely, since the poisoning had been caused by an earth mage, he had been able to counter it.

If she thought about it and considered what she had read in the village's records, the danger in the water might have been simply a concentration of metals of some kind, which would explain how he hadn't felt the consequences. An earth mage, though not as well as a metal mage, could still interact with metals or at least sense them.

Much like a water mage can feel ice and snow, and in small part, they can use them, but not as easily as an ice mage. There are probably even more interactions like that, but knowledge of other elements is simply too fragmented.

Their return had seen much fuss, as Yaomi blasting off in a fiery corona was not a common sight, but people were reassured and even jubilant to find out that their chief had dealt with the threat.

The Witch enjoyed very high popularity among her tribesmen, but an occasional victory of this kind went a long way in quelling dissent. Yaomi was the strongest mage of the region, and that was unquestionable, now more than ever.

Dorea, for her part, found herself swarmed by Whitecliff's contingent as they wanted to know more. That the fight had happened so close to the forest only enhanced their curiosity, so she found herself back in the communal tent, recounting everything that had happened that day.

"And that's how the fight ended. It was honestly a bit anticlimactic since the man's newest construct looked and felt extremely menacing, but I guess it was a good thing to put a stop to it before he could do anything dangerous."

She sipped from a cup of tea that had been proffered to her, humming in satisfaction when she found it to be of the more floral kind. Dorea smiled at Nora gratefully, surprised that the girl had remembered her tastes after just a few breakfasts together.

"Is she truly as powerful as the stories say?" asked Tom, who had been much more interested in hearing about Yaomi's spells than the Ubag's. He had been happy to hear the matter with the salamanders was resolved, but curiosity got the better of him.

"She was, and to be honest, I'm pretty sure she wasn't going all out either. Be it because we were still close enough to be caught in whatever else she had in her arsenal, or simply because the enemy wasn't strong enough, the way she behaved makes me think that she barely took him seriously," Dorea revealed, thinking back about the casualness with which the woman had taken everything that the Ubag mage had thrown at her.

"What happened to the forest fire, then? And the salamanders?" asked another.

"Oh, she put out the fire with just a wave of her hands, and after making sure that we would be safe where we were, she went to check on the salamanders." She took another sip, feeling the day's exhaustion weigh her limbs down. Dorea was honestly contemplating just going back to bed, even though it was still the afternoon.

"She then came back and told us it was handled. After that, Masi asked if it meant that she had killed them, and she slapped the back of his head and told him that just because they had been agitated, it didn't mean that they deserved to die. She actually made an interesting point about preserving the balance of power within the forest," she finished, draining the last of her tea.

Before she could even ask for some more, Nora brought her another cup, alongside an assortment of cold cuts. The brunette then turned to glare at everyone else, making it understood that they weren't to bother Dorea until she had eaten and rested.

With a stifled laugh, the blonde tucked in.

The fight between Yaomi and the earth mage had been the talk of Camp for a couple of days, and people still speculated wildly about what the man had been doing in their territory, apparently not buying the explanation they had been given.

"We can't reveal the worth of the salamander's blood. Otherwise, a few foolish mages are sure to try their luck to get some, and it's just not worth losing manpower over at the moment." That had been Yaomi's words, and Dorea and Masi had followed her command.

That meant, however, that the people were left without a real reason for why the man would brave Yaomi's wrath, so they had come up with all kinds of weird explanations.

"My favorite so far has been that he was one of our own mages during the Great War, that he lost his mind after his companions were killed and had just regained enough of his memories to return, but his madness drove him to attack you."

Dorea drily snorted, not nearly as fascinated as Tom about all the theories. "That has to be the stupidest one I heard. He was of a different race! Yaomi at least would have recognized him then."

"Ah, but you see, that's the fun part. The more they stray from reality, and yet people still believe in them, the more fun these stories are." The boy chuckled.

They were currently on patrol, walking through the southern reaches of the grasslands as they looked for any sign of activity coming from the desert.

Nothing had happened lately, and they weren't expecting anything to start up now. However, care still had to be applied in these situations, especially as the enemy mages got more skilled and developed ways of hiding themselves from their senses.

Dorea had finally completed the technique herself, having brought her usage up to fifteen minutes, which would make it usable in a live situation.

She had been itching to go train some more, but her destructive spells weren't exactly suited to be used too close to the settlement, and she couldn't justify leaving Camp by herself for long stretches of time like she did in Whitecliff, as she had a duty to the people under her command.

Still, she had managed to train a few subtler skills, amongst which was magical stealth and Jonah's Whispering Wind.

To think that her awkward and fearful friend would be one of the cornerstones of her village's safety—both thanks to his incredible sensing range and his knack for creating utility spells that he would then teach to others—was still unbelievable to her, but she felt proud of him nonetheless.

Still, these last couple of days that she had been on forced rest had been hard on her. Her failure to do anything against the Ubag mage grated on her pride, even though she intellectually knew that she couldn't have done anything even if given the time to prepare—the gap between them was far too high!

That said, she had been feeling the need to let go in a proper fight for a while, wanting to test herself like she hadn't since the time against the sea serpent. And even then, the difficulty had come from an unfamiliar terrain rather than her opponent's power.

Luckily for her, if what her senses were telling her was correct, she'd get her wish quite soon. "Enhanced beast coming from the southwest! Lightning! I think it's some kind of deer!" she called out, readying herself for battle with a grin that might have had a touch of madness, given how the others gulped.

Soon after, a creature that was related to a deer but was evidently not one emerged from the grasslands. With two sets of horns, one forked and located above the eyes and a second, longer and straight, on the back of the skull.

Standing at six feet in height at the shoulders and reaching almost nine thanks to the sparking horns, the creature looked less like a deer and more like a drunken drawing of one.

"That's a hayoceros!" exclaimed one of the Heidel scouts that was accompanying them.

Everyone immediately recognized the name, as it was one of the most delicious meats served at Camp. The creatures were considered challenging to hunt, thanks to their sheer speed, but given that this particular specimen was charging straight at them, Dorea doubted it'd be that difficult to engage.

When she felt its horns light up with electricity, much stronger than she would have expected given how little mana it had been emitting so far, she hurriedly called upon her magic to cast a shield made of conjured water.

Although her Bulwark was more resilient, she had been taught by Voggo in her early days to recognize when to use the most suitable spell, and since conjured water didn't allow lightning to travel through it easily, it was the better choice.

A powerful enough bolt would simply vaporize the liquid and still pass through, but she packed a lot of mana behind it, and luckily it held.

Her recent battles might have seen her take a backseat, being a mere spectator of fights between old monsters, but the truth was that Dorea had grown a lot lately, both in skill and in power, and when put against an enemy in her weight class, she could swing very hard.

Indeed, as soon as the hayoceros's attack was over, she rapidly condensed the water that made up her shield and turned it into Bullets. Around her, the others had barely had enough time to realize that the beast was much stronger than it had appeared, and barriers were starting to flicker into being.

Knowing that she could trust the defense to them—especially Tom, who had started focusing on protective magics since the debacle with the Mondeans in the forest—she concentrated on the attack.

Her Bullets ripped through the air, unerringly directed toward the animal that had attacked them.

Unfortunately, rather than staying still and taking on the punishment, the beast lit up again with power, this time all over its body rather than just on its horns, and flickered away, moving at such speeds that only her mystical senses allowed her to track it.

Still, the barrage had not been for nothing, as she had managed to drench the battlefield with puddles, allowing her a much greater reach than usual.

It felt weird, going back to using the basic tactics she had used during her first real fight—against the smilodon to protect her family's anoas—but she wasn't above reusing an idea if it proved to work.

Using its enhanced body, the hayoceros charged at them, moving very quickly. It zipped through the grasslands, closing the distance fast enough that it avoided most of the puddles.

Still, Dorea was able to use the last three, sending jets of compressed water crashing into the beast.

The lightning that coated its body prevented its skewering, but it was still sent crashing away from the group. Considering the speed it had been moving at, it had to have been hurt even if it had managed to protect itself from the direct consequences of being hit.

Dorea didn't give it the time to gather itself. Instead, she crafted another Bullet, and with accuracy given by using a single one rather than her usual barrages, she hit its head, pulping it.

It's kind of uncomfortable how often I end my fights with a headshot. Sure, it's an excellent way of eliminating anything, but the gore . . .

"Oh, man. That's nasty!"

Dorea turned to give Tom the stink eye. They had both been through much more unsettling situations than this, and there was no need to point that out.

Sounds of agreement were made by the others, and she had to give it up as a bad job. It was pretty nasty, after all, but she didn't feel too bad.

With a wave of her hand, water flew in from all the puddles she had created while fighting and converged on the slain beast, severing what little remained of its head and cleaning the carcass.

One of the things that really makes my life as a mage worth it is that I don't really have to get my hands dirty if I don't want to.

Indeed, by now, she was an old hand at dressing a carcass of the field, cleaning it thoroughly with half of the same water that had killed it. It was a very efficient process.

The boost she got from killing the hayoceros wasn't enough to change things, but she would take all she could get, especially since they were getting close to the borders of Heidel territory, and having her mana reserves filled was always a good idea.

The interruption hadn't taken more than a few minutes, butchering and cleaning the body included, and they resumed their patrol, spreading out once again with the newly acquired meat safely encased in a bubble of water.

"Do you want me to take care of that?" asked Tom, gesturing toward the floating carcass.

Dorea shook her head, not bothered in the slightest. Hoisting the therium hadn't been much of a problem for her, and considering how the hayoceros wasn't even a tenth of its weight, she could keep it up indefinitely.

The boy shrugged and took back his position. Tom had always been of a friendly sort, but ever since she rescued him from the Mondean wood mage, he had held her in very high regard. He wasn't sycophantic—having expressed more than once differing opinions than her—and for that, she was very grateful, but he was firmly on her side, and she knew she could count on him.

Still, while he had made significant strides in his magical training, splitting his focus while on a possibly dangerous patrol was not the kind of thing she felt comfortable allowing.

Her concerns were validated shortly after that, as one of the Heidel mages taking part in the patrol flagged that he had sensed several people's presence.

In these desolate parts of the grasslands, so close to the desert, there is only one group of people that it could possibly be.

Indeed, a few minutes later, she, too, felt their presence—they made no effort to hide, she noted—and soon after, she saw them.

Ten men and two women, all of the Heidel race as was common in the south, but darker in skin than those from Yaomi's tribe, came closer to their group, looking as if they were simply taking a stroll with how casual they were.

At their head, a young man with a well-groomed beard led the way. From what Dorea could feel, he was a water mage. His hair was long, held up in a topknot in a style she had never seen before. His skin was the color of dark amber, and his beard reached his chest—which was a feat, considering how he didn't look a day over twenty.

He constantly replenished a very thin film of liquid on his skin. It was as wide as a hair, but she could sense a significant quantity of water and mana packed within.

It reminded Dorea of Melu's water armor, though the girl's was much thicker. Hers served as a constant defense, ready to catch powerful spells head-on.

The one she was currently studying was different than that. Though the water was condensed enough to provide some protection, at least from mundane attacks and stray hits, it didn't feel sturdy enough to protect the caster against direct blows.

It was possible, she considered, that the man was simply too weak to cast a proper defensive spell, but she doubted it. Going by the others' body language, he was obviously the leader, and she didn't think the notoriously strength-focused southern barbarians would allow a weakling to lead them.

It had to have another reason for existing, but from a cursory observation, she couldn't glean its purpose. Unfortunately, she couldn't dedicate much more time to it since she needed to keep her senses trained on all of them and farther out, to prevent any ambush or foul play.

"Halt!" she called. It was what she had seen done by the senior Heidel scouts. If met with other tribes' patrols, they would call for them to stop, ask for an explanation for their presence, and if deemed unthreatening and truthful enough, they'd simply escort them away from their border.

If the response wasn't satisfactory . . . well, she was no stranger to forcing others to see her point.

CHAPTER TWENTY-SEVEN

Thankfully, the southerners stopped when she called for them to do so, lowering the tension that had risen as they got closer.

"You are entering alliance territory. State your provenance and reasons!" she asked, using the winds to ensure her voice could be easily heard.

As she had expected, the young man at the front took point, signaling that he would speak. "We come from Kamadar, the restored city. We have noticed increased activity from your side of the border in the last few weeks and have come to ensure nothing nefarious is going on."

The candidness of his words took her by surprise. To claim that he suspected them of foul play, even if he hadn't directly stated it, was a bold move. Especially if he wanted to avoid any escalation.

Dorea snorted. "We have no intention of leaving our lands. Your so-called cities are little more than ruins held together by hopes and dreams. There is nothing there we would want."

She decided that since he wanted to put their cards on the table in an effort to take her by surprise, she would follow suit. She wasn't one to be easily intimidated, having stared death in the face more times than she cared to remember.

The bearded mage chuckled, apparently not offended by her description of his home. "It is true that we are still a long way from bringing Kamadar back to its glory days, but at least we have the foundations of a city. Can you say the same, Sapiens?"

Cities were a big deal because they meant an organized society. They couldn't survive by themselves and required resources from all around, from immense fields to cultivate grain to complex mining operations.

Magic might simplify many things, but the basics remained the same. To claim that they would one day rebuild Kamadar back to what it was centuries before was bold.

Dorea sincerely doubted that they'd be able to do it, at least not in the near future, but she wouldn't be baited into revealing the state of their infrastructure.

It's not a bad way to get information. Just push the right buttons of an ornery person, and they'll tell you all you need to know by themselves. Unfortunately for you, I'm not that easy to fool.

When she felt Tom's mouth open, likely to reply to what had just been said, Dorea gently shut it with the air, the click of his teeth coming together audible in the silence, and gave him a nasty look.

It seemed to work as the boy raised his hands in surrender, quelled for the moment.

"You can have all the suspicions you want, but that still doesn't give you the right to trespass," she replied, not wanting the conversation to shift away.

The bearded young man smirked. "We have not entered your so-called alliance's land. This area has been for generations where the southern tribes would gather in the hottest days of the summer, seeking refuge in the waters of the river that runs just a few miles east of here."

Smart, I can't say I know anything about the history of this specific stretch of land, so his claim will have to go uncontested. Or maybe . . .

Dorea turned to one of the older scouts, seeking his opinion. Though she was the nominal leader of the patrol, she was smart enough to know that sometimes, you had to bow your head and ask for another's help, especially if you didn't know enough about the subject matter.

Considering the southerner's words, the middle-aged man rubbed his chin. "The river has always been no man's land; that is true. At least since the Great War. But where we are now is our territory, and no one tried to contest this before. I don't know if they ever snuck through between gaps in our attention, but that doesn't make it theirs." Though he usually would have been heard by everyone, Dorea had contained the sound around them, not wanting to give a possible adversary an advantage.

Satisfied with his answer, she turned to reply to her interlocutor. "The river you speak of belongs to no one, and we have no intention of preventing your people from reaching it."

At that, the man smiled, looking almost triumphant. "But," she continued, freezing his expression, "the same is not true for where we stand now. This is alliance land. That is not up for debate."

And Dorea was ready to enforce her words. She had seen too much suffering at the hands of those who thought themselves conquerors, who'd readily take another's place just because they wanted to. She wouldn't allow anything of the sort to happen under her watch.

Luckily, the group of southerners made no move to react negatively. Instead, their leader relaxed, looking amused. "It's good to know you have some courage in you, despite your appearance."

While internally indignant, Dorea wasn't about to blow a gasket over such a childish insult. She very much would have liked to reply that his—admittedly well-groomed—beard did nothing to hide his youth, but she refrained. The situation was already tense enough, and now that the hurdle of territorial claims seemed to have been dealt with, she didn't want to add other problems on top of that.

"I'm glad you think so. Now, are you ready to leave? We will escort you back outside the border, and if you really want to reach the river, you can do it from there."

She made to go but noticed that the southerners hadn't moved at all. "What now?" she asked exasperatedly.

"We are ancient allies," the bearded leader answered. "Our people fought together against Ergasters depredations in the Great War. We bled and died alongside one another. For that reason alone, we have come here to share what we know of our ultimate enemy's movements."

And there is the real reason. All that song and dance about passing through no man's land, and you spring this now? Ugh, this is why I hate diplomatic missions.

Unfortunately, Dorea couldn't exactly reject his offer. Firstly, she knew that her allies would want to learn as much as possible about what was going on in Ergasters' land. Secondly, she was smart enough to know that establishing good relationships with at least one of the two cities being resettled in the south would be fundamental for their chances to keep the peace.

"Well then, we can begin now and establish a date to meet again and share more information." Her proposal also had the benefit of establishing further diplomatic relations. Though Dorea would never be a fan of the politicking that came with it, she knew that it was by far the better option.

Thankfully, the man agreed, "That's fine. We didn't expect the first people we'd find to have been made aware of everything, but even the most widely known bits of information can be useful."

Dorea concentrated, recalling everything that had been shared at the summit and all she had learned while being at Camp.

I don't know precisely how much Yaomi will want to share, but giving them the broad strokes should be fine.

Just to be sure, she checked with every team member to see if they had second thoughts or suggestions, but they all seemed willing to trust her. That their chief had selected her for testing to see if she could become a future leader had gained her a lot of respect with the Heidels, even those that had seemed more reticent at first.

"Very well, I'm not the most well-informed, so if you want more up-to-date news, you'll have to come back, but as far as I know, the Ergasters are mostly embroiled in a quiet civil war. The new generation of mages is trying to gain power, but the older functionaries are not letting go easily, so we don't expect them to turn to expansionary military actions for a few years."

The southerners looked shocked at that. "Do you have spies inside their cities?!" one asked, finally breaking the silence everyone but the leader had maintained.

Dorea just smiled mysteriously. She wasn't sure of the answer herself, but letting them think they did only had upsides. After all, if they believed that the alliance had such wide-ranging intelligence operations, they'd be much more careful not to provoke them.

"Well, do you have anything you can tell me?" she asked instead, not bothering to address the question.

The leader shook his head and refocused, chuckling at her words. "All right, I guess we can't reveal everything about our capabilities either. We have noticed that one of the generals in charge of the eastern border has been replaced with a younger one—which now makes sense if a shadow civil war is happening—and the troops under him have begun drilling more seriously. If what you said about internal conflict is true, then it's possible that their target is not us but one of their own."

Or it's an upstart who wants to gather some military accomplishments against an easy target to then angle for a higher position. But we can't know that, unfortunately. Or, well, maybe Yaomi really has spies everywhere in the Ergasters' territory. Who knows.

"Well, we'll obviously have to verify that on our own, but if it's true, then it's valuable information. I guess we can set a new meeting date a week from now here so the elders can decide what to do," she finally replied.

The day had been surprisingly productive, and if she had truly managed to open a channel of friendly discussion with one of the two major settlements in the south after the Heidels hadn't done so for months, well, she might just have a knack for diplomacy, no matter her dislike for the practice.

"Just one last thing," the bearded southerner interjected, making her instantly warier. "While we of Kamadar are more than willing to open talks with your alliance, you shouldn't expect Katmasou to be so friendly. From what I know, those people are much more insular and have set their sights on this stretch of grasslands, since it's a direct path to the river."

The unexpected meeting broke up shortly after that, and they both reiterated their willingness to repeat it in a week's time. Dorea's team then escorted the southerners outside of the grasslands.

A solemn mood had fallen as everyone considered the implications of what they had just heard.

"It's possible that they were bluffing, is it not? Just a way to make us indisposed to open talks with their rivals?" Tom asked, interrupting the silence that had lasted since they left their new theoretical allies.

"I wouldn't put it past them, but it's true that the tribes that congregated at Katmasou are known to be more aggressive," one of the older scouts replied.

And so went on the discussion. Everyone was relieved that a point of contact had finally been established with at least one of the two cities from the south, but the news they had learned brought the mood down.

That one of the Ergaster generals was moving was worrying enough on its own, even if there was a good chance that he was simply taking advantage of the internal chaos to take control of a regiment.

But hearing that the tribes of Katmasou might have aggressive intentions toward them was a heavy burden. No one felt the need to go to war to protect an unused stretch of land, but they all knew that they couldn't simply allow them to take what they wanted. That way laid constant compromise with an emboldened adversary.

It was a relief when they finally got back to Camp. Dorea made a quick detour to drop off the hayoceros's carcass that she had been floating along and was thanked for her contribution.

Then, she quickly walked to Yaomi's tent, eager to drop the weight of responsibility on someone else.

Inside was organized chaos. The quiet she had experienced the first time she came and the professional atmosphere of the second time had been replaced with a much more relaxed state of affairs, though it still seemed to be a productive environment, given the snippets she overheard.

She was met by Lindus at the entrance, the man's impeccably groomed mustache making him easily recognizable, and was quickly bustled to the back of the maze of tents.

In the grandest pavilion, Yaomi was sitting on her comfortable sofa, quietly discussing something she couldn't pick up with her natural hearing—she didn't dare aid herself with magic, as she had no doubt that the older woman would notice—with Seshi, the portly earth mage.

They both greeted her distractedly, but when they saw her solemn face, they set aside whatever they had been talking about and turned to give her their attention. Dorea briefly considered asking if the man had to be included in her report before setting the notion aside. Seshi was an Elder with the capital E. Someone who was trusted by both the community and Yaomi and handled much of the day-to-day running of the village.

At their return, she had impressed upon her team that everything they had learned during their mission had to be kept secret until it was decided they could talk about it, but she expected bits and pieces to start floating around soon enough.

"We have encountered a team from Kamadar, established a friendly rapport, exchanged vital information, and set a new meeting for a week from now."

She might have enjoyed the two elders' gobsmacked looks a bit too much, but Dorea was not above a bit of payback after being so easily rattled during their last meeting.

After they composed themselves, Seshi chuckled, amused. "All right, you got us. Now explain."

She launched into the tale, briefly mentioning the fight against the hayoceros before concentrating on the important matter: the talks with the southerners.

Though she was sure they must have had questions, the two elders didn't interrupt her, allowing her to finish. "And then I told them very sternly that nothing of what had happened today after the fight could be spoken of, not even amongst themselves—the tents are really not good at keeping anything private."

"Well," Seshi began, after a look at Yaomi, "you did well in keeping a lid on this. In truth, you did well in everything. It was a delicate situation, and you managed to bring home an important victory."

Dorea wasn't one to fall to flattery easily, but she could tell that the strangely young-looking old man was being truthful. He really believed that she had done something good. She smiled in thanks, feeling relieved now that she had pushed the problem off on them to deal with.

"That said, we now need to send missions out to the southeastern and eastern borders to verify what the Kamadari told her," he continued, this time speaking to his chief.

Yaomi had been quiet so far, only nodding once in a while when she went into further detail. Finally, she broke her silence. "You did a good job. A leader's duty is to ensure their people's prosperity; to do that, you need to strike a balance between diplomacy and aggressiveness. Considering our current situation, with a war up north that's only just begun, we really can't afford to open another front."

Then she turned to her counselor. "We need to check on that info, but it wouldn't surprise me if it were true. The southerners have always aimed to get control of that stretch of the river since it would grant them access to resources they severely need, especially now that they are rebuilding the ruined cities."

Seshi nodded in agreement. "That's true, and to get there, they either need to lengthen the journey by going through the canyon that connects the grasslands to the desert, or they can bypass it by entering the grasslands sooner, in our territory."

So there are geographical reasons as to why they want that stretch of land. I expected as much, but it's nice to have confirmation.

"It wouldn't surprise me if they wanted to deviate some of the river's water to make a new lake." The portly man continued, "They can't take everything, since that would be a threat to the Ergasters, as they rely on the river's waters to cultivate their easternmost lands, but some would be better than none. And they can't last forever on desert oasis, no matter how easy having a water mage makes finding them."

Dorea hadn't considered that, but it seemed obvious now that she had heard it. She knew that the ruined cities must have had some sort of underground water supply. Otherwise, they could have never been built in the middle of the desert, but that must have been centuries ago. Who knew in what condition those wells were.

"So, we need to check on both the Katmasousi's movements and send word to our people at the eastern border to learn more about this new general. And to explain why exactly this information wasn't already known to us," Yaomi concluded, sounding tired.

"And we need to raise the alert level, Chief. While we shouldn't take everything said as gospel, we need to be ready in case the other southerners try to take that stretch of land." Seshi didn't seem to enjoy the prospect any more than they did, but it was the unfortunate truth that allowing any piece of territory to be taken was unacceptable, and to retain control of it, they needed to increase their numbers there.

CHAPTER TWENTY-EIGHT

Ever since the Mother's Wrath gave her powers, Dorea had felt mixed emotions about the rain. In part, she knew that it wasn't logical to associate its presence with the loss of Rupert and the others, but it still reminded her of those who weren't there anymore.

On the other hand, she was much more powerful in the middle of a storm. Her control over the three elements meant that she could pretend to be a goddess in her little domain, and no one who wasn't a Master could threaten her.

So, when she was given a mission to deal with an enhanced wolverine on the eastern border while it rained cats and dogs, she wasn't sure how to feel. It would certainly make it all easier to accomplish, and given the reports that this particular beast had sent a patrol packing with great waves of mud, she felt that it would be a good fit for her.

Evidently, Yaomi felt the same because she intercepted her before she could leave. "I know that wolverine. It's from the previous generation and until now, it has never caused any problems. I want to know what has got it in such a tizzy—if there even is anything. Consider this a leadership test. You have shown yourself capable of diplomacy, and the men respect you. Now show me you have the power and courage necessary for the position."

She had then swept away, not allowing Dorea the time to ask any questions.

In a way, I suppose that this is another method of testing me. Drop me in the middle of a situation I know nothing about and see how I deal with it.

She was somewhat worried that a beast that gained its powers during the previous generation would be too much, but she knew Yaomi wouldn't send her to her death, which meant it should be defeatable.

Looking at the flashing sky overhead, where dark clouds poured rain down on the grasslands in a classic summer storm, Dorea decided that even if the wolverine was truly dangerous, she wouldn't find a better condition to fight it in.

She quickly walked to her tent, unbothered by the rain, which slid off her form as if she wasn't there. Inside, she found Nora sitting on her bed. The two girls had become better friends as they were forced to spend more time together, and if anything, Dorea was glad to have had the chance of getting to know the brunette better.

Despite her initial awe and shyness, Nora demonstrated a quick wit and dry sarcasm that never failed to make her laugh. Dorea had come to appreciate her running commentary on everything, from Tom's absurdly loaded breakfasts to the clumsy ways he tried to hit on a Heidel girl.

She had become something of a confidant lately, and Dorea was genuinely grateful that the girl didn't seem to mind listening to her ramblings. The absence of Beth and Jonah was making itself heard, and while Tom was also becoming a good friend, they weren't on the level where she could freely complain about her periods.

"You are conflicted. What else did they drop on your lap?" Nora asked as soon as Dorea entered the tent. That was another thing she appreciated about the girl. She was always ready to fight for her and take her side, even without knowing anything.

Dorea chuckled, shaking her head. "Well, since my last test was a flop, thanks to that damn Ubag mage, Yaomi has finally found something to use as a substitute."

She dropped herself on the cot next to Nora, picked up her rucksack, and emptied it on the floor, where she could check that everything she needed was there.

"I'm going to the eastern border to deal with a powerful beast that has been making a nuisance of itself. A wolverine that can use earth magic and likes drowning its enemies in mud, apparently," she explained, picking up her bedroll and unfurling it, using the air to remove any accumulated dust and then pushing the little cloud outside the tent.

"Isn't that too dangerous? A beast that has lived long enough to have been there when the last Wrath arrived means that it has to be much stronger than anything you have fought before." Nora's worries were painted plainly on her face. And in a way, she was correct. Dorea had never before successfully defeated a beast from the previous generation.

"Yaomi assured me it's not a Master-level. You forget that animals plateau much more than humans, and when they reach enough strength to not fear the nearby threats, they generally stop pushing," she answered distractedly, referencing Voggo's lessons from months before as she checked on the sharpness of her hunting knife.

She had never had to use it, since her magic made it redundant, but it had been a present from her father before she departed for Camp, and she preferred having an option beyond hand-to-hand fighting in case her mana was exhausted.

Nora sighed. "Well, I suppose nothing I can say will change your mind. Good luck, Dorea." With that, the girl stood up, patted her cheek, and left.

I appreciate her concerns, I really do, but what is too dangerous for her is not the same for me. I'm not being arrogant when I say that we are not on the same level.

That was something she had been noticing with time. Her exploits seemed almost fantastical to the other mages her age, and the few that could relate—Mark the Blue being the prime example—weren't exactly the friendliest sort. This meant that Dorea ended up feeling isolated even when in good company, as her experiences were not at all relatable to the others.

All right, enough whining. It's not that bad. Yes, there is a gap between me and everyone else, but it's only evident in a few situations. Otherwise, Nora, Tom, and the others have been terrific friends. Not everyone is gonna share every experience with me, and that's perfectly normal.

Even to her, it sounded like she was trying very hard to convince herself, but she buried that little voice and turned her attention to finishing her preparations. With a gesture, the pounding rain outside gathered in a perfectly spherical ball and flowed into her waterskin.

Though she was also a water mage, perfectly capable of either conjuring her element from the air or, in case she didn't want to drink it pure, gathering it from the atmosphere, it never hurt to be prepared.

It was a strange feeling, knowing that you'll be getting into a fight with a powerful opponent for almost no reason. She didn't choose it to test herself, nor did she pick that specific beast because it would grant her greater power—in truth, Dorea wasn't sure of what would happen when she defeated it and attempted to draw in its mana. It had not threatened her or those she cared about. It was a task given to her by another.

She would fulfill it because if not her, then someone else would have to go and deal with it, and putting Yaomi aside, she was by far the best suited to do it, especially with such favorable weather, but she still felt contemplative.

Her hand unconsciously closed around her grandmother's pendant, which she wore religiously. It hadn't helped against the Ubag mage, though she hadn't expected it to, since hiding her at that point would have been almost pointless, but she would never part with it.

It had saved her during the Trial, and she was confident that she would have never left Old Titan's territory alive without it. That alone was enough of a reason to wear it, but she did it also because it was the only thing she had of Doressa, the great earth mage, and to know that someone in her family had gone through what she was currently experiencing was more relieving than she liked to admit.

Done with the preparations, Dorea passed by the communal tent set aside for Whitecliff's contingent, distractedly waved at those few who had taken refuge from the rain there, and grabbed a few packs of rations, stuffing them in her bag.

She expected the trip there to take almost a day, which meant that taking into consideration the time to fight, then explore the border to see if something specific had spooked the wolverine, and then the trip back, she would be out for a couple of days, and though she was a mage, making a fire in the current conditions felt a bit too much even to her.

I could do it—cut down some trees, remove the water from them, create a bubble around the camp, spark a fire, and keep it up for as long as needed to cook. But why would I do that when there are perfectly good rations here that don't require any of that?

With that done, Dorea was finally ready to leave.

Running in the rain was more liberating than she had thought it would be. Her Air Boost would generally not allow anything to touch her, but she purposefully made an exception and let in a few drops once in a while, just to enjoy the feeling of the rain hitting her skin.

Of course, at the speed she was going, even just that could be dangerous, but it was the work of a moment to accelerate the drops of water at the same speed she was moving at so as to not get hurt.

It was a wasteful usage of mana, especially when she had a critical mission to accomplish, but Dorea allowed herself this little treat. Though she had made peace with the notion that she would have to take on more responsibilities as time went on, it still weighed on her mind, and she needed a release occasionally.

A good fight would help, and indeed, she looked forward to battling with the wolverine—she had spent most of the long hours of travel thinking up counter-measures for any possible tactic it would employ—but little moments of joy like this were also important.

Voggo had been very clear, at the beginning of his lessons, that they should try their best to maintain the wonder they had toward their magic for their whole life, as it would make their path as mages much easier. While Dorea very much enjoyed spending long hours experimenting with her powers—and she had several new ideas for possible wards that she couldn't wait to test when she finally got back home—she also loved the simplicity of using her magic to run through the grasslands in the middle of a storm, uncaring of the fury of the elements.

It was a heady feeling, having it all under her control. If she wished, it would take just an instant to fly up in the sky and take control of the clouds and winds. She would have the entire thing for herself, and that much power was enough to do many, many things.

Dorea wasn't above daydreaming of flying north, taking the storm with her like an angry elemental, and crashing upon the Mondeans, destroying them through the might of nature.

Her rational mind luckily reasserted itself in those moments and told her that she simply didn't have the power nor the control to grip the entire storm, not to speak of moving it for hundreds of miles.

Even if I somehow managed to catch it, I'd probably lose my grip while close to Whitecliff or something, considering my luck.

Shaking the thought off, she continued her path eastward, noticing how the grasslands were slowly turning into less of a loose collection of hills and the occasional copse of trees and more into a uniform plain.

She knew that if she pushed even farther east, she'd enter the central plains proper, where the Ergasters built their civilization. Curiosity burned at her, but she had a duty to do, and she'd need her whole attention for it.

Hours after she had departed from Camp, she finally arrived at what had been described as the place where the wolverine had attacked the patrol.

It was a recognizable spot only because it housed the ruins of an old outpost from the Great War. The building, a squat and ugly thing, had evidently been made by earth magic. It emerged from the ground in a single piece, an impossible technique without magical intervention.

Her senses told her that most of it was underground, as she could feel water and air almost a hundred feet deep. By now, it had been abandoned for decades, with moss and vegetation growing all over it, but the foundation was still sturdy, unbowed by the elements.

I just hope we won't have to use it anytime soon. Between the Mondeans and the southerners, we already have our hands full. If the Ergasters ever pull their heads out of their asses, they'll pick us all apart.

It was unfortunate, but as things stood, she really couldn't see any way for the tribes that had once stood shoulder to shoulder against their eastern enemies to put their differences aside.

Rather, it's more likely that some will try to take advantage of the situation and attack us from another front.

Shaking those thoughts aside, Dorea refocused on her mission. Once that was done, she'd have all the time she wanted to explore the ruins, even if her senses had already revealed that they had long since picked clean.

She dismissed Air Boost, only keeping a tenuous hold on the atmosphere surrounding her so as to be ready in case anything attacked her. She then walked for a couple of minutes, until she reached the exact spot that had been described to her as the place of confrontation. There, evidence of a fight was all over the place.

Great clumps of earth told her that the wolverine had used more than just waves of mud, and she immediately adjusted her plans. She also made a note to complain to whoever had given the report, as it was turning out to be woefully inadequate.

Scars in the area showed that the two mages that had been part of the patrol had at least tried to respond to the beast's aggression, but they had evidently been overpowered and barely managed to keep the thing at bay long enough for everyone to evacuate.

Dorea observed that slashing wind attacks seemed to have had little effect on it, as walls of earth had been built to block them, and they showed little more than superficial scratching.

That implied some intelligence on the wolverine's part—something that she had initially doubted, given its hyperaggressive behavior—and more than a little experience in dealing with different elements, but she had already known about that since the beast was so old.

She continued her survey, surprised to find little evidence of subterranean tunneling. As far as she knew, that was the most common way for both beasts and mages, after they reached a certain level of power, to deal with larger numbers, as it allowed them to remain unseen and protected by dozens of feet of packed earth.

Instead, the wolverine seemed to prefer a more aggressive style, attacking from the surface, in plain sight. She had seen Old Titan employ that style, but that monster was strong enough that he could do anything he wanted and probably tough enough to take on his enemy's attacks head-on without worries about being overwhelmed by larger numbers.

Yeah, I can't really compare this wolverine with the master of the forest. It'd be like trying to find patterns between how I fight and how Yaomi does. We just have very different capabilities.

Still, the fact that the animal she was tracking showed such confidence and aggressiveness, even while employing strategies that should have been above it, told her that something was afoot. Why would such an intelligent beast, who had enough experience to develop its own unique style and who had lived, if not in harmony, at least with begrudging tolerance, suddenly attack a patrol?

It wasn't even that it had been pushed away from its lands like the salamanders had risked with the Ubag mage, since the wolverine had been known to have resided in the area for decades.

No, Dorea would have to dig in deeper. If she ever found out the truth, she was sure it would be simpler than she expected, but until then, her mind ran with all kinds of possibilities.

The most obvious thing is that the Ergasters did something to spook it, likely the new general in charge of the eastern district, but that still doesn't explain why it would attack us. It should recognize the difference between races if it's bright enough for such tactics.

As she was standing above one of the very few holes in the ground, where she expected the beast to have taken refuge from one of the more powerful attacks that the Heidel patrol had managed to unleash, she felt something.

Instinctively, she conjured a Bulwark around herself, the air converging on her position so quickly as to make a loud rushing sound.

A ton of rock crashed against her barrier a second later.

CHAPTER TWENTY-NINE

Dorea stumbled back, not because she had been directly hit, since her Bulwark had managed to protect her, but because of how unexpected the attack had been.

She had been keeping her senses fully extended for several minutes and hadn't noticed anything wrong until the very last second.

The feeling of another huge boulder coming her way shook her out of her daze, and she redoubled her mana commitment to the Bulwark, empowering it enough that it barely shook when the rock crashed against it.

That's right. You can't just stay away and try to take me down like this; my defenses are better than your attacks.

Feeling vindicated at having spent so much time perfecting the spells she already had rather than dedicating herself to crafting new ones, Dorea looked for her enemy, not making the mistake of assuming it would be where the projectiles had come from.

Indeed, she quickly found the wolverine a couple hundred feet away, and it was closing the distance fast. It seemed that instead of the long-range battle she had initially expected, the beast had decided to fight much closer.

Its fur was gray with age, but its movement would have fooled anyone into thinking that it was in its prime. The wolverine was not a particularly large specimen, standing at three and a half feet, nor was it more corpulent than the nonmagical variety, unlike other enhanced beasts she had seen. Still, the power contained within it was enough to give her a pause.

The beast was not a Master, but it was still the strongest Journeyman-rank being she had faced in a fight. Even the mighty therium she had battled weeks before had not been brimming with as much mana as it was.

Deciding that she would have to give it her all if she wanted to defeat it, Dorea released any notion of holding back.

She then took hold of the battering rain that still raged on and crafted a dozen Bullets with it, shooting them toward her target. Even as she did so, another part of her mind was already reaching for more, ready to end it all in one mighty barrage.

The beast reacted quickly. As soon as the first Bullet was completed, the mud at its feet rose to cover it as it aborted its run.

With a staccato of bangs, her spell crashed into where it had stood, sending mud and grass flying everywhere. Then, the second round hit, and the explosions it caused started digging into the earth, where she could feel the wolverine's presence.

Without letting up, Dorea shot a third series and then a fourth. The storm's might around her fueled her power, limiting how much mana she had to expend and allowing for a greater than usual firing rate.

So it's not that you never fight from underground. You just felt cocky with the patrol, eh?

All through that, she still kept up her Bulwark and was rewarded for her attention when another huge boulder came hurtling toward her, followed by a second in the first's shadow.

She held them both back, not struggling now that she knew what to expect, but didn't allow herself to think that was it. Indeed, shortly after that, she felt the water that had sunk into the ground beneath her feet move as the mud converged toward one spot a hundred feet to her left.

Dorea sank mana into the ground a dozen feet below her and forced a small area to stay still by taking control of the water particles.

A wall of mud, higher than Whitecliff's, rose up, with the wolverine at its top, riding it as if a dolphin in the sea. It looked much worse now than at the beginning; its fur was marred with blood, but it was still alive and well enough to fight, so Dorea prepared herself to continue.

Rather than taking its attack head-on, she did what those poor mages from the patrol that was attacked couldn't do and rose into the air, thus entirely avoiding the wave that crashed where she had just stood.

Knowing that she had just made herself a much bigger target now that she was levitating, Dorea didn't allow the beast the time to react to her movements, zipping away.

Her flight might not have been as fast as her speed on the ground, but having at her disposal 360 degrees of movement made her much more unpredictable, as shown by the boulders that were sent flying her way hitting nothing.

When I was on the ground, you could use the point of contact between my feet and it to localize me, but now that I'm flying, it's not so easy, huh?

Indeed, the accuracy of the wolverine's shots had dramatically lowered. Instead of continuing on the foolish path, the beast again showed its cunning mind as it adapted. Rather than the enormous boulders it had preferred at the beginning of the fight, it began to use much smaller balls of mud, condensed enough to pack a punch but so large in numbers that she simply couldn't avoid them all.

Of course, their individual strength was not enough to break through her Bulwark, but all together, they made flying around a much trickier prospect.

With an angry shout, Dorea grasped every raindrop for hundreds of feet and used it as counterbattery, annihilating the mud balls and forcing the wolverine into the ground once again.

Then, she restarted her barrage of Bullets, aiming to crush it through the sheer force of the explosions they created when they hit.

The most frustrating thing about fighting earth mages—something that had been remarked upon by everyone to have ever faced one in the village records— was that, unless one was immensely superior, they could easily slip away into the ground and use the tons of packed dirt as protection to run away.

It was what the Ubag mage had attempted to do during the fight with Yaomi when he understood just how much he was out of his depths, but then the difference in power had been so significant that the Witch of Immolation simply melted down everything between the two of them.

The wolverine that Dorea was fighting could have simply left, and she wouldn't have been able to do anything about it. She simply didn't have the punch to hit it when it was so deep. Fortunately for her, the beast seemed to have no intention of running away, and as soon as she let out with her barrage, it emerged once again, looking worse for wear but still combat capable.

It growled angrily at her, almost daring her to get closer. Though Dorea would have really liked decking the annoying animal on the snout, she refrained, keeping her favorable position in the sky.

For a moment, neither attacked as they evaluated their chances. It was obvious that the beast, though powerful, couldn't actually break through her defenses, empowered as she was by the storm. That said, Dorea couldn't seem to truly hurt it either.

It was battered, yes, but being knocked around by explosions didn't mean it would go down anytime soon, and considering the legendary stubbornness and persistence that wolverines were known for, she expected that the fight could go on for many hours if they kept up the rhythm.

Then, the quiet was broken as the beast started up another barrage of smaller projectiles, looking to saturate her defenses and, if her suspicions were correct, her senses. Keeping track of so many mud balls being thrown her way was extremely difficult, and if she had fully dedicated herself to it, she would have easily missed that the wolverine was preparing something.

Deep below the ground, where the battering rain allowed her to extend her senses, she could barely feel a great deal of churning. A vast amount of dirt was being condensed in one point, pressed together by mystical force in a section as large as a building.

If the beast was truly able to shoot her with that amount of mass, she doubted she'd be able to resist, Wind Bulwark or not. That meant that Dorea needed to go on the offensive.

So far, she had been content with disrupting her opponent's plans and occasionally attacking, using her Bullets as a deterrent. But now she saw she couldn't win if she kept up her passiveness.

The wolverine would not allow her to slowly whittle it down. It was too bright for it, though something—be it pride, anger, or the threat of something foreign—kept it from leaving a fight that it couldn't easily win. That meant it had to be preparing a spell to overcome the defenses she had shown so far. It was simply too intelligent to fight a losing battle, and that led her to believe it thought that whatever it was doing at the moment would be enough to hurt her.

Dorea wouldn't be able to live with herself if she had to run away from a damn wolverine. While she entertained the idea of using her Bullets again to break its concentration, she could feel that it had burrowed deep enough that she couldn't entirely disrupt it.

Well, then, I just have to do something even bigger than what it's doing. And luckily for me, I have just the thing.

Dorea had felt extremely frustrated ever since the "fight" with the Ubag mage, since her newest spell had been burning a brand in that little corner of her mind. If she had been able to cast it and had it hit, she might have actually damaged the man.

But she hadn't had the chance. Without the correct atmospheric conditions, setting it up would take long minutes she simply didn't have, and using it would have left her completely wiped. That would have meant being at the complete mercy of her enemy if he had survived the hit.

And though Dorea was confident that very few things could take it on and live, a Master mage was always a dicey prospect.

The entire thing was moot anyway since she hadn't had the time to set it up. That was not true for the fight she was currently in. The raging storm around them would supply the raw materials for the spell, and she would just need to concentrate on the matrix.

She had tested it out once, in a desolate valley found in the eastern rocky hills, and the results had been more than satisfying, though the bone-deep exhaustion she had felt afterward ensured that she wouldn't use it carelessly.

The fact that she had gained the insight necessary for this specific spell from witnessing the fight between Old Titan and the majestic eagle, and that the eagle—whose final attack had been what she had tried to replicate—had lost terribly, made her feel a bit weird, but Dorea supposed that when one was in the situation she was in, besieged on all sides by powerful enemies, they couldn't really complain.

Thus, she grabbed hold of the winds, the rain, and the electrical charges that made up the squall. She took advantage of the time the wolverine was dedicating to crafting its own final weapon to make something that she shouldn't have been capable of.

The three elements that made up her mana had always been distinctly separate until she developed this spell. She could craft combination attacks of two, but they were never made into one.

This, she believed, was her greatest breakthrough to date. Twisting the three different mana types together, grinding them into one singular mass until it felt too wild for her to hold within herself.

Slowly, a glowing ball of churning power exited her chest, almost painful to look at. It tugged at her surroundings, calling upon the storm to feed it. And it answered, funneling toward its new center.

In a majestic display, the dark, ominous clouds that had been traveling through the grasslands stopped as the winds that had pushed them changed direction. The rain, once falling mercilessly upon the earth, now started turning her way, sucked in by the glowing sphere.

One bolt of lightning that should have hit a copse of trees miles away arched toward her, greedily absorbed by her spell.

This is not a normal spell. It's something more.

Indeed, now that her magic could grow by sucking in the strength of the world, it had taken a different taste. What had once been the condensation of her own mana into the compressed replica of an entire storm was now taking on a more conceptual structure.

It felt as if the very idea of a storm was being held within her hands, and Dorea had spent enough time traipsing between Whitecliff's ancient records as she tried to learn warding that she realized, in a flash of insight, that what she had created was a hybrid between her original spell and a powerful ritual.

She hadn't thought of it initially, but all the components were there. She was calling upon the elements that made up a storm while standing in the middle of one. Her purpose was clear, as she wanted to crush her enemy into dust; her method was pure, utilizing only her personal mana to manipulate external elements.

No one was trying to interfere with her casting—one of the fundamentals of rituals, as even the slightest hint of foreign mana could disrupt the whole thing—since the wolverine was too deep into the earth to touch her, and too focused on its own creation to even attempt such a thing.

Somehow, she had ended up getting much more than she had expected. Heart of the Storm was an incredibly powerful spell, and it would have been enough to drill down to where the beast was hiding, crushing it into nothingness and taking its construct with it.

It was by far the greatest spell in her repertoire, and though it took a long time to set up, thanks to her still lacking skills, it would have been enough by itself. Instead, she now had on her hands a Master-level spell. Something that, by all rights, she shouldn't have been able to even come close to. Somehow, she had done it.

Dorea doubted that she'd be able to easily replicate it, even if another storm of this intensity passed by. Still, for the moment, she needed all her concentration to tightly grip the immense power she had called upon.

It felt like if she allowed herself to be distracted, even for just a moment, the spell would blow up. And that would end with her getting erased. Nothing she could do would protect her from it, which meant she needed to send it away as soon as possible.

The ritual, however, was still ongoing. More and more of the storm was being funneled between her hands, and she had no idea how to stop it. At the rate it was accelerating, it would take in everything, and at that point, she would still be hit by the blast.

She needed to find a way to stop the gathering of power, both because she'd get killed by her own spell if she didn't and because she could feel that the wolverine was almost done with its own.

Pitting her will against the storm's might was not easy, but Dorea didn't need to do that. Since the mana that powered the whole thing was her own, she just had to shut that off.

It felt like trying to hold sand in her hands as it kept falling off, but she was a stubborn girl who wouldn't allow her journey to end like this. The air around her trembled as she pushed with everything she had against the immense sucking force of her spell.

No great mage was ready to intervene this time; her grandmother's pendant couldn't help her. It was just Dorea against the world.

And slowly, bit by bit, she pushed back. The flow stuttered and then finally stopped. The enhanced Heart of the Storm felt incredibly unstable and far more potent than the one time she had used it, but she couldn't allow herself second thoughts. If she let up for just one more moment, it would either explode in her hands or start taking power from its surroundings again, and she couldn't allow that.

Therefore, she aimed at where she could vaguely feel a great mass emerging from the earth, sure that it was the wolverine's final attack, and let it go.

As the spell left her hands, it almost felt like it was taking a piece of herself with it, but she knew it was just because she had poured so much mana into it.

A great roar shook the grasslands as the condensed concept of a storm was unleashed upon it. Dorea's vision flashed white, and she poured everything she had left into her Bulwark, feeling it heavily stressed under the shock wave.

It lasted several seconds, and even though she kept a grip on her barrier, she felt herself traveling through a great distance as she concentrated only on defense, rather than staying stationary.

Finally, the pressure stopped, and she wearily opened her eyes.

Before her was a destroyed landscape. Where once there had been flat plains dotted with the results of the occasional fighting, now it was just a crater. It was big enough that it encompassed even some of the underground compound from the Great War, and to Dorea's surprise, one of its rooms was wholly caved in.

Of the wolverine, there was no trace. Its construct was gone as if it had never been made, and any hope of figuring out its behavior quickly vanished alongside it.

Then, the rush of mana hit her, and she had absolute confirmation that she had accomplished her mission.

CHAPTER THIRTY

Dorea had been curious about what would happen if she killed an enhanced beast of an element she couldn't use since she had understood what exactly her condition meant.

The first inkling that it might not turn out to be anything spectacular was when she attacked the wood mage in the Mondean camp. In the chaos of things, she hadn't managed to ascertain whether she had truly killed him, but it seemed more likely than not that she had.

And since she hadn't gained much that time, she had feared that the experience would repeat itself with anything that didn't have her three elements.

The rush of mana that followed her unleashing of Heart of the Storm was welcome for more reasons than simply replenishing her starved reserves. The wolverine's leftover mana that had been released into the atmosphere with its death felt like a drink of water on a hot summer day.

Unsurprisingly, it didn't feel exactly like every other time she gained more power. Rather than immediately being absorbed within her system, most of the foreign energy dispersed throughout her body. It didn't feel like anything dangerous, but she sat down in the middle of the crater she had created to meditate and check that she hadn't done irreparable damage to herself.

As she was coming down from the excitement of the fight, it took her a few minutes to get into the correct state of mind, but eventually, she did. She found that instead of breaking down the mana to make more of her own, she was somehow stripping it of its elemental flavor and using it to enhance every facet of her body.

At the rate the process was going, it would take several hours to finish, and she feared she might lose a decent part of her loot, but this being the first time she had gone through anything of the kind, she decided to let her body do its thing and to occasionally check in to see how things were going.

Though she wouldn't know for sure until the process was over and she had the time to run a few experiments, Dorea suspected that her particular mutation reacted to elemental mana that wasn't directly compatible with her by using it as fuel for enhancing her body, rather than her metaphysical system.

Or that might be simply because it's earth mana that's being used here. It is well known that earth and metal mages have sturdier bodies than most other Gifted. Other elements, like fire, might have entirely different effects.

It was a fascinating subject, and had it not been happening to her, she would have easily enjoyed speculating about all the possible reactions to different stimuli.

Since it was her, however, she was considerably more tepid about it. She relied heavily on her incredible growth, and for it to be possibly affected by external factors scared her in a way that she hadn't expected.

My mutation is what made me special. It's what catapulted me to the highest ranks in Whitecliff and the whole alliance. My capacity to become stronger faster than anyone else is what everyone, from Voggo to Yaomi, is relying upon to see to our people's future. This was actually incredibly reckless, and if it hadn't worked or had done some irreparable damage, I'd have become useless.

Dorea was well aware that without her special little quirk, she'd just be a decent mage with good control. In a few years, she might have eventually become worthy of notice after she spent long hours working for the tiniest increment in power.

Still, she couldn't have avoided this kind of situation forever. Rather, learning her limits now that they were in relative peace was paramount so that when things kicked off again—and they would, she was sure of it—she could be more secure in her position.

There is one thing that worries me a bit. I can feel some of the earth mana not leaving my body, nor being used for anything else. It's just sitting there, as if waiting for something . . .

Prodding it with her own had no effect, and Dorea was forced to conclude that she'd need to wait and see if anything else happened with time.

With her meditation done, she decided to do a cursory sweep of the area to try and glean from the environment what the wolverine's uncharacteristic behavior had been caused by. Unfortunately for her, nothing presented itself. She spent a couple of hours checking from the ground and the sky, but the cause remained frustratingly elusive.

Something told her that things might become clearer if she pushed farther east, but she didn't want to tempt fate. The Ergasters being focused on internal matters was the best possible scenario for the alliance, and she didn't want to give them any excuse to turn their attention to the outside world.

Thus, she made the return trip only halfway successful, but still satisfied. Her biggest fear had been mostly put to rest—nothing seemed to be going wrong with assimilating the wolverine's mana, even if not much of it was fueling her reserve's growth—and a dangerous threat had been dealt with.

By the time she had gotten back to Camp, the light of the sun was illuminating the grasslands, chasing away the last of the storm.

Dorea had a suspicion that her last spell had contributed to weakening it, as from what she had felt, it had enough strength to keep going for a while more. However, she wouldn't voice it as she didn't want to seem too arrogant. Controlling the weather in such a manner was not easy even for Master mages, and to claim to have that kind of power wouldn't endear her to anyone, even if it was partially true.

At the village's gates, she was met by the ever-unflappable Lindus, Yaomi's assistant. The man was easily recognizable, given his tall, thin frame and perfectly groomed mustache.

"Have you been waiting for me?" she asked curiously once she had come to a stop.

"Chief Yaomi informed me that you were getting closer a few minutes ago and instructed me to bring you to her as soon as you arrived," he replied, immediately turning and walking off into the settlement.

Baffled, Dorea followed him. She had known that Yaomi's sensing capabilities were by far greater than hers, but for her to have sensed her minutes before her approach when she was using Air Boost to travel meant that her range must have spanned a dozen miles. That was much farther than even Jonah, who focused almost entirely on that ability.

Well, she did feel that something was amiss while we were running from the Ubag. That should have told me enough. Still, scary.

Undoubtedly, Jonah would eventually eclipse the woman if he kept up his rate of advancement, but it was still very impressive.

When they got to the chief's pavilion, Dorea shook herself out of her contemplations. Inside, she could feel that only Yaomi was present in her tent, without either of her counselors, which told her that it would be a more private conversation.

She walked through the tents, noticing that even in the early morning, the workers seemed to be very active. She didn't pay them any more mind, though, as she got to her stop soon enough.

"Please, go in. The chief is waiting for you," Lindus said, bowing slightly in respect before taking off.

Dorea nodded absentmindedly, ducking in. As she had sensed, only Yaomi was inside, and she appeared to be in the middle of preparing some tea. The woman gestured for the couch opposite hers, and Dorea gratefully sat down, suddenly exhausted after the extended mission.

Though she had spent some time resting as she ate her meals, it hadn't been enough to recover fully from the fight, and the run back hadn't helped. She needed to wash herself and sleep, but the bed would have to wait.

First, she needed to give her report and hear whatever new plan the Witch had cooked up in the meantime. Then she'd need to have a talk with Whitecliff's contingent to keep them abreast of things.

She had decided early on to do it periodically, and it had shown promising results so far. People enjoyed being consulted before big decisions that affected them were made, and even when it came to the little things, having their leader show that they valued their opinion mattered.

After that, though, a war would have to break out before she'd leave her bed.

"I assume you were victorious," the older woman commented lightly as she poured the tea in two copper cups.

"I was. The wolverine was powerful, but being in the middle of a storm gave me the advantage, and since it decided not to run away, I eventually managed to kill it." She didn't mention her spell simply because then she'd need to reveal much of her capabilities. Though Yaomi was someone she had come to trust, Dorea knew the importance of keeping an ace secret.

"And what of the reason behind its behavior?"

Dorea sighed, frustrated at her lack of success in that area. "I scoured the land for anything out of place but couldn't find it. Of course, since I didn't cross the border, I might have missed an obvious clue."

Rather than being disappointed, Yaomi merely nodded in acknowledgment of her words. She then sipped more of the acidic red tea. "I expected as much. Not everything is as clear-cut as the situation with the salamanders. Still, I'm satisfied that you have proved your strength and resourcefulness. You passed this trial as well."

Oh, that's right. I almost forgot the entire reason why I went there.

"Thank you, Chief Yaomi," she replied, not knowing what else to say.

The woman waved her off. "Bah, don't think too much of it. This is mostly mummery to show the people that their leaders are ensuring their future safety. I already knew you were capable enough for the position. Otherwise, I wouldn't have chosen you in the first place."

Dorea just blinked, too tired to get angry at having been sent off to fight a dangerous foe for such a vapid reason.

"We'll talk more about this in the future, but I wanted you to know I'm confident in my choice. Keep pushing yourself, Dorea; power will come to you by itself."

You have no idea how right you are.

* * *

Whitecliff's mages were more considerate of her state than Yaomi had been, and after a short debrief, they had pushed her to get some rest.

Nothing too important was on the horizon, so she could take a few hours to nap. Nora had evidently been the mind behind it, having convinced the others that they didn't need to keep her for too long, and Dorea gratefully nodded to her as she exited the communal tent.

The atmosphere had been festive as word spread that she had passed Yaomi's test and defeated a powerful beast, and she could see the curiosity in her friends' faces to know how exactly she had done it.

That they had contained themselves was a greater gift than she had expected, and she gratefully went off to rest. As soon as she had cleaned herself with some conjured water and had lain down on the bed, she immediately fell asleep.

It seemed that she had been even more exhausted than she had thought because she didn't dream of anything—lately, her worries for Whitecliff's safety and the possibility of another front opening in the south had been disturbing her sleep.

When she woke up, the sun had passed its zenith and was now well into its descent. The heat of the summer, especially in the grasslands, where there was little natural shade, would have been almost debilitating, but magic made short work of that kind of concern.

Thus, Dorea exited her tent refreshed and ready to face the day's responsibilities. Before she could reach the communal space, a familiar signature's approach stopped her in her tracks.

Masi, it seemed, had homed in on her and was quickly walking in her direction. The boy didn't have the luck of having either the wind or water at his beck and call, but it seemed that being a Heidel gave him some sort of resistance to the heat since he didn't have any sweat on him.

"Dorea!" he called, waving from the distance. The streets were surprisingly busy, given the time of the day, but she supposed that with it being summer, most people would wait until the hottest hours had passed before going about their business.

"I heard you've come back and wanted to congratulate you."

Dorea silently looked at the boy, trying to discern his angle. Masi had been behaving weirdly since their ill-fated battle with the Ubag mage, and it seemed that that trend would continue. "Thank you. It wasn't easy, but I managed."

He looked hesitant, as if he wanted to speak of some great secret or as if afraid of offending her with his words. Rather than waiting for him to gather his courage, the blonde simply decided to take things into her own hands. She grabbed his wrist and pulled him alongside her, not giving his sputtering any mind.

She walked for a few minutes before stopping at the river's bank. Though it was mostly used for drinking, if one went downstream, they were allowed to bathe and clean their clothes. Dorea wanted to do neither, but she'd gladly take advantage of the cool breeze and relaxing atmosphere.

Finally, she plopped down on the sandy shore and looked up at Masi expectantly. A few seconds of silence later, he sighed. "I was being a bit weird, wasn't I?"

"We are friends, Masi. If you need to tell me something, you can just go ahead and say it," she replied.

He dropped next to her, sitting cross-legged as he watched the river flow by. "Sorry. It's just been a difficult period. I thought I had my life kind of figured out. It turns out that I had made a ton of assumptions and needed to reevaluate most things."

Even as he spoke, it sounded like he was still processing his thoughts, so Dorea remained quiet and gave him the time he needed. She had nothing urgent to do, and though they hadn't known each other for that long, she considered Masi to be one of the few people who could understand the weight she was under.

The boy ruffled his hair, huffing in frustration. "What I'm trying to say is that the things that happened in the last few weeks have made me reconsider my place in the tribe and the alliance in general."

It didn't take a genius to realize that he had been spooked by his inability to do anything to help against the Ubag mage and that seeing how much Yaomi was openly relying on her had shown him that he wouldn't end up as chief.

"The things we are facing require complete unity to win against, and though I had believed that I could eventually become strong enough to shield our people, it is now evident to me that you are much more suited to that duty than I," he finally stated, looking directly at her.

He seemed to have found some courage, and the resolution in his voice firmed up as he spoke. Dorea took a moment to let his words hang in the air, considering all their implications.

It sounded to her that, more than a simple acknowledgment, Masi was fundamentally recognizing her bid for leadership and saying he wouldn't oppose it. He was even open to supporting it.

I kind of hate that this is what I have to deal with all my life now. Instead of chatting with my friends and talking about inane things, I need to negotiate and do all I can to secure power. I know why I have to do it, but I still hate it.

"Does that mean that you'll be endorsing me?" she asked quietly.

Though Yaomi's will was paramount, and most Heidels wouldn't dare gainsay her even on such matters, if she could get the most obvious candidate from their tribe to support her, she'd have a much easier time when things came to a head.

"That's what I'm saying. I saw just how much more than anyone else you work. Saw how much you care. And to be led by someone like you would be an honor," he solemnly replied.

For all that magic made things much easier on women, Dorea knew that men generally didn't like being led by the fairer sex. It was only in cases of absolute supremacy, like with Yaomi, that no one complained.

Masi was a young man with a bright future. He had been groomed for leadership, and Dorea knew that the promise of power could do terrible things to people. For him to voluntarily concede that his bid was unrealistic and, even more, to throw his support behind her, touched her deeply.

"Thank you," Dorea said sincerely. "This means a lot to me. I respect you, both as a mage and as a person, and your support makes my heart full."

They were two teenagers enjoying the breeze on the river's banks. They were two powerful mages who had just decided the future of the alliance. Both were true at the same time.

Dorea decided, at that moment, that too much was at stake for her to do this half-heartedly. She would stop grumbling, even to herself, and try to adopt a more positive outlook. People she trusted believed in her, and that meant it was worth seriously trying.

CHAPTER THIRTY-ONE

Even as she sped through the grasslands, Dorea lamented the need to slow down to allow the other mages to keep up with her.

She was taking two people along with her Air Boost, while Masi was blitzing by thanks to his Lightning Enhancement. Since the nature of his spell made him dangerous to be close to, he couldn't bring anyone else with him, which meant that they had to wait for the remaining six mages to catch up every once in a while.

When the alarm had sounded that a patrol in the stretch of land where they had met the Kamadari group had been attacked, Dorea had been ready to go there by herself, unburdened by anyone else.

Yaomi, however, had a different idea, and since she was still very much in charge, they all had to obey.

Thus, a contingent of ten mages had been gathered, all capable of using their own mobility spells, and sent to retake the occupied territory. The unfortunate fact was that, though everyone could travel much faster than a normal human, or even one riding a horse, there was a significant difference between Dorea and Masi and everyone else.

Still, she gritted her teeth and went along with it. No one was in danger at the moment. The attacked patrol had returned to Camp, where Yaomi's presence would shield them, and though it was frustrating to think of the southerners taking what they wanted as if they had a right to it, it wasn't an immediate emergency.

The trip took them six hours, much longer than it would have had she been alone, but when she got there, she realized that having some backup might not have been such a bad idea.

Dorea finally dropped Air Boost atop a hill that overlooked the flat plains. She then lowered Nora and Eol to the ground, ensuring they touched down softly.

"Ugh, I never want to have to do that again," her friend complained, holding her stomach. The taciturn Heidel, on the other hand, merely grunted in discomfort. He was a good battler, but his skill at moving around still required some work, which meant he had to acquiesce to being pulled along as if he were a package.

Dorea could have taken everyone alongside her—she had done it while flying away from the Mondean camp in the forest, after all—but the speed would have been even slower than what they made. Though it wouldn't have taxed her too much, she still wanted to be fully ready for the battle that was sure to come.

While I have a good way of refilling my reserves, that doesn't mean I should rely on it to always save my ass. Getting to a fight already tired is just plain stupid.

From the hill, it quickly became apparent that a bigger contingent than they had been told about had taken residence. Dorea counted more than twenty people, most feeling like mages. The few nonmagicals were relegated to the back lines, where they were working on setting up a camp in what appeared to be an effort to occupy the zone for more than just the short term.

That, of course, couldn't be allowed. While the alliance didn't necessarily need the territory now, it still held strategic importance in case the Ergasters ever decided to move against them, and having it stolen from beneath their noses would be a significant loss.

In the end, they couldn't leave them be, even if the fight looked to be much harder than what they had expected. If they waited for much longer in an effort to scout them out, Dorea fully expected them to set up defensive structures and maybe for even more people to arrive. If that were the case, their only recourse would be a shameful retreat. Yaomi would have to get involved, turning a border dispute into an all-out war.

And that's something we really want to avoid. Though we can't just ignore them, and I fully intend to make them pay for attacking our patrol, for the Witch of Immolation to come here would be taken as an existential threat by the new city.

And these people were from the city. Katmasou was known to be the colder of the two, standing beneath the shadow of a great red rock, and the clothing of the invaders appeared to show that.

For desert people, they dressed heavier than she would have expected, which meant that they generally didn't expect to be under the sun for long.

Of course, since the city's settling was such a recent thing, it was impossible to tell if these were the genuine article, a group from Kamadar meant to deceive them, or even from an unrelated tribe. Still, given their coordination and the quantity of mages present, Dorea believed it could only be one of the first two possibilities.

Considering how well the trade and diplomatic relations with Kamadar had been going ever since she had managed to establish a point of contact—incidentally, in the vicinity of the now-occupied area—she doubted they were involved. They simply had too much to lose in case they were discovered, and the gain they'd get if their possible deception succeeded was too small.

Having met and talked with Tobu, the leader of the Kamadari mission that they encountered almost two weeks before, Dorea knew that such foolishness didn't belong to them.

No, the most likely explanation was that things were exactly as they appeared. The Katmasousi needed freshwater, and the strategic position of the stretch of land that directly connected the desert to the river was significant.

Now that they had finally managed to build up their city enough to be functioning, they were turning their eyes outward, ready to fulfill their long-term needs.

She suspected they had something that gave them the confidence to survive Yaomi's wrath—possibly a Master mage of their own, though even then, few were the woman's equal—and they were now probing to see what the alliance's response would be.

That meant they needed to bring swift and complete retribution. In such cases, being too soft simply meant that the enemy would continue taking until one had nothing left to give.

Dorea didn't want to completely wipe them out, as that could possibly show too much aggressiveness. Yaomi had, much to her surprise, agreed with her assessment.

If possible, she would kill a couple, hurt a dozen, and let the others live to bring their comrades back, alongside a message not to mess with the alliance.

Masi had been more for complete annihilation but had acquiesced when she had explained her plan. Shock and Awe would be the name of the game, and Dorea wanted the whole thing to be over in just a few minutes.

That, more than the death of everyone, would send a message. That they were perfectly capable of killing them all but had refrained for the moment. It would show the Katmasousi that they weren't there to play around, that their territory wasn't up for grabs, but also that they weren't bloodthirsty maniacs like the Mondeans.

Knowing that the enemy at your border is ready and willing to exterminate your people is a very good motivator to throw yourself in the fight. If, instead, that very enemy, though powerful and brutal when provoked, shows no intention to hurt you, well, then the rational thing to do is to wait until you build up your strength enough to defend yourself and, in the meantime, to keep as low a profile as possible.

It was a big gamble, Dorea knew. If the fight didn't go as planned—and that was a genuine possibility, given the numbers involved—they could have a new front to which they needed to dedicate their resources.

But no other choice was possible; on this much, everyone had agreed. Even Seshi, the elderly but strangely young-looking earth mage, had admitted it was a good plan.

He had then personally committed himself to the defense of the south in case the whole thing was a diversion to get them to split their forces. Dorea didn't exactly know what the man planned on doing there or how he intended to hold off an entire invasion alone, but he had shown himself to be strangely resourceful, and she trusted him to keep his word.

Yaomi, as always, would serve as the last defense for Camp and the entire southern area of the alliance. In case of an Ergaster incursion, she would be the first to take the field.

But there were no signs of that for the moment, and as such, Dorea refocused on the current situation.

The camp building looked to be proceeding slower than she expected, mostly because none of the mages seemed interested in helping the nonmagicals. Indeed, they even looked disgusted at their presence the few times they bothered to glance at them.

It was a fascinating, if slightly sad, look at how things could have gone in Whitecliff if she or one of the others with influence with the Gifted had allowed such behavior to take root.

It had seemed unconscionable to her, treating her dad, mom, and sister as lesser people simply because they hadn't been in the correct age range to receive the Mother's Gift. But not everyone shared the same opinion.

If she hadn't made it clear early on that such behavior wasn't acceptable, the same thing could be happening in her village too.

Shaking her head to refocus, Dorea checked if everyone else in her group had recovered from their long trip.

Not all have the same luck as me or Masi in the quantity of mana. While these are all good mages, it doesn't mean that they don't have weaknesses. And my job as their leader is to dampen those as much as possible.

It took another fifteen minutes before the last one gave her the sign.

"All right, people, you all know what we are here for. Hit hard, hit fast. Make sure not to be too directly lethal, but allow them no quarter. If you ever feel overwhelmed, send the signal we agreed upon, and I'll come to your rescue as quickly as possible."

Everyone looked grim. Though they were all veterans of several battles, it was never easy to throw yourself in danger—especially against a numerically superior enemy—and the jitters were to be expected.

"Do not target the nonmagicals unless they take up arms. Keep your senses peeled, even in the chaos, as getting hit from a different enemy than the mage you are fighting is the most common way for anyone to die on the battlefield," she finished. It wasn't a grand speech, but that was more Voggo's forte. Her thing was incredible power and tenacity, and she was more than ready to unleash both.

She raised her hand, counted to three, and lowered it in a quick movement. With that, the fight began.

Spells flashed by, accompanied by her own Lightning Sphere aimed at what looked like the Katmasousi leader.

Dorea didn't stop to see what happened to the man and instead cast a barrage of Bullets immediately after, aimed more at confusing the already chaotic scene.

Screams erupted from the camp as people were thrown back after being hit, whole limbs were sent flying away, blades of air descended upon them with viciousness, and lightning crackled, blackening the soil.

Shields started flashing into existence shortly after, but the damage was already done. Though the Katmasousi had been arranged in a decently defensive formation, the gaps created by the sneak attack ensured that several more spells could find their targets.

The detonations of her Exploding Water Bullets didn't directly affect anyone, as she had planned, but they did send a group of three mages that were putting up a good combination air shield flying, disrupting their defenses even more.

Dorea felt good. The mana she had absorbed from the wolverine had not directly increased her reserves but empowered her body. She was sturdier than before, now able to arm-wrestle Tom fairly. She still lost most of the time, but it was a world of difference compared to before.

That increased physicality was what saved her, as her senses screamed that something very dangerous was hurtling her way. Dorea dropped and rolled away, barely avoiding something extremely heavy as it hit the ground next to her.

With the corner of her eye, she was surprised to notice an ice chunk before she snapped to attention and raised her Bulwark. Several more hailstones hit it, making the barrier wobble, but she managed to protect herself and Nora, who was standing close to her.

Dorea pushed herself up and looked around. There, at the back of the camp, where she had believed only the nonmagicals were, a burly man was standing. His hair was white as snow, as was his skin, save for the tribal tattoos around his ribs.

He wore simple linen pants that cut off above the knees and nothing above that, showing off a scarred but muscular torso.

Above the man's head rotated three more large hailstones, as big as a pig's head. They hummed dangerously, and Dorea knew that being hit by one, increased strength or not, would mean her death.

She realized she had made a severe blunder, but luckily, no one had to pay for it. Therefore, she focused all her efforts on ensuring it would remain so. However much she would have enjoyed casting Heart of the Storm, there wasn't enough time for it, nor was she strong enough to protect her allies from its catastrophic power.

There was much that she could do beyond that, though. She rose up into the air, stopping a hundred feet above her companions to make herself a target. It seemed to work, as immediately, she was pelted with attacks of all kinds alongside several of the dangerous balls of ice she had seen before.

Though Dorea had never fought with an ice mage before and didn't have at her disposal its natural counter element, fire, she had several options to choose from, thanks to what she had read in Whitecliff's archives.

When fighting away from snowy mountains, ice mages had little to work with from the environment, meaning that they needed to expend much more mana to cast their spells.

Unfortunately, she couldn't draw him in a slugfest since she wasn't alone. However, she could deliberately target his constructs, rather than him—he was much more likely to prefer abandoning them rather than attempting to shield them—and force him to expend himself.

That, however, wasn't to her tastes. Thanks to her advantages, Dorea had built her style by boldly attacking, never backing down and surpassing all her enemies. Using Water Bullets might end up giving him more ammunition, so she was left with her first and original spell.

Lightning Spheres roared through the air, looking like miniature suns falling upon her enemies. For once, Dorea let go. She allowed herself not to worry about keeping some mana in reserve. After all, if she failed here, the entire thing would end up in a rout, and she couldn't allow it.

That meant she pushed everything she had accumulated in many months of hard work into an unending barrage of Lightning Spheres.

The light coming from the spells was so blinding that even some of her companions had to stop what they were doing and protect their eyes. Still, she kept going. Where her reserves had once been a puddle, they were now a lake, and she would use it all.

The danger of an unknown element, alongside the greater numbers of their enemy, meant that she couldn't really go at it with the soft touch she had wanted to. Still, she tried to aim only in the general direction of the ice mage so as to hopefully leave enough alive that her message would still be sent.

Power flowed through her veins at speeds unmatched before. Even her usage of Heart of the Storm had been more external. This time, she was the one supplying all the power.

The air was thick with ozone as the continuous buzzing of her spells resounded, interrupted only by the eventual angry crackling when they hit their target. Dorea pressed for even more. She wasn't sure if the man was still alive, but she would do so since this was about sending a message—even if not precisely in the way she had envisioned.

She had long since lost all sensation in her hands, as the sheer amount of mana that flowed through them numbed them down, coupled with their vicinity to such powerful lightning spells.

With a primal roar, Dorea unleashed the final barrage. Five more Spheres left her hands, draining her almost to the bottom. Their trajectory was too quick to follow with naked eyes, but the light they left behind showed their path.

They all went where she had wanted to. However, a dust cloud covered the battlefield, meaning she couldn't see if they had hit their targets.

Exhausted, without even the mana left to conjure a gust of wind to clear the air, Dorea finally felt a rush of cooling power entering her system.

The ice mage was dead.

INTERLUDE

Tobu

The campfire's smoke lazily drifted up, lending the area a hazy atmosphere as if it were a dream.

It wasn't the first time that Tobu had seen Tutanq work his craft, but it still had that mystical quality that made it seem almost impossible.

Magic was something he knew very well by now. He had become famous for his own skill with the winds between his people. But what the shaman was working on baffled him and fascinated him at the same time.

Tobu could easily defeat the man in a fight; he could conjure blades of wind that could cut through stone. But using a campfire's smoke to peer into faraway lands was somehow much more magical.

"It's almost ready, boy. Come over here if you want to have a good look." Tutanq's soft voice shook him out of his contemplation. He was a tall man, though hunched with age. His skin was weather beaten, giving it an ancient quality, but his eyes were a luminous amber, showing his bright intellect.

Tobu smiled at the elderly man and joined him in four quick strides. He sat on the log next to him, ready to experience the magic of far-sight again.

"However much you might have changed with the years, this still remains the same, huh?" Tutanq commented, a melancholic smile painted on his features.

The old man was not directly related to him, but he had served as a surrogate grandfather, being his natural one's best friend and taking on the role when the man had been killed many years before.

They had spent long hours during Tobu's childhood just spying upon the great beasts that held the ancient cities. Some might have considered it too much for a young child, but his fascination with magic had been well known to everyone.

I'm still eternally grateful to the Spirits that I managed to make the cutoff for the Trial. I don't think I could have lived with myself had I missed it.

Tobu was self-aware enough to realize that, even had he been too old for conventional wisdom, he likely would have tried. He would have died in the process, but that was a better fate than being magic-less while his friends received the Gift.

"You know me. If magic is being done, I want to know everything I can about it." The young man grinned, stroking his beard.

Finally, the smoke seemed to condense into actual images. There were no colors, just as he was used to, but given the short distance between their camp and the events they were spying upon, the detail was excellent.

Small figures, easily recognizable as the Katmasousi contingent, were busy setting up a semipermanent camp or as lookouts.

On the other side, behind a milky white hill, a smaller group emerged.

Even with the great detail of the smoke figures, it took Tobu a while to recognize the leader as Dorea, the girl he had encountered days before.

She appeared to be very trusted and, given the dangers involved in the upcoming fight, also quite powerful if the command had been given to her.

"Are you sure we cannot help them?" Jang asked from the other side, curiously peering at the smoke.

"I have already explained why. Too much can go wrong here, and though the Katmasousi were always going to throw themselves at the alliance, if we manage to reduce the scope of the conflict, we'll all be better off," Tobu replied. Emotionally, he wanted to agree with Jang, but he had to consider too many other moving parts, and getting Kamadar involved in the upcoming fight was not a good idea, even if abandoning their new allies so soon left a bad taste.

It was an old argument, and Jang wouldn't do more than grumble about it, but the boy still didn't like having to sit back. He had managed to grow into a powerful water mage in his own right—mostly thanks to his efforts in beating back the beasts of the desert and patrolling the walls of their city against bandit raids—and having to watch a fight without intervening must have been against his instincts.

Still, he settled back down, tugging at his dark locks as he watched the alliance group set up for a blitz attack.

"Smart of them, trying to hit them hard and fast. Given the disparity in numbers, they have to do something like that to get the upper hand," Tobu commented, observing the smoke.

"The girl seems to have something up her sleeve," Tutanq shared, pointing with an aged finger to where Dorea appeared to be setting up.

His words turned out almost prophetic, as all hell was unleashed upon the Katmasousi. Spells flashed by, the smoke struggling to give them shape before they touched the ground.

The absence of color made it difficult to recognize what elements were being used, but even this much was extremely valuable information.

What they gathered watching the battle rage on was almost priceless. The best of the alliance's new guard against one of Katmasou's infamous assault teams. Whatever the result ended up being, Tobu was sure that both sides would suffer some losses.

Then, the tide shifted. The Katmasousi—seemingly almost done for—gained some space as a mage from the back lines started pelting the alliance with large spheres. It wasn't possible to understand what they were from the smoke, but considering how much they shook the shields they hit, Tobu would wager that they were solid constructs.

"Seems like the rumor that they have an ice mage is true, then."

The others nodded, their eyes fixed on the still raging battle.

Surprisingly, instead of being pushed back and having to flee like he might have expected, Dorea's smoky figure seemed to rally. Spells started flashing from her, dozens and dozens of them, all coming from the same source.

It became almost impossible to see what was happening on the Katmasousi side of the battlefield as the magic rained down upon them like the wrath of an angry goddess.

Silence had fallen upon the group as they struggled to take in the absurd sight. Finally, Tutanq shook himself out of his stupor and waved his hand through the smoke, removing the curtain hiding the bombardment's consequences.

A desolate sight greeted them. The landscape had been turned into a wasteland as the extremely powerful electric currents burned everything down. Everyone within their radius had been annihilated, so much so that Tobu struggled to even recognize their remains.

Of the ice mage who had been standing in the middle of it, nothing was left. He had simply ceased to exist. Such was the might that had been leveled against him that he probably didn't even have the time to realize the error of his ways.

"What the absolute fuck?!"

The sentiment was a shared one, as they all attempted to reconcile the confident but still young girl they had met with the monster they had just witnessed.

"Is she a Master?" another asked, still staring incredulously at the desolate crater that was where once had been the beginning of a settlement.

"No, not yet. But she's closer than anyone I know," the elderly shaman replied, his eyes unerringly pointed upon Dorea's form.

The girl wobbled a bit before one of her companions came to her rescue and offered her some help. She had evidently exhausted herself with such a terrifying show, but what she had displayed today would mean a redrawing of their plans.

We can't afford to alienate her. No, more than that, we need to get on her good side. I don't know if she was abnormally strong from the beginning or if she's a freak that grows faster than anyone I know, but this level of power cannot be ignored. She'll become a Master if she continues like this, and she won't take long either.

To their further surprise, the girl needed only a couple of minutes before she was good enough to stand up by herself, seemingly having shaken the exhaustion in another baffling display.

"That's not possible. It can't be possible, right?" Jang asked.

It wasn't, everyone knew. And still, Dorea walked up to the few survivors—looking as if she hadn't just dumped enough mana to fill four normal mages—and started speaking to them.

Smoky Vision did not allow sound to travel, and as such, they would never know what exactly she had told them, but from the looks of it, the Katmasousi didn't appear to find anything worth fighting about with her demands.

After a display like that, she would be entitled to ask for a lot, having shown herself perfectly capable of taking all their lives if needed, but rather than beginning the traditional negotiations for ransom, she appeared to wave them off.

Apparently not worried at all about possible reprisal—not that they would be able to do much since they were likely all too exhausted from protecting themselves from the backlash of her anger—Dorea then left them there, standing in the ashes of their comrades, cradling their injuries.

She simply gathered her companions and left without a backward glance.

CHAPTER THIRTY-TWO

We shouldn't expect the southerners to show any intelligence now, after having been bereft of it for so long." Mort's words were tinged with a personal distaste, and generally, Dorea would have been inclined toward rejecting such broad statements out of hand, but she knew all too well that you couldn't expect your enemy to act accordingly to logic.

"I agree." She sighed. "I would like to think that I have left enough of an impression on them, but I sincerely doubt that the ice mage was their only surprise."

She was sitting at the ornate table at the back of the administrative tent, where Yaomi resided. It had been a couple of days since she returned from the punitive mission, and things had finally settled down enough that a meeting to discuss their future moves had been called.

"If they have truly managed to claim a city for their own and have gathered enough people under their banner to fill at least the basic population needs of one, we should expect them to have much more than what they showed us," Seshi commented, reminding them all that they weren't facing isolated tribes anymore.

Mort seemed to agree with that as he nodded while stroking his mustache. "Their numbers can make our lives difficult, especially if we have to maintain readiness for possible attacks from the north and the east," he commented, looking at his chief to see if she had anything to add.

"Open war should still be a last resort, but we need to keep an eye on the border and be seen doing it, to discourage them from getting any ideas," was her answer. It wasn't a particularly satisfactory one to the elders, Dorea knew, as they had been getting increasingly frustrated with Yaomi about her decision to dedicate an almost equal force to patrolling the east—where nothing seemed to be moving—compared to the south, where the possibility of a conflict was very real.

It was an old argument between them, but the Witch of Immolation didn't appear to be any closer to changing her mind.

In a way, Dorea could understand her. Yaomi was the only one who could put up a fight if the Ergasters ever attacked, and having gone through the last war, she likely wanted to prevent its horrors again.

Still, that didn't mean Dorea agreed. There was a difference between being prepared and overly cautious, and she said so. "We should relocate a few of the teams patrolling the eastern border down south. Of course, some should still be left, but in the unlikely case of an Ergaster invasion, twenty more mages won't do anything, while they are sorely needed for a possible fight with the Katmasousi."

She braced herself for a verbal smackdown—until now, Dorea had only ever given suggestions when asked and had carefully steered clear of looking like she wanted more control over how things were run in Camp—but it unexpectedly didn't come.

Instead, Yaomi chuckled, looking all too pleased. "See, I told you she had some fire in her. She's not just a pretty face with a strong punch."

The two elders, too, looked happy, evidently having been waiting for her to intercede on their behalf.

Huh? What? Wait, does this mean that this whole charade where they went back and forth, arguing for what was obviously the better option but never convincing her was just another test to see if I would have the courage to disagree with Yaomi?

In a way, it made sense. Dorea had shown herself capable of leading men in a fight, overpowering powerful beasts, and negotiating important deals. Those were all fundamental qualities for a future leader.

But until now, she had yet to actively disagree with Yaomi—the woman who, with just a word, could put an end to her aspirations—especially in a matter that chiefly regarded the Heidels.

Dorea was well aware that Voggo and the others in Whitecliff's council wouldn't necessarily have taken it well if Masi had disagreed with them in a meeting where they were discussing their defensive strategies.

The three elders had baited her with an inane argument just to see if she would stay silent in an effort to remain on Yaomi's good side. And she had passed, luckily. It seemed like the tests they planned for her were not necessarily limited to her magical might, but she should have expected it.

"All right," she sighed. "Now that I have met your expectations, can we actually get to the planning bit?"

The planning, it turned out, had already been done. Three teams would be sent to the contested stretch of land on a semipermanent basis, much like what the Katmasousi had attempted to do when she ambushed them.

They would keep an eye on things, show that the alliance had an active interest in the area, and hopefully head off any more confrontations.

Yeah, right. If people could be so reasonable, we wouldn't be here in the first place.

Power, it turned out, only made humans greedier for more. The Mondeans' success in conquering their neighbors hadn't sated them at all. Instead, they had embarked on a war to get the entire region beneath their feet.

Dorea was afraid that the same might be happening here. The Katmasousi didn't appear to have the same bloodthirsty leadership, but that didn't mean they wouldn't do it too.

People did horrible things for all sorts of reasons, and conquering an important natural resource and strategic area would be more than enough as motivations went.

"Are we sure our presence will be needed after all you've done to them?" Nora asked from her side.

The girl was the only other mage from Whitecliff present for this operation, and after having witnessed Dorea's might firsthand, she was sticking close by. Several chunks of ice that would have taken her head had been stopped by the Wind Bulwark the blonde had employed, and the brunette was very grateful for it.

"Hope for the best, prepare for the worst," Dorea replied. It was a motto she was becoming increasingly in tune with. If nothing happened in the valley, and she could spend the last week of her rotation in peace, she would do so gratefully, but she expected at least a few probing attacks to come.

More realistically, the Katmasousi would send a punitive mission of their own to avenge their people. Considering how she had killed a valuable ice mage, they must have been furious.

That's also a reason why I agreed to come here again. Information about the southerners—as Voggo asked me to collect—is essential, but more than that, I don't want anyone to get hurt because of my actions.

It wasn't a logical thought, she knew. Skirmishes and grudges had always existed between these people and would continue long after she was dust, but still, she wanted to be present to at least take on the bulk of it herself.

The valley they arrived at was exactly as she had left it, sans the corpses of the men far enough from her bombardment to not be vaporized but close enough that shielding didn't help.

Either someone had buried them, as was proper, or the wild animals had taken them. Dorea hoped it wasn't the latter but decided she had bigger things to worry about.

"Let's start setting up, people. Tents first, then we'll begin the rotations, as I explained before. If anyone needs anything, you know where to find me."

That said, she set off to find a good spot for her tent. They had decided to settle high up on the hill where she attacked from so as to give them a better view of their surroundings and also because no one wanted to sleep where a dozen people had been incinerated.

The real objective of the Katmasousi—the wide river that curved eastward from the grasslands, taking in all its rivulets and streams to make a singular impressive body of water—was a few miles to their east.

They could have set up directly there, of course, but since it technically wasn't in alliance territory, to do so would mean losing the moral high ground.

It might not have seemed very important when dealing with barbarians, but Dorea agreed with Yaomi that they shouldn't lower themselves to their level. Also, equally important, they had no need for the river, and taking it just to establish an outpost there and have to constantly supply it was an expenditure they could do without.

Had the alliance not been so pressed to repel the Mondeans, they might have been able to dedicate time and effort to putting the entire grasslands under their control, but as things stood, it was just a dream.

Camp was the only permanent settlement of the area, but several more nomadic tribes lived within it, and though none of them could put up much of a fight against their might, if they joined together they might become annoying to deal with.

That, and Yaomi simply doesn't have any desire to expand the territory under her protection. With the forging of the alliance, she has already pushed her ability to act to the limit. Adding even more would mean renouncing her decision to protect every inch of land she considered hers.

It was a weird hang-up, but Dorea respected it. Not many Masters were willing to forsake conquest and glory just to defend their people and their way of life. It did the old woman honor.

"We're basically done with the standard encampment. To make it more permanent will take a couple of days, considering the patrolling schedule, but things should proceed on time," Nora informed her from the other side of the hill, using one of Jonah's many nifty spells, Whispering Wind.

I miss him. For all that he's not suited to direct combat, having him here would allow us much greater security. Just his sensing, without needing to move, would let him monitor a good bit of the river from here.

That kind of absurd range couldn't be acquired by simply working on it. No, the boy had a monstrous talent for it and had dedicated himself to wringing it for every drop.

"All right, give the go-ahead, and let's get this thing started," Dorea replied, using the same spell.

* * *

A day after they had arrived at the valley, the patrols picked up some movement from the south.

It had been what Dorea and Camp's leaders had expected their enemies to do—avoiding a direct confrontation by taking the long way to get to the river—but there wasn't much they could do about it.

The river wasn't in their lands, and so they had no intention of fighting the southerners over access to it. That had been their promise to the Kamadari, and they intended to keep it.

Still, just because they had gotten there peacefully didn't mean their intentions were good. It would require simply too many resources—even for a city with several water mages in its employ—to divert the river's course through the desert. That it would also affect the Ergasters and thus bring their unwanted attention meant they were unlikely to do it. That left just the option of passing through alliance land.

That could be achieved in only one of two ways. Through a diplomatic agreement, like the Kamadari had done, or through force, like the Katmasousi had attempted once before, and like what Dorea expected them to do again.

Not now, though. They seem perfectly content just setting up close to the river for the moment.

"How long do you think we have before they start poking at us?" Nora asked.

Dorea turned to face her friend, taking in her furrowed brow and clenched fingers. "I'd say a day or so. Just enough for them to get the lay of the land, learn something about our numbers, and prepare a plan."

The brunette hummed, looking in the river's direction as though trying to peer at what the Katmasousi were doing.

"Should we do something before that, then? Try to scare them off?"

Dorea sighed. She would have liked that to be possible, but if they hadn't gotten the message after what she had done to the first group they sent, she doubted anything would do it.

"We don't know if they have any hostile intentions yet," interjected Eol, the air mage she had first met during the initial exchange between Camp and Whitecliff. The teen had grown up a lot in the last few months, going from a short five-foot-two to almost six feet, and didn't appear to be stopping anytime soon. He had also gotten less quiet as he got to know them better and felt more comfortable.

Still, Dorea considered him to be a bit naive. "I wish that could be true, but they really don't have a good way of accessing the river by going through the long route south. They need this stretch of land, and since they don't appear interested in negotiating, force is all they have left," she explained.

He didn't seem that convinced, though—surprisingly so, given that he had participated in the last battle as well. " Just because they need it doesn't mean they'll do it. And I'm not convinced they actually do need it. We don't know what their subterranean reserves are like," he said, looking at her weirdly, as if trying to gauge her reaction.

Eol seemingly switched tracks when he saw that she was listening but didn't appear too engaged. "It might be that they simply wanted this place as a strategic staging point against the Ergasters."

Dorea gave him a long look to see if he was actually serious. "I can understand your first point, but do you genuinely think that a newly settled city, still in its infancy and with all the problems its newness brings, would seek conflict with a foe they know they cannot defeat? I could understand if they mobilized against minor tribes, as absorbing their people and taking their resources could help, but this is foolish."

The Heidel teen didn't appear to take that too well and quickly stormed off, a pronounced frown on his face.

"Was that too harsh?" Dorea asked Nora, confused at the reaction.

The brunette sighed, patting her hand in comfort. "He was trying to impress you with his knowledge and insight, but then you went and destroyed his point. He'll get over it, don't worry."

It took Dorea an embarrassingly long time before she realized what exactly she meant by that. Eol was, apparently, interested in her as a girl and had tried to show off his knowledge to look attractive.

Dorea was no stranger to that kind of interaction, but ever since she had gained her powers, relationships had been the furthest thing from her mind.

Rupert's death was still a wound on her heart, barely scabbed over and threatening to open again. The thought of seeing someone like that was simply too much.

She hadn't minded Masi's proposal too much, but that was simply because he had been so matter-of-fact with it. He had stated the way he saw things and given her a deal. It had felt more like a diplomatic matter between tribes rather than the emotional mess she was used to. He also hadn't pushed her when she made it clear she wasn't about to accept immediately.

Eol, for all that he was turning into a handsome young man, had never crossed her mind as a potential partner—not that others had, to be entirely honest.

"Ugh. I can't deal with this right now," Dorea complained, scratching her head in frustration. She had been given command of the operation, and if she wanted to have any hopes of preventing all-out war and keeping the incoming conflict to a low simmer, she'd need her whole mental faculties.

"What is going on inside his head?! Does this look like the place to be wooing ladies? We are a few feet away from the site of a massacre, for the Goddess's sake. Just, just . . . Argh!"

Nora laughed silently at her complaining, apparently delighting in seeing the unflappable leader so rattled by such a small matter.

"We're all teenagers, Dorea. Though no one dared bother you before, it's perfectly normal to do this kind of thing. We do it in Whitecliff, they do it here, and I don't doubt even the Mondeans do it. It's just the way of the world, I'm afraid," the brunette explained, twirling a lock of hair.

"Does that mean that when I'm not there, you guys spend all the time flirting and stuff? Ugh."

This time, Nora's laughter was audible as she held her stomach. "Oh Goddess, that's too funny. Imagine, the moment you leave, we all turn into lovestruck fools." She wiped a tear from her eye, still chuckling. "No, it's not that bad. It's just that you can be a bit intimidating to boys, and no one wants to look bad in front of you. We all respect you too much for that."

That was an unexpected consequence of her fame. Dorea hadn't considered that she might have become unapproachable. *Well, that's not true. I did notice that not many people sought to talk to me, but I attributed it to me simply being too angry and emotional all the time—because of my mutation—and hadn't considered that they might simply be intimidated by me as a person.*

Their talk, unfortunately, was interrupted by a shout from the lookout. "They have started moving in this direction. Everyone, prepare!"

CHAPTER THIRTY-THREE

Dorea might have expected to have more time before a confrontation, but she had still prepared in case things started off immediately.

"Everyone to your positions. Hold your fire until I give the signal!" she called out, helped by her wind manipulation in making sure everyone heard it.

Though she doubted the Katmasousi were coming for a chat, she still wouldn't attack first. Technically, they were trespassing, but she would try to give them a chance as long as they weren't overtly hostile.

It might be naive to think that peace is still an option, especially after what I did to the group they sent here to settle the land, but I have to try. And if they show themselves to be hostile, well, I will have no mercy, then.

Not all of the southerners that had settled close to the river appeared to be coming in their direction, but from what the lookouts told her, Dorea expected that they had left behind only the nonmagicals.

"The ones still there are continuing with the construction operations. It seems like they have acquired thousands of bricks, but we had no knowledge of those before," Tumul, a water mage, told her. The eighteen-year-old was a good fighter, specializing mostly in long-range spells, but his main strength was information gathering.

His sensing, though not nearly as extensive as Jonah's, was accurate to an incredible degree, and he had developed a spell to show with his waters what he was feeling.

If he had not known about the bricks before, and since no one had been observed to be coming in, the only possible explanation was that they had a mage capable of making those bricks on the spot.

"Likely an earth mage, then," Dorea commented out loud. "Are you sure they weren't made of metal or ice?" she asked Tumul.

He shook his head in denial. "No, if they were ice, I'd be able to feel them much better. If they were metal, I'd feel nothing at all. I think it's clay, and they have enough water in them that I can sense them now that I know they are there."

Clay meant earth magic. A specialized kind of earth magic, even. Just like not all air mages liked making gusts of wind, not all earth mages wanted simply to move the earth beneath their feet.

Of course, they'd still be perfectly capable of it, especially if they were from the previous generation. Still, she would have to readjust her tactics if they had specialized in a subset of earth magic—there were many, as she knew from reading the village's records.

A typical earth mage would control the environment, attempt to entrap their enemies, and, if they took to the air, take them down with a bombardment of stones. A clay mage would likely have much more specific spells. She knew of only one such example—Beth's grandfather, if she remembered correctly—and he had developed magic to animate and strengthen clay figures to fight for him.

They were different from normal earthen constructs in that they weren't simply being manipulated directly by the caster but had a built-in autonomy.

I should be careful, though. Just because some signs point to a clay mage, it doesn't mean there is one, or even if there is, they don't have to use the same tactics as Beth's grandpa.

Starting a fight thinking that you knew what to expect from your opponent, only to find out that you were wrong, was not a good idea, and Dorea much preferred being overly cautious in this aspect.

I figure I'll know soon enough. They must have brought someone strong enough to deal with what I did last time, which means he's a powerful Journeyman, and since he's from the previous generation, he has much more experience than me.

That was the main problem, as she saw things. Dorea was confident that between her peculiarities, skill, and talent, she could face almost every mage in her class and win. But fighting someone who had lived for more than half a century as a mage meant they would have many hidden tricks and likely had picked up several ways of dealing with Gifted of all elements.

If the man wasn't a Master—and she sincerely doubted it, as such a powerhouse would have simply taken the land they wanted rather than do all this mummery—she was sure she could deal with him. She just needed to avoid any stupid mistake.

Finally, the Katmasousi group entered alliance territory, thus officially trespassing. From that point, Dorea would have been justified to attack in the eyes of gods and men, but she decided to wait.

She could feel the eyes of her comrades on her as they readied themselves for conflict. Still, Dorea tried not to enter the confrontation with such a mindset. Often, Voggo had told her that when someone expected things to go one way, they'd subconsciously behave to make it happen.

"Halt!" she called out, enhancing her voice with the winds.

It's better to make them think I'm just a wind mage so that I can take them by surprise. Also, I feel like I've done this one too many times, honestly.

The Katmasousi kept walking until they were within hearing distance and stopped there, though given their hard faces, they, too, expected a fight to break out.

"You are trespassing on alliance land. Explain yourselves at once, or be removed." Her words weren't exactly conciliatory, but there was only so much she could do about it. Being too soft would be even worse than being too harsh.

The elderly man at the head of the group, whose head was covered in a turban that hid most of his features save his long white beard and wrinkly mouth, spoke up in return, "The river Dansa once passed through this very stretch of land, curving until it touched the desert and only then flowing south, to sate the Ergasters' thirst."

Aaah, it seems like we are going to get a conveniently reformatted retelling of the truth, then. He's gonna tell me that since the river's course once touched his people's lands, they should still have access to it. Honestly, have a little imagination.

"Our people freely drank its waters and used it for animals and crops alike back then. After the Great War with the enemy, Dansa's course was changed, and thus we have today's borders."

Dorea smiled to herself, satisfied that she had gotten it right. The Katmasousi seemed to want to be on the right side, and to do that, they needed to establish a just cause for their aggression.

"Our ancient right has been put on hold for too long," the old man continued. He held a staff in his hands, and by the look of it, the prediction that it would be a clay-specialized earth mage was correct. "But no more! Today, that ends. From now on, we no longer have to fear the long draughts of the desert. The waters of the river Dansa are open to us once again!"

His exhortations seemed to have fired up his people, and seeing a few dozen mages—enough that had they attacked Whitecliff before they first started their diplomatic efforts, they would have crushed it—all hungry for battle was not a good sight.

Still, Dorea didn't falter, and the people around her, seeing her stalwart figure, kept their positions. They were almost evenly matched in numbers, and any significant victory would come from the leaders duking it out.

Though the old man's answer to her had turned into an impromptu speech, he was still technically addressing her, so she replied, "No one is trying to deny you access to the river. The desert is open for you to go through, and if you really wanted to pass here, you could have attempted to reach a deal. Instead, you occupy our land and paint yourself as the victim."

By now, Dorea had become an old hand at dealing with pompous fools. For all that she wasn't underestimating the old man when it came to magical abilities, it seemed he was not particularly sharp on the rhetorical side of things.

"You lie, girl! You attacked our people out of nowhere, and now you try to say it is our fault for simply taking our natural rights?" His face had steadily become redder, and now that he wasn't covered by his cloak anymore, she could see just how ugly he was.

He had a bald head filled with spots, a crooked nose, and a long, dirty beard. His eyes were flinty and filled with hatred, which told her that the outcome of these talks had long since been decided. This was a man who had a plan, and he didn't care what he had to go through.

"Prepare yourselves," she whispered to her companions.

Indeed, not even a minute later, the ground started to rumble. At first, Dorea thought that she had been mistaken about the man and that he was a more traditional type of earth mage, but as soon as the first clay statue emerged, she knew she had it right.

First a couple, then more and more until a hundred statues with the features of different people, from a fisherman to a soldier, all marched in lockstep until they stopped next to the old man.

"You cannot win. Surrender now, and we'll show mercy," he called out, sounding as if victory was in his grasp.

Fighting a mage from the previous generation was always a daunting prospect since they would necessarily be more experienced and likely stronger than any of the current ones, but Dorea had a different belief.

The true monsters survived, and those I cannot do anything about, but another class of people who lived through the war are those who simply couldn't fight in it. Voggo is a shining example of this, as his skills aren't good in a battle. But this man is neither strong enough to have lasted this long on that alone, nor does he seem suited to war.

That meant one thing only. He was a coward.

And his skillset seemed to compound that assessment. For a mage to focus so much on only one specific subset of their element like he had to and develop it enough to make it useful in a fight while keeping their distance, meant a significant aversion to engaging directly.

And so, Dorea decided that she would deny him the pleasure of setting the rules. If she fought against all his creations, she was sure he'd eventually be able to wear her down, and the losses they'd face would be great.

Instead, she blasted off the ground, spinning Air Boost and Wind Bulwark into existence at the same time, and bypassed the clay statues entirely.

They tried to stop her, of course. Arrows and stones pelted her form, even as the other mages had barely managed to realize that the battle had truly begun.

But her protections were simply too strong. She had withstood much more that they could bring to bear at such distance, and with her speed, she needed to last only for a short amount of time.

Before anyone could react, she had reached behind the clay army and launched herself at the old man with murderous intent.

Meanwhile, he had built himself a clay armor similar to those of his creations, but much more ornate, and three clay spears levitated around him, looking like very angry wasps, ready to sting.

Not giving him the time to do anything, Dorea blasted him with a barrage of Exploding Water Bullets, sending him flying back with the force of the blow.

Unfortunately, it seemed he wasn't down for the count yet, as the armor appeared to have protected him enough that he was only banged up.

Dorea lifted off again as the clay statues quickly converged on her position. She needed to avoid being swarmed by them, and she also couldn't allow herself to be flanked by the enemy mages and the statues and be crushed between them.

So she zipped around the battlefield, aiding her companions where she could and taking every shot she had at the old man, who was getting increasingly frustrated with her ability to vanish from his grasp.

His defenses held much better than she had initially projected, but she should have expected it once she recognized him as a coward.

Lightning Sphere was unfortunately not particularly effective against him, as his armor—though charred and cracked—mostly held up.

He must have spent a long time devising his spell in a way that would cover him from as many elements as possible. *For a coward, he's very thorough. He must really not want to get hurt, huh.*

Still, for all that it was taking longer than she might have wanted, she was making progress. It was evident that her opponent, despite his enhanced physique given by earth magic and the power of his defensive spell, was slowing down.

His main strength was obviously the clay army; her ignoring it entirely had removed it from the board.

Of course, she wasn't completely free from harassment from the constructed soldiers, but it took only a couple of seconds to relocate and start again with her attacks.

Dorea, though, was feeling the lack of a finishing spell. Lightning Sphere worked well against unprotected enemies, but she needed something that could burst through barriers and armor alike and put an end to things.

Heart of the Storm was the perfect candidate, of course, but its requirements were simply too steep. If she stopped to gather all the necessary power, she'd get swarmed by the clay soldiers.

She had been working on a modified, lesser version, though. She hadn't had enough time to truly start on the practical side, but she felt she could use something from her preliminary ideas.

Combination element spells were something that no one talked about, simply because no one beyond her could attempt such a thing.

The closest she had gotten from the archives was the story of two twins, a fire mage and an earth mage, who would fuse their powers to create lava constructs.

But it still wasn't what she wanted. She had achieved it with Heart of the Storm, but it wasn't efficient in an active battle, and the area of effect was simply too widespread.

The principle behind it, though, was something she could work with. Her first forays in combining water and lightning had resulted in explosive failures, as she found that the isolating properties of pure, conjured water did not go well with the crackling energy of electricity.

Instead, she theorized that she could use the pure form of one element's mana in combination with another and obtain something that wasn't necessarily the classical expression one would expect.

I'm trying a new combination attack. I'm attempting to surpass the limitations of singular elements! I did something like it before, and it's just a matter of scaling it back enough to be immediately useful now.

A battlefield might not seem the best place to start experimenting with volatile and untested magics, but Dorea always found that her very best came out in such moments.

Thus, she set out to accomplish what she had not even attempted to do yet while being chased by an army of clay soldiers—though by now only sixty or so remained, thanks to her companions' efforts—and, in turn, chasing an elderly earth mage.

All the while, she had to dodge the attacks of the other Katmasousi Gifted, who tried to kill her whenever they had a clear shot.

Dorea entered a state of hyperawareness. Her mind expanded beyond its physical limits, beyond even its magical senses. She touched deep within herself and drew inspiration from the chaos of nature and the battle around her.

Lightning and water mana bloomed into being, twisting and turning around each other but constantly repelling the other in the end.

With a huff, she dismissed her first attempt. She needed to do something different to get results dissimilar from what she always got.

Thinking about the principle behind Heart of the Storm, Dorea contemplated its matrix. Most of it had come to her in the form of a bout of inspiration, which she got from witnessing the fight between the eagle and Old Titan.

It worked by taking the very concept of an element and aligning it with a similar facet of another one. It was simple, in the end. She just needed to find a way to get a stable concept to twist two elements around, much like the Storm did for all three together.

In the end, it was witnessing a surprising interaction between spells on the battlefield that made her find a way. A blade of wind hit a whip of water, and rather than the explosion she had expected, they merged for a moment. For just an instant, the two spells coexisted in the same spot as the compressed water and air fought for control. Then, the pressure got too much, and they separated explosively.

But she had gotten the spark of inspiration she needed.

Dorea waited until she had gotten far away from the main bulk of the Katmasousi army, far from even the old clay mage, and turned her hand to the doll soldiers.

She called upon the concept that she had just witnessed, and rather than allowing it to form in a combination of the two elements, she pushed at it until its energy melded into one.

It took a lot of mana, more than she would have preferred with the possibility it would not work still present, but she was committed now and needed to see it to the end. She added a conceptual weight, taking inspiration from something she had witnessed many times in her childhood.

The roaring power of a Waterspout condensed into a singular deadly beam. It cut through the clay statues like they weren't even there.

It went beyond them, carving a deep furrow in the ground. So mighty was it that for just a moment, it looked as if the sky had dimmed. The sounds of battle quieted immediately as everyone struggled to comprehend what they had just seen.

Dorea, on the other hand, just smiled.

CHAPTER THIRTY-FOUR

Death was always a harsh thing to accept.

Dorea considered herself lucky, as her closest friends and family had mostly gone through the hard times they found themselves in with little trouble.

The only person she had a good relationship with who died was Rupert, and since that happened during the Trial, it felt different than losing someone during a battle.

As Dorea stood over the corpse of Eol, a weird numbness came over her. The boy would have looked peaceful, had he not been missing the left side of his torso entirely.

His expression was shocked, as if he couldn't believe what had happened to him. His hair was matted with sweat, dirt, and blood. For some weird reason, Dorea fixated on his eyes.

They were a deep amber, she realized, and though death had robbed them of their light, if she pushed her imagination just a bit, she could see them spark as he tried to impress her.

The boy had not been given a good death, being hit by a sneak attack from behind as he tried to help his comrades assaulting a breaking shield formation, but at least it had been quick.

A sphere of ripping void, not unlike what Nora used, had removed his heart, and after that, nobody had been able to do anything to save him.

Even had she known about it, Dorea couldn't think of anything in her supplies that would have helped. Even the method she had seen used to save Nettle, that of forcefully keeping one's blood inside the body by manipulating the water within it, did not apply, as Eol was an air mage and such deep magics couldn't be worked on another's body.

Not without long preparations or severe consequences. And at that point, I don't know what would have killed him quicker. The absence of a heart or another's mage magic inside his body.

What Voggo had done to her to check on her "condition" was the furthest one could push the technique, and that was only possible thanks to the shaman's extreme skill and finesse. Had he been even just a little more clumsy, he could have done irreparable damage to her.

Of course, she found this out later during her studies to understand warding. When confronted, Voggo's response was that since he did have that kind of skill, there had been no reason to mention all the possible, excruciating deaths that could have befallen her.

"Clean him up. We'll send a small team with his body back to Camp to inform them of our victory here," Dorea told Nora, who was waiting respectfully a few steps behind. Just uttering the words made her mouth feel like ash, but she had a duty, and by the Goddess, she'd complete it.

If one ignored the personal loss of Eol and another water mage she didn't know, the battle fought today was a resounding success.

Not only had they killed at least a dozen of their Gifted in the skirmish, but she had severely injured their leader—the old clay mage—and thoroughly broken the Katmasousi's morale by destroying their secret weapon.

The army of statues would have changed the tide of any battle, but especially since they did not know to expect such a thing, it would have been a deadly blow.

Instead, her decision to jump into the fray and deal with them herself, while keeping the strongest caster's attention, had allowed her companions to fight without worrying about being crushed between the two forces.

But it also meant that I couldn't protect Eol with my shields. I made a choice, and now I must bear its weight.

Dorea knew it wasn't necessarily correct to say it was her fault the boy had died. Death couldn't be avoided easily in a battle such as the one they just fought.

Still, she felt she was somehow responsible for it. Maybe it was simply because she had rejected the boy shortly before they started the battle, or maybe because she had given the others the impression they'd have more time before having to fight and when the Katmasousi finally attacked, they had been taken by surprise.

For all her guilt, though, Dorea wasn't one to let it affect her performance. Thus, she kept making the rounds, visiting the triage tent where the injured had been taken, reassuring everyone that they'd be able to use her own stash of ointments and potions, which came directly from Voggo himself, and touring the battlefield.

The old basin where they had fought looked less like the verdant valley it had once been. The lush green grass had been either trampled by the mad chase the clay army had engaged in as they tried to catch up to her, or burned and flattened by the many spells thrown around.

It made her sad that their passage meant death and destruction for nature, but she knew that the environment was much more resilient than this. Even without a wood mage to make things right immediately, in just a few weeks it would look much less like the barren mess it now was.

That is, of course, if we don't have to keep fighting here. There is no reason to believe they will stop now. That clay mage is simply too stubborn to back down, even when faced with a more powerful opponent.

He was likely to lick his wounds and come back with another strategy now that he knew what she could do.

Of course, if he believed that her Waterspout was the most power she could unleash, he'd have a very rude awakening. It had been reckless of her to try out a new manipulation in the middle of the battlefield, but she had judged that she could do it by applying principles she was familiar with, and that the fight needed to end soon to limit the losses as much as possible.

Her gamble had paid off in the end, as the proto-spell had leveled the clay army in one go—admittedly, she had been left much more drained than she had expected, though not on the same level as its parent spell—and ended the battle.

The Katmasousi had broken then, and while she might have enjoyed the thought of chasing them down and killing them to the last man, they were far too numerous to do so easily, and had she pushed them to the brink, they might have regained their vigor.

Turning a victory into a meat grinder would have been terribly foolish. So she called a halt to the advance, beyond sending a few people to ensure their enemies would leave alliance land, and ordered the dead and wounded to be gathered.

As for their enemies' bodies, they would have to be searched for anything of value and then dumped at the border, where the Katmasousi could pick them up.

Dorea wouldn't have minded burying them in the soil here, but she had been warned that the southerners had different traditions regarding death, and she didn't want to give them any more justifications for their aggression.

"I'd say this victory should gain us a couple of days of peace, shouldn't it?" Nora asked after having relayed her orders.

"It should. The clay mage needs at least that much to prepare something new if he even wants to try his luck again," Dorea replied, looking in the distance at the flowing river.

Humans were unfortunate creatures, she knew. They needed constant resources from the environment and were forced by their instincts to keep growing, making more of themselves, and thus needing even more resources.

This brought chaos and destruction to the world until either balance was achieved as they found enough to settle, or something else took offense to their actions and struck them down.

Right now, Dorea was feeling very much like that something. The Katmasousi were simply seeking more and better things for themselves, and she was the impenetrable wall they would crash against.

"Do you think he'll make the same mistake of engaging only you the next time? If he had used at least some of his soldiers to attack us, things might have gone very differently," the brunette continued. She had been one of those focused on the offensive, as her signature void balls swarmed the enemy ranks and broke through barriers.

"We shouldn't ascribe to him powers we don't know he has, just like we shouldn't underestimate him. If he had been capable of using the soldiers in such a sophisticated manner, he probably would have. He didn't strike me as the patient type." Dorea would forever remember the sheer look of hatred the old man had worn as he ordered the retreat.

For someone like him, whose power must have meant a position of great respect for a long time, being smacked down by a teenage girl must have been a terrible blow.

Well, I'm not going to hold back to save my enemy's feelings. If anything, it's something I can use in the future if I ever meet him again. And I think I will.

Dorea fully expected to spend her whole time here in between constant skirmishes. Probably not like the one they had just fought, as the sides needed to take the other's measure, but peace would likely not come cheap.

Therefore, she made sure that a rotation was set up to always have someone to keep an eye on the Katmasousi and the southern border—she wouldn't put it past them to try and pincer them from two sides—and someone without any duty, so that when the time came for them to act, they could be fully rested.

As Dorea had predicted, the Katmasousi showed a distinct lack of regard for her sleeping patterns.

A night attack just a day after the initial fight had almost taken them by surprise, but the patrols she had insisted on had managed to pick them up as they attempted sneaking through the border.

With the alarm raised, a force had been sent out, and the enemies retreated after seeing that they couldn't proceed with whatever plan they had in mind.

Dorea had made it very clear to everyone that she didn't want them to keep up the pursuit after the border, though she had only said that it was because their entire reason for being here was that they wanted that line to be respected.

The other reason she had only shared with Nora so far was. If the Katmasousi started believing themselves safe after exiting alliance land, the one time that pursuit didn't end there, they'd be taken unprepared.

It wasn't in her plans to mount a full-on assault on their position, yet she reserved the possibility to do so if things became unbearable, or to even just prepare the ground for the next commander, who was slated to come and take her place in less than a week.

She would have preferred to have the situation dealt with before then, but since the scouts had observed signs of earth magic at work in raising buildings alongside the river's banks, she expected things to go on for quite a bit longer.

The third skirmish happened openly, as an army of clay beasts marched upon the camp they had set up.

The older mage who controlled them had been nowhere to be seen, but his presence could be felt as clay bullets rocketed from different directions, breaking shields and allowing his constructs to do much more damage than they should.

A contingent of mages kept to the back, where they mostly just acted as defense for the inhuman army, protecting them from wide-area spells that would have slowed them down.

Dorea could have used Waterspout again, and she considered it for a moment, but she soon realized that it was the old mage's intention, to draw her out like that.

Since he wasn't immediately visible, if she made a stationary target of herself he'd probably have the whole mage contingent and his army converge on her and trap her in one spot, where they could overwhelm her and deal a terrible blow to the alliance.

Of course, it was only her theory, and no confirmation was likely to ever come, but her hunches were often correct, so she went with it.

Dorea left dealing with the clay army to her companions and unleashed her fury against the enemy mages.

Her usage of Lightning Sphere in such quantity might not have been a surprise anymore, after she had used it to deal with the first Katmasousi group, but it was very effective nonetheless.

The sheer volume and destructive force she was able to unleash by herself was enough that it stopped the advance entirely and even began pushing back.

The layered defenses were too much for her to break entirely, but she purposefully concentrated her attacks in the weakest spots, getting some hits in.

Anyone who was touched by her first original spell was almost certainly doomed. She had not thought of it like that when first working on it, but its explosion meant that pain and suffering couldn't be avoided, even for those who managed to dodge its initial effect.

That battle turned out to be more about attrition than the first one, but in the end, the alliance mages—thanks to her monopolizing the enemy Gifted's attention—had simply inflicted too much damage, and the enemy had to retreat once again.

If there is one thing they have, it's strategic patience. They aren't in a rush to get us out of here. They probably even know that we have more enemies to deal with and are banking on us not wanting to waste too many resources for this uninhabited stretch of land.

Of course, clearing the field would take someone like Yaomi very little time. She would even be back in just a few hours. The sheer might she had displayed during the fight with the Ubag mage had shown Dorea that, had she wanted to, the Witch of Immolation could have dealt with any opposing force by herself.

But there are considerations and consequences and blah blah blah. I know she can't and that it's not that simple, but sometimes, it feels like it should be, and we are just overcomplicating things.

It was a frustration shared by others as well, but Dorea always made sure to shut them down. She gently explained that Yaomi moving would send a signal to all the other tribes that could end up with them facing a unified front, which they desperately needed to avoid.

Still, not everyone was satisfied with that explanation, and as the deaths slowly piled up, she couldn't find the strength to reprimand them too harshly.

"We have an incoming group from the west!" a scout relayed through the wind.

That had been one of her better ideas: sending messages to a fixed place where someone would always be ready to receive them. It made it so that even at much greater distances, information could be exchanged at high speeds.

"That's weird. There shouldn't be a team coming to relieve us for a while yet," Nora commented, turning to look toward the horizon.

"Has something happened to Camp?" another girl wondered, levitating up to get a better view.

Dorea soon joined her, curious about the reason herself. Though she didn't have a way to actively increase her sight—light magic, unfortunately, was the domain of legends—flying higher made it easier to distinguish the approaching figures.

The first thing that told her something was wrong was that only one man was traveling with the help of his magic. The others were all riding horses.

And considering how careful the Heidels were with their horses—they had adamantly refused to take them to the battlefield, as they would get immediately targeted by the enemy mages just like what had happened during the Great War—their need to get here fast must have been overwhelming.

Rather than waiting for them to approach, Dorea blasted off toward them. Thanks to Air Boost, it took her only a couple of minutes to cross the distance. She stopped a hundred feet ahead of them, giving the riders the time to stop the animals.

She barely remembered to pulse her mana, receiving one back in order to confirm their identities. "What's going on?"

If anyone minded the lack of propriety, they made no mention of it. Everyone looked tired and drawn, and a sinking feeling started to form in her gut.

"We have been ordered to relieve you and your team immediately, Dorea. You are needed back home," their leader began.

She recognized him as one of Masi's friends, though she had never taken the time to learn his name. Still, she could remember his face well and had never seen him without a smile.

He was pale and grim, looking like the bearer of bad news. He was also determined, though, which at least told her that all was not lost, whatever it was that had happened.

"Home as in Camp or home as in Whitecliff?" she asked, but she already knew the answer. Anything that would have required her presence in Camp could have been solved by others, and with how close she was to the end of her rotation down south, she sincerely doubted that Yaomi would have recalled her now.

"Whitecliff. You are needed north, Dorea. Your home was attacked by a Mondean force, and Chief Yaomi was called to help with the defense once it was clear that a Master-level mage was present. She ordered that you be told immediately and gave you authorization to leave your post."

CHAPTER THIRTY-FIVE

The wind whistled as Dorea passed by, pushing speeds she hadn't ever managed before. She was traveling through the grasslands at a high enough altitude that she didn't need to stop to take her bearings.

She hadn't even contemplated going back to her post once she heard of what happened to Whitecliff. Still, she was grateful that Yaomi had the presence of mind to officially relieve her of command so that she could leave without tainting her reputation.

She would have done it anyway, but it was still nice.

If I have the energy to have that kind of inane thought, I have the strength to push harder.

And harder she did push. By now, she was like a streak, cutting through the landscape and scattering flocks of birds.

Dorea had considered for half a second leaving for Camp to pick up the others and her things, but she immediately rejected that option. Firstly, she had nothing of import she needed, and secondly, she fully expected the others to be already on the way to Whitecliff.

She'd simply lose time, so after leaving Nora a message to organize the passing of the post to the new commander, she had blasted off toward the north.

Normally, she'd expect to take a day or so to get to Whitecliff from where she had been stationed, but with time so tight, she had left behind any reticence she had at doping Air Boost as much as possible and simply let go.

Her ability to fly freely with Wind Bulwark meant she didn't need to worry about any obstacle. That allowed her to push away any thought of maneuverability—she just needed to keep the correct course, which the ocean and the mountains up north made very easy to do once she got high enough—and focus entirely on speed.

It wasn't the first time she tweaked with a fully formed spell, but it certainly was the most involved. She needed to actively ignore that part of the matrix that had been burned in her brain which dealt with control and instead supplant it with even more power supply.

Once, it would have been impossible for her to maintain such a spell active for even a few minutes, but now she had been flying at high speeds for hours and was still comfortably full.

It truly made a difference, the level of mana one possessed. In a fight, one would think that the more skilled mage would win, and sometimes, they truly would, but the majority of confrontations were decided by how many more spells one could throw around.

As she finally left the scorched border of the grasslands behind—a reminder of what a Master mage could do, even just by accident—she entered the forest.

Immediately, she felt more at home. Had it not been an emergency, Dorea would have dropped down and taken the time to truly appreciate the beauty of it.

Unfortunately, her dreams of walking barefooted on moss would have to be put aside for the moment. The fading column of smoke she could see in the distance reminded her harshly that she needed to deal with much bigger issues first.

She rushed above the canopy, uncaring of the squawking of annoyed birds and squirrels. Even with the urgency she felt, she wouldn't dare rise too high up in the air above the forest, for some of its mightier denizens could mistake her for a snack.

At the level she was currently at, Dorea had little to fear from the average enhanced beast, but she couldn't allow her path to be impeded, even for just a few minutes.

Finally, many long hours after she had been informed of the attack, the village of Whitecliff came into sight. The walls were still hidden beneath the mighty trees, but she could see signs of damage everywhere.

The southern side of the village seemed the least affected, but the farther north she looked, the more she could see that a battle had been fought within the very walls.

Entire houses had been demolished, with signs of powerful spells having been used. Most fields had been spared, but those closer to where the main gate should be looked burned.

The newer constructions all suffered some damage, while most of the older ones were still standing, though some were notably not.

The kind of power required to damage a house built by a skilled earth mage was great, making her worry even more.

There seemed to be no active fighting when she touched down close to

Voggo's house, though a closer look at what her senses told her showed that the entire main gate was missing.

It looked to have been sheared off, as if a giant shovel had simply dug beneath it and taken the gate alongside the ground beneath it, leaving a gap in its place.

Following the signatures she could feel, Dorea ran to the back of the shaman's house, finding Yaomi, who looked dirtier and worse for wear than she had ever seen her; Voggo himself, though half of his face was hidden beneath thick bandages; and Ed, the lead hunter.

"Dorea!" the older man exclaimed, making as if to rise before dropping back down in his seat with a wince.

The shaman looked terrible. His always sparkling eyes were now dulled with sadness, and his arms trembled. He looked like an old man. And Voggo had never been one to be called weak.

As far as Dorea remembered, he had always been filled with an almost manic energy. He would look for new things to capture his interest, much like a curious animal. His hands would seek to touch, feel, and discover the secrets of whatever new interest he had found.

Now, on the other hand, he was just lying there, looking barely awake. Bloody splotches marred his bandages, and given his ability to heal himself, that told her exactly how tired he was.

Dorea didn't doubt for a moment that he had pulled every hidden card in his arsenal to fight back. He must have done everything possible to keep the line until Yaomi could arrive, but Voggo was not a frontline fighter. He simply wasn't made for it.

Shame burned within her at having been away during Whitecliff's darkest hour. Dorea knew she couldn't have known, but seeing her grandfather like that ate at her.

The blond girl rushed to his side, carefully hugging the old man. "What happened?" she asked, already resigned to what she'd hear.

"Treachery and foulness, that's what happened," was the reply. She had always known Voggo to be capable of keeping his emotions in check when necessary, so the sheer bile in his tone surprised her.

Dorea was no stranger to anger, and the flame that had bloomed in her the moment she had heard of the attack burned hotter now. She had been carefully keeping it contained, worried that if she lost her cool, she wouldn't be able to help once she got there, but it took an effort of will to keep herself contained once she heard of what truly occurred in her absence.

"A couple of days ago," Voggo began, his voice tired but strong, "we tracked another group of refugees. They were following the same tracks as the ones you found last. Now that I think about it, their stories were suspiciously similar. Too similar. They must have learned what to say to get welcomed somehow . . ."

Though Dorea was impatient to know more, she didn't interrupt her mentor. She had long learned he could make surprising leaps of logic from little evidence.

Less than a minute later, he shook himself. "Well, that will have to be looked at by someone else. As I was saying, we took in a group of refugees. I did the usual checks to see if anyone had ill intentions toward Whitecliff, but somehow, they evaded notice."

Dorea observed Ed's face take on an even grimmer cast as Voggo spoke. The man had been the most outspoken critic of taking in so many strangers, and now his reticence had been vindicated.

Still, he had the good sense not to gloat about it. Rather, he seemed even more pissed off than the others.

"Yesterday, things changed. A few new mages claimed to have fallen ill, but I found nothing wrong with them when I checked. Since they had supposedly just escaped from certain death, I allowed them a day of rest anyway," Voggo continued.

It wasn't uncommon for people coming from traumatic events to need some alone time; the Goddess knew that Dorea had. Still, with hindsight, she could see how the subterfuge had taken place.

"They used that time to prepare a ritual, taking advantage of their camp's closeness to the main gate. And when night fell, they set it off. You have seen the results, I imagine."

She had and nodded. The gate had been a symbol for all of Whitecliff of their Gifted's might, even in times when only Voggo had been able to do magic.

"The gate has no real strategic value beyond being a staging point, but in a surprise attack, the only reason to attack it is to crush our morale," she commented, getting a tired nod from the shaman.

"Were there too many?" Dorea asked. If the Mondeans had finally brought to bear their true strength down south, there was little Whitecliff could do. Qualitative superiority only worked so far against overwhelming numbers, unfortunately.

But it doesn't make sense. They would have razed the village to the ground, then. Yaomi wouldn't have made it in time to do anything, then.

His next words confirmed her thoughts. "No, though they were a sizable group, they were nowhere near the thousands we'd expect if their main army came south. Rather, this was another strike group meant to remind us of our place until they can truly deal with us."

"Then was the surprise that effective? Even then, I can't imagine how they could have had the time to do that much damage to our buildings." Her question made sense. Though Dorea had not been present, Whitecliff had several powerful mages ready to fight for it. Mark the Blue alone should have done enough to interfere with that.

"There was a Master," Ed finally spoke up. He had been silent so far, only brooding darkly, but his words chilled her to the bone.

Dorea looked at Yaomi, now finally understanding why she had been needed. The Witch of Immolation wasn't one to simply leave her home easily, as demonstrated when she stayed in Camp for the Battle of the Rocky Hills.

Masters were not simple existences. They were not just powerful mages. A Master was someone whose sheer level of control over their element gave them absolute dominion over their surroundings.

For a Master to take the field, if there was no one of equivalent power on the other side, meant that the fight was already over.

"Ghionn the Invisible Hand is an old Master-level ice mage." The old man sighed. He looked tired down to his bones, as if the energy that had always animated him, the spark that made Voggo himself had been extinguished.

Dorea had heard of the man, of course. Though he wasn't a hidden Master, he was the closest thing in the region. An ice mage so powerful that he could control entire mountains' worth of his element. A monster whose territory simply could not be crossed by anyone he didn't personally allow.

That such a person had been enticed to leave his village just to attack Whitecliff was not easy to swallow.

"I have no idea how they enticed him to participate in this, as he had always seemed like a reasonable person to me, and since he refused to speak to Yaomi even when she engaged him directly, we'll likely never know," Voggo explained.

"I told you, the old bastard just wanted a fight," the elderly woman said, boredly picking at the bandages around her hand.

"What?!"

It took Dorea a moment to realize that the strangled voice had been hers. She couldn't understand how someone who was not directly involved in their conflict with the Mondeans would choose to visit destruction upon them just because he wanted a fight.

"Ghionn's son died during the Great War while he was battling against the Ergasters, and a beast attacked his village," the old shaman told her, his hands shaking imperceptibly. "He swore then that until the time came that someone could protect his people, he'd never leave. He has stayed up there in the mountains until now, but apparently, the Mondeans offered him something."

Dorea knew that political considerations were not the only reason behind people's actions, but to hear that a Master had bound themselves to a place for such a foolish reason and, when given a chance to finally leave it, had immediately decided to attack her village . . . That was simply too much.

"Did you kill him?" she whispered, staring directly at Yaomi.

To her credit, the old woman seemed to understand the deadly seriousness with which Dorea had spoken. "I didn't, unfortunately. He's a slippery bastard, and with the threat of him destroying even more of Whitecliff, I couldn't give it my all. I needed to get him away from the village to save more lives."

It was a reasonable response, but at the moment, Dorea didn't want reasonable. She wanted blood and vengeance. She wanted to find the people responsible for her home's state and make them pay.

"How many have we lost?" she finally asked the question she had been dreading ever since she had been informed of the attack.

"Thirty dead, and a dozen have been taken captive," Ed said.

It was a gut punch. In all their skirmishes and battles with the Mondeans, they had never lost that many people.

It always ended up relatively light in deaths, and Dorea had started to think that it would forever be so. Hearing that thirty people she had bled for, whom she had laughed, feasted, and cried with, were gone was too much.

The flame of shame and rage she had so carefully suppressed, which had burned brighter and brighter with every new piece of information, now roared like an inferno.

Dorea wanted—no, needed—to do something. Her mana was boiling, begging her to be unleashed upon her enemies. Her brain was firing at maximum capacity as she thought of all the possible ways she could ambush the ice Master while he was still away from the mountains and kill him.

Thirty people were dead, and she had done nothing to prevent it. That fact gnawed at her mind, making her feel close to madness. She had sworn, again and again, that she'd grow stronger so that she could protect her family and friends. So that none would have to suffer the pain of loss.

She had failed. Her oath lay broken at her feet, and she was left with ashes in her mouth and tears that refused to fall.

I don't deserve to cry. I won't cry until every last person is avenged. Until I have brought back the bones of everyone who dared attack my people.

Thirty people was just too many. Too many to bear. The thought of going through the funerary rites and explaining to parents and friends why she had let this happen . . .

Instead of thinking of that, of asking who exactly was gone—she couldn't stand the thought of those closest to her having been killed when she was not there to save them; her mind simply rebelled at the thought—she focused on the latter part of his statement.

"Who was kidnapped, and where?"

The three adults looked at each other before Voggo sighed. "We believe they have deliberately targeted the younger mages. Those who can be broken and remolded into soldiers for their cause. As far as we know, they'll likely take them to the same place we once observed their army resting."

Dorea kept silent, staring at the old man to tell him she wouldn't let go of the matter.

With pursed lips, he finally replied, "Of your friends, Jonah was taken."

INTERLUDE

Jonah

The sound of an explosion woke him up abruptly, sending him flying off the bed. Subconsciously, Jonah extended his senses, seeking the origin of the noise. Even when he was deafened and half-awake, it took him only a handful of seconds to realize they were under attack.

A large host of mages was moving through the forest toward the gate, and where there should have been a team guarding the entrance to the village was now just a crater.

Jonah didn't even stop to think of his options. If Whitecliff was under attack, everyone would be needed, even those whose roles usually kept them away from the front line.

With just a thought, Whispering Wind was cast and sent to the village's leaders to alert them of his preliminary findings. Even as he moved through the house, checking on his father and neighbors, he kept a wary eye on the missing gate.

People were swarming it by now, mostly mages and warriors, but they seemed disorganized, confused as to how they could have been attacked without any notice.

Jonah gathered everyone in the vicinity as quickly as possible and started leading them toward Voggo's house, where the basement would serve as a place to hide until they had gotten the situation under control.

Meanwhile, he kept updating the shaman about the situation, along with shorter messages to Mark the Blue and the others setting up a defensive formation where the gate had once been.

He had barely gotten the nonmagicals to the shelter, sharing a long, meaningful look with his father, which meant much more than a thousand words, when the Mondeans—and they had to be Mondeans—finally arrived.

Initially, their advance was held back with little trouble. For all that his people had been taken by surprise, they were trained well enough that the few short minutes they had had were enough. If battles between mages of the same caliber didn't end through subterfuge or external factors, they usually ended up as attrition fights, as the two sides attempted to crush the other's shields.

Unfortunately, that state of affairs only lasted a short while.

Glimmering lights in the night sky, thousands of them, were the first sign they had that something was different this time. Jonah's senses were sharp enough to grasp what they were early enough to feel horror before they smashed upon the layered shields, breaking them immediately.

The feeling of his friends' lives being snuffed in an instant, as ice shards flying at speeds he could barely conceive fell upon them in waves, was almost too much.

Desperate, Jonah sought to find their creator, wanting to do something to end the monstrously powerful attack. Thanks to his keen senses, it only took him a short while.

The man, who was flying high up above the forest, was old. His entire aura told of age and power, sparkling like an ancient iceberg in the sun. Around him were arrayed countless more deadly shards—enough that Jonah fell to his knees.

He barely had the presence of mind to relay what he had discovered to Voggo, even as he contemplated exactly how desperate their situation was.

Little was left of the initial defenders when the barrage of ice was finally over. Those few who had been in the back line had been spared, but over a dozen people had been killed just like that.

Immediately after, the Mondeans surged forward, emboldened by the massacre of their enemies.

The first man had just stepped within the village proper when a blinding light bloomed from the central plaza. More than just a physical feeling, the sheer power in the corona of light was enough that Jonah had to retract his senses, sure that he would have somehow been burned if he had gazed at it for too long.

The cry of a bird could be heard, sounding much like the sorrowful song of the dying. The light intensified further, and the image of a gigantic owl was projected above the skies.

It was like nothing Jonah had ever seen before, but he knew, deep within, that this was Voggo's doing.

The shaman did not enjoy fighting, and his specific style of magic was not well suited to it, but apparently, he had prepared something in case of a true emergency.

When the light dimmed and the image finally disappeared, the floating form of Voggo became visible above the breached wall.

Ghostly purple wings emerged from his back, and his hands and feet looked as if they had become talons of some kind. Jonah was too far to see with his own eyes, but timidly, he extended his senses enough to realize that the old man's signature had been profoundly changed.

If before it had been a steady and warm campfire, now it was a raging wildfire, burning everything in its path and threatening to snuff itself out at any moment.

Voggo then blasted off toward the ice mage, who was still calmly floating above the forest and engaged him in a brilliant show of lights.

Power that Jonah had not known the old man to be capable of was thrown around as if it didn't matter, as the two ancient mages battled in the sky.

Meanwhile, the Mondeans had resumed their march into Whitecliff, now that they knew they weren't about to be attacked directly by the suddenly powerful shaman.

Battles erupted everywhere as people who hadn't managed to get to the shelter ran for their lives, screaming.

At that moment, Jonah realized that even though he had never wanted to fight, the choice had been ripped away from him. He couldn't simply stay there, a silent witness to the rape of his people.

He picked himself up from the ground and quickly marched toward where he felt the closest fight.

Without even trying to take prisoners, he sent a blade of wind, too weak by itself to break any shield, but extremely successful when unnoticed, and cut off the head of a particularly ugly man who had been leering at Beor, the short lightning mage, getting a grateful nod.

The red blood that spilled on the grass looked almost black, illuminated only by the fires of burning houses. Jonah spat at the headless corpse, too angry to form words.

Not bothering to stay and chat, the two immediately split off, seeking other fights.

For the next few minutes, Jonah ghosted through Whitecliff, the village looking almost unrecognizable with all the blood and bodies everywhere. Friend and foe were recognizable only through his senses, and the boy felt extremely grateful for all the training he had put into the skill.

It allowed him to put an end to fights long before his approach could be felt, and he saved five more people before a blinding explosion of light illuminated the night sky.

In a panic, Jonah realized he could no longer feel Voggo's blazing signature. Ever since he had lifted off into the sky, the man's presence had felt like a layer of security, keeping the monstrous ice mage at bay.

But now, nothing stood in the man's path.

A frantic search finally revealed that Voggo was still alive, lying in a crater just inside the village's walls. He felt weak and diminished, but he was still breathing, and that was all that mattered.

The Master mage, however, didn't take to the field. He just hovered there, a silent menace threatening to end everything Jonah had known and loved in an instant.

His attention was then ripped away as a group of Mondean mages pushed farther into Whitecliff, and he ran in their direction, afraid of what they might do to the three young Gifted they were about to meet.

The following fight was much more confusing than he ever experienced before. His air spells were ripped away from him as three mages worked in concert to contrast his grip on the atmosphere.

Nothing he tried seemed to work, and Jonah was getting increasingly desperate. The three he had attempted to save had already been knocked out and administered some kind of liquid, which made them feel muffled to his senses.

Ultimately, he had little recourse but to try and break through. Picking up a broken piece of wood, Jonah spun up a couple more spells, which were predictably arrested in their paths soon after.

Still, he had gotten close enough to one of the mages by then that there was nothing he could do as the blond boy thrust the sharp branch into his eye.

The man collapsed in agony, clutching at his ruined face.

Jonah just had the time to smile vindictively before a powerful blow to the back of his head made his vision go dark.

CHAPTER THIRTY-SIX

What?"

Voggo and Yaomi looked at her with pity in their eyes, as if she was the one suffering. "It seems like they used the confusion of the fight to kidnap some of our younger mages. Considering their modus operandi so far, I expect them to try and turn them into soldiers," the old man carefully explained.

Even when heavily injured and terribly tired, Voggo made sure to treat her kindly, but at the moment, Dorea was not in the right state of mind to appreciate it.

Her mind was stuck on his previous words, repeating them in a loop. Not only had some of her precious tribesmen been killed and horribly injured, but some had even been kidnapped?

Abruptly, she stood up. Dorea had finally found a clear path forward. She had been late to the fight, and her absence had meant suffering for all, but she had one chance to make things better.

I need to get them back. It doesn't matter where I have to go or who I need to fight. I will save them.

That thought crystallized into an absolute certainty of purpose. There simply didn't exist a world where she wouldn't go after them. Dorea was not capable of stomaching such a thing.

"We are already organizing an expedition to try and rescue them," Ed interjected, seeing through her intentions. "We'll be ready in a day or less. If you wait that long, you'll be fully rested and much more capable. If you go now, you'll just kill yourself and doom us all."

Dorea turned to face him, his words piercing through the haze of her thoughts but not moving her. "We'll all die, then. If Ghionn the Invisible Hand is there, nothing we could do would work, and I doubt Yaomi is gonna help us much further, right?" With that, she turned to the only other woman in the room, to find her looking sad but determined.

"This is not a matter of survival of the alliance. I came immediately when called because a Master attacking Whitecliff is terrible for all of us. However, I will not engage in a protracted campaign to save a few people when the southern border is reaching a boiling point," the Heidel chief replied, just like Dorea knew she would.

Yaomi was not a cruel person, for all her fame as the Witch of Immolation. The blonde had gotten to know her pretty well during her stint south and had found her to be an intelligent and pragmatic woman.

It was precisely because of that, that she hadn't expected further help from her. Already, having to fight a Master-level mage to defend a village not her own had been extremely generous—though arguably necessary if she wanted to even have an ally afterward. Asking for her to hunt down a dozen kidnapped kids while the Katmasousi tried to take her territory was just too much.

Dorea held no ill will toward her. She understood that their priorities were simply too different. And luckily, the older woman seemed to get her meaning, because she deliberately nodded while locking eyes.

"Why go to die in the mountains, then? If you stay here and get stronger, you might be able to actually do something in a few years. Now, it would just be suicide," Ed countered, though to her, it seemed less like he was trying to steer her away and more like he was testing her conviction.

"I doubt Ghionn will actually stick around. He was looking for a fight, and he got it. No reasons to babysit the Mondeans now," Yaomi said, interrupting her response.

That actually changed things. If the lone Master was not there anymore, she might have a real chance.

I'm already pretty experienced in rescuing kidnapped people. What's one more time.

Before she left, though, Dorea needed to ask one more question. She had been purposefully avoiding it, too afraid of what the answer might be, but the uncertainty was gnawing at her. "What happened to my family?"

Voggo's expression softened at that. "They are alive. Hurt, scared, but alive. Your father has lost a hand and your sister has been inconsolable, but your mother is unscathed and has been taking good care of them."

A weight she hadn't known about dropped from her shoulders, and she could finally breathe a bit easier.

Now, I can focus on my goal.

* * *

Passing through Whitecliff and seeing all the bodies being pulled from the rubble; the weeping families who watched their homes crumble; and the long line of injured only solidified Dorea's resolve.

They would rebuild, she knew. Her people were resilient, and this wouldn't break them. They would bury their loved ones and create an even better society, always keeping those who lost their lives in mind.

That was their duty, while she had hers.

She was supposed to protect them from such suffering. She had promised such to herself again and again. And she had failed in her self-assigned task.

However, if she couldn't protect them, she would at least avenge them.

Dorea's blood was boiling in her veins, and she had to make a concerted effort not to let mana spill into the air, such was her fury. Her control had always been the best in Whitecliff, and for it to be under such strain, her emotions had to be extremely intense.

When she finally got to her family's ranch, the sight almost took her breath away. It was like she had been punched in the gut.

The barn she and her father had rebuilt after the Wrath had been entirely burned down. The main building, luckily, seemed intact, but the two enclosures next to it had also been hit by stray shards of ice.

The bodies of several animals had been left there, as the people who should have dealt with them lay in a pool of blood.

The two refugees had shown a deep thankfulness to her and her family for taking them in, giving them honest work and the possibility of integrating with their new home. They were simple people, dedicated to handling the animals and all the tasks needed to keep a ranch running without ever complaining.

Their deaths would go mostly unremarked in the general despair, but Dorea would keep them in mind. She remembered their hesitant smiles, rough hands, and thankful nods.

She would remember that they had been taken away.

Dorea hadn't been close to them, only ever having exchanged a couple of words with Monty, the taller of the two. But seeing them there, cut down by magic that hadn't even been meant for them, further inflamed her resolve.

She spent a moment praying for their souls and then buried them, carving into the soil with conjured water.

She should have gone to visit her family, she knew. They would have appreciated seeing her unharmed, and it might have given them peace of mind. But she was afraid that if she did, she wouldn't leave them.

Dorea felt the need to keep moving, to push toward her goal, and anything that might slow her down needed to be put aside for the moment.

Voggo will tell them I'm alive. They'll forgive me when I come back with the others.

She knew it wasn't a good excuse, but it was what she had to give.

With the burial over, she had nothing else left to do in Whitecliff, so she cast Air Boost and launched herself forward in pursuit of the Mondean host.

The rocky hills had become a familiar landscape to her during the many patrols she went on, but they had somehow always managed to maintain an air of danger, leftover from the days when she was too young and weak to ever attempt walking through them.

Now, nothing there could stop her advance. Only to the far east lived beasts with enough power to threaten her, but they had no reason to impede her passage.

Dorea searched for the tracks that had to have been left behind by the Mondean army, and though she had to push farther east than she had expected, she finally found them.

They were relatively fresh, not even a day old, and given the speed at which they could realistically move, especially since they had prisoners, she believed she'd catch up in just a few hours if she wasn't slowed down.

The journey across the rocky hills turned out to be more annoying than she had expected, as beasts of all kinds tried to make a meal out of her.

I expected them to be in hiding after the Mondeans passed, but apparently, long enough has passed that they feel they can reassert their control by killing me.

Such considerations might have been intellectually engaging at any other time, but currently, they only served to annoy her further.

Dorea wasn't directly opposed to fighting, as she could grow even stronger in preparation for the most challenging mission of her life, but the time it took her to dispatch angry smilodons annoyed her greatly.

Nameless wind blades carved deep into the last beast to try its luck, spilling its lifeblood on the dusty ground.

This one had at least attempted to hide itself before ambushing her, which she considered a step up from the frontal assaults she had to face earlier.

That also served as a reminder that she would have to engage in her hiding technique before getting too close.

For all that the Mondeans were sloppy, she couldn't expect them not to have designated lookouts, and if she got found out immediately, her entire mission would fall apart.

And Dorea was simply too angry to allow that to happen. As she flew through the desolate landscape, the righteous anger that had enflamed her so much slowly morphed into a colder, more vicious sentiment.

She was still incredibly determined to walk the path she had chosen, but she had come to realize that her initial plan of approaching the Mondeans as if they were the group she had fought in the forest needed to be revised.

First, Dorea wasn't confident that Ghionn the Invisible Hand had really left. If he ended up being there, she'd need to rethink her entire approach, if she could even dare to try.

She pushed down the little sly voice that told her that a Master would die all the same as any other human if their head got removed from their bodies.

I can't think like that. If I fall into that trap, I will simply lose. I must keep in mind that my goal is the safety of the kidnapped people, not bathing in the blood of my enemies.

Dorea sharpened her focus as she followed the tracks, considering and discarding various options. In the end, she couldn't settle on anything before she got there, as depending on the situation on the field, she would have to change plans.

But the exercise had served her well. Now that her mind was clearer, no longer obfuscated by the roar of outrage and pain, she felt more in control. Her chances, she felt, were better.

After leaving a still-smoking Whitecliff behind, she had honestly considered just throwing herself at the enemy, taking as many as possible down with her, but time had allowed her much-needed clarity.

The Mondeans wouldn't care if she killed thirty of theirs. They wouldn't care about a hundred, possibly even about a thousand—unless to lament the lack of manpower.

They weren't like her. They didn't feel as she did. To truly hurt them, she'd need to attack their capabilities of waging war.

But that was a matter for another time. Her plans to sabotage, infiltrate, and assassinate as many as necessary would have to be shelved for the moment, though not to be forgotten.

Instead, she needed to focus on rescue efforts. Leaving Jonah and the others to be broken and forced to fight for the monsters that killed their friends was simply unacceptable.

Since the rocky hills were starting to slope upward, morphing into higher and higher peaks to make up the mountain ranges, Dorea stopped for a moment.

The traces she had been following were getting fresher, and she expected the Mondean host to be about a couple of hours of Air Boost away. That meant she needed to start focusing on stealth.

To approach them unseen would allow her precious time to gather information and build a definitive plan. If she wanted her self-imposed mission to succeed, it was paramount that she wasn't noticed.

Therefore, she focused inward, pulling at her mana gently. Total invisibility to mystical senses was not something she could hope to achieve, unfortunately, but if she could manage to blend in enough that anything less than a direct search would find her, she'd be golden.

She had not practiced magical stealth much, but her great control and natural talent had allowed her to pull ahead of her friends, even though they were much more dedicated to it.

She had been introduced to it early on, during Voggo's lessons, but had left it to the wayside in favor of flashier styles of magic until she was confronted with her evident lack of skill. That had burned, but her immediate leaps in skill had soothed her ego—Dorea wasn't above admitting that she had developed a bit of self-importance.

Still, she had thought about it several times, both out of simple curiosity and because she wanted to experiment with practical uses. Her end results had been somehow both disappointing and exciting at the same time.

It turned out that maintaining complete stealth while casting spells was almost impossible—she had only managed it when keeping Air Boost at its lowest intensity, like she was currently doing—and it would have to be revisited as a strategy when she had grown further.

However, her ability to blend in with the environment thanks to her three-typed mana turned out to be great. Indeed, Nora and Tom, whom she had asked for help during her experiments, had trouble locating her even though she was directly in front of them, and when she took their blindfolds off, they almost did not believe her.

In such instances, Dorea wondered whether she would have taken an entirely different path, had she not been "blessed" with her weird mutation.

Her natural skill, apparently, laid in delicate manipulation and finicky bits of magic. *I probably would have made a good enchanter, or even an assassin.*

With her mana fully under a veil, she started following the tracks again.

Though Dorea had wandered through the rocky hills many times, she had never been part of the scouting teams sent up north, and thus, she entered the mountain ranges for the first time in her life.

A vast valley opened before her eyes as soon as she crested the last hill, looking surprisingly lush, given the grayish color of the stone it was surrounded by.

The trees here were different than those of the forest, less dense and with foliage that appeared akin to needles. Their trunks were stout, and she could feel all kinds of animals around them.

Bushes of berries were also surprisingly common, especially close to a brook, which gurgled quietly.

At another time, she would have been delighted to explore the environment further, taking joy in Mother Nature's different expressions.

Now, however, Dorea only saw the footprints of her enemies moving through the valley and into the next through a gully. She followed them, keeping her mana expenditure to a minimum. The tracks were getting fresher, and she started itching for a fight.

The next valley was less lively than the last, looking more like the gray dusty landscape she had been told about. Few trees dotted the mountainsides, and she could sense only a couple of smilodons residing in a cave, though given their deep, even breaths, she believed them to be sleeping.

Trekking through the mountains as one person was relatively easy, and since the Mondean host was made of dozens of people—close to a hundred, if Voggo's count was correct—their speed had to be much lower than hers, even though most of those who made it up had been living in and moving through these paths since they were born.

Once she had reached the highest point of the path, Dorea allowed herself a single moment, breathing in the fresh air and looking south to where, beyond the gray and brown of the rocky hills, the forest stretched as far as she could see, emerald green and as beautiful as anything could possibly be.

That done, she turned back to her task.

If this turns out to be the last time I see it, I think I can be satisfied with it.

After she went through its exit point—a narrow path between two large rocks, which had evidently been carved by humans—she felt the first person.

Immediately, she stopped moving, zeroing all her senses in on that signature. More and more started to appear as she focused intensely.

She had finally found them.

CHAPTER THIRTY-SEVEN

Now that she knew where her enemy was, Dorea needed to approach close enough to study them without being noticed.

It was lucky that they had stopped, as evidenced by the tents being set up and the fires being lit for cooking.

Marching for almost an entire day must have been exhausting, especially for people who just had to fight. For all that they didn't face any organized defense, the people of Whitecliff are not ones to go down without raising hell.

That the Mondeans had decided to only stop when well into the mountains told her they were not foolish enough to expect the alliance to stay still.

They had succeeded in their punitive mission, killing many and destroying Whitecliff's morale, but they had to know that if they remained close, they would get picked apart by the organized might of the three villages.

Even had she managed to complete her warding scheme and cast a protection over the entirety of Whitecliff—Dorea could admit that she was still nowhere close to that, as more pressing matters had occupied her time—their subterfuge would have rendered them useless.

Their plan to use infiltrators had been ingenious—it hurt to admit, but from now on, they'd need to be much more careful about whom they took in, which would hurt their expansion efforts—and the presence of a Master mage meant that they couldn't face defeat unless they truly screwed up.

Still, that they had left so soon gave credence to Yaomi's belief that Ghionn had only come along to have a good fight. The old monster was probably not interested at all in the Mondeans' conquest plans.

Well, I can't just assume he won't be here. If I go in and he pops out of a tent, I'll just be dead meat. I need to scout this camp properly.

Again, Dorea pushed down the boiling rage that wanted to come out, cooling it into a more productive, deadly resolve. While flying in and raining death on the Mondeans was very tempting, her true objective was to save the kidnapped mages.

Thus, she set off up the mountain she was standing at the base of. There was no other path she could realistically take that would give her a vantage point on the entire camp, while at the same time helping her keep away from the lookouts that had no doubt been placed.

Being unable to use Air Boost significantly slowed her down, as she was forced to use her physical strength to scale the steeper parts.

I could take the flatter path and get up there much more quickly, but I'd be visible from the valley. Well, I'd be far enough that they wouldn't be able to tell it's a person and not a beast, but it's better not to risk it.

Every once in a while, she stopped to regain her breath. Dorea had always been an active person, but the many months of relying on her magic had not done her any favors, and she suspected she was managing only because of the strength boost she got from killing that wolverine.

During one of her little pauses, something touched the edge of her senses in a way she hadn't experienced before. It almost felt like an oily hand had touched hers. An impenetrable sphere entered within her range, only to immediately back out.

Dorea panicked, terrified that she had been found out. She pulled on her mana even tighter, attempting to completely blend in with the environment.

As she did that, she steeled herself to the possibility that she might have to go through with her initial plan. If she had been discovered so early, she'd try to kill as many Mondeans as possible while she made her way to the prisoners' camp.

She wouldn't make it far, she knew, but she had to try.

Still, she wouldn't make their life easy, and so she hunkered down, ready to fight if she had to. Fortunately, it turned out not to be needed.

Whatever she had felt, it had seemingly decided not to bother her. And now that her heart wasn't beating madly, she realized that it had come from the opposite side of the mountain, far away from the Mondean camp.

That didn't mean it wasn't one of them, but it significantly reduced the likelihood that it was. After half an hour of complete stillness, Dorea decided she had waited enough.

Her curiosity burned as a part of her wanted to change direction and immediately look for the thing that had surprised her—it wasn't often that such an alien feeling appeared to her senses!—but her rational mind reasserted itself quickly.

With a sigh, she started her trek up the mountain again. She had a specific spot in mind, a cluster of tall rocks that oversaw a steep drop, below which the entire camp should be visible. She would have a perfect vantage point if she managed to make it there without interruptions.

She moved even slower than she had initially, still somewhat spooked, but finally reached it. Her hands were full of scrapes, and her legs hurt from the exertion, but she felt only satisfaction when she settled between the rocks, perfectly hidden from below.

As her senses had been telling her, the camp was lively and still in the process of being set up, though it was much further along now than when she first noticed it.

When she saw them like this, the Mondeans looked less like the monsters she saw in her mind and more like simple humans going through the motions.

The fact that they chose to set aside that humanity to inflict so much pain and suffering on innocent people only infuriated her further.

Or maybe it is precisely because they are human that they can do so. Our history is dotted with people of all kinds gaining the tiniest bit of power and engaging in bloody conflict to get more.

It had been a recurring thought in her meditations that her enemy might not simply be an ontologically evil force she needed to eradicate.

Her anger had clouded her recently, mostly because she didn't want to see the Mondeans as anything more than an enemy to destroy. Still, observing them like that, laughing together as they prepared a meal, crying over their injuries and lost friends, made her reflect.

People didn't naturally set out to hurt others without reason, and even though the attack on Whitecliff had been brutal and horrifying, and retribution of some kind had to follow, she knew that it hadn't been a collective choice.

The Mondean chief, about whom they still knew frustratingly little beyond the basics, was a warmonger. More than that, he was an efficient warmonger.

He had developed a system through which the people he conquered would be assimilated within his forces in surprisingly little time, and then he'd use them to attack more tribes, thus building a self-powering machine.

Dorea knew that the ultimate fault resided in him. He was the one whose choices had led to the attack of Whitecliff. He was the one with blood on his hands, possibly even more than those who had done the actual deed.

Personal responsibility had always been an important value her parents had tried to teach her, but there was a limit to how much it could be stretched. With a system that involved thousands of people actively working against her, pointing fingers didn't help.

Unfortunately, Dorea didn't have the time or the skills to dismantle such a system from the inside. The amount of damage the Mondeans would surely do if left to themselves for as long as it took her to do something about their recruiting methods was simply too high.

Infiltration was something she had thought about several times. Dorea didn't consider herself the most subterfuge-oriented person, but she knew she'd only trust herself to get out of such a situation.

Somehow being recruited by the Mondeans without suffering whatever brainwashing they put the conquered mages through, gaining a position of high enough standing to learn important information, using that position to start undermining the system . . .

Those were all dreams. In the real world, she couldn't solve everything by herself. Especially not without shedding a drop of blood like she did in her fantasies.

She had neither the skill nor the temperament for it. However, one thing she had in spades was determination and mana, especially if she was allowed to replenish herself by killing her enemies.

Her natural inclination to battle, and more importantly, the urgency of saving her comrades now rather than later, meant that that path had been shut closed before it could ever open.

They might not all be individually responsible for the decision to attack Whitecliff, but they all took part in it. They killed, injured, and destroyed. Given their numeric superiority and that they might have a Master helping them, I have no choice but to be as brutally efficient in killing them as possible.

Of course, that all hinged on how the rescue attempt went.

If she was successful—she gave this a low level of chance—her duty would be to simply guide the saved prisoners back to Whitecliff, and to stay there to prepare for the inevitable new attack from the northern barbarians.

If she managed to get to the prisoners but was discovered during the rescue— this was much more likely, in her opinion—Dorea would have to fight her way out while defending the helpless mages. That would probably mean her death, but she'd take down as many of the bastards with her as she could.

And if possible, wake Jonah and the others so that they could try and run away by themselves, but that depended on how much they had been drugged.

The other possible course of action—waiting for Whitecliff's reinforcements to arrive in a day or so and mount an assault together—was the safest. It also ran the risk of being too late, since the Mondeans didn't look like they were setting up a permanent camp.

No, it was much more likely that they would have a short rest from their forced march and then continue deeper into the mountain ranges, after which any attempt from Whitecliff to rescue their people would be doomed from the beginning.

If they get close enough to their other armies, it's over. The window of time we have to act is very short and closing rapidly. Less than a day, I think, given how quickly they managed to move even while encumbered by all the wounded and prisoners.

That urgency set a hard limit on how much she could scope out the enemy forces—which mostly meant trying to understand how wounded the mages were and if Ghionn the Invisible Hand had stuck around—and it meant waiting for the troops Ed had promised would come was not a good idea.

Though she had left the village seeing red, seething with anger at the sheer destruction the Mondeans had enacted, Dorea was slowly realizing it had been the right choice all along.

Their slowness in gathering their forces had been why the sneak attack had succeeded—not counting the betrayal the latest group of refugees had enacted.

If Yaomi hadn't been alerted immediately, and had she not dropped everything to come to the rescue, Dorea didn't doubt that she would have found only smoking rubble rather than a scarred but still living village.

She hadn't waited long enough to ask how exactly they had managed to hold Ghionn back until the Witch's arrival. Still, given Voggo's extensive injuries and total exhaustion, she suspected the old man might have used something he had been keeping in reserve for an emergency.

Whatever it was that he had done had made him too weak to be of any use during the rescue operation—the very fact that he was sitting in his house rather than directing the healing of his people meant that he was worse off than he appeared, which was saying something. Dorea felt that, though her methods might have been a bit too abrupt, she had made the correct choice by leaving so soon.

Ultimately, the real choices were simply about how much she wanted to wait and whether she should set off a distraction, like she had done during her last rescue mission, or simply drop in and try to sneak by the guards.

As she sat there, hidden by the large rocks she had specifically chosen as a vantage point, Dorea observed the movements down below.

East of her position, close to the center of the camp but not exactly, was the tent she believed housed the prisoners.

It might have been the lack of a wood mage, but the Mondeans had learned from their last attempt that leaving their captives out in the open was not a good idea.

The presence of four guards told her enough. The girl cast her senses in that direction, still somewhat fearful of being found again by that weird, oily sphere she had felt earlier.

Luckily for her, nothing impeded her. As she had figured out, inside the guarded tent were her companions, all seemingly sleeping, likely under the influence of some drug meant to keep them down until they arrived at a safe place where the indoctrination could begin.

Dorea didn't want to think that any of her tribesmen were weak enough to fall under whatever sorcery the Mondeans had cooked up, but the thought of having to face Jonah on the battlefield sent shivers down her spine.

She simply couldn't allow that to happen.

She lingered on his signature for a bit longer than the others, noting all the bits of dried blood stuck to his skin. Her friend was injured but seemingly not in a dangerous manner.

With a sigh, Dorea restarted her surveillance. Nowhere she looked was an old man who fit the description given to her by Yaomi of Ghionn the Invisible Hand, which was an immense relief.

Other mages, however, seemed much less tired than she would have liked, and she counted more than a dozen conducting surveillance of their own on the surroundings to prevent sneak attacks.

Her stealth skills were seemingly sufficient to hide from their senses at the distance she was at, but she didn't know how they would fare if she got any closer.

This camp seemed much more organized than the one she had encountered in the forest so many months ago, and after half an hour of searching, she finally located the man responsible for it.

A short, ugly brunet sat at the head of a stone table—which immediately set her on high alert, as it was unlikely that the Mondeans would lug such a heavy thing around—and was seemingly busy giving orders to a constant stream of visitors.

He had, she could feel even with just her senses, gnarled features, a prominent brow, and surprisingly large hands. Though his appearance wasn't pleasant, he sat there with ease that could only be acquired with experience, deftly coordinating the setting up of the camp.

If, as she suspected, the man was an earth mage, things would get complicated quickly. He was too old to be of the new generation, that much she could tell even without seeing him, and the fact that he was given control over such a mission in a militaristic society that valued strength above all, meant he must have possessed some personal power.

It was obvious, then, that he was a mage from the previous generation. She didn't understand why no one had told her anything about an earth mage's presence during the assault.

The only thing that could explain it was that he had simply not taken part, preferring to keep to the back lines and allow his people and Ghionn to do the dirty work.

A smart enemy was worse than a powerful but stupid one. That was something Voggo had spent a long time explaining to them, and something which Dorea had been able to confirm through her own experience.

If the suspected earth mage was not particularly strong, he must have had other prominent qualities, otherwise the other Mondeans would not have accepted his lead. Considering the successful raid—the first of its kind since they started the hostilities—and the efficiency she could observe with her senses,

Dorea strongly suspected that he had been chosen for his strategic skills directly from above.

Nothing else could explain the evident respect she could sense around him. He didn't have the palpable aura of power Master mages had, nor were the people fearful of his wrath.

Such a capable foe would mean she needed to rethink her approach. He couldn't have ignored the possibility of Whitecliff sending people after them the moment they got their bearings, which suggested she needed to be even more careful.

I need a miracle.

CHAPTER THIRTY-EIGHT

Dorea was afraid she might have erred too much on the safe side as she watched the Mondean host pack up their camp and move deeper into the mountain range.

Her surveillance had unearthed several important pieces of information, which she would not have been comfortable without, but the thought that they might join up with another bigger army still ate at her.

Not only had she found out for sure that the man she believed to be in charge of the whole operation was, indeed, an earth mage—though one not known specifically for his prowess in battle—but also that the guards she had overheard talking believed that in two days, they'd get to a staging point where they'd meet the rest of their forces.

Apparently, the whole raid on Whitecliff had been little more than an after-thought for the Mondean leadership. Mostly, they had been interested in getting Ghionn the Invisible Hand on their side, and they had used the occasion to promise him a decent fight if he took part in the operation and ensured it didn't fail like those before it.

It had been incredibly frustrating to hear that. Dorea had to grit her teeth and breathe deeply to stop herself from jumping down and raining death and destruction on the people who had hurt her tribe so much.

Still, once she had recovered her calm, she was able to paint a more complete picture of the enemy operations.

The Mondeans were still embroiled in the war of conquest they had started in the spring. Still, unlike the beginning—where village after village had fallen quickly, putting up little resistance to their brutality and combined might—things had started to slow down.

The tribes in the eastern mountains had, according to what she learned by manipulating the winds to bring sound to her position, joined up together in something close to the alliance Whitecliff had with Camp and the Forest tribe.

It was apparently comprised of a dozen villages, all banded together to resist Mondean depredations.

Well, they hadn't put it exactly like that. It was more like "Those treacherous bastards, turning against the hand that protected them in the past and stabbing us in the back. How dare they call us aggressors when they obviously meant to attack us?!"

The logic wasn't particularly sound, but then again, I didn't expect it to be. To do the things they do, they need to be far removed from reality, otherwise they wouldn't be able to sleep.

Though not necessarily all important, the conversations she overheard reaffirmed her earlier conclusions. The Mondeans did not see themselves as evil. Rather, they thought they were a force of order, meant to end the chaos and division within the Sapiens tribes, all thanks to their glorious leader.

They didn't exactly say glorious when they spoke of Olnar—who she was finally learning was a water mage of great power and with little compunction for the lives of his enemies—in awed whispers, but they were generous with their compliments.

The mages who had taken part in the assault on Whitecliff either considered it simply part of their duties, showing the same deep disconnect between their words and reality as they hoped that killing and hurting so many people would somehow bring together everyone, or reveled in it.

Dorea made a note of all those who had no compunction in openly enjoying what they had done to her tribe. She would remember them, and if things went awry and she ended up having to fight like she suspected she would, she'd make a point of taking those out with extreme prejudice.

In a way, those people were the most logical. They simply liked bloodshed and fighting, and after having their assaults repelled several times, they felt good about finally showing the uppity southerners where their place was.

They were brutish barbarians who cared not for the pain they caused. They even reveled in it. But at least, there was no fake higher moral ground. They didn't think of themselves as doing the right thing for the people they oppressed.

It made them less unbearable to listen to. They were just enemies she'd need to destroy and with which no kind of argument could be had.

The others, who believed they were doing the right thing, were insufferable. They either believed that whatever their chief told them to do would eventually lead to the best outcome for everyone, without ever stopping to think about the impossibility of it—these were the new converts, from what she could glean—or simply thought of themselves as so superior that anything that would lead to the other tribes coming under their control was justified.

She might have spent too much time listening to these conversations and memorizing the feel of each and every one of those people. Still, since Dorea was becoming increasingly certain that she wouldn't manage to sneak in and back out alongside the prisoners, she had subconsciously decided that if she had to go, she'd clean the table before she died.

Unlike the camp she infiltrated in the forest, there were several dedicated lookouts, all mages, who constantly exchanged information between themselves.

The general organization, all thanks to the earth mage who led the host, was simply too well done for her to hope for a miracle. She had spent many long hours in wait, listening, feeling, and watching for a gap in the camp's defenses that never materialized.

Still, before she committed to an outright assault—if she didn't find another solution before a day was up, she'd need to do so, as waiting until they rejoined with the larger Mondean army would mean that Jonah and the others' fates would be sealed—Dorea wanted to try one last thing.

She had been thinking about the oily blackness that had touched her senses earlier for a while. Since no movement had happened in the camp below to indicate that it was their doing, she had ended up with two different hypotheses.

Firstly, which would mean she was already doomed, she had somehow touched upon Ghionn's aura. If the Master mage was present and knew of her, then it was already over. Nothing she could do in so little time would do anything to him.

Still, she wasn't convinced. Not only was he an ice mage, and therefore he should have nothing to do with the weird sensation that presence gave her, but the man was called the Invisible Hand for a reason. His skill in stealth magic was such that he could work several spells above an encampment without being noticed, and rain death upon them before they could realize they were under attack.

The possibility she most hoped for was that it had been someone or something else. A being strong enough to elicit such a reaction in her had to be a Master, and if she could bring its attention to the Mondean camp, she might be able to complete her mission while they were otherwise occupied.

Of course, I know this has a high chance of me dying anyway. If it's something similar to Old Titan, like I suspect, it might simply decide to kill me on the spot, and then this whole thing would be over.

But she had come too far now to stop. Dorea had to face the choice of certain death for herself—which surprisingly didn't scare her much anymore, beyond a dull pain at the thought of never seeing her family again—and likely continued imprisonment and brainwashing for her captured companions, or possible death and a decent chance of saving her friends.

In the end, the choice had already been made the moment she thought of it. She would do her best to locate that presence, assess if it was possible to ally with it or simply turn it against the Mondeans, and then go through with her rescue mission.

If it turned out to be something else, or she simply couldn't make it help her, she'd commit to a frontal assault and try to kill as many mages as possible before she was taken down herself.

With a sigh, Dorea finally stood up from her position above the encampment. She had stayed there for many long hours, and her limbs needed a good stretch before she could start her search.

The Mondeans were moving again and would likely stop only after an entire day of marching. That meant she'd need to catch up with them once she located her target, and the sooner she found it and convinced it to help her—or more likely enraged it enough that it would hunt her and lead it to her enemy—the less she'd have to travel to catch up with them.

Now that the scouts and lookouts had finally lowered their guards, Dorea had a fleeting thought of blitzing down the mountain and trying to go for the stealth approach all the same, but a look at the well-hidden communication happening between various people at the edges of the host told her that surveillance hadn't dropped at all.

If anything, it had increased in scope now that they were on the last stretch.

It was extremely annoying, having competent enemies. It severely limited one's possibilities and made simple plans even more alluring, though she knew it was a trap.

With her last observation over, she set off, carefully lowering herself from the outcropping she had camped out on and spinning up her Air Boost, though at low intensity to not spook anything that might be in range.

The fresh morning air felt fantastic on her skin, revitalizing her after a long night of surveillance, where she drifted off only for a few minutes at a time.

If I ever make it alive out of here, I want to come back and just enjoy the scenery. It's too beautiful not to.

Dawn painted the peaks around her in pink and gold, giving them an otherworldly feel. From the height she was at, she could see the ranges developing north for hundreds of miles, the sea to the west stretching as far as she could see, and to the south, the just waking forest.

As she levitated there, just taking in the beauty of nature all around, something once again pinged the edge of her senses.

Immediately, Dorea focused on that feeling, determined not to let it slip away. This time, the presence remained still rather than vanishing after unsettling her.

The girl decided to get closer to learn more, concentrating on prying all she could from just her mystical senses.

As she got closer, it started moving away, though slowly enough that she could easily follow. The suspicion that she had been noticed was confirmed when she stopped for a moment, only for it to stop as well, as if it were waiting for her to start moving again.

With a sigh, Dorea decided that if the presence had already known of her and was smart enough to want to communicate, she might as well go with it.

If it's Ghionn, I'm already dead. If it's a Master-level beast, and it hasn't already killed me, I might as well find out what it wants.

Powerful enhanced animals could have human-level intelligence, that much was known to all, but seeing one was not a common thing.

Even Old Titan, who was known as the most powerful denizen of the forest, had not shown that spark, for all that he was evidently an intelligent creature.

For an hour, Dorea drifted through the peaks, going almost parallel to the Mondean host, but always hidden from their direct sight by rocks or even the occasional lone tree.

Eventually, the presence touched down at the mouth of a valley. It was so well hidden within the mountains—and impossible to reach without magical assistance—that Dorea was sure nobody else could have found it without knowing about it first.

With some hesitation, she caught up.

It's too late now to back down. I chose this path; I might as well see it through.

The oily presence she had been following finally became visible to her eyes. As she got closer, she realized that her theory about it being either a mage or a powerful beast had been more correct than she could have possibly realized.

Standing on two hooved feet, with powerful, bulging muscles that belonged on a warrior; a short dark-blue furry coat that covered its entire body; humanlike hands; and two majestic ram horns, a goat man waited for her.

Dorea had known about the existence of in-between beings, not quite animals but not human either, as many cautionary tales spoke of them as either demons—though she learned from her studies that it was the wrong label, as real demons were an entirely different kind of being—or benevolent spirits.

Reality, as usual, was somewhere in the middle.

Jyūjin, beast men, abominations, spirits. You can call them any way you want. As long as they have a high intelligence, treating them all the same would be like treating all humans as if they were the same. Not a good idea.

"Hello there," she greeted as she touched down a couple dozen feet from it.

For all that she knew it wouldn't necessarily attack her immediately, Dorea was still wary. It was the first of its kind she had ever encountered, and considering her situation, she felt justifying being a bit on edge.

"Good morning, little Sapiens," the goat man greeted back, its voice deep and surprisingly intelligible. It had something close to an accent but not quite, likely given the slightly different shape of its vocal cords.

Dorea tentatively smiled, still trying to understand if the being was a friend or a foe.

It might have smiled back, or it might have threatened her life. Given how wide its lips pulled back, it was impossible for her to know.

The creature had a jarringly human set of teeth, of a brilliant white color, but its square pupils gave off no emotions.

It was only now that Dorea realized just how much people depended on micro-expressions to figure out others' moods, and being faced with something that lacked more than half of those felt unsettling.

It gave no other sign of possible aggression, though, and turned around, showing her its back in a way that no normal animal ever would.

It's either much dumber than I thought, and I doubt that, or so powerful it doesn't have anything to fear from me.

She hurried to follow as the goat man walked through the narrow gorge that served as the entrance to the hidden valley.

They walked silently for a few minutes, its strides much longer than hers, given its height of at least seven feet, forcing her to half-run to keep up.

Finally, a slice of paradise was revealed to them. If the plant life and animals of the mountains had been beautiful to look at, what was on display here blew them out of the water.

Brightly colored trees, as tall as the oldest oaks of the forest she lived by, gave the valley an otherworldly feel. A flock of birds she had never seen before, made of green, pink, and purple specimens with short and wide beaks, trilled happily atop them.

Fat fruits, looking ripe and juicy, hung from almost every tree in what would be an impossible sight without careful care.

The entire hidden valley, Dorea realized, was a private orchard. And its owner was the goat man she had followed.

Her senses didn't work as they should have, as things she could see with her eyes felt hazy and indistinct. She would have suspected it all of being an illusion if she hadn't been able to run her hands on the trees' bark or even touch one of their many fruits that weighed on the branches.

"Beautiful, isn't it?" her guide asked in its peculiar, unsettling tone of voice from just a few feet behind her.

Dorea turned to face it quickly, surprised that she had lowered her guard enough to let it get so close. With her mystical senses not working as they should, impeded as they were by something in the air, she hadn't even noticed it moving.

"It is. I would have never expected something like this here," she answered, trying to keep her tone steady.

It smiled again, seemingly pleased with her compliment. "I have worked hard to foster this kind of environment. Many years of research in the outside world and all its different habitats went into creating this perfect little garden."

The more it talked, the more Dorea realized that the goat man was older than she had first thought. The wistfulness in its tone strongly reminded her of the village elders when they spoke of their younger days, while its fur, which she had initially believed to be a uniform dark blue, actually had hints of gray and white at the edges.

It was still an imposing being, and the power that it must have been capable of stilled any thought she had of pushing it immediately. Still, she got the distinct impression that it didn't often have visitors, and letting it show off its creation was a good way to get on its good side.

"It took me a long time to get the waterfall just right. At first, too much water was coming out, and the small lake at its feet would have swallowed a good chunk of the valley," it droned on, gesturing to the western side of the valley, where a small stream tumbled down the rock wall, creating a perfect miniature of the main one at Tumbling Lake.

Finally, after another half an hour in which the goat man regaled her with all the trial and error that went into creating the valley, it stopped, seemingly having exhausted itself.

The short silence was finally interrupted when he spoke up in a much more serious tone, "But I don't want to bore you too much. We have important things to speak of."

Dorea looked at it curiously, projecting her willingness to hear it out.

Another unsettling smile followed, tinged with a hint of recognizable bloodlust. "We have a common enemy, little Sapiens. I want those who dare use my lands as if it were theirs gone for good, and I know you do too."

Dorea smiled back, lips peeled and magic thrumming in her veins. Revenge was close.

CHAPTER THIRTY-NINE

The goat man had a name, it turned out. Peve'nar was surprisingly sheepish at having forgotten to introduce himself and apologized profusely, saying that it had been at least a decade since he last had a guest.

Still, their purpose was the same, and an agreement was quickly reached.

Dorea was surprised to find that, so far, the Mondeans had deliberately avoided the straightest path across the mountains to get to them because of Peve'nar himself, who was known not to suffer intruders to all the mountain tribes.

Lately, they had gotten more arrogant and had seemingly forgotten what the angry goat man could do when his territory was trampled, in their quest for absolute dominance.

It was a great relief that she didn't have to convince him to see the Mondeans as enemies, as it had been one of her biggest worries. That her new ally wanted to bring the fight to them immediately was almost suspiciously good luck.

As Dad always says, don't look into a gift anoa's mouth. Trying to find a good thing's faults is a quick way to lose it.

Considering how desperate she was, Dorea couldn't afford to alienate Peve'nar. No, his very presence, as a Master-level being, made a mission that should have been totally impossible into a reasonably complex one.

The girl had almost given up entirely on succeeding. Thoughts of how exactly she should die had been increasingly common, and she had even started wondering what her last words should be.

No, she couldn't afford to say no. After she had agreed to help him, Peve'nar had quickly explained why he had approached her in the first place, which had been a pressing concern of hers.

It turned out that the goat man had very, very keen senses, and even from a great distance, he had been able to discover her three-element mana, and more than that, that there was something unique about her.

He had been curious about it but, upon seeing her hesitance, had immediately backed down. That such a peculiar creature could show that level of understanding and social grace was incredible to her, but Dorea was nothing if not grateful for it.

His plan, it turned out, was to use her as a secondary scout, since though he considered himself fluent in human speech and customs, he was afraid he might miss something crucial.

Once she had confirmed that the coast was clear and that no trap or unexpectedly powerful mage was present, they would launch their assault together.

When she confessed her desire to first save her friends and then to engage the enemy, Peve'nar had brushed her off, saying that as long she got them out of the camp and quickly came back, he'd be happy to play the distraction.

Afterward, they'd both unleash their full might and send an unambiguous message to the Mondean leadership.

Dorea felt very weird about the whole thing. She had somehow managed to meet a Master-level being, found him to be entirely agreeable, and he also had the very same objective as she did!

She knew that the hard part was still to come. She had agreed to come back and fight, to take on the entirety of the army that broke Whitecliff with only the goat man as backup.

But she had built up the complexity of the mission so much in her head that something actually going right unsettled her.

Still, she wasn't about to renege on her word. Dorea set off from the hidden valley after a terrifying moment in which she realized she couldn't have left it on her own, as her magic refused to answer her call.

Only when she walked through the narrow path that led away from it was she finally able to regain control of it.

Somehow, Peve'nar had created wards that could stop a mage from accessing their powers entirely. That such a thing could exist at all was terrifying, and Dorea promised herself she'd finish her warding studies so that she could find a way to protect herself.

Catching up with the Mondeans was the work of a couple of hours of low-power Air Boost as she followed the traces of their passing.

Once she got there, she dropped her spell, keeping her senses peeled so as to notice any outrider or scout who might ping her position.

She kept to the mountain paths, high enough that they wouldn't be able to see her, though she had to push herself to keep up since the road was so often broken by fallen trees or steep climbs.

For a few hours, the host kept moving, though without the urgency that had led them away from Whitecliff, as they started feeling more secure now that they were deep in their territory and only a day away from the main army.

When they finally stopped, sooner than she expected given the efficiency she had observed previously, Dorea became suspicious that something had changed.

It only took her another hour of surveillance before the reason for the changed behavior became clear. Another person now sat in the central tent, where the short, ugly man she had observed earlier used to give orders.

Long hair, wrinkles, and a glass made of ice in his hands made it immediately obvious who it was that had changed the routine. Only one person's presence could give the Mondeans enough safety that they no longer felt the need to hurry back to their main army.

Ghionn the Invisible Hand, the Master-rank ice mage who had battled Voggo and Yaomi above Whitecliff, had returned.

The man's presence changed everything. Though she doubted he'd be willing to protect each and every one of his nominal allies, he wouldn't allow her to run roughshod over the camp, and even the assault she had planned out with Peve'nar's help would have to be rethought.

Must it? Do I have the time to go back to the drawing board and plan it out differently? No. No, I can't. Jonah and the others would be gone if we allowed them to join the main army. They'd be as good as dead.

Lies were necessary in any civilized society, as people couldn't always be trusted to handle the unvarnished truth. They were the bread and butter of anyone with political ambitions, as they'd need to carefully calculate exactly how much they could reveal.

Dorea had, so far, managed to remain honest and truthful, at most having to deflect away from probing questions. That part of her that had rebelled against the idea of having to dirty her conscience to do the right thing was now facing its toughest challenge.

The right thing would have been to stop, seek Peve'nar immediately, alert him to Ghionn's presence, and find another way to save her comrades.

The more experienced, calculating side of her knew that if she were to do such a thing, it would mean the end of her rescue attempt. She simply would never get another opportunity like this.

A strong, dedicated ally ready to take on all the heat while she infiltrated the camp and removed the prisoners; the Mondeans tired enough that they wouldn't be able to fight at full power and far away from reinforcements that unless a miracle happened, they'd be far too late to do anything.

The conditions were all perfect. If she alerted Peve'nar of the ice Master's presence, he'd likely not want to go through with it.

Dorea felt something within herself, something innocent and important, shatter as she decided to keep her mouth shut.

The goat man had been nothing but friendly and courteous; he had decided to help her even when he didn't need to and allowed her to alter his plans to achieve her objective.

But the safety of her friends came first, and when she put that on a scale against her new ally, there was no contest.

With a heavy heart, Dorea stayed still, waiting another long hour until she received Peve'nar's questioning mana pulse.

She didn't hesitate, having put aside all of her gripes and doubts. A clear, unmistakable go-ahead later, she felt the beast man approach the camp.

Dorea knew that if he were to survive the coming fight, she'd have a tough time explaining why she had kept quiet, if he even gave her the time to. However, she had made her choice and would have to deal with the consequences if she managed to make it out.

Shaking off any distracting thought of the future, the girl set about doing her part. Now that she was committed, she'd have to do her very best to pull it off, otherwise the sacrifice she had imposed on her ally and the damning of her conscience would be for nothing.

As soon as the first explosion resounded through the valley where the Mondeans had set up, Dorea jumped in, keeping her mana tight beneath her skin and flying close to the ground.

Rocks and shrubbery passed beneath her feet at great speeds, even as she tried to disturb as little dust as possible. As she got closer, shouts of surprise and anger started being audible, and she knew that Peve'nar was doing his part.

The lookouts closest to her position were all busy checking out the situation developing on the other side of the camp, though they had not left their post in a surprising show of professionalism.

That didn't help them against the sharpened wind blades she had prepared, and both men's heads soon rolled on the ground. Dorea didn't stop to grant them even a stray thought, such was her concentration.

Once she had gotten in, she dismissed her magic and made sure to act as if she belonged, looking harried and distracted by the developing fight on the eastern side.

Typically, such a simple disguise would not have worked, as people from the same tribe would immediately recognize her as not belonging. However, the Mondean habit of absorbing conquered villages and building heterogeneous armies meant that no one batted an eye at her presence, especially because she made sure to curse under her breath and look very harried, as if she had something important she needed to do.

In a way, it was the truth.

Only when she got close to the tent where the prisoners were being held did she slow down. Having had the chance to observe the Mondean leader's methods for several hours, Dorea was sure that the man would not be incompetent enough to allow just anyone access to the kidnapped Gifted.

Likely, the earth mage had ensured the guards knew not to let anyone whom he hadn't personally allowed in. It meant she couldn't come up with any old excuse to convince the four obstacles that she should be let in.

A direct assault was also considered shortly—it was her preferred method, as too much subterfuge had already gone into this mission for her tastes—but set aside, as many Mondeans were still around, not having been fooled by the singular attack vector.

It's incredibly annoying to contend with a competent enemy commander. It makes it necessary to constantly adapt to their actions. He must have ordered them not to leave their post if they get attacked by a small force from one side.

Dorea knew that Peve'nar could bring much more destruction if he wanted. He'd easily be able to wipe the camp from the face of the earth if he truly let go, but he had agreed to keep to hit-and-run tactics and only minor damage until she had gotten her friends out. That consideration also meant there wasn't enough urgency between the enemies, and she would have to rethink her approach.

Since lying and direct assault were out, Dorea only saw the stealth approach as possible. She made her way into a tent close to the prisoners' and entered it after ensuring it was empty and concentrated.

The main principle behind her stealth technique was that of holding the weight of her mana back from affecting the world around her. It might have felt simply like she was stopping mana from leaking out, but the theory was clear.

If she just kept a hold on her power, she would still be immediately identifiable to any sensor, though they wouldn't feel her coming before she entered their range.

True stealth meant preventing another mage from feeling her entirely. That meant a much more involved process, whose side effect was that she also became unnoticeable to the naked eye.

Humans relied on many more senses than they realized, and though she couldn't become invisible, if she could achieve the true, perfect actualization of the technique, she'd essentially be imperceptible unless standing right in front of the observer.

She had only managed something close to it during training, though, and even then only for a short time. However, Dorea was no stranger to improvisation, and high-stakes situations brought out the best of her.

Before she could even attempt what would have been a technically challenging and highly complex operation, however, a much bigger explosion than any before it rang out.

With a chill, Dorea realized what it meant. Peve'nar wouldn't have needed to use that much power unless confronted with someone stronger than expected.

She pushed down the shame she felt at that. Her deception would cost the friendly, if weird, goat man much, possibly even his life. But if she allowed that to stop her now, it would all be for nothing.

Now that it was evident that a much greater assault was underway and the entirety of the army was under threat, the Mondeans' attention was pulled to the east, where the two Masters battled it out in the sky.

Rather than stop and stare like everyone else, however much she might have wanted to, Dorea used the hate and anger she had buried deep within to fuel herself.

Without hesitation, she strode out of the tent she had taken refuge in.

I have no idea how long Peve'nar can hold off against Ghionn, which means the slow and stealthy approach is out. Back to the basics it is.

It wasn't such a sacrifice anyway since Dorea much preferred fighting things out.

Now sure of the path forward, she quickly strode toward where she felt her companions being held. People were swarming by now, either running away from the clash of titans or, in a few specific cases, toward it.

The press of bodies made it easy to get to her target unnoticed, and though she was tempted to unleash her full might while in the middle of the enemy encampment, she held herself back.

First, I save them. Second, I come back and kill as many of these fuckers as I can.

Unfortunately, the four guards assigned to the prisoners' tent were still there, not having been spooked enough to leave their post.

Three of them, however, were entirely focused on the fight developing in the sky above them, while the last only occasionally glanced at his surroundings.

As silently as she could, Dorea prepared wind blades for each. The manipulation was coming easier than she expected, and if she could dedicate the time to it, she wouldn't be surprised if it turned into a proper spell with just a few hours of work.

Still, it worked well enough, even for her purposes. Efficiency and power could be simply made up for by an abundance of mana, and she had it in spades by now.

The first guard dropped silently, barely managing to open his mouth to call to the others. Without stopping, she cut down the second and third.

"Intrud—"

The last one had managed to let out half a shout before she killed him too, mercilessly staring into the boy's eyes.

He was younger than she had first believed, probably not even out of his teens yet. Dorea, however, felt nothing if not cold satisfaction.

The time for philosophical and ethical considerations had long since passed, and she was well and truly committed now.

The little mana she had expended to remove the four obstacles was immediately refilled and then some. The girl felt her reserves expand slightly and sighed at the stretch.

With that over, she walked into the tent that housed her friends and was relieved to see them with her own eyes.

She lingered on Jonah's still form for just a moment, drinking in the sight. Though she had felt him breathe with her mystical senses, using her mortal ones to ensure he was alive meant more.

With a deep breath, she crafted a Wind Bulwark around them, lifting them from the bare floor where they had been dumped and cocooning them in her power.

Then, with a mental push, she blew out of the tent, shredding it to pieces.

CHAPTER FORTY

A great battle raged above the Mondean encampment. Majestic ice snakes, whose glittering scales reflected the light of the setting sun, crashed against dark waves of power.

Their beauty was more of a weapon than their might, as they hid countless shards of sharpened ice, which rained down upon their target, uncaring of any who might have been below it.

The valley's landscape was changing with the rhythm of the battle as the great fighters of the region duked it out. Shadows cast by the tall peaks rose from the ground, crossing the threshold between the world of dreams and that of the living, and formed an impenetrable barrier as mighty as the mountains they were born from.

A ferocious blizzard picked up, blanketing the entirety of the encampment in freezing winds, spelling the doom of many more than would have died had the ice mage not interfered at all.

But Ghionn doesn't care about them. Yaomi was right; he's only here because he wants to face strong opponents. If it means there are some dead as collateral damage, he wouldn't even notice.

Dorea gave one last prayer to the Goddess to protect Peve'nar, the friendly goat man who had agreed to serve as a distraction while she rescued her kidnapped friends.

He ended up having to face a much harder task than he had imagined, and though she knew that if he survived, he'd be very cross with her, she still hoped he'd make it.

That moment over, she pushed all distracting thoughts away and focused on maintaining her traveling speed. Though not as fast as when by herself, Dorea was using her combination magic of Air Boost and Wind Bulwark to its limits, taking twelve other people with her.

She had entirely given up on stealth, as the circumstances didn't allow for anything less than her absolute best. Her magic roared out, unbound for the first time since she started her chase.

Her true objective was not getting back to Whitecliff, however much she might have liked to do so. She was not naive enough to believe she wouldn't be chased down as soon as a semblance of order was restored within the Mondean ranks.

No, I just need to push far away enough that whoever is sent after me won't be able to get reinforcements. Then, as soon as I have put the others somewhere safe, I can truly cut loose.

Dorea wiped the slightly deranged grin from her face. She'd get her moment, but it was not there yet.

She glanced back at her friends, noticing their rough state, but their even breaths as they slept off whatever drugs they had been given calmed her.

Compared to the first rescue she had to mount, their journey was as smooth as silk. Everyone had their own individual cocoon of air that kept them still, and if they were to end up under attack, the Bulwark that covered them would stop anything.

Half an hour of hard travel later, Dorea touched down. It wasn't as close to the spot she had picked as she would have liked, but it would have to make do.

Carefully, she placed her friends inside a crevice, where they should be out of direct spellfire. Unfortunately, it wouldn't serve to hide their presence, but it was the best she could do.

I'll just have to stop anything that gets too close to them myself.

Dorea hadn't stopped her flight without reason. Though she had pushed herself hard to get as far away from the army as possible, she had kept her senses focused on any possible pursuer, and finally, something had come into her range.

Since Dorea sincerely doubted that they'd allow her to continue flying as much as she wanted, and engaging a group of unknown Gifted in aerial combat while protecting her friends was something she had learned the hard way not to do, she had picked a spot to have the confrontation herself.

Had the drugged prisoners woken up, she might have simply sent them on their way and placed herself in the path of any pursuer, acting as an unmoving rock against the river.

However, the situation was different. Dorea needed to act as both a defender and an attacker, as she couldn't allow any of the Mondeans that had found her trail to go back and alert their companions about where to find her.

That meant a short, brutal fight, where she would have to have absolutely no mercy.

I can't lose too much time in case this is just the vanguard of a bigger group. I can only hope that Peve'nar has managed to keep their attention on him all this time, and these are the only ones who thought to pursue me.

Three mages finally touched down, all held in a similar construct to what she had used with her friends. Dorea immediately pegged the long-haired brunette in the center as an air mage and the most dangerous one.

The versatility required to develop such spells, especially in a society as focused on outright offensive power as the Mondeans' made the girl a real threat.

Though she was aching to fight, to finally let loose all the anger and frustration she had been bottling up for so long, Dorea forced herself to take a moment to observe her enemies.

The two boys on the sides looked very stereotypically northern, with leather coats and animal bone and teeth adornments. Their plain appearance, however, was coupled with a shrewd look in the left one's eyes and an expectant grin on the right one.

Though these three couldn't be older than twenty, they had seen much bloodshed and had taken part in the assault on Whitecliff. They might even have personally killed some of her tribesmen.

Without a doubt, they had a share of blame for their deaths.

From what little she could glean with a cursory observation, Dorea could sense that the two boys were lightning mages. It was rare to have so many in one team—something that almost never happened in Whitecliff—but she guessed that when a host reached the thousand Gifted, simple considerations like keeping a balance in a team's composition went out the window.

"You can't escape. Already, we have sent messengers to the main army. Give up quietly, and you'll keep your life," the leftmost one said dispassionately.

Though his words implied there could be mercy if she complied, Dorea knew the barbarians' methods all too well.

Death would be the only fate awaiting her if she followed their commands—not that she had any intention of doing so, even had their words been genuine—possibly only followed after a long period of suffering.

Dorea wasn't afraid of death. She knew her end would come, sooner rather than later even, if she continued taking so many dangerous missions.

Then again, considering what she was about to do to them, maybe they weren't the only overly brutal ones.

Rather than answering to the provocation and engaging in what would have no doubt been a fruitless discussion meant only to waste her time, Dorea responded in a different way.

"Scatter!" the girl yelled, her eyes widening at the unexpected attack.

A hail of Exploding Water Bullets bombarded the three mages, sending a shock wave with the power emitted. A hasty wind barrier was the only thing that saved the more attentive girl as her two companions were blown away.

"Aaargh!" the left one yelled, clutching the stump of his leg.

As a spell, Exploding Water Bullets had acquired enough power to blow through a sturdy tree. Fueled by the unending rage she had been feeling ever since word of the attack on her village had reached her, Dorea unleashed an even more powerful variant, pushing almost too much mana into it.

That led to a destabilization of the matrix, and she had to manually keep the compressed marbles of water together. The end result was worth it.

A shower of rock shards had hit the lucky two mages who had managed to avoid a direct hit, rendering them incapable of responding quickly.

Taking advantage of their confusion, Dorea shot another precisely aimed Bullet, ending the wounded mage's life.

Immediately after, she gathered the headless body with the air and threw it to the remaining man, absorbing the lightning bolt he had crafted.

A wind blade smashed against her Bulwark, strong enough to cut her in two but useless before her barrier.

The two remaining mages split apart, trying to encircle her. They took aim, sending simultaneous bolts of electricity and blades of wind, trying to pin her down.

Though she had proven her defense to be mighty, any shield would eventually fall under a concerted effort, and it was apparent they were trying to exhaust her like that.

Dorea didn't allow herself to fall to such a tactic and flew up into the sky, the winds kicked up by her move conjuring a cloud of dust that covered her enemies' sight.

In a battle between mages, the physical senses were much less useful than the mystical ones, but losing access to sight was still a heavy restriction.

She swiftly maneuvered against the clumsier shots, a bolt passing harmlessly beneath her feet even as a gust of wind blew away the cover.

In midair, Dorea called upon the latent electricity of the atmosphere and crafted several Lightning Spheres. Her first spell answered readily, and the fury she had been feeling inside fueled its might.

The male, who shared the element she was using, had enough time to realize what was coming. He opened his mouth to shout, desperate to alert his companion.

The roar of her magic being unleashed overwhelmed his voice, and the result of it made the attempt useless.

The crackling cage of electricity that resulted from Lightning Sphere hitting its target, multiplied by a dozen, rendered the rocky battlefield into an otherworldly sight.

For just a moment, it was as if they had all been lifted inside a thundercloud, where mighty arcs of power blew through any opposition.

Little was left of the two mages she had been battling after that.

Only their residual power, which Dorea drank to replenish her resources, attested to their presence, as their remains were charred beyond recognition.

The blonde allowed herself only a moment of stillness. She breathed in harshly, not particularly winded by the effort so much as by the casualness with which she wiped three people off the face of the earth.

Dorea then walked over to where she had hidden her still sleeping friends, somewhat surprised that they were all still unconscious after all the fighting, and crafted another Bulwark around them.

They must have really been heavy-handed with the drugs this time. I hope Voggo will be able to help them with any side effects . . .

Rising back up into the sky, Dorea glanced at the direction she had come from, where she had left Peve'nar to fend for himself against a Master and the entire Mondean army.

The only thing that spurred her on her path was the thought that reinforcements could be coming soon, from what she had been told by the lightning mage she had just killed.

Honor demanded that she leave her friends there, now that she had ensured their immediate survival, and fly back to help her ally.

But Dorea couldn't be sure more were not coming—instead, she strongly suspected she would have to face more mages before she got to safety—and the lives of the people she was charged with saving had to come first.

Therefore, with a heavy heart, Dorea pushed on, flying at breakneck speeds toward the only place she knew to be safe in the mountains.

Her journey was undisturbed, the wildlife seemingly understanding that to get in her path would mean certain death, until she had almost gotten there.

All of a sudden, Dorea felt the very air drying out.

It was like someone had sucked away all the moisture, blinding her water senses entirely.

A foreboding feeling gripped her as she knew of only one person whose control allowed for such a thing. The one mage below the Master level she had decided to avoid if possible.

Refugee groups from the tribes that had fought against the Mondeans all reported one thing. That the young chief, the person who had started the entire campaign of conquest, was a monster in human flesh.

Dorea didn't stick around to wait and see if her feeling was correct.

She grabbed her friends and shot off, flying directly toward her destination.

If it's who I think it is, I need to get the others to safety before I can fight him. But this might actually be good.

The conflict against the Mondeans had always been one-sided, as the northerners sought to bring the entire Loisos region under their control.

If it were up to the alliance, they'd simply live their lives in peace, warily observing the much graver threat posed by the Ergasters. Instead, they were all forced to fight off the growing presence up north.

That impulse of conquest was not something that could simply be taken back once it started, Voggo had been very clear. Merely killing the Mondean chief wouldn't necessarily mean the end of the hostilities—rather, it might mean a more concerted effort to bring the ones who killed him to ruin as revenge—but if one managed to survive the initial chaos after his death . . . Well, at least on that specific border, things might be finally over.

Dorea hadn't even entertained the idea of taking off on a foolish mission to go and kill a man who was supposed to be the closest Journeyman to Master rank. But if he was coming to get her himself, well, an opportunity opened up.

Since her survival had always been in question during this mission, Dorea didn't feel like she was taking excessive risks.

Her only problem was that her companions were all still out of it and would just be a liability in such a high-stakes fight.

Before realizing whom she was being followed by, her plan had been to drop them off in a safe location—and there was only one truly safe place in the mountains.

Her flight was surprisingly undisturbed. Either her hunter was not as fast as she was—an unlikely thing since she was so burdened—or he had decided to let her get to where she wanted to. If it was the latter, it meant he was extremely confident.

Well, the more he believes he'll win, the more surprised he'll be. I'll take any advantage I can get.

The mountainous landscape would have been too confusing to navigate, especially since she was trying to go as fast as possible, but Dorea had taken the time, when she first left Peve'nar's valley, to memorize the path that led to it.

Even then, when she hadn't known of Ghionn's presence, she had wanted to secure a truly safe place to leave her friends so that she could go back to fight alongside the goat man without worries.

That caution served her well now, as she sped through valleys and peaks. The absence of any evident pursuer didn't make her relax. If anything, it made her even warier.

Dorea was sure she had felt her control over water slip for a moment. That meant the Mondean chief couldn't be too far, and his traveling speed must have been well above average to have caught up so quickly.

Finally, she touched down before the narrow path that led to Peve'nar's abode. Night had well and truly fallen by then, and the only light available came from the moon and stars as they twinkled uncaringly.

All the death and destruction of the day, every spell she had ever cast, the effort she had put into her craft. They meant nothing in the grand scheme of things, she knew this much.

But Dorea had long since made peace with how uncaring the universe was. Life happened without rhyme or reason.

She had chosen what her most treasured things were: her family, her friends, and Whitecliff, the village she belonged to.

To defend those, she'd do anything.

Dorea gently pushed her companions deeper until her magic abruptly stopped working. She smiled, happy to find that Peve'nar's wards were still working, and turned around, determined to face what could be the last fight of her life.

"Are you ready now?" a smooth, deep voice came seemingly from the air.

Dorea didn't start. She had realized, during her long flight, that burdened as she was, she couldn't have possibly escaped her pursuer.

That implied he had deliberately allowed her to get there. It also meant he could have attacked her from behind, and she would have been in a terrible position to respond.

"Thank you for waiting," she answered, unsurprised to see a young man appear, a thin coating of water coming off his skin to reveal his features.

Finally, Dorea laid her eyes on the man responsible for all the pain and suffering her people had gone through. The root cause of all that had happened to Whitecliff.

She only had one thing to say.

"I thought you'd be taller."

CHAPTER FORTY-ONE

You are just as beautiful and direct as I have been told," he answered, seemingly amused by her remark.

That he had known about her beforehand put her on high alert. Dorea had believed, until now, that the alliance had been almost an afterthought in the general Mondean strategy. They had seemed much more interested in conquering the neighboring mountain tribes than pushing south, and all the attacks that did come were more meant as punitive measures.

If the leadership had kept a close enough eye on the situation to know about her, they were much more involved than she had originally believed.

"You should get to know someone before you start handing out compliments like that. You'll make them think you give them to everyone," she responded.

The boy—and it was a boy, for all the terrible things he had done and the power he wielded, both political and magical—threw his head back and laughed.

It was a bright, happy thing. His blond hair flew around, the long braid he had tied them in doing little to stop their escape. His eyes, an icy blue, gained a warmth that had not been there.

He smiled widely, forming dimples and showing off his pearly white teeth.

All in all, the monstrous chief of the Mondeans, who had been terrorizing the entire region and whose exploits were recounted with hushed whispers, was a pretty boy.

"Oh, that's a bad habit of mine, you see. When I meet a beautiful and fierce girl like you, it just makes me lose control a little bit," he explained, his eyes abruptly becoming cold again.

The warmth that had been there, that made him look like any other boy his age, was suddenly gone.

Left behind was an intense, bordering on maniacal stare. His smile became tinged with a touch of insanity as he kept looking at her, hardly blinking.

The abrupt shift in personality threw her off, but Dorea did her best not to let it affect her. After all, she had known there had to be a dark side to him.

"It seems you already know me, but I've been taught to present myself properly when first meeting someone. My name is Dorea of Whitecliff. Pleased to finally meet you."

Just as quickly as the unsettling expression had come, it was gone. Again, he was just a handsome teenager.

"Oh, you are correct. If my father has ever taught me anything of use, it was manners. I'm Olnar, the chief of the tribe that lives below Mondeo, the mountain of the Gods." His hair, sent flying by his previous bout of laughter, put itself back into order without any overt input from him. "I have heard many things about the young mage who defended her quaint little village. Truly, an amazing story. I was surprised you weren't there for the last act."

Dorea carefully observed what he was doing and was surprised to find that a thin, almost imperceptible film of water covered each and every strand.

That level of control is insane, even for me. He can't be holding everything together with simple manipulation, but who would spend so much time crafting such a spell?

That Olnar was not right in the head had been clear from the start. But for someone whose explicit goal was to bind all the Sapiens tribes under his banner to waste his time on a vanity spell . . . Unless, of course, the magic was not limited to simple effects like the one she just observed.

Because she was distracted by studying his every movement, it took her a moment to finally register his words.

The roar of her blood boiling at such a provocation, coupled with the fact that she finally had found someone she could hold wholly responsible for everything she had to go through, made it very difficult to hold back.

But hold back, she did. Dorea was not in a situation where she could be careless with her actions, and she had long since mastered her more impulsive side, especially after Voggo's ritual cleansed her of the accumulated taint.

"Hmmm . . . I would have thought you'd get angrier. It seems like the reports I got weren't as accurate as they should have been," Olnar casually commented, observing her like one would a bug.

There was something deeply unsettling about the way he behaved. Dorea had met many megalomaniacs, crazy people, and even righteous crusaders. The Mondean chief was none of those things.

Though she hadn't known him for long, already a picture was forming in her mind.

For someone to be able to kill their own father the moment they became powerful enough to deal with the aftermath and to immediately go on to wage war on all his neighbors in a clinical, almost systematic manner made for a very specific type of person.

Voggo had told her, during one of his private lessons after a council meeting, that she was likely to meet all types of people for as long as she acted as a leader. To prepare her for that, he had given her a few ways to deal with the crazies.

Well, people with genuine illnesses of the mind would require specific approaches and the usage of medication, but for those who somehow gained power, she needed ways to deal with them in the short term.

Methodical, cold, rational, but prone to bouts of extreme emotions. All the categories fit into one specific archetype she had been told to be wary about.

Moral Insanity was, according to the old shaman, an unfortunately common thing among powerful mages. Not everyone was built to belong in a society, after all.

Some said it was a result of demonic possession. Others believed it came from damage to the mind during the Trial. Voggo, on the other hand, said it was merely a human condition.

Already, she could fit together many more pieces of the puzzle that had always seemed not to make sense. The relentless drive behind all the actions up north, the sheer efficiency of the slaughter, and the surprising little trouble the Mondeans had with absorbing conquered people into their forces.

The person she was about to fight did not care about honor, tradition, or fairness. He was a relentless machine fueled by delusions of grandeur.

Is it still delusions if he has managed to take control of half the mountain range?

Olnar was not someone she would have liked to face without a good plan, especially because he seemed very likely to have one of his own and perfectly capable of improvising on the spot.

"It seems like you've been keeping an eye on me. What, is your campaign going so poorly that you have to distract yourself from the losses?" she provoked, still seeking to learn more about him.

Instead of the explosion of rage Dorea had expected, Olnar just smiled. A delighted expression that looked entirely out of place. "Complications were to be expected. Apparently, not everyone is happy about coming under my rule. Can you imagine?"

Seeing that their talk was going nowhere and deciding that stalling further would only help him, Dorea put an end to the banter. "This has been lovely," she snarked. "But we should both do our jobs, don't you think?"

The boy sighed dramatically. "And here I was, thinking we were both enjoying our chat. Truly, you break my heart." His eyes, differently from his warm tone, were cold. Hard as flint, they roved over her body, cataloging every minute twitch.

From what she had been able to learn about him, Olnar had achieved a level of control over water that put him at the border between Journeyman and Master. In a few years, when he had the time to grow his reserves further, he'd probably fall into the latter category without needing to do anything.

That meant using his favorite element against him was more likely to do harm than good. Though Exploding Water Bullet was a fast-moving spell, and she didn't expect him to snatch control of it from her, he'd be able to use the leftover liquid to significant effect.

Not that he needs it. I can already feel his grip on every bit of moisture in the atmosphere. In a way, it reminds me of the aura emitted by the Ubag Master, though it's not exactly the same thing.

In the end, she'd have to trust her two other elements to do the job, and if it became necessary, she had a couple of trump cards she could use. Dorea wasn't one to keep her best to the last moment without reason; surprising the enemy with overwhelming might right from the start was a valid strategy, after all.

But she had a feeling that she'd regret not using those spells at their best possible form, which required some setting up beforehand.

Without further ado, Dorea snapped out a Lightning Sphere, the power answering eagerly to her call. It roared out, quickly crossing the distance, only to be met with a thin veil of water, which dispersed the angry electricity with little trouble.

Of course he knows about conductivity. Well, it was worth a try.

Rather than being discouraged, Dorea grinned, bloodlust pumping. So far, she had managed to keep a leash on her darker instincts, as there was always a more important goal she needed to achieve.

However, that was no longer the case. Her friends were safe, ensconced behind Peve'nar's wards. Nothing short of another Master could hope to penetrate those defenses.

Her duty was to defend her village, and she had the architect of all their sufferings in front of her. She'd ensure a great success if she could manage to kill him.

That meant she no longer needed to hold back.

More and more Spheres materialized from her mana, arching around Olnar's shield like angry bees. Dorea pumped them out with little care for collateral damage, as they were in an uninhabited valley.

Though initially defended against by the veils of water Olnar kept raising, the spells exploded into bright arcs of electricity, blinding her opponent's sight and even forcing him to dodge hurriedly.

All through her barrage, Olnar kept a calm and collected look, swiftly reacting to an attack that would have been difficult to face for anyone.

Seemingly done with being passive, he raised his hand toward her, and with a flick of his fingers, whips of water formed up, snaking toward her with great force.

Dorea raised her Bulwark but didn't stop there, not wanting to become a stationary target. Air Boost lifted her up, easily allowing her to dodge the hits she decided not to take head-on.

And so the battle raged, Dorea flying through the air, acrobatically avoiding most of the whips that would have cut her in twain, while the remaining ones splashed harmlessly against her shield. All the while, she kept up her barrage of Lightning Spheres, forcing Olnar to move around the battlefield, even as he managed to keep the worst of the damage down thanks to his water veils.

This is a battle of endurance. If I try to go in for the kill now, I'll just waste a tremendous amount of mana and he'll most likely survive it. I need to keep attacking him while I prepare for the next step.

Her opponent, too, seemed happy to keep going as they were. More than once he had the opportunity to push her harder, but he kept the pace, apparently sharing her same train of thought.

Had Dorea been an average Gifted, her fate would have been sealed then and there. The fight against the three pursuers and the long flight with her friends as baggage should have, by all rights, exhausted her.

By then, it would have taken just a short bout to bring her to her knees. Instead, thanks to her weird mutation, Dorea was able to keep going as if she had just rested for hours.

The mana she had absorbed from the three Mondean mages had refilled her reserves and even expanded them slightly—the increases were getting slower as she got stronger, but anything was better than nothing—which meant that she was full by the time Olnar revealed himself.

Dorea deliberately started slowing down, tanking more hits than she was dodging and making her Lightning Spheres sloppier. She put up a front of someone reaching the end of her rope and saw the glint of victory in her opponent's eyes.

Olnar widely gestured with his hands toward her, and the waters accumulated on the ground rose in response. Twin liquid dragons were born and roared out their might for all the world to hear.

They then set their sight on her and flew, leaving the earth behind to crash into her Bulwark, snapping at it with great force and throwing themselves at it, in an attempt to bring her back to land.

Dorea, however, kept her eyes on the prize. All of a sudden, her tiredness and sluggish demeanor disappeared, revealing the act for what it had been. Before Olnar could realize the deception, she took advantage of it, catalyzing the leftover energy from all her Spheres into one mighty bolt of lightning.

The blinding energy left her hands, traveling through the air at speeds that boggled the mind, leaving behind just the smell of ozone and the crack of thunder.

A flash of light erupted when it hit, blocking her from seeing the result.

Relying on her metaphysical senses, Dorea returned to the air, gaining altitude to prevent retaliation from reaching her.

Before sight could return to her, she felt a great deal of power being dumped into the water below, signifying that the blow had not been enough to take Olnar out of the fight.

A colossal wave rose, fueled by mana to grow and grow until it reached the sky, becoming almost as tall as the nearby peak.

Shocked by the speed at which it had formed, Dorea flew away from it, escaping its grasp just barely. In exchange, she ended up in the path of a water whip, which smashed into her Bulwark with enough strength to crack it.

She was sent tumbling down, and for a moment, the girl believed she was done for. However, when she touched the wave, rather than sucking her in like she expected it to, it disappeared like fog beneath the summer sun.

Immediately, Dorea realized she had been had. Illusion magic was not something she had ever had to fight against before, but she should have known that sooner or later, it would happen.

Just as she had that realization, another whip crashed into her shield, cracking it again after it had just sealed up.

Dorea spent the next couple of minutes dodging increasingly powerful attacks. The gloves had come off, it seemed, and Olnar was no longer trying to assess her.

His illusion—Dorea set the part of her that was raging at such underhanded tricks to the side; there would be time for that later when she had won—had managed to give him the upper hand in the flow of battle.

Still, she made sure to sneak in a Lightning Sphere of her own once in a while to ensure he didn't have the time to try something more complex.

Dorea kept her calm. Even though she had made a mistake, she was powerful enough to survive it, and her overall strategy for the battle hadn't changed.

While she frantically dodged what now were jets of compressed water, which had lost their form to become even more deadly, Dorea kept prepping the field.

Then, the high-speed chase stopped, and she looked down to see that Olnar seemed to be concentrating on something. Going by the sheer amount of mana she sensed being used, it had to be big.

Not wanting to give him a free shot, Dorea manipulated some of the charge left in the atmosphere to shoot another blindingly bright lightning bolt at him.

Another veil of water rose to intercept it, dispersing the energy harmlessly. That, however, had not been her real attack. Under the cover of a much flashier move, Dorea had prepped something that would surprise her opponent.

At the same time, whatever Olnar had been preparing was finished, and they both unleashed their magic.

Thunderclap—now a proper spell thanks to long hours of training—burst out in a deafening rumble, much greater than what the previous lightning bolt had generated.

Though the distance between her and Olnar was too great to inflict serious damage with the shock wave, the absurdly loud sound could deafen anyone if not adequately guarded against.

As soon as it passed, a feeling of absolute stillness gripped the air as every particle of water stopped moving, locking everything into place. Unfortunately, it seemed like he had been able to shield against her spell.

Dorea pushed back against it, grateful for the presence of her Bulwark that prevented what would have been a gruesome end. Instead, she found herself stuck in the air, as the water vapor, under Olnar's spell, didn't budge.

This might get ugly.

Mark the Blue

Traveling through the rocky hills while tired and angry had been difficult. Scaling mountain passes and dealing with the complexities of moving so many people through rugged terrain was hell.

Mark was not well suited to a command position; he had always known that much. He didn't seek one, nor did he allow himself to get trapped into the miserable role of a future leader, unlike that poor girl Dorea.

He was a simple man, he knew. He enjoyed exploring the world, feeling the high of a hunt, getting stronger, and facing powerful people. Nothing beyond that was necessary for him to be happy.

So when he had been told, in no uncertain terms, that he needed to gather a good chunk of the mages fit for combat and head north into the mountains to attempt a foolhardy rescue, the only bit Mark had complained about was that he would need to organize the operation.

Luckily, after seeing him struggle with the logistics of it, others had subbed in for him, and they had managed to set off in short order.

Finding the tracks had been easy enough, as hiding the passage of dozens of people was not a simple task, and once they managed to get their stride, they made good time. Entering Mondean territory had been a relief, as Mark had always believed they should bring the fight to them rather than passively waiting for their enemy to attack.

We should be getting close. Maybe a little more than an hour of marching, and I'll get my hands on those bastards.

A silly grin had been trying to make its way on his face for a while now, but he forced it down. Not everyone shared his giddiness at the coming fight, after all, and it wouldn't do to make them think he wasn't taking it seriously.

I'm probably much more serious about this than anyone else! Just the thought of being able to fight freely without holding back makes my blood pump.

Luckily for him, his main duty would be to directly assault the camp, drawing in their attention while the others attempted to get to the prisoners.

If he had been asked to take part in rescuing them, he'd have blown a gasket. Mark was not one to be distracted from the real prize—a free-for-all without collateral damage!—but luckily, no one had even suggested it.

As they trudged closer to where they believed the Mondeans had struck camp, plumes of smoke became visible behind the last mountain pass they needed to get through.

Those are not the kind that comes from a campfire. Probably Dorea's work, then, huh? That girl has some fire in her.

"The battle has already started! People of Whitecliff, ready yourselves! Have no mercy and save our comrades!" he yelled, finally letting go of his composure and allowing a large, slightly manic grin to come over his features.

Mark tied back his medium-length blue hair—the only part of his appearance he truly cared about—and started running, electricity flooding his muscles to enhance his speed and strength. He crested the path, power thrumming beneath his skin and ready to smash against any opposing force, when the sight of a desolate, broken, and burned-out camp stopped him in his tracks.

The force that had assaulted Whitecliff, that had broken their gate and entered their village, was no more, and he had no idea how that could have happened.

With a huff of discontent, Mark released his grip on the spell he had been preparing. He ignored the disbelieving cheers of his companions, resigning himself to the tedious next few hours.

Finding out the origin of the destruction had been relatively easy. They simply needed to follow the path of the damage and were led to a mountain of bodies with a monstrous creature in the middle.

Signs of destruction were all around. People with entire limbs missing, mages with chests caved in by large fists, expressions of horror forever etched on their faces. For all the death, though, the being at the center of it seemed almost peaceful.

A goat with the body of a human, covered in fur and taller than any man. The cause of death was easily recognizable as a sword of ice, which still impaled its heart. Its limbs were littered with cuts everywhere, and it appeared the humans had made its rampage as tough as possible, even when they were hopelessly underpowered. That was, apart from the person who killed it, Ghionn the Invisible Hand.

The entire valley showed signs of the two Masters having battled it out. Canyons had been carved into the mountainside, while enough ice to make a new glacier had been used as artillery, littering the space.

When they looked at the scene, it was quite obvious that the Mondeans had been attacked by the goat man for some reason, and Ghionn had battled with it in the skies, uncaring of what damage they'd do to the camp.

"Have you found any sign that the old bastard might be dead?" Mark asked one of the mages who was accompanying him. If the goat man had also managed to kill the ice mage, they might have to build a statue in its honor. Already, Mark considered the being very highly.

It has probably been provoked by the Mondeans; they are annoying bastards like that. But to die after taking an entire army down with yourself . . . Well, there are much worse ways to go.

"No, no sign of his body. It might have been one of the unrecognizable ones, but we suspect he made it out." That was the answer. The mage looked disappointed, probably wishing all their problems would get solved that easily.

Mark didn't hate Ghionn, despite the man having attacked his village. He could understand his desperation for a good fight. To live your life to the fullest until the very end. It was why he didn't understand why the old man had retreated rather than dying to Yaomi.

The thrill of putting your life on the line, unleashing all the power you have been given by the Goddess. Death didn't scare Mark; dying without having had enough good battles did.

The thought of going like his grandfather—old, frail, and ill—gasping for air, coughing and in constant pain for months as his mental faculties declined inexorably . . . That was what fear was like.

Dying to a skilled opponent in the prime of his life after fighting to the best of his capabilities and coming just short . . . It wouldn't be the worst.

"What could have made it so angry that it'd attack an entire army? Usually, Master-rank beasts are smart enough to stay away from large congregations of humans."

Mark huffed a laugh. If they wanted to understand the workings of an animal's mind, especially given how smart it must have been, they would spend years trying.

No, they needed to look at the consequences of the goat man's actions. The Mondean army that had attacked Whitecliff was no more. Only Ghionn was still alive, and who knew where the old man might have gone.

I'd expect a few have managed to run away. They might not have cared about collateral damage during their fight, but I doubt they deliberately targeted those fleeing.

"Don't waste your time. Go look and see if our people managed to run away as well during the chaos or if they were amongst the victims," he commanded, tearing his gaze away from the still figure. "And someone prepare a burial for this creature. It might not be human, but it took care of our enemies for us and we should still show our respect for the apex of magic."

The fight must have been something spectacular, and a part of him was sad he had missed it. Though he was a lightning mage, Mark was sure he would have learned something by watching the two Masters battle it out.

Well, I probably wouldn't have survived had I been here for the whole thing. But what a way to go, heh?

Mysterious gouges into the earth and barely melting ice chunks littered the valley, as the entirety of it had been involved in the fighting.

Briefly, Mark wondered what the goat man's element had been, as it didn't look like the result of earth magic, but he put that thought aside. He'd have time to ask more learned people about it.

He observed the goings for a while until a scout approached him. "We have found evidence to believe that someone took the prisoners by flight. The tent was flattened by a huge block of ice, but the shock wave of some kind of wind magic is still visible."

Immediately, Mark understood what had happened. He had been curious as to why they hadn't seen traces of her, as he had expected her to take part in the fighting, given how angry she had looked when she left.

Dorea. It has to be her. Could she have led the goat man here?

"We have also found something else," the scout continued, looking a bit hesitant. "Though most of the traces away from here lead north, deeper into Mondean territory, at least three people left for the southeast, the direction we believe the prisoners were taken in."

Mark grinned widely as the picture became suddenly clear. Dorea had to have roused the goat man to anger in some way and led it to the camp, where it was engaged by Ghionn. Using that cover, she must have sneaked in, taken the prisoners, and left. A few people must have noticed and followed after her.

"So there is still a fight to be had." He turned to face the scout and asked, "Which direction did the traces lead to?"

With the path forward secured, Mark hurriedly gave the command to Harlan—the old, grizzled scout that had taught him everything he knew about moving in the forest and dealing with wildlife—much to his exasperation.

He reactivated his magic, pumping energy into his spell. A few seconds later, he shot off in the direction he had been given at incredibly high speeds, almost flying between steps as his every muscle and nerve were enhanced by his power.

Wait for me—I'm coming.

CHAPTER FORTY-TWO

Locked in the air, Dorea pushed with all her might against Olnar's spell. Slowly, the combination of Air Boost and Wind Bulwark let her move somewhat, but her speed was too low to possibly dodge anything.

Therefore, she couldn't do anything but look at the incoming jets of water that struck her barrier with immense force, pushing her back in the air even through the grip of the immobilizing spell.

A dozen hits happened in a moment, all concentrated on the same spot, aiming to break through the Bulwark and end her life in one shot.

Dorea could have simply put all her mana in reinforcing her only protection, pitting her defenses against Olnar's destructive power. Still, she had never been one to passively let things happen.

Instead, trusting in the strength of her magic, she concentrated on something that should allow her to turn the tides. She had only used it once in battle, but it had great results, and further tinkering had brought it to an even higher level.

The concept of a Waterspout, the merging of sky and sea into one extremely destructive funnel of death, condensed into one point until the very magic that made it couldn't hold still any longer.

Endowed with a meaning, magic could do much more than she had thought possible before, and Dorea was sure it would be the discovery that would push her to Master level in time.

She held onto it for the moment, deliberately waiting until the last possible moment to continue pumping it with magic.

Surprisingly, the water mana that made up half of it didn't resist being used, implying that for all his terrifying control, Olnar could only access what had been actualized into his element.

Making a note to remember that if he somehow managed to survive what she was about to unleash, Dorea poured all her frustration and anger into her magic, turning it even more unstable.

Finally, as one last powerful jet of water struck the Bulwark, cracking it beyond repair, she let go.

The immense power she had held within her hands just a moment before eagerly left her will's constraints, breaking into the real world with a roar.

The condensed concept of a Waterspout, though not as powerful as the actual weather phenomenon as she wasn't yet a Master, still contained so much power that the stillness spell Olnar had employed couldn't do anything to stop it.

The beam broke through several of the water veils that had frustrated her efforts during their entire battle and finally touched down, striking true against the figure coordinating the barrage of water jets.

The Waterspout went through as if there was no resistance, carving a deep gouge in the ground below.

Once she was sure it had done its job, Dorea stopped feeding it, allowing the potent magic to disperse.

She allowed herself a sigh of relief, more because it had been so challenging to conjure such a thing than for any belief it was already over.

Still wary of any possible trickery after the illusionary wave, she touched down gently, coming to a stop before the mangled body.

Immediately, it became apparent that it was not the true Olnar she had struck, nor an illusion.

Instead, her Waterspout had hit an imitation of her opponent, if only a bit paler, and with the insides made of water, which was now freely leaking as if blood.

The sound of clapping seemed especially loud in the silence that had fallen upon the valley. Dorea turned to face its origin and was unsurprised to find Olnar, hale and healthy, once again appearing from the air, a thin film of water coming off his skin.

"That was majestic, I have to say," he commented, looking genuinely impressed. Considering how intense their fight had been, he seemed perfectly presentable. His hair was still without a lock out of place, no speck of dirt marred his skin, and his clothes were unrumpled, as if he had just put them on.

Dorea found that she was more annoyed at that than her Waterspout failing. She knew he couldn't possibly be as unaffected as he was portraying, but the mere fact that he managed to look like it while she no doubt was grimy from climbing mountains and fighting to the death—her occasional washes aside, she hadn't put much effort in her appearance, fueled as she was by righteous anger.

"What even was that?" she asked, gesturing to the fake body that was still "bleeding."

Olnar smirked, evidently enjoying her bafflement. "My forays into illusion magic were enjoyable, but I soon found the need to give them some substance. So I married the two disciplines, illusory arts with true elemental manipulation, and got this. I call it Water Clone. It's me, but a bit less. Still very useful, and it can even use some magic of its own."

The level of skill required to craft such a spell boggled her mind. Dorea tried to think of how long it would take her to build it from nothing and immediately realized it simply wasn't possible. "So you had records of water spells to start from, huh?"

Her question hadn't even been meant as insulting, being just the logical conclusion she had arrived at—it would probably take years of hard work to invent an entirely new discipline, merge it with conventional magic, and then craft such a complex spell!—but Olnar evidently took it as such.

His face contorted into an angry visage, his beautiful features turning ugly, as rage consumed him. "I did it! I'm the one who achieved greatness. Those old fools merely learned what their ancestors told them to and never looked beyond it! Without me, the discipline would have never been anything!"

The abrupt shift was jarring, but Dorea had already understood that the Mondean chief, for all his magical and tactical brilliance, was very perturbed. It didn't surprise her that something as harmless as that could set him off.

Consumed with anger, Olnar evidently decided that the time to speak was over. He gestured forward with his hands, and two whips snaked forth, striking the hastily rebuilt Wind Bulwark.

The whips evidently don't require more time or focus than the jets and are even more unpredictable. Then why was he just using those? Wait, he said the Water Clone could use spells. Is that when he switched? Ugh, I fought with that thing for minutes! I wasted so much mana on it.

They exchanged several shots, though since Olnar didn't use his stillness spell again—which Dorea conjectured he had been able to use only because of his Clone's presence taking the brunt of her attention—she was able to avoid most of the damage.

Still, his spells seemed more potent than what he had shown in the beginning or what the Clone had been capable of. They forced her to dodge much more than before, allowing her little time to counterattack.

A particularly well-hidden lance of water, coming directly from above her, managed to avoid her senses long enough that when she felt it approach, she was forced to tank the hit, sending her tumbling down toward the ground.

Without being able to right herself, Dorea spun uncontrollably, only the mighty Wind Bulwark protecting her from the many consecutive hits she received.

She barely had the presence of mind to realize that something big was coming, as her senses screamed that large amounts of water were approaching her position. The problem was that she had been thrown around too much and couldn't orientate herself quickly enough to react beyond dumping even more mana in her shield.

All of a sudden, the ground below her broke as a geyser of scalding hot water burst out, sending her back into the air and further damaging her protection. The speed at which it had hit her and the force behind it was greater than any single attack Olnar had produced so far, and the fact he had been able to manipulate the environment so quickly while still keeping up his barrage made her grit her teeth.

This damn bastard . . . If I had the time to stop and attack him, things would be different, but he's deliberately not letting me get my bearings!

It was an unfortunately effective strategy, and frustration mounted within Dorea. For all the mana still within her, she was forced to use it to supplement her only defense.

She had built up significant reserves thanks to her long months of constant training, hunts, and battles. Her control had always been great, but she hadn't slept on her laurels and managed to push herself even in that field. All of that was useless if she couldn't find the time to get a shot in.

Then, the constant assault stopped after a blinding flash of light.

She didn't waste the moment of reprieve and immediately righted herself in the air, pumping more mana in the Bulwark and preparing to start her own offensive.

Down below, she was surprised to find a different fight was taking place. Given the extremely recognizable hair, she instantly realized that Mark the Blue had come to her rescue, likely after reaching the Mondean camp and finding traces of her flight.

Large bolts of lightning flashed as her ally ran at incredible speeds toward Olnar, who had been forced to raise several veils of water to tank them.

Not wanting the opportunity to go to waste, Dorea started sending down compressed wind blades, whose cutting power made short work of the Mondean chief's protection.

With an angry shout, he lifted his hands up, gathering all the water emitted by the geyser and forming a churning sphere around himself, similar, in a way, to her Wind Bulwark.

The powerful lightning bolts sent his way by Mark all were effortlessly tanked, much to her ally's frustration. Dorea grimaced in sympathy, having spent the entirety of the fight trying to get at least one good hit in.

The water sphere seemed impenetrable, not even budging after being hit by her wind blades, which had easily cut through people like they were made of butter.

Seeing that Mark was gathering power for a piercing strike, Dorea decided to support him by upping the rate at which she was sending her attacks, focusing entirely on that and leaving the preparation she had been doing in the background since the beginning to the side.

Things are almost ready anyway. I just need to finish getting the charge right, and I'll be able to end this.

Lightning Spheres roared out from her hands, looking like miniature suns falling out of the sky. Though the defenses Olnar was employing were mighty, the stress of deflecting that much energy kept him pinned down, unable to move away and restart his assault.

Finally, Mark completed his spell. A lance made of blinding light rested in his hands. It hummed menacingly, and to her senses, it was even brighter. This, she knew, was a finishing move. A conceptual spell based upon something the elders called a fulgor: a single bolt of lightning possessing exceptional brightness and strength, usually wielded by powerful mages in stories.

That Mark had completed such a spell wasn't surprising, considering the aptitude he had always shown and his vast reserves. Still, Dorea felt her attention be drawn away from it, as for all its might, something more significant was happening.

Within the still churning sphere of water, Olnar had not been idle. Similarly to when she had been caught in his stillness spell, and even more so than when she had first felt him approach, her grasp over the waters in the valley escaped her. As if she had never been able to use the element, she could only passively observe as all moisture started being pulled toward him.

Simultaneously, the Fulgor was released, and with a rushing sound, every particle of water was yanked to the valley's center. Dorea felt it happen, even as she desperately tried to pit her own control against Olnar's, fruitless as it might be.

She simply didn't have the skill necessary with that specific element, and contrary to her, Mark didn't have any active protection going.

Dorea would never know what would have happened had he been just a bit more cautious. It was possible that he would have saved himself with a decent defensive spell, or it might not have mattered any.

He wasn't, unfortunately, and thus he was helpless against Olnar's greatest skill, which they had been warned against by multiple refugees who had witnessed the terror of it being unleashed.

Without being able to emit a single sound, Mark dropped down, his body devoid of any moisture, looking as if it had been left to dry for months. The boy she had competed against, who had tirelessly worked alongside her to defend Whitecliff and whom she had come to respect for his strength and dedication to the pursuit of it, was dead, and she had been powerless to stop it. Again.

The Fulgor he had unleashed, however, was still active and it quickly crossed the distance, finally breaking through Olnar's enhanced defense and hitting the boy within with great power.

Numbly, Dorea observed her opponent scream in agony as the might of Mark's last spell—though severely weakened by both the churning sphere and an additional veil of water that had been resting on the Mondean chief's skin—coursed through him, turning one of his limbs into a charred mess and sending him into a painful fit of seizures as the electricity ran wild.

The gory sight was enough to shock Dorea out of the daze that had fallen upon her, fury building up within her core, hot like a star being born.

Too much had been happening these last few days. She had endured again and again, simply too worried about other people's fates and the consequences of her actions. She had held back because she had duties.

That was over now. Everything she had been pushing down rushed back in, the cold fury she had been using to propel herself forward igniting into an inferno. She could no longer ignore it, at the pain of insanity.

In that moment, the certainty that she needed to do anything in her power to kill Olnar there and then, to end the scourge that had been rampaging across Loisos once and for all, crystallized.

Mark's last-ditch effort, his Fulgor, might not have been enough to finish the job, but it certainly had managed to complete the conditions for her to do it.

Without further hesitation, as she knew Olnar to be too crafty to simply be out of the fight this easily, Dorea pushed all the turbulent emotions rampaging through her into her mana, taking advantage of the similarity in concepts between them and the fury of a storm.

Tears she hadn't noticed falling from her eyes were pulled away as all three elements under her control eagerly responded, concentrating into a singular point between her extended hands.

She cradled the newborn spell, fueling it with her own mana and using the conditions she had set up since the beginning of the fight to substitute the lack of an actual storm.

The waters, now free from Olnar's control thanks to Mark's sacrifice, were abundant enough that she didn't need to supplement them. Their chaotic nature, as they had been summoned with the clear intention to do harm, allowed her to easily use them to fuel her work.

The winds, having been stirred up all along by her quick movements and deadly blades, whirled gleefully around her, their purpose clear and uncontested.

The electrical charges, which she had been disseminating all along with her Lightning Spheres and which had been given the last power-up necessary by the Fulgor, jumped to her commands, ionizing the air and rushing to the central point of the vortex she was holding.

Dorea realized with a start that the power she was gathering was even greater than what she had unleashed against the wolverine. The might of the storm she had used to fuel her magic then had been immense; in a way, it had been too much.

She was too small, on a metaphysical level, to grasp all of it, and her attempt to do so had led to most of it being wasted, and only a small part ended up fueling her spell.

What she was working with now, however, was well within her range. She had been the one to create most of the elements she was using, and their purpose had been to be used by mages for battle since the beginning. Nothing fought her grip now, and her uncontested control, coupled with a more advanced skill level, brought Heart of the Storm to a higher level.

The spell finally actualized, a whirling blue marble of incredible power with enough strength to devastate the entire valley.

I can only hope that Peve'nar's protection will prove strong enough to save the others from this. But I know I'll never get another chance at killing him, and if he's allowed to go, he'll never rest until Whitecliff is erased from existence.

Her choice had been made before she was even conscious of it. Risking her life and that of the friends she had rushed here to save was not worth stopping. She needed to end this. Now.

She unleashed Heart of the Storm with a sigh of relief.

CHAPTER FORTY-THREE

The moment Heart of the Storm left her hands, Dorea knew it was simply too powerful for her to be left unscathed. The ease with which she had managed to build it to completion, compared to what length she had to go to during training, had made her careless.

She had grasped this spell by watching the Master-rank eagle, who had fought and lost to Old Titan, attempt a last-ditch effort. Its conceptual weight was unparalleled compared to anything else in her arsenal.

Dorea had known that it was more than what she could normally produce since the beginning, given the complexity of the required matrices, but the sheer power she had just unleashed scared her.

Blinded by her rage at Mark's death and all her suppressed feelings, she had barely stopped to consider the consequences of her actions. Her only hope of survival—and to ensure her friends wouldn't get swept away by the monstrous spell she had unleashed—was to forcibly retake control of it and prevent it from leaving the valley.

Olnar, too, seemed stunned out of his pain by what he was feeling. Even from the distance, Dorea could make out the white of his eyes as he gazed at the coming death.

As she extended her metaphysical grip toward Heart of the Storm, she felt him do the same in an attempt to redirect it away.

Together, they managed to slow its approach somewhat, gaining precious seconds before the spell released its contained might. Considering how she still very much wanted to kill him, it felt weird working together with the water mage, but the magic she had created was simply too strong.

Dorea had managed to touch the Master rank, if only with a great deal of preparation and luck.

Inexorably, Heart of the Storm continued on its path. Though slowed, the spell couldn't be stopped, and the two mages attempting it were simply too spent to challenge its might.

Already, she could see signs of breaking down from Olnar. The injury Mark had inflicted upon him was too heavy, and he appeared to struggle to even stay standing.

Considering how he was attempting to control a spell made up of lightning, wind, and water mana, he had to put even more effort into achieving what little he was getting.

The strain of holding the sphere of death away was doing the job she had made the thing for. Olnar was dying simply because he was pitting his will against a power much greater than him.

Dorea slowly let go of her grip, deciding he could do it alone if he wanted to struggle so much. Instead, she flew toward the mouth of Peve'nar's valley, placing herself before its entrance and readying her remaining reserves to defend it.

Without her help, Heart of the Storm shot toward Olnar, almost unimpeded in its path. Before it hit, Dorea noticed an almost relieved smile on the Mondean chief's face, as if he was welcoming something.

It's almost like he was waiting for this. What could he possibly do now?

Then, all hell was let loose.

The concentrated power of an entire storm was unleashed upon the valley with the crack of thunder, several times stronger than anything she had created with her Thunderclap, heralding its arrival.

Winds of incredible power rushed out of their containment, strong enough that even hidden in the crevice as she was, Dorea was forced to supplement her Bulwark with more mana to prevent it from breaking.

A dark, ominous cloud spread following them, covering her sight completely. Cold, freezing air pushed around her as rain so heavy that it felt like her Bullets pelted the area, turning it into a cracked, desolate wasteland.

What little vegetation had survived the previous fight was immediately erased from existence. Lightning, of an intensity she didn't believe was possible in nature, flashed everywhere, blinding her completely and forcing her to rely entirely on her mystical senses.

When she was finally hit, it felt like an anoa had kicked her in the stomach; such was the power.

It pushed through her defenses and only her control over the elements stopped her from ending up like her opponent after Mark's Fulgor.

Rather than curling down to cry like she wanted to, Dorea pushed through the pain, extending her senses to once again try and corral the beast she had unleashed.

The storm was still growing in intensity, with little to make her think it would stop anytime soon. Since the valley behind her was starting to be affected—she could feel the heavy blows of the rain, the constant winds, and the occasional lightning bolt stressing the wards into overheating—she needed to do something, or her helpless friends would end up like Olnar. She'd never forgive herself if she caused that to happen, even once she was in the Mother's embrace.

Her mana system creaked in pain and warning as she attempted to take control of a phenomenon that had long since escaped her grasp. Dorea realized that she would be doing damage to herself if she continued and that running away—like she had thought Olnar stupid for not doing—likely was the only way for her to survive.

But she was even more stubborn than he was. Rather than attempting to pick apart the threads of magic or directly facing the storm's might with her defenses, Dorea chose a different battlefield.

On a conceptual level, Heart of the Storm reflected her in every facet. It was the magical actualization of her struggles, victories, defects, and qualities. It was her in a spell, given form by observing the eagle's magnum opus.

Which meant that she had a connection to it that went deeper than the control she could exert with mana. The spell was tied to her on the metaphysical level.

Dorea closed her eyes and trusted that the power she had dumped into Wind Bulwark would protect her while she tried to meditate in the middle of the insanity around her.

Reaching the level of concentration required to touch the edge of her system, where reality itself went a bit wonky, was not easy in a calm environment. To do it with the pressure and anxiety she was feeling should have been impossible, by all rights.

But Dorea had always prided herself on doing what others thought no one could. Necessity and sheer willpower had seen her through all kinds of situations, and she was ready to bet on them this time too.

She mapped her channels, again observing how they didn't have a physical presence, but they still occupied space. The flow of mana was turbulent, owing to the great deal of power she was still using to support her defenses and how much she had received from the three mages' deaths.

Oh, that just gave me an idea. Why have I never thought of doing this before?!

Following that new mana, she reached that liminal place between dimensions. Where her metaphysical self touched upon the realm of magic and received the power of those she killed.

There, with eyes that couldn't see and senses that didn't work, she tentatively reached for the outside, immediately recoiling at the fierce resistance she got.

It made sense how the rules of that reality didn't allow one to push outward, otherwise so many mages would simply break themselves without even knowing why.

But at the moment, she needed to do so, so she redoubled her efforts, slowly inching out of her shell and into the wider plane.

The sensory feedback she got was not something she could easily describe with human language, but the closest thing she could think of was the weird dissonance one felt when putting one hand in a cold pot of water and the other in a hot one.

Contrasting feelings, all different from one another, pushed at her sanity, but Dorea held steady. She didn't allow herself to be distracted from her task and tirelessly searched for what she had come for.

Finally, one of those feelings seemed more familiar than any of the others, and she jumped on it, seeking more from where it came from.

The thread brought her to a mass of power she immediately recognized as Heart of the Storm. Even in this world, what she had unleashed was simply too great for her to control wholly, but then again, she didn't need to.

Here, she could simply appeal to her signature's similarity with it and corral it away, leading it up into the sky, where it could accomplish its true purpose of becoming a real storm.

It was simpler than she had expected, but things here followed different rules, and invoking its original concept seemed to have entirely bypassed the need to use force.

Her job done, Dorea returned back to herself, slowly waking as if from a long slumber. Everything ached in a way that screamed she had pushed herself too much. She was unsurprised to find that Wind Bulwark and every active magic she had going on had disappeared, as even the thought of moving her mana into a spell made her lock up.

What she had done—pushing her consciousness so far away from her body, pitting it against Heart of the Storm—had consequences. She knew it would but had done it nonetheless.

Slowly, Dorea opened her eyes, blinking repeatedly as she tried to get used to the sunlight after being in complete darkness for so long. The stormy clouds had risen up and shifted to the west, revealing the afternoon sun.

She stayed there momentarily, contently enjoying the warmth, before a cracking sound attracted her attention. When she painfully pushed herself up, wincing at the sensation of total weakness in her limbs, she saw something that sent a shiver down her spine.

An enormous cocoon, as if made by a man-sized caterpillar, sat where she had last seen Olnar. Its surface reflected the light in every direction in what should have been a beautiful display. Instead, as she watched the icy surface slowly flake apart, Dorea felt only despair.

Heart of the Storm had been the last resort. A spell so powerful that it had taken everything in her to avoid getting dragged into it too. She had been so sure it would be enough to deal with the Mondean chief, despite all his personal power, that she had forgotten he was not the only enemy she needed to think of.

Her fears proved correct when the cocoon finally broke apart, revealing two figures inside. One, the young man, whom she had fought so desperately against, was unmoving, save from the very shallow rise and fall of his chest. The other, a tall old man with a long white beard and a snow-white cloak, was the last thing she wanted to see.

Ghionn the Invisible Hand—and it could be no one else, given the ice magic and the power employed to survive her last spell—looked at his feet, where Olnar rested, and grunted in dissatisfaction. "I thought he had gotten good enough. I suppose I was a bit too greedy."

His voice was deliberately loud, as if he knew Dorea was there and wanted her to hear. He then stepped around the still form of the boy, slowly walking toward her.

As much as she might have wanted to stand up and fight, pushing herself up had already taken all her strength. Her limbs were almost unresponsive, and she could just barely move her fingers. Her magic was even worse, as even the slightest attempt to move mana sent a shock of pain all through her.

When Ghionn finally stopped before her, he wore a curious look. Like she was a fascinating bug. He kept observing in silence, taking her in. "It must have truly taken everything you had to give to craft such a spell, eh?"

Dorea licked her lips, summoning the strength to speak. "It wasn't easy, I can tell you that." The cheeky reply had the intended effect, extracting a chuckle from the old man. He didn't seem immediately intentioned to kill her, and she wasn't one to beg for her life anyway.

"I thought you might have used an artifact of great power, but it was all you. Really, old Voggo was hiding such a gem in the rough." Ghionn shook his head, seemingly amused. "I'm sorry to have intervened in your fight. For what it's worth, you are the clear winner. I'll make sure the kid respects that. It should give you some breathing room."

"Does that mean you won't kill me?" Dorea asked, her voice coming out as a weak rasp.

"Oh no, you are like an unripe fruit, my dear. Just a little more time, and you'll be perfect for plucking, but taking you off the tree now would be a waste. You'll live, go back to your family and friends, struggle, grow, and once you have reached the next realm, you'll be good enough for me to fight, if you don't kill me first," the old man said with a bright grin, as if he weren't discussing their possible death.

Still, something in Dorea relaxed a bit at his words. She was glad she wouldn't die, to be sure, but more than that, she had the confirmation he was truly a battle maniac, caring only about his next fight.

"But why interfere, then?" She found the courage to ask now that he had assured her of her safety.

"Ah, I'm sorry to say I'm a bit of a hypocrite. This kid, you see, is something like an apprentice to me," he revealed, gesturing to where Olnar was lying. "I put many long hours into his training, and to have him die now, before he can achieve what he's so close to . . . Well, that'd be a right shame. I want to see how far he'll go, and if he dies now, he'll never get there."

Dorea sighed, already feeling herself starting to slip off into unconsciousness. Gritting her teeth, she forced herself to stay awake and asked another question. "Was the reason why you led the attack on Whitecliff that you just wanted to fight Yaomi, then? Couldn't you have simply traveled south by yourself?"

She was treading on dangerous grounds now, she knew. But Dorea wouldn't forgive herself if she did not ask. She wanted to know if the death of her friends and tribesmen had come simply because of this man and his wants, or if there was more to it.

"Yes, I wanted to fight, but not with Yaomi. She was a good opponent, to be sure, but not the one I went south for. Can you think of who I really wanted?" Ghionn asked, in that leading tone teachers used when they wanted their pupils to get to the correct answer by themselves.

It took only a moment for Dorea to realize the implication. "Voggo. You wanted to fight Voggo. And to draw him out, to force him to use all his strength, you needed to threaten the village. That's why you led the Mondeans south. So that you could battle with him without worrying about anyone interfering. Until Yaomi arrived."

"Until the Witch showed her ugly mug, that's right. I knew Voggo was more than he appeared, but he never once put himself in a situation where he'd need to use all his power. Always so sly and crafty, that man. Well, I had to find out, even if it meant drawing him out."

Dorea would have liked to curse him out, to ask more questions, but her eyelids were closing against her will, and exhaustion took her.

When she opened her eyes, night was starting to fall again, but there was just enough light to see a large group of people trudging out of the mountain pass in her direction. Thankfully, her passive senses still worked and their signatures were recognizable enough that Dorea didn't even attempt rising from the slump she had fallen in, simply too tired to even think about moving.

She saw them visibly take in the landscape before them when they crested the mountain pass.

For all that the range had a wide variety of ecosystems within and that every valley was not the same as another—with several being arid and almost desolate—what her Heart of the Storm had done to this one went much beyond it.

Craters littered the entirety of it, looking as if a shower of meteors had fallen from the firmament. The mighty winds had blown away all traces of life, turning it into an otherworldly view. Cracked, charred earth was the only color present, as the immense lightning strikes had glassed the ground.

After a couple minutes of stunned silence, Dorea saw who she recognized as Harlan, the old scout from Whitecliff she had gone on a few patrols with, shake himself out a daze and bark orders at the others, gesturing toward where she was propped up against the entrance of the gulley.

"Looks like you got chewed up and spat out, girl," the old man gruffly told her.

Though his tone was rough, he was very gentle as he helped her up, holding her steady when her legs almost gave out from under her, as if she were a newborn fawn.

"You should see the other guy. Unfortunately, Ghionn saved him at the last moment, but I had him. I really had him," she answered, frustrated that the solution to so many of her problems had been taken away.

He granted her a smirk, apparently darkly amused at her humor, as he carefully brought her to a rock she could use to sit on. "Where did you put the kids? I know you wouldn't have made this much mess with them around."

His trust warmed her, and Dorea slowly raised her hand and gestured farther into the gully. "This path will take you to a hidden valley. It has powerful wards that limit magic usage and stop direct assaults. I put them there when I realized I was being chased by Olnar, the Mondean chief."

A moment of silence followed her words as everyone digested the implications. "You mean to say that you almost killed the chief bastard, and Ghionn stopped you at the last moment?" Lara asked, sounding as if she couldn't believe it.

Dorea nodded and, with great effort, recounted most of what had happened after she left Whitecliff in a rage. She left her discussion with the ice mage out, deciding that Voggo could choose for himself what should be made public.

Shortly after, people started coming out of Peve'nar's valley, holding the rescued mages, who were still sleeping off whatever drug they had been fed to keep them down. Seeing Jonah's face after her long, tiring fight was a balm, and Dorea allowed herself to finally relax a bit.

"To think that the goat man would help us so much. We should hold a feast in his honor when we return to Whitecliff," Harlan distractedly commented, reminding Dorea that she still didn't know what happened after leaving the Mondean camp.

When she urgently asked, he frowned. "We arrived after things were already over. A great fight had broken out between this Peve'nar and Ghionn the Invisible Hand, and they had destroyed the camp as they tried to off each other." He paused to scratch his chin, looking slightly out of his depths.

Harlan was an experienced scout, but that kind of destruction and power were still outside his expectations.

"As you might expect, the old bastard won in the end, but I can tell you this: the goat man didn't go down without a fight. He took down almost every Mondean with him."

Dorea had known this would be the most likely scenario. For all his might, Peve'nar was still one being against the entirety of the army and his death had been almost inevitable. Still, feeling the wards still up, she had hoped he had survived.

They are likely being powered by something similar to the Forest village's. No need for him to stay around all the time that way . . . I only hope he has been embraced by Mother Nature.

The goat man had been powerful and intelligent but also naive. Trusting a human had been his last mistake.

"Oh, by the way. Mark the Blue should have come this way. Did you see him?" someone asked from behind. Dorea didn't even turn to look at who it was, but the expression on her face must have been enough because Harlan grimaced and shook his head to the gasps of those around.

"Olnar killed him. He died to give me an opening to end him," she finally answered. Mark's death marred the whole expedition, and the fact that the Mondean chief was still alive only made it hurt more.

That said, Dorea decided she had spoken enough. The ache in her mana system was significant, and she feared the consequences of her spell would be grave. She needed to rest if she wanted to start her recovery, so she gave Harlan one last smile and then closed her eyes, exhausted beyond words. Sleep took her immediately.

EPILOGUE

The scent of herbs was heavy in the air. Lavender, sage, willow bark, and other medicinal ingredients Dorea was so familiar with slowly pulled her from the deep slumber she had been in.

With great effort, Dorea pried open her eyelids, heavy with sleep. A haze of background pain—something that went deeper than just her body, touching every bit of what made her, her—and medication dulled her senses, but she was alive.

That realization, which she had not dared hope for, revitalized her enough for her brain to start working. Memories crashed over her—the long hunt, Peve'nar, the flight from the Mondean camp, the short fight with the first three pursuers, the thunderous battle with Olnar, Mark's death, Ghionn.

It was too much, and she shied away from the vortex of emotions those memories evoked. She'd have the time to revisit them later, but she wasn't in the condition to do so now.

As her vision focused, Dorea saw the white canvas walls of a tent. She heard the rustling of the wind outside and the murmur of voices farther out. She was in the healing tents of Whitecliff, her home village, where Voggo and her mother cared for the injured and sick.

Though her mystical senses were hazy and unfocused, she managed to notice a row of beds to her left. Looking over with great effort, she saw the kidnapped mages she had rescued, all laid out on their own cots.

Some were still sleeping, though she didn't know if their slumber was natural or forced. Others looked to be awake, if tired and weak.

The closest bed to her, she was overjoyed to find, housed Jonah. His blond locks matted against his forehead and his usually vibrant blue eyes shadowed with exhaustion. At his bedside stood Beth, dark hair cascading over her eyes to cover them, and her hand holding her boyfriend's tightly.

Dorea watched the two in silence, warmth spreading in her chest. Her best friends were safe.

Jonah stirred, his eyes darting to Dorea instantly. "You're awake," he whispered, voice hoarse.

Beth looked up, relief flooding her face. "Thank the Mother. We were so worried," she murmured.

They kept their tone low so as to not disturb the others, but the happiness in their voices couldn't be concealed.

Beth released Jonah's hand and went around his bed, coming to a stop before her. Gently, as if Dorea was made of frail glass, she gathered her in her arms and hugged her, shaking.

The blonde gripped her best friend tighter, a surge of emotions she couldn't easily define flowing through her. She had been so certain she would die, again and again, that being back home with her best friends, safe, was simply too much.

Silently, Dorea cried. Tears of relief flowing out and feeling like a burden had been lifted. She released her fears, her certainty she would die. Beth cried with her, overwhelmed and happy.

Once they were finally done, they pulled back, trying and failing to make themselves look less like a mess.

"Nothing you can do about it now," Jonah commented, though he, too, seemed to be trying to cover a few tear tracks.

Before they could answer, the tent flaps were gently pulled aside and in strode Voggo. He looked slightly better than when Dorea had last seen him, but a bone-deep tiredness still seemed to remain.

Whatever it was that he did to stand up to Ghionn must have had a terrible toll on him. He has aged more than in the last ten years.

"You gave me quite the scare, little Dory," he greeted, his voice crackling and low.

Dorea put aside her worry for him and answered, "I had to. I couldn't let them take our people like that."

Going on such a harebrained mission might not have been the smartest thing she could have done, but for Dorea, there had never been another option. She needed to save her friends and, if possible, carve into the Mondeans' memory what would happen when they attacked what was hers. She might not have killed Olnar, but she doubted he'd soon forget her anger.

Jonah attempted to sit up but winced in pain, settling back into his cot. "It was stupid and reckless, but we'd be worse than dead without you. Thank you," he said, seeking her gaze with his earnest one, willing her to understand his feelings.

"I'd do it again," Dorea replied, smiling weakly. "That's what friends are for."

Voggo approached, interrupting the moment. He sat on the chair beside her bed, his gaze piercing. "What you did . . . Your mana system wasn't made to channel that much power, nor could it handle your attempt to retake control of the storm. It came at a cost, unfortunately."

Dorea looked down, having already known that her recklessness had damaged something important within her. The weakness she felt was only a warning her system was trying to give her to not use mana. She was sure she'd feel excruciating pain if she tried to draw on some. "What have I done to myself?"

"You pushed so far beyond your limits that it's a miracle you haven't burned yourself out from within," Voggo explained, sounding a bit more like his old self now that he could talk about his area of expertise. "Not only did you use too much mana all at the same time to build your spell. Attempting to take back control of it strained you deeply, and then, what you did to push it away almost broke your mana pathways."

Beth, looking extremely worried, asked, "Can she recover? Will she be able to use magic again?"

Voggo took a deep breath, but his tiny smile rekindled the flame of hope within Dorea. "It will take time and a lot of hard work, but thanks to a few rituals I have been preparing, she should be able to go back to where she was."

A weight Dorea hadn't realized she'd been carrying lightened slightly. "So, there's hope?"

Voggo nodded. "Yes, but it won't be easy. It will require discipline, patience, and trust. We will have to rebuild your magic system from the ground up, reinforce the pathways, and help your internal reservoir recover."

Dorea gripped her sheets, determination burning in her blue eyes. "I'll do whatever it takes."

The old shaman graced her with a smile and the pride reflected within it warmed her greatly. "What you have done for Whitecliff and the alliance means you'll always be a hero, but if I know you as well as I think, you won't rest until you have regained the power necessary to live up to your new fame. Defeating the enemy chief in magical combat is something people will talk about for decades."

Letting out a sheepish laugh, Dorea scratched her head. "It wasn't all me. Mark gave me a free shot I would have never gotten otherwise. Olnar was much more powerful than I expected." Her chest tightened at the memory of the overwhelming force she had to unleash to finally defeat the Mondean chief. And how complete victory had been snatched from her hands by the ice Master.

Beth's grip on her hand tightened, lending her strength and pulling her away from the memories.

"Do we know anything of what is going on up north? Now that I beat Olnar, and Ghionn took him away?" Dorea finally asked the question that had been burning her since she woke up.

The old man sighed, tired but still strong. "We won't know for sure until the scouts we sent return with more than just the preliminary information they have gathered so far, but something we can all agree on is that Olnar's defeat has left a power vacuum. Generals that had been cowed by his might are probably looking to strike out on their own, and his continued absence is not doing the Mondean host's cohesion any favor."

"And someone is gonna fill that void," Jonah commented from his cot with a serious expression as he contemplated the consequences of her victory.

Voggo nodded distractedly. "Absolutely. Half the mountain tribes were either absorbed or driven away. Without him there to keep things running, and with Ghionn gone for the moment, it will be chaos." Then he shook his head, turning to look at Dorea. "That doesn't mean what you did was wrong. All the troubles that will follow are nothing compared to an organized and well-run army bearing down on us. Unless Olnar reappears soon and pulls the frayed and disaffected army back together, we are looking at their inevitable disintegration."

The blonde smiled, grateful that he had taken the time to reassure her. She knew, intellectually, that even in the haze of her rage she had made the correct choice, but having faced her own mortality and, more importantly, that of her friends, she had been having second thoughts.

Still, taking Olnar out of the equation, even if just temporarily as he recovered from the injuries she had inflicted, was a victory. That was indisputable.

Jonah drummed his hands on the bedsheets, looking contemplative. "His commanders will not sit idle. They have tasted victory and won't stop now."

Voggo nodded. "Exactly. Without him there to keep the reins, his generals will likely vie for dominance. They might form alliances or, more likely, turn on each other. The mountains will become even more of a battleground. And Ghionn won't raise a hand to keep the peace, I can tell you that much."

Beth coughed, claiming their attention. "Won't they try to get easy wins by taking revenge on who defeated their leader? It would be a perfect way to claim renown and consolidate more people behind their host."

Everyone looked at her in surprise. Beth was not a stupid girl; rather, she had always shown a quick wit and sharp mind, but she had never appeared interested in the outside world beyond what was strictly necessary for her duties.

For her to speak on the subject, it must have been bothering her for a while now.

Dorea and Jonah shared a look, wordlessly agreeing to try and reassure her. It was true that Whitecliff would be vulnerable because of the power vacuum but no more than they were before she battled Olnar.

Voggo cleared his throat, drawing the attention of the room. "We must be proactive. Strengthen our defenses, fortify our borders, and perhaps most importantly, gather intelligence. But that is my concern. For now, little Dory, you just need to worry about resting and recovering. We expect they'll need a few weeks to sort themselves out anyway."

That said, the old shaman stood up, his knees creaking with the effort. He then patted Dorea's cheek affectionately, smiled at Jonah and Beth, and left.

For all that Voggo was obviously weakened and tired, he still managed to keep things running in the village, and that, more than anything, reassured Dorea that they would be fine. It was unlikely that they'd have to face more Masters, since Ghionn had given his word he'd wait for her to reach his level before he came back, and each Mondean general's numbers were not nearly as threatening as the entire army working as one.

Especially since we still have our allies. Well, the Heidels are likely to be busy in the near future with the mess at the southern border, but things should start looking up from now on.

It might have been a naive hope. The Mondeans could simply regroup under Olnar as soon as he recovered and continue their campaign of slaughter and conquest. But the instinct Dorea had long since learned to trust told her that at least that problem would not be as pressing. He had been hurt too badly to shrug it off, and no healer of the caliber he needed was likely to be available to cure him. Voggo certainly could, but he would never.

Coming back home was more emotional than she had expected. The last she had seen it, her family's ranch had suffered heavy damage under the Mondean assault, and the death of the two workers still lingered in the air.

However, someone had been hard at work to remake it into what it once was, and little evidence of the depredations remained, sans a bigger, better grave for the two dead.

It was probably several people working on it at the same time. Knowing the villagers, it's to repay me.

Her home was not the same as when she had left it to go south. There were some visible scars, while others would remain hidden, even as they worked hard to heal them.

Much more important than the building, however, were the people coming out of it to greet her.

A familiar laugh rang out and a blur of blond curls came hurtling toward her. "Dorea!" Lia, her younger sister, raced forward, her blue eyes sparkling with a mix of relief and excitement.

Dorea braced herself, expecting the usual forceful hug, but was pleasantly surprised when Lia approached with caution, wrapping her arms gingerly around her waist, taking care not to aggravate her still healing body.

Pulling away, Lia looked up, her face a mirror of adoration and concern. "I missed you so much," she whispered.

Dorea smiled, brushing a strand of hair behind Lia's ear. "I missed you too, you little rascal."

The familiar voices of her parents pulled them away.

"Oh, my darling." Lilian approached, her hair in a loose ponytail as dark bags hung below her eyes. "We were so worried," she murmured, embracing Dorea.

Dodro, always the steady one, simply placed his only remaining hand on Dorea's shoulder, his touch firm yet gentle. "Welcome home," he said, his voice rough with emotion. She felt a pang of pain at the sight but soon shrugged it off.

The walk back to the ranch was slow, as they all savored each other's presence and even through many hardships, they had all made it. They were back together.

Inside, the familiar aroma of roasted meats, fresh bread, and baking pie wafted through the air. The dining table was set with ceramic plates, filled with a hearty meal: a pot roast with root vegetables, fluffy rolls with honey butter, courtesy of Joe's bakery, and a fresh green salad tossed with berries and nuts, sprinkled with some of Dodro's more aged cheese that had survived the attack. As the family sat down, Lilian poured a golden cider into their glasses, the fresh, sweet, and dry fragrance mingling with the other aromas.

They ate in comfortable silence, interspersed with Lia's recounting of what she had been up to these last few days while Dorea recovered. By unspoken agreement, they decided to leave the heavier topics for a later moment, simply basking in the warm atmosphere of a reunited family.

With every bite, Dorea felt the warmth of home seep into her bones, healing her in ways the medical tents couldn't.

After the meal, as the night cast soft shadows around the room, Dorea sat back, reflecting on her journey these last few months since the Wrath. The naive, eager girl who had first started exploring her magic seemed a world away. In her place sat a woman who had faced one of the greatest threats to her village, tapped into powers she hadn't known were possible and had paid the price for that strength.

The weight of responsibility was heavy, and Dorea now knew very well how much it could take to live up to it. She finally realized why her parents had been so reluctant to let her take such an important role in the village's ruling and defense.

Still, even after all she had been through, looking at her current self, bandaged and weak, not even capable of lifting the water from her bedside with her magic, she'd do it again. Not only had she experienced things she hadn't even known were possible before the Wrath had changed her life, but her presence meant Whitecliff managed to defend itself repeatedly.

This last attack had been much more brutal, but they had survived it, and the rebuilding, much like her healing, was a certainty.

Watching her daughter from across the room, Lilian seemed to read her thoughts. "You've grown so much, Dorea," she said softly, pride evident in her voice.

Dodro, standing next to his wife, nodded in agreement, adding, "We always knew you were destined for greatness. But watching you now, seeing the woman you've become, fills my heart with so much happiness. Your grandmother would have been so proud of who you are, much like we are now."

Life, Dorea knew, would never be without strife. More problems would arise—the southern border, the Ergasters in the east, and Olnar and the mess up north being simply the closest ones—and things wouldn't be easy. But looking at her loving parents, feeling her little sister's sleeping form in the room next to hers, remembering the warmth of her friendships, Dorea was confident they would make it.

In the tranquil embrace of the evening, with the stars outside twinkling merrily as her only light, Dorea felt a deep gratitude. She had faced the storm head-on and survived it, and as long as she had her sanctuary to return to, she knew she'd be able to brave all the future ones.

About the Author

Persimmon is the author of the Sapiens series, originally released on Royal Road. He has written fantasy stories for more than a decade and more recently began to specialize in the gamelit and progression fantasy subgenres. His work centers on themes of magical experimentation and adventure as well as exploration of the human psyche.